MAY 2006

By Rochelle Krich

Where's Mommy Now?
Till Death Do Us Part
Nowhere to Run
Speak No Evil
Fertile Ground

IN THE MOLLY BLUME SERIES

Blues in the Night
Dream House
Grave Endings
Now You See Me...

IN THE JESSE DRAKE SERIES

Fair Game
Angel of Death
Blood Money
Dead Air
Shadows of Sin

SHORT STORIES

"A Golden Opportunity"
Sisters in Crime 5

"Cat in the Act"
Feline and Famous

"Regrets Only"
Malice Domestic 4

"Widow's Peak"
Unholy Orders

"You Win Some..."
Women Before the Bench

"Bitter Waters"
Criminal Kabbalah

Now You See Me...

Now You See Me...

A NOVEL OF SUSPENSE

Rochelle Krich

BALLANTINE BOOKS / NEW YORK

A Ballantine Book
Published by The Random House Publishing Group

Copyright © 2005 by Rochelle Majer Krich
Reading group guide copyright © 2005 by Random House, Inc.

Published in the United States by Ballantine Books, an imprint of The Random House Publishing Group, a division of Random House, Inc., New York.

BALLANTINE and colophon are registered trademarks of Random House, Inc.

Library of Congress Cataloging-in-Publication Data

Krich, Rochelle Majer.
Now you see me— : a novel / Rochelle Krich.— 1st ed.
p. cm.
ISBN 0-345-46812-0
1. Blume, Molly (Fictitious character)—Fiction. 2. Teenage girls—Crimes against—Fiction. 3. Los Angeles (Calif.)—Fiction. 4. Women journalists—Fiction. 5. Kidnapping—Fiction. I. Title.

PS3561.R477N69 2005
813'.54—dc22
2005046478

Printed in the United States of America

www.ballantinebooks.com

2 3 4 5 6 7 8 9

FIRST EDITION

Book design by Dana Leigh Blanchette

To my Monday night mah jongg partners—
Anna, Arlene, Ellen, Frieda, Judy, Mimi B,
and Mimi M—

It's more than the game.

Acknowledgments

Many thanks to those who were generous with their time and expertise for this work of fiction:

Rabbi Yitzchok Adlerstein, Chair, Jewish Law and Ethics, Loyola Law School, was my sounding board for discussions about teens at risk. Dan Kline of CM Meiers Auto Insurance provided information that stumped Molly. (I thank Dan—Molly doesn't.) D. P. Lyle is the author of two invaluable resource books that I keep on my bookshelf: *Murder and Mayhem* and *Forensics for Dummies*. Doug is my CSI and makes science intelligible and fun. Debbie Shrier, General Studies Principal of Yeshiva of Los Angeles High Schools, helped me plot my first mystery (*Till Death Do Us Part*) and, for this novel, gave me insight into the challenges students and teachers face today. Mary Hanlon Stone, Deputy District Attorney, made the law fit my story and promises that we'll get together as soon as our schedules permit.

For his keen eye, steadfast faith and support (and the crème brûlée), I thank my editor, Joe Blades. I'm indebted to my wonderful agent, Sandra Dijkstra, and her staff; to Eileen Hutton and everyone at Brilliance Audio; to Marie Coolman, Gilly Hailparn, Heather Smith, and Margaret Winter and all my other friends and supporters at Ballantine; to Daisy Maryles; to Carolyn Hessel of the Jewish Book Council and all the book fair chairpersons who have invited me to participate in their programs; to Theda Zuckerman of Hadassah Women; and to my film agent, Liza Wachter, who is determined to bring Molly Blume into your homes or to a theater near you.

My "aunt" Regina Rechnitz, and my mother, of blessed memory, met in a labor camp during the Holocaust and forged a lasting friendship. Regina shared many stories with me, including her poignant reunion with her husband, my "uncle" Henry—a story in which my mother played a part. I thank Regina and Henry for allowing me to tell their story through the voice of Molly's grandmother, Bubbie G.

I am blessed to share my life with my husband, Hershie, our children and their spouses, and our grandchildren. Special thanks to Chani, who taught Molly a few things; to Daniel and Meira and her Daniel, for giving me a reason to visit New York; to Eli, for the uplifting humor; to David, who always finds the right biblical chapter and verse, and Michelle, who makes the best potato kugel in the world; to Josh, my computer go-to guy; and to Sabina, who literally allowed me to push her around, over and over, so that I could construct one of the final scenes in the novel.

Rochelle Krich

A Note on Pronunciations

Yiddish has certain consonant sounds that have no English equivalencies—in particular the guttural "ch" (achieved by clearing one's throat) that sounds like the "ch" in Bach or in the German "Ach."

Some Yiddish historians and linguists, including the Yiddish Scientific Institute (YIVO—Yidisher Visenshaftikhe Institut), spell this sound with a "kh" (Khanukah, khalla). Others use "ch" (Chanukah, challa). I've chosen to use "ch."

To help the reader unfamiliar with Yiddish, I've also doubled some consonants ("chapp," "gitte").

"Zh" is pronounced like the "s" in *treasure*.
"Tsh" is pronounced like the "ch" in *lurch*.
"Dzh" is pronounced like the "g" in *passage*.

Here are the YIVO guidelines for vowel pronunciations, which I've followed in most cases, except for those in which the regional pronunciations vary (*"kliegeh"* instead of *"klugeh,"* *"gitte"* instead of *"gutte"*):

a as in *father* or *bother* (*a dank*—thanks)
ay as in *try* (*shrayt*—yells)
e as in *bed,* pronounced even when it's the final letter in the word (*naye*—new)
ey as in *hay* (*beheyme*—animal)
i as in *hid,* or in *me* (*Yid*—Jew)
o as between *aw* in *pawn* and *u* in *lunch* (*hot*—has)
oy as in *joy* (*loyfen*—to run)
u as in *rule* (*hunt*—dog)

With a little practice, you'll sound just like Molly's Bubbie G.

—Rochelle Krich ("ch" as in birch,
but that's another story)

Now Dinah—the daughter of Leah, whom she had borne to Jacob—went out to look over the daughters of the land. Schechem, son of Hamor the Hivvite, the prince of the land, saw her. He took her, and he lay with her, and violated her. He became deeply attached to Dinah, daughter of Jacob. He loved the maiden and spoke to the maiden's heart.

—Genesis 34:1–3

Now You See Me...

Chapter 1

On a Sunday morning in November, a day before the Monday Hadassah Bailor never came
home, her alarm rang at five-fifty. She shut
off the alarm within seconds, but her older sister, Aliza, who had returned late from a date,
groaned, *"C'mon, Dass,"* even before she saw
the clock radio's green liquid crystal numbers,
eerily bright in the dark room. Like cat's eyes,
Aliza would say, though that was probably
an afterthought inspired by the Harry Potter
novel lying on the nightstand between the two
beds.

Aliza jammed a pillow over her head. Later,
with some prodding, when insignificant details assumed urgency, she remembered hearing the splash of water as Hadassah, using the
white plastic tub and two-handled laver that
she'd kept at her bedside for most of her eighteen years, rinsed her hands and eyes before

she murmured her waking prayers. Also with some prodding, Aliza was able to recall the hum of the computer and the staccato clicking of Hadassah's fingernails on the keyboard, and the muffled drone behind the closed door of the bathroom, where Hadassah dried her long curly strawberry-blond hair, which she liked to wear loose but had secured with a black velvet scrunchy.

At seven-forty Hadassah roused her three younger brothers. She helped Yonatan, the seven-year-old, find a tennis shoe and a yarmulke, both wedged between the bunk bed and the wall. While they dressed, she put snacks into brown paper bags (she almost forgot to decorate Yonatan's with a smiley face) and handed the bags to the boys as they tore out the side door to their waiting carpool.

Hadassah put on a buttery yellow, cable-knit hooded sweater and a gray wool skirt that revealed a few inches of slim legs encased in gray tights too warm for what promised to be an unseasonably balmy day. After prayers and breakfast (two rice cakes, sliced red pepper, a glass of nonfat milk), she returned to her computer, muting the volume in deference to her sister's restless tossing.

Two hours later she shut the computer and went downstairs. She had slipped her black backpack, heavy with books, over her black quilted jacket and was hoisting the strap of her overnight bag, which, if anyone had checked, was packed with more than her school uniform and a change of underwear, when her mother, one hand stifling a yawn, padded into the kitchen.

Nechama Bailor didn't think her daughter had seemed different that morning. "In a rush, maybe," she said on reflection, "but teenage girls are always like that, aren't they?" Nechama was almost certain Hadassah had kissed her good-bye.

"Dassie *always* kisses me before she leaves," the mother said, using the present tense from habit and hope and touching her cheek gingerly, as though she didn't want to disturb the airy brush of her daughter's lips.

Chapter 2

Wednesday, November 17, 7:42 p.m. Melrose Avenue near Spaulding. A man approached a 14-year-old boy and grabbed his left shoulder from behind. The suspect said, "Do you want to die of AIDS?" before producing a syringe with a long needle. He then fled the scene.

"The face," my grandmother likes to say, "tells a secret." It's an old Yiddish proverb that I have found to be true more often than not. But you have to really *see* a face to read its secrets. And some faces are like masks, hardened by misery or guile to reveal nothing, or like mirrors, reflecting what you expect or want to see.

If you had looked at my face that Wednesday, you might have detected loneliness. I was on an overnight book tour, and a tour, even one that's only a two-hour drive from home, can have lonesome moments. Not during the reading, when you're caught up in the thrill of sharing your words with people who know your name even if you don't know theirs. And not immediately afterward, when you may cherish the solitude and anonymity. But at some point—when the euphoria has evaporated, when the people who came to hear you are in their homes, chatting with family or friends about the day's happenings, and you're in your hotel or in a restaurant and everyone around you seems to be part of a couple or a group, sharing drinks or laughter—at some point you're filled with melancholy, with a sense of being disconnected, invisible.

I was in San Diego that night, in a hotel room that, though not the Del Coronado, was more than adequate, but I missed Los Angeles and the comforts and contours of my house and my bed. Mostly, I missed my husband of eight months, especially since this was the first night we'd been apart since our wedding. So when I saw a familiar face in the lobby of my hotel, my spirits lifted.

He was sitting on a sofa opposite the elevator I'd just exited. I smiled, ready to greet him, unable to place him. His eyes were lowered toward the magazine on his lap, and he was wearing gunmetal-framed bifocals and a black cap that obscured his forehead.

I *knew* him. Where did I . . . ?

It took a moment for his identity to register (the other times, I realized, he'd worn a yarmulke and no glasses), another for surprise to twist into shock, then alarm.

He was following me.

I had first noticed him Monday at my publication party for *Sins of the Father,* a true account of a man who had injected his son with the AIDS virus. More than half of the people at the Dutton's Brentwood event were friends and family and, like me, Orthodox Jews, so his black suede yarmulke had been one of many. He was in his midforties, I'd guessed, judging from the dusting of gray in his thinning light brown hair. He had kept his distance while I greeted guests and steered them to the chocolates and wine I'd set out in the courtyard. Inside the store, he listened intently while I read from the first chapter of *Sins,* his dark brown eyes narrowed in concentration, his nods punctuating my sentences and making me flush with pleasure at his approval—or maybe it was the wine. Later, he joined the advancing queue of people holding books for me to sign. I was certain he would comment on the book or my reading, but he set a copy of *Sins* in front of me, said, "Signature only" in a low voice, and slipped away before I could ask his name.

Tuesday afternoon he was in the back row of chairs in a Thousand Oaks mystery bookstore. He listened with that same flattering concentration while I spoke about the research I'd done for the book, about the people I'd interviewed, the conclusions I'd reached. After my talk he was the first to approach me, a copy of *Sins* in his hand.

Maybe he was a collector, I'd thought. Collectors often buy two copies of a hardcover—one for their collection, another to read—though they generally buy both at the same time. Or maybe he was picking up a copy for a friend.

"It's nice to see you again," I said, smiling warmly as he handed me the book. "Do you live in the city or the Valley?" I continued when he didn't reply. His was the only yarmulke in the room, and I admit I felt a kinship.

"City." His curt tone didn't invite conversation.

So much for "kinship." Uncapping my pen, I turned to the title page. "What's your name?"

"Signature only, please."

With someone else I might have quipped that it was an odd name, but I didn't think he'd appreciate the humor. He sounded somber. Nervous, too, now that I look back.

"Would you like me to write the date?" I asked.

"Please."

I wrote "Morgan Blake" (my pseudonym for my true crime books), "November 16," and the year. In my byline—I'm a freelance reporter and pen a weekly "Crime Sheet" column for the local tabloids—I use my real name, Molly Blume. (Molly Blume *Abrams* since I married Zack, my former high school sweetheart, who is now a pulpit rabbi.)

He showed up that night at the Mystery Bookstore in Westwood. From my stool behind the tall black desk at the rear of the store, I saw him hovering near a front table, leafing through books and darting glances in my direction. On some level I was flattered, but I kept my eye on him while I chatted with people and signed copies of *Sins*.

Minutes later he was standing in front of me.

"Signature and date only, right?" I opened the book he handed me. "I take it you're a collector?"

He seemed surprised by my question. "No."

"Then you really *are* a fan. I wish I had dozens like you." I wondered if he was giving the copies as gifts for Chanukah, which was only weeks away, or for Christmas.

"I admire your work. Your passion for truth, your determination, your integrity. It all comes through in the book."

"Thank you." It was the most he'd said since we'd met—practically a speech—and I was struck again by the gravity of his tone. "What's your name, by the way?"

"Reuben." He stepped closer and leaned over the desk. "Can I buy you a cup of coffee when you're done?"

I assumed he wanted advice about getting published, or a critique of his work, or both. I try to repay the kindness others have shown me on my road to publication, but the man's intensity made me cautious.

"I wish I could, but my husband is waiting for me," I said, grateful for the excuse and the man who provided it.

"What about tomorrow morning?" he said with an urgency that confirmed my wariness. "I need to discuss something with you. It's important."

"I'm sorry, I can't. My schedule is *really* hectic." I smiled to soften the rejection.

"I know, but—" He stopped, then scribbled a phone number on a slip of paper that he pushed toward me. "In case you change your mind," he said, and turned to leave.

"You forgot your book." I held it out to him.

His third copy.

I love devoted fans, but I read *Misery* and saw the movie. So in spite of the yarmulke—no guarantee of character, and for all I knew it was camouflage; anyone could buy one—I asked the store manager to accompany me to my car, and I didn't fully relax until I was home.

"Three signings in two days, and two on the same day?" Zack said after I'd told him about my new fan.

"He probably wanted writing advice, or a referral to my agent. Or a blurb." My caution seemed silly now that I was nestled in the crook of Zack's arm, a position that after eight months had lost its novelty but not its appeal.

"Did you keep the phone number he gave you?"

I found the scrap of paper in my purse and handed it to Zack. He dialed the number, listened, and hung up a moment later.

"No name, just a recorded message. Three books, huh?" The expression in his gray-blue eyes had turned pensive.

"I think he was trying to butter me up."

"Maybe. So are you going to call the guy?"

"No." Zack was trying to sound casual, but I could hear his concern. My ex-husband, Ron, would have told me what to do—or, in this case, *not* do. "Now if he'd bought *four* books," I said, and we both laughed.

I didn't feel like laughing now. Less than a minute had passed since I'd stepped out of the elevator, and the man still wasn't aware of my presence. Common sense told me to return to my room and contact security, but anger and the safety net of potential rescuers propelled me across the marble floor.

The clacking of my heels echoed loudly in the high-ceilinged lobby. His head whipped up from the magazine, and he jumped to his feet, smoothing his startled expression and his navy sports coat. He was about four inches taller than my five-six, but my Jimmy Choos erased the difference.

My heart was thumping. "You're stalking me," I said, raising my voice to attract the attention of the guests in the next bay of sofas. "I want to know why."

Color worked up his neck like a spider's web. "I'm really sorry. I didn't mean to frighten you, Miss Blume. As I told you last night, I need to talk to you. It's urgent."

"Well, you *did* frighten me." I wasn't surprised that he knew my real name—practically everyone at the Dutton's signing had called me Molly. But I wasn't thrilled. "Since you know *my* name, what's yours?"

"Reuben Jastrow."

"Show me some ID, Reuben Jastrow."

Tucking the magazine under his arm, he removed a wallet from the pocket of his gray wool slacks and handed it to me. I examined his driver's license. Same name, same face, a little less gray in the hair. He was forty-eight, several years older than I'd guessed.

I fished a pen and pad out of my purse and made a show of writing down his name, driver's license number, and an address in Beverly-wood, an upscale neighborhood near Beverly Hills.

"Why are you stalking me?" I repeated after I returned his wallet.

"I wasn't—" He glanced around. "Can we talk somewhere private?"

My heart was still racing. My stomach muscles were knotted. "I don't think so. Right now I find crowds really appealing. Why the disguise, Reuben?"

He looked confused. "The disguise?"

I pointed to his head. "A hat instead of the yarmulke. The glasses. You weren't wearing them the other times."

He lifted his cap and revealed a black suede yarmulke. "My contact lenses are monovision. One is for reading, the other for distance," he said, replacing the cap. "They're okay, but not perfect, especially at night, when I'd be on my way back to L.A."

His explanation rang true—my mother wears monovision contacts and complains about their limitations. But that didn't mean it *was* true. "What *shul* do you go to, Reuben?"

He named an Orthodox synagogue in Beverlywood.

"Who's the rabbi?" I asked, testing him.

He told me that, too. "You can ask around about me, although I'd prefer you didn't. We don't want talk."

"*We?*" The word had a vaguely conspiratorial sound.

"My family. This is a delicate matter."

I raised a brow. "Stalking me is delicate?"

A beefy man standing nearby had been watching us. Now he approached and folded his arms. "Is this guy bothering you?" he asked me, glowering at Jastrow and the magazine, which Jastrow had twisted into a tight roll.

Hardly a lethal weapon, even if words *can* kill. "No, I'm fine," I told my defender. "Thanks, though."

"Okay, then." He seemed disappointed and gave Jastrow a long warning look before he walked away.

"I read your book," Jastrow said. "I came to your signings to hear you, to see if you're the right one."

"Three L.A. events didn't do it for you?"

"*I* was sure, but—" He broke off. "It's complicated."

"Delicate *and* complicated, huh?" In spite of my annoyance, I was intrigued. Then I frowned. "How did you know I'd be at this hotel?"

"I looked up your schedule on your website and followed you here from the book signing."

"You were there?" The fact that I hadn't known made me feel vulnerable again.

"In my car. There were so many people in the store—I knew I wouldn't have a chance to talk to you. So I followed you. I figured you'd come down eventually to get dinner."

I studied him. "So you drove two hours to talk to me?"

"I'm in insurance. Some of my clients live in the area. I made appointments." Unfurling the magazine, Jastrow slipped it into a black briefcase and took out a business card that he handed me. "I was out of these last night. This isn't something I wanted to discuss on the phone."

I glanced at the card before dropping it into my purse. "Which clients did you see?"

He named two. "You can call them. They'll verify that I met with them today." He looked around again. "Can we sit somewhere? Give me five minutes. If you're not interested in what I have to say, I won't bother you again."

I chewed on my lip. "What's delicate and complicated, Reuben?"

"My daughter ran away three days ago. We want you to find her and bring her home."

Chapter 3

We found a table at the back of the hotel's restaurant. Jastrow was silent while the waitress took our orders—the man was obsessive about privacy, though I doubted that anyone nearby was interested in our conversation—so I followed his lead.

"You should be talking to the police, not to me, Mr. Jastrow," I said when the waitress left. "Have you contacted them?"

"We don't want to involve them. And it's not a police matter. My daughter wasn't kidnapped. She ran away. And she's eighteen, legally an adult." He pushed his glasses against the bridge of his thin nose. "We know you've helped the police. That's one of the reasons I came to you."

Over the past year I had become involved in several criminal investigations, a fact I still find hard to believe. The first two times, I'd been drawn by intriguing items I'd read while collecting data for my crime column. The third had been personal. Each had ultimately been a harrowing experience, and while I didn't regret my involvement, my brushes with violence and my mortality still gave me nightmares. I wasn't eager to incur more.

I didn't feel the need to explain all that. "I've never tried to find a missing person. I wouldn't know where to begin. You need a professional."

"You found Aggie Lasher's killer. The police didn't, for almost six years."

Aggie was my best friend. Her murder was the personal investigation. Though I had found a measure of solace in the truth that eluded everyone for so long, and in the knowledge that justice was finally served, thinking about her brought a stab of fresh loss. So I was offended by what I saw as Jastrow's manipulation.

"New evidence came up," I said, making light of a situation that had been anything but. "I was lucky."

"From what I heard, you were persistent. And smart." He leaned toward me. "And discreet. That's what I admired about your book, too, and your comments at the Thousand Oaks's signing. You protect your sources."

His flattery was car-salesman cloying. "What if your daughter didn't run away?" I said. "Have you checked the hospitals? She may have been involved in a car accident."

Or worse, I thought, blinking away a kaleidoscope of gruesome images. Collecting data for my column has made me uncomfortably aware of how vulnerable we all are.

"She's with a man she met on the Internet, in a chat room. She phoned her sister Monday, and again this morning. She doesn't want us to worry." Jastrow grunted. "It's an Orthodox Jewish chat room, so she thought it was safe," he added, the irony tinged with bitterness. "Dinah thought *she* was safe when she left her family's tent to see the town."

The biblical Dinah, Jacob's daughter, raped by Schechem and then held against her will. I've heard too many stories about teenage girls and adult women, lured into danger by men they've met on the Internet. Like Kacie Woody, who was kidnapped, sexually assaulted, and murdered by a forty-seven-year-old man who befriended her in a Christian chat room.

My heart ached for the man sitting across from me. "So you think your daughter was . . ."

"We're trying *not* to think. We're praying that he didn't . . . that she's. . . ." Jastrow had been playing with his knife. He set it down, clanking the foot of his water goblet. "She doesn't realize this could ruin her life. Not just *her* life. Her older sister and brother are of marriageable age, and there are younger siblings. If this gets out. . . ."

This was the "delicate" part. The Orthodox community I know and love is close-knit and supportive, but a hint of unconventional behavior can be the kiss of death for a family when parents vet prospective spouses for their children. And a teenage girl who runs away with a man . . .

"If your daughter left three days ago, Mr. Jastrow, people must know by now."

"Outside of the family, only the friend where our daughter was supposedly spending Sunday night."

"What about people at her school? Where does she go, by the way?"

"Torat Tzion. Only the Jewish studies principal knows. He won't say anything."

I was familiar with the modern Orthodox high school. "And the secular studies principal?"

"Dr. Mendes. She doesn't know. The official story is that my daughter flew to New York for a cousin's wedding. She developed bronchitis and can't travel until she feels better. Next week is Thanksgiving, so that gives us more time. And we're praying she'll be home before then."

A good story, I thought, but one that would work for only so long. "How do you know about the chat room?"

"From the friend. She claims she doesn't know this man's name, but she may be protecting my daughter, and herself." His pursed lips indicated what he thought of the friend. "We're hoping you can find out what she *does* know."

I was moved by his plight. I wanted to help. I doubted I could succeed. "I am *so* sorry about your daughter, Mr. Jastrow. I understand your concern about keeping this quiet, but you really need a private detective. I can ask my police contact for recommendations."

"A detective is a last resort," he admitted. "This friend won't be as forthcoming with a detective as she'd be with you. Her parents may not even let her *talk* to a detective. You're *frum,* Miss Blume. You're part of the community. You'd know what to say, what not to say. And as you mentioned, you have police connections. Maybe you could get them to help you, unofficially. Also—" Jastrow stopped.

Out of the corner of my eye I saw our waitress approaching. Jastrow fidgeted with a napkin while she set down his iced tea and my coffee. From his strained smile and thank you, I could tell he was eager for her to be gone.

"It's not just *finding* my daughter," he said when we were alone again. "It's convincing her to come home. She's more likely to listen to you than to a stranger. You were her counselor in B'nos. She was five at the time, but you made an impression."

I added sweetener to my coffee and stirred. I hadn't thought about the *Shabbat* afternoon program in ages. During my four years of high school, I'd probably been in charge of hundreds of ponytailed little girls who had come for the games and stories and nosh. Twenty-some years ago, I'd been one of those little girls.

"She follows your work," Jastrow said. "She admires you." He removed an envelope from his briefcase and took out a photo that he slid toward me. "That's her."

It was a glossy five-by-seven with a swirled blue background similar to the one my three sisters and I had posed against when we were seniors. Jastrow's daughter was pretty, with curly shoulder-length strawberry-blond hair, bright lively blue eyes, full lips that allowed a timid smile, a hint of dimples. Heavy makeup (de rigueur for the yearbook, aka a *"shidduch* book" perused by parents seeking mates for their sons) made her look glamorous and sophisticated, closer to twenty-two than eighteen.

In spite of my reservations I was being drawn in. "What's her name?" I asked with reluctance. A name would make it harder to walk away. I took a sip of coffee.

"Hadassah. So you'll do it? You'll help?" His tone was imploring, urgent.

I nodded and hoped I wasn't getting in over my head. "Hadassah Jastrow," I said. "I have to be honest. I don't remember her."

He returned the photo to his briefcase. "Actually, her last name isn't Jastrow."

"She's your stepdaughter?"

He looked uneasy. "My niece. I was afraid if I told you right away, you wouldn't give me a chance to explain."

For a moment I was too shocked to speak. I glared at him. "You *lied* to me?"

"She's not my daughter, no. But everything else I told you is true. Her last name is Bailor."

"Why would I—" I jostled my cup as I set it down. Coffee sloshed over the rim and onto the table. "Rabbi Bailor's daughter? *Chaim* Bailor?"

The Judaic studies teacher I had adored, the man who had later made me feel that I was a disappointment to him, to the school, to the community, to the world.

Jastrow's silence was an answer.

"So Rabbi Bailor sent you," I said, my face tingling. "He was afraid to approach me himself."

Set the hook, reel me in. No wonder Jastrow was confident that the Jewish studies principal of Torat Tzion would keep Hadassah Bailor's disappearance under wraps. Rabbi Bailor *was* that principal.

"My brother-in-law doesn't know I'm here. When I heard about your Dutton's signing, I thought, This is *bashert*. I told Nechama and Chaim, but they were sure Hadassah would come back on her own. Now they realize she isn't going to."

My mind was whirling. I blotted the table and saucer with a paper napkin. "Maybe he doesn't want my help."

"He does. He's certain you'll say no. I'm hoping you'll prove him wrong."

The man was good. "If I agree to help—and I'm not saying yes," I said, raising a warning hand. "If I do it, I'd have to have access to Hadassah's things. Her computer, papers, books. Her friends."

Jastrow nodded. "The one friend I told you about, yes. I don't know about the others. The more questions you ask, the more talk there will be. That's what we want to avoid."

This, I guessed, was the "complicated" part. "I can't exactly find Hadassah if I don't ask questions."

"You can ask about her indirectly. Maybe you can say you're doing an article on Jewish chat rooms or the school. Something like that."

I doubted that the idea had popped into Jastrow's head. He'd probably been confident that I'd agree. That annoyed me, but I had to admit his suggestion had merit.

"I'd have to ask the family questions that might make them uncomfortable," I said.

"I don't know that you'll find answers. Hadassah is a good girl. None of us saw anything that would explain why she would run away."

"Good girls run away sometimes," I said. "And they usually don't decide to do it overnight."

Chapter 4

From the lobby I watched Jastrow fold himself into a dark blue Volvo that the valet had brought to a screeching halt in the semicircular driveway. Minutes after Jastrow left, I walked to my car and drove to Sheila's, a kosher restaurant, where I enjoyed a salad, grilled chicken, and a giant chocolate chip cookie. I was the only lone diner in a restaurant packed with families, but Sheila treats customers like friends, and she stopped by frequently to chat. I bought several more cookies and half a dozen biscotti to take back to the hotel. When you're on tour, comfort food is essential, and I needed extra comforting.

I was in a tank top and pajama bottoms, lying on my bed and watching *Law and Order,* when Zack phoned me on my cell phone. I had talked to him throughout the day, including several times on my drive down to San

Diego and once after the book signing. Hearing his voice eased my loneliness and intensified it at the same time, if that makes any sense.

I lowered the volume on the TV. "Now I understand why the rabbis say you're not supposed to be apart during the first year of marriage."

"Rabbis are smart," Zack said. "How was dinner? How are *you?*"

"Fine and fine."

"You don't sound fine. You sound glum. Something on your mind?"

Hadassah Bailor. But there was no point in telling Zack about her over the phone. "I wish I were home."

"Me, too. Where are you right now?"

"In my room, on a king-size bed that's *such* a waste." God, I missed him. "How's Mrs. Kroen?"

"I left her a few hours ago. Her brother is with her, plus several friends. I don't think the reality of her husband's death has struck yet, but she's a strong woman."

"Please tell her I'm sorry I can't be at the funeral tomorrow morning. I'll pay a *shiva* call on Sunday."

Though as the rabbi's wife I'm not obligated to attend every congregant's funeral, I knew Mrs. Kroen and wanted to be there for her. But I had a newspaper interview and two radio interviews scheduled for tomorrow.

"I'll tell Mrs. Kroen," Zack said. "So what are you doing right now?"

"Watching TV and eating chocolate chip cookies—my idea of multitasking. I'd offer to save a cookie for you, but I have no willpower."

"At least you're honest."

"Speaking of honest, how was my meat loaf?"

"Speaking of honest, I froze it. My parents invited me to dinner."

I frowned. "But you told them I prepared dinner, right? I don't want them to think I'm neglecting you."

"I did. They don't. I'm the one who pushed you to go, remember? They're proud of you, Molly. They send their love. So does your family. Edie, Mindy, Judah, your mom. They all invited me to dinner. And Joey asked if I wanted to play a pickup game."

"You're not annoyed, are you?"

As an only child Zack is still adjusting to being part of my large, boisterous family. There are seven of us Blume siblings—four female, three male. I'm number three, and sometimes *I* feel overwhelmed.

"Actually, being doted on is fun," he said. "I could get used to this."

"Don't."

"Right." He laughed. "Ask me what I'm doing right now, Molly."

If I knew Zack, he'd taken advantage of my absence to unpack the boxes that were occupying most of the space in the second bedroom, even though we'd moved into our house six months ago. That's what I told him.

"A good idea, but guess again," he said.

"Polishing your *drash* for *Shabbos*."

"Already polished, with your edits. Living with a writer has its perks. FYI, I undangled the participle."

"Participles should never dangle. So what *are* you doing?"

"Making a delivery."

"What kind? I assume you don't mean a baby."

"That would be correct, and lucky for the baby and mother. Why don't you open your door?"

I turned my head toward it. "Why would I do that?"

"Because the bell is ringing."

It was. My heart skipped a beat. "You're kidding, right?" I scurried off the bed and hurried to the peephole.

He was wearing navy Dockers and a powder blue V-neck sweater that showed the white of his T-shirt. His black velvet yarmulke was off-center on his black hair, the way it usually is.

"I can't believe you drove two hours just to be with me," I said when he was inside the room.

"Chocolate chip are my favorites."

He put his hands on my waist and licked the crumbs off my lips. He's over six feet tall, and I was barefoot, so he had to bend down to kiss me. It was a long kiss that left me breathless and curled my toes and probably gave him a permanent crick in his neck, but he didn't complain.

Later, lying next to him, I told him about Reuben Jastrow and felt his muscles tense.

"I didn't want to spoil the mood, Zack, but I had to tell you."

"So I wasn't the only one to drive two hours to see you," he said, his gray-blue eyes somber. He folded his arms beneath his head. "I can't imagine what the Bailors are going through. I wish I could do something." He turned to me. "Should I call Rabbi Bailor?"

Rabbi Bailor had been Zack's teacher, too. Zack had been a grade ahead of me at Sharsheret (the high school has a coed population but separate buildings for girls and boys), along with my ex-husband, who is on the board of the synagogue where Zack is rabbi. Life is complicated.

"Definitely not. Jastrow didn't even want me to tell *you*. I told him I don't keep secrets from my husband."

Zack nodded. "Anyway, Rabbi Bailor might feel awkward if I called him. It must have been hard for him to ask you for help."

"Technically, his brother-in-law asked. I'm not even sure Rabbi Bailor *wants* my help. And I have no idea where I'd start looking for his daughter."

"You're a reporter, Molly. You're good at getting information out of people. And Andy Connors may be willing to help you."

"Maybe."

Connors is an LAPD detective with whom I've become friendly over the past five years. He's generous with information when he can give it, but I've never asked him for a personal favor. I explained that to Zack.

He raised himself on one elbow. "This isn't about Connors helping you. You don't want to do this, do you?"

"I have mixed feelings."

He linked his fingers with mine. "Why are you resisting? Is it because she's Rabbi Bailor's daughter?"

"That's part of it. I don't like the fact that Jastrow lied to me, for one thing."

"Jastrow explained why. If he'd told you right away that he was here on behalf of the Bailors, would you have given him the time of day?"

"I don't know," I admitted. "Meeting with Rabbi Bailor will be awkward, Zack. And yes, I'm still hurt by what he did. But that's petty, considering what he and his wife are going through. I feel terrible for them."

"I guess you have your answer," Zack said.

"What if I can't find her, Zack?"

"Then the Bailors are no worse off than they are now."

"They could be wasting precious time. I still think they should go to the police, Zack. I told that to Jastrow again, before he left. Just because Hadassah told her sister she's safe doesn't mean she is."

Chapter 5

==

There were two things Hadassah hadn't antic-
ipated: how much she would miss her family,
and how much the lies would trouble her.

The secret had been enough, at first, to
block out both concerns. From her waking
moment on Sunday, the secret had enveloped
her, had filled her consciousness, had made it
difficult for her to think of anything else as her
fingers flew across the keyboard, knowing that
his fingers were on a keyboard just miles away,
typing words that made her heart sing while
she dressed and packed her bag and woke the
boys and said good-bye to her mother.

See you tonight, sweetie.

Hadassah had worried, because how was it
possible that no one would detect the excitement that surged through her like electricity?
She must look different. She *felt* different. But
Laban, she remembered learning in class, had

seen Rachel and Leah every day and had detected no sign that his daughters were about to steal away with his son-in-law, Jacob, and their families and possessions.

And anyway, Aliza had been drunk with sleep and dashed hopes, and her mother had been oblivious. "Did the boys brush their teeth?" she'd asked.

Later that night, and early the next morning, Hadassah's excitement had been muted with panic that buzzed in her head and tightened her chest until she was perspiring and nauseated with fear.

What had she done?

He had calmed her, the way he always did. It was natural to be nervous, he'd told her. She had never disobeyed her parents, had never made a decision on her own even though she was eighteen years old, legally an adult, something her parents seemed not to recognize. If they hadn't kept her back a year, she would be making her own decisions, wasn't that so? What she wanted to do with her life, who she wanted to marry?

Some girls her age were already engaged to men they'd known only weeks—less time than he and Dassie had known each other. And yes, both sets of parents had checked out the other family and the young man and woman, but that wasn't a guarantee, was it? You never really knew someone until you lived with that person—what was truth, what was exaggeration or lies.

And Dassie's parents wouldn't approve of him, even though he loved her and cherished her. They would never think he was good enough for their daughter. A rabbi's daughter. They probably wanted her to marry a rabbi's son, someone like her brother, who learned Torah all day. They would lie. "Let's wait until after Aliza is engaged, sweetheart." And who knew when that would be? Two years, three? And in the meantime they would try to change Dassie's mind, and set her up with young men they chose for her.

"You know that's what will happen, Dassie."

Unless Dassie didn't love him? Or maybe, like her parents, she thought he *wasn't* good enough? "If you're not sure," he'd said, "if you want to go home . . ."

Today had been bad. With each day that passed she felt more like a prisoner, though she understood that it was risky for her to leave the apartment, or go on the balcony, or open the blinds.

"My neighbors are nosy," he'd said. "We have to keep a low profile until the time is right. . . ."

But she felt isolated and lonely, especially when he was away, sometimes even when he was with her. More than once she'd been tempted to phone her family, or Sara. It wasn't a good idea, he'd told her. They would try to convince her to come home. He was right, of course. So she'd given him her cell phone.

"Only if you want to," he'd said. "I'll give it back whenever you say. The nice thing is, my charger works for your phone. Another bond," he'd joked.

There was no other phone in the apartment. He'd moved in a few months ago and planned to get phone service, but he had his cell phone, so he was in no rush.

It was a nice apartment, nicer than she'd expected, and he'd tried hard to make it her home. He'd scattered rose petals on the large sleigh bed that first night. He'd filled the closet with clothes he'd bought her (some of the clothes weren't to her taste, but she hadn't told him) and stocked the fridge and small pantry with foods she liked. He'd bought several of her favorite CDs, which she'd played, keeping the volume low, on the sound system he kept in a teak wall unit in the living room. He had a large mix of CDs, classical to heavy metal. She found most of the ones he favored depressing, especially the sound track from *Romeo and Juliet*. "I Would Die for You." He played that song over and over and knew the lyrics by heart.

"That'll be *our* song, Dassie," he told her.

She would have chosen a different song, one that didn't talk about death and twisting knives and bleeding hearts, but she didn't want to hurt his feelings.

Also in the wall unit were hundreds of books and knickknacks, including a black marble owl that stared at her knowingly and a thirty-two-inch TV. During the day, while he was out, she spent hours watching TV, letting other people's faces and voices fill her head so there was no room for her thoughts. Katie Couric and *The View*, and Ellen De-Generes and Oprah and Judge Judy, reruns of *Seinfeld, Friends, Will and*

Grace—so many shows that she'd seen at Sara's or some of her other friends. Not at home. Her parents had never owned a TV.

She wondered what they were doing now. If she were home, she would be helping her mother, braiding the challas and brushing them with an egg wash after the dough rose. If she shut her eyes she could smell the yeast, and the dill her mother sprinkled into the soup. Chicken this week, last week it was split pea. Her father was probably at the dining room table, learning the week's Torah portion with Yonatan and the other boys, unless he was at a meeting, or talking with Gavriel, who had barely said ten words to her when he was home in October for Sukkot, because he was always out on a date. Aliza was, too. Hadassah knew they were angry at her, would blame her if the *shadchonim* stopped calling because she had brought shame to the family.

And the lies, so many lies. One had followed the other. They nibbled at her now like tiny insects, made her face hot and her skin itch when she allowed herself to think about them.

"Sometimes you have to lie to protect yourself," he'd told her. Abraham had told the king that Sara was his sister, not his wife. Isaac had done the same. And Jacob had conspired with his mother, Rebecca, and lied to his father to steal the birthright from Esau.

"You're not stealing anything, Dassie, are you?" he'd asked.

Peace of mind, she had thought but hadn't said. Trust. Things she could never return . . .

But she trusted him, too. And loved him. And he loved her.

Those *weren't* lies.

Chapter 6

Thursday, November 18, 7:03 p.m. Along the 8100 block of Santa Monica Boulevard. A woman reported that an unknown Caucasian male thief stole her wheelchair that she had left just outside a store while making a purchase.

The Bailors lived on Cardiff in Pico-Robertson, an Orthodox Jewish neighborhood that, Zack and I joke, will soon have more kosher restaurants than residents. I parked in front of the two-story house, a dark gray stucco with a lighter gray trim and a narrow but tidy flower bed thickly planted with pansies. Aside from the addition of a black wrought-iron gate in the driveway and the two cars parked in front of it—a black Honda and a silver minivan—nothing had changed since the first time I'd been here fifteen years ago, when I was one of thirty-plus girls at a sophomore barbecue in the middle of Sukkot, the eight-day harvest holiday that starts five days after Yom Kippur.

At the time I had been Rabbi Bailor's student for less than two months, but I'd had a crush on him since my freshman year. I wasn't alone in my infatuation (I had to share him with most of the girls in my school), and I'd had to adjust my fantasy to include a wife and children. If I couldn't have Rabbi Bailor, I wanted someone just like him.

He was in his early thirties then, younger than our other male teachers and, despite the bump on his nose, better looking, too—slim and broad-shouldered, with a square chin darkened by a perpetual five-o'clock shadow, and straight, jet-black hair that he was always pushing away from his eyes. It was the eyes—dark brown, soulful—that held you spellbound and pinned you to your seat, eyes that made you squirm if you weren't prepared and, if you were, made your heart soar when he smiled at you as though you were the only one in the room and said, "Very good," in a heavy Brooklyn accent that conjured up the high school basketball court where, we'd heard, he'd obtained the nose bump and the small scar on his chin.

He was a restless man, always in motion. When he wasn't attacking the blackboard with his bold, jagged script, he was striding between the rows of desks, sometimes backward, keeping us on our toes while he bounced on his, constantly adjusting the black velvet yarmulke that migrated to the side of his head, jiggling the keys in his pants pockets, tossing his chalk from palm to palm as he pondered an answer or a question. He spoke rapidly, too, and would wait for us to supply the missing word or syllables of a phrase or sentence, maybe because his mind was racing ahead to the next thought. I don't think he was conscious of his trait or our contribution. The one time we let him flounder for several long, excruciating seconds, he looked confused until someone (I think it was Aggie) came to his rescue. He laughed good-naturedly, but his face was pink, and we never had the heart to tease him again.

From the way he eyed me when he laughed that day, I think he suspected that I was behind the prank. I wasn't, but peer loyalty and the horror of being a goody-goody prevented me from telling him so. I didn't blame him for thinking I was the instigator. Unlike my two older sisters, Edie and Mindy, class valedictorians who had earned glory for the Blume name, I had earned frequent visits to the principal's office, prompted by teachers' complaints.

I was "excessively exuberant." I was too inquisitive, too persistent. I was argumentative and lacked respect for authority. My appearance and behavior didn't reflect the modesty of a true *bas Yisroel,* a daughter of Israel.

But in Rabbi Bailor's class, I was a model student, and he was my champion. He not only tolerated my endless questions (about the Bible and Jewish law, about philosophy, about the temptations of the secular world) but encouraged them and my spirited arguments—some of which, I'll admit, were a ploy to get his attention. If he didn't have an answer, he'd say so and research the subject. And while I'm sure he disapproved of the brevity of my uniform skirt and the dark crimson polish on my nails, he never said anything—at least, not to me. His acceptance and honesty and dedication inspired me. I wanted desperately to please him, to make him proud. That's why his betrayal was so devastating.

I tried not to think about that now as I sat facing the rabbi and his wife at the white-cloth-covered dining room table where, before things soured, I'd enjoyed several *Shabbat* meals. It was Thursday evening, and preparations for the Sabbath were in evidence. An eight-armed silver candelabrum and tray occupied one end of the table, and a mélange of aromas wafted in from the kitchen. Gefilte fish, beef seasoned with garlic and onion, dilled chicken soup, the yeasty perfume of freshly baked challa.

The room was as I'd remembered it. With the exception of a modest china closet that displayed an assortment of silver chalices, a Chanukah menorah, and other ritual items, the pale peach walls were lined with floor-to-ceiling dark wood bookcases crammed with gilt-lettered, oversized, leather-bound volumes of the Talmud and its commentaries. In the adjoining living room there were more texts on the coffee table, more filled bookcases. The furniture, mismatched, seemed incidental.

Rabbi Bailor had aged well. His black hair was streaked with silver, and there was more gray than black in the trim beard that hid the scar on his chin, but he was still handsome. I couldn't remember when I'd first noticed the beard. Ten years ago? Twelve? Over the years I had seen him at a wedding or a funeral, in one of the kosher markets or bakeries. I'd avoided looking at him, and I suspect he'd avoided looking at me, too.

I had occasionally seen Mrs. Bailor, too. She had her runaway daughter's vivid blue eyes, the strawberry-blond hair, the angular chin. In high school, after coming to terms with the fact that there *was* a Mrs. Bailor, I had liked that she was pretty. Rabbi Bailor *deserved* pretty. Now she looked tired and drawn, her pallor unrelieved by lipstick or blush, her eyelids puffy and red. Her hair was covered with a black crocheted snood instead of her usual wig, and she looked different. Younger, actually.

Many Orthodox married women cover their hair. I do it, for Zack. As my mother and Mindy had promised, it's less cumbersome than I'd expected, but after eight months I'm still eager to remove my hat or wig the minute I'm home, and I miss feeling the wind in my hair, the sun on my head. And it isn't second nature. Several times I've left the house bareheaded and have had to return for a covering.

I wear hats more often than my wig, which is almost identical to my shoulder-length highlighted blond hair, but that evening I'd opted for the wig, and a navy skirt that covered my knees, coupled with a long-sleeved cowl-neck gray sweater. Practically a school uniform, I'd realized as I finished changing from my travel clothes. Freud would have had a field day.

"My wife and I appreciate your coming here," Rabbi Bailor said. "It's good to see you, Malka."

"Molly."

Malka is the Hebrew for Mala, the paternal Polish-Jewish great-grandmother I never knew. I'm proud to carry her name, and it's what all my Judaic studies instructors had called me, but I suppose I wanted to assert my independence. *I'm not your student.*

He nodded. "Molly."

His eyes, surrounded by a network of crow's-feet, hadn't lost their intensity, and the look he gave me—a little hurt, I thought—made me feel small. I was thirty years old, but I folded my hands in my lap and felt as though I were back in school.

"*Mazel tov* on your marriage," Nechama Bailor said, filling the awkward silence. "We were happy to hear your good news. That was six months ago?"

She didn't sound happy. She sounded burdened with the effort of making small talk. I didn't blame her.

"Eight. Thank you." Zack had wanted to invite the Bailors to the wedding. I had nixed it, just as I had nixed inviting them to my first wedding.

"I'm glad you and Zack found each other," Rabbi Bailor said. "I hear that his congregation loves him. I told him he had great potential, even though he wasn't exactly serious about my class." A half smile played around the rabbi's lips. "I knew you had great potential, too, Molly."

"*Did* you?"

"Yes," he said, ignoring my sarcasm. "And I was right. You've had several books published. You write a weekly column. *Kol ha'kavod.*" Kudos.

"Thanks."

There was another silence. Mrs. Bailor turned her attention to the wedding band she was twisting.

"I was so sorry to hear about your daughter," I said. "You haven't heard from her since yesterday?"

"We keep trying her cell phone. She doesn't answer." Rabbi Bailor's voice had become husky. "We're living a nightmare. Every morning I wake up and look in Dassie's room, expecting to see her."

"Was Hadassah upset lately? Did she quarrel with either of you or her siblings?"

He cleared his throat. "We have the typical father–daughter disagreements. Sometimes Dassie's moody. Sometimes she doesn't want to talk. That's how teenagers are. Lately, she seemed *less* moody. And she's never given us cause for concern. This is so out of character."

"Why would she *do* this?" the mother said, her voice breaking.

Rabbi Bailor reached for his wife's hand. She pulled it away. Above the beard a hint of color tinged his cheeks.

As a writer I found the scene revealing. As the rabbi's former student I felt unsettled, witnessing an intimate moment, and I shared his embarrassment.

Rabbi Bailor passed me a yellow Post-it. "That's the address and phone number for Sara Mellon, the friend Dassie told about the chat room. She's willing to talk to you. I know you've just returned from San Diego, Molly, but if you could go there tonight?"

"Of course." I glanced at the Post-it. The girl lived on Reeves, only blocks from the Bailors.

"Sara could have told us *weeks* ago." The mother's voice was brooding. Anger pinched her colorless lips. "If she had, Dassie would be home, not off who knows where with some piece of trash."

"Dassie might have run off anyway, Nechama. And teenagers don't tattle on their friends." The rabbi's weariness suggested they'd discussed this before.

"Even if the friend is in danger?" Her eyes flashed. "Dassie said she's safe, but how do we know that's true, Chaim? Who knows what this man is planning?"

The tension in the room was incongruous with the *Shabbat* candlesticks and the serenity they promised. We lapsed into another silence which Rabbi Bailor interrupted with a long sigh.

"Dassie knows chat rooms are off limits," he said. "She understood why. This is so out of . . ."

"Character," I finished for him.

"Yes." He looked at me sharply. "He tricked her. He brainwashed her." The rabbi's hand formed a fist. "You have to find her, Molly. You have to convince Dassie that we don't care what happened. We just want her home, *now.*"

"You didn't notice anything unusual about Hadassah that morning?" I asked. "Or during the days before?"

"That's what we keep asking ourselves. I'm not home much. That's not an excuse, but . . ." He looked at his wife.

"We have a busy household." Nechama was prickly with defensiveness, which she tried to soften with a tight smile. "The younger children need constant attention. Our two oldest are dating, and—well, you know what they say. '*Kleine kinder . . .*' "

I nodded. *Kleine kinder, kleine freiden; groisseh kinder, groisseh laiden.* Small children, small joys; bigger children, bigger sorrows.

"I try to give Dassie her space," Nechama said. "But if something was bothering her, we would have known."

From my own experiences as a teenager, I wasn't sure that was so. "And Sunday morning?"

"Chaim was in *shul*. I saw Dassie when she was leaving for Sara's. She got the boys ready for school and prepared their snacks. My weekly Mother's Day gift, she calls it." Nechama smiled again, more genuinely.

"Did she have luggage with her?"

"Her backpack and an overnight bag. My husband picked them up Monday night from Sara's. Dassie said she was spending the night and needed her uniform for school the next day." Nechama's face clouded.

I could hear the hurt in her voice. "Speaking of school, your brother mentioned that Hadassah is eighteen. Was she kept behind?"

"Her birthday was in September. We thought it would be better if she was one of the older girls in her class, not one of the youngest. Also, with two grades between Dassie and Aliza, her older sister, there was less competition."

Having two older, accomplished sisters, I understood about competition. "Was Hadassah having difficulty with her classes or with the other students?"

"Dassie gets along with everybody," Rabbi Bailor said. "She's doing well in all her classes. Not straight A's, as she hoped, but it's a heavy double schedule. We don't expect A's. Just do your best. That's what we tell all our children. I don't know if she believes us."

"She *is* tense about school," the mother said. "Term papers, midterms, SATs. All those applications."

"Applications for seminary, you mean?"

Most Orthodox girls spend the year after high school in one of many Jerusalem all-girl schools. I had done it. So had my three sisters.

"And for college," the rabbi said. "She plans to go after her year in Israel."

"She might change her mind about college," Nechama said. "She might meet someone."

I sensed that she hoped her daughter *would* change her mind. It's not uncommon for Orthodox girls to marry soon after their year of seminary, but it's not typical of young women from Torat Tzion, which prides itself on the high number of graduates who get into the Ivy Leagues. I was surprised the Bailors had allowed their daughter to attend a school with a liberal philosophy and coed classes.

"Hadassah wants to be a defense attorney," Rabbi Bailor said when I asked him about it. "She needs an academic program that will give her the best chance of getting into a top college and law school. And since I'm at Torat Tzion, that made the most sense."

"Even though the students are more modern?"

"We weren't worried."

"*You* weren't worried," his wife said.

The rabbi flushed. "Dassie knows who she is, what her values are. Some of the girls dress and behave inappropriately. Dassie's sleeves are so long you can't see her wrists. If anything, *tznius* has become *more* important to her."

The laws of modesty. Skirts well below the knee, sleeves covering the elbow, necklines that expose a minimum of skin, general decorum. Those are some of the rules I continue to bend, though because of Zack, I've compromised.

"But it must be difficult for Hadassah," I pressed. "Most of the students socialize, go on dates. . . ."

"Dating was out of the question," he said, impatient. "Dassie never pressured us about it. So all of this . . ." The rabbi's shoulders sagged. "You must think I'm a fool," he said quietly. "Obviously, Dassie felt pressured. Maybe we made a mistake." He glanced at his wife. "Maybe *I* made a mistake."

Nechama turned her head away. It was another private, painful moment that made me wish I were somewhere else.

"She wrote a beautiful essay," the rabbi said. "She had help, but the ideas were hers, and the style."

"Who helped her?"

"Mrs. Wexner. Many of our students hire her for help with the application process—the competition to get into a top college is intense. And Mrs. Wexner didn't charge us, because I'm studying with her son."

"Using hours you could put to better use," his wife said. "You barely have time to breathe, Chaim."

"The young man wants to deepen his understanding of Judaism, Nechama. How is that a waste of time?"

"It's not." She lowered her eyes, embarrassed. "I'm sorry. I'm just so tense."

He made a move to take her hand. Instead, he curled his fingers into a ball that he pressed against his mouth.

"Do you have Mrs. Wexner's phone number?" I asked. "Hadassah may have told her something she wouldn't tell her parents."

"I used to think she told us everything." The rabbi looked at his wife. She was lost in thought. "It's a good idea, Molly. Dassie likes Mrs. Wexner. I have her number at school. I'll get it for you tomorrow. I'm sure she'll be discreet," he added, glancing again at his wife.

I asked whether Hadassah had kept a journal. Nechama told me she hadn't found one.

"If she *did* have one, she took it with her," she said.

Disappointing, but not surprising. "I'd like to see the essay she wrote."

"It won't tell you anything," Rabbi Bailor said. "She talks about her desire to protect society and the rights of the individual. Nothing in it explains why she ran away."

"True, but it may give me a sense of your daughter's personality, her interests."

He adjusted his yarmulke. "And how is that relevant?"

"I don't know that it is." I was back in Rabbi Bailor's class, forced to defend my position. In high school I'd enjoyed being challenged. Now I bristled. "As I told your brother-in-law, I've never tried to find a missing person. You should really hire a detective."

"I thought you understood our situation, Molly." The rabbi sounded pained.

"That's why I'm here. But I need your cooperation, not your resistance." I couldn't believe I was talking with such chutzpah to the teacher I had revered.

He drew back, bewildered. "I'm not resisting."

"*Chaim.*" Nechama sighed his name.

He faced his wife. "Since when is asking questions 'resisting'?" To me, he said, "Of course, you can read the essay, Molly. I just didn't see the point. What else?"

He was right. I'd been seeking a justification to vent my resentment from the moment I'd arrived. "I'll need to talk to Hadassah's siblings. Who's the dark-haired young man who was leaving when I arrived?"

"Gavriel. He's twenty-three, our oldest." Nechama named with pride a top-ranked New York yeshiva where her son was studying. "He came home Tuesday to give us moral support. He hasn't talked to Dassie in weeks. Longer, really. And our three younger boys don't know about Dassie."

"Is there anything else I should know?"

"I can't think of anything." She turned to her husband. "Chaim?"

"No, nothing," her husband said. "That's it?"

I had detected a beat of hesitation and wondered what, if anything, the rabbi was withholding. And why. "I'd like to see Hadassah's room."

"Fine. Whatever you want."

He sounded defeated. The former student in me was uncomfortable. Another part—a part I'm not proud of—enjoyed the moment, and I was flustered by my petty victory.

Nechama pushed her chair away from the table. "I'll get the essay."

She left the room through a doorway that led to the hall and shut the door behind her. I was alone with the rabbi. For over a decade I had fantasized about confronting him, but this wasn't the time.

"Tomorrow is *Shabbos,*" he said. "I keep wondering where Dassie is, what she's doing. What kind of *Shabbos* will she have?"

I didn't know how to respond to that.

"It's been many years since you've been here, Molly."

"Fourteen." I broke off a cluster of flame grapes from the platter on the table and slipped it onto a plate.

"To be honest, I wasn't sure you'd come. I know you're still angry with me."

I plucked a grape and silently recited the blessing before biting into it.

"It wasn't my decision, Molly."

"You allowed the school to suspend me for something I didn't do. You let Rabbi Ingel harangue me in front of all my friends and teachers."

For a moment I was back in the large, crowded cafeteria. Ingel, tall and rotund with blond hair cut so short it was almost invisible, loomed over me, his blue eyes sparking with fury that contorted the otherwise ordinary features of his clean-shaven face. His words, thundering with a ferocity that bounced off the walls in that awful silence, torched my cheeks and pierced my heart. I couldn't breathe. I willed the floor to open up and swallow me.

"Rabbi Ingel was agitated, Molly. He—"

"He called me a liar and a cheater, and you didn't say anything." My cheeks flamed. My voice quivered with fourteen-year-old hurt. "He said my children would be liars and cheaters."

Rabbi Bailor sighed. "Rabbi Ingel told me the next day that he wished he could take back what he'd said. He was agitated. He said you got hold of a copy of his final and circulated it before the exam."

I shook my head.

"Why would Rabbi Ingel accuse you of something you didn't do, Molly?" he asked gently.

"Because he never liked me? Because I asked questions he couldn't or wouldn't answer? Because he didn't want to give me an A? Because he couldn't imagine that one of the 'good girls' who sucked up to him could have done what he accused me of doing?" I took a breath. "The answer is, all of the above."

"Rabbi Ingel told us he had proof."

"And you believed him. That's what hurts. You *knew* I'd never do something like that. But you didn't defend me."

"The truth is, Molly—"

Nechama entered the dining room. I wondered how long she'd been on the other side of the door, what she'd heard.

She handed me a manila folder. "Here's the essay, and Hadassah's yearbook photo." She glanced at her husband, then at me. "Is everything all right?"

"Everything is fine," I said.

Chapter 7

Aliza had talked to her sister around seven on Saturday night.

"I was getting ready for a date, and she was on the computer," Aliza told me. "Dassie's *always* on the computer. And I'm always going on dates." There was a hint of sadness behind the wry smile.

She was nineteen, petite and more striking than Hadassah, with her father's dark eyes and a long sleek waterfall of dark brown hair that she kept pushing behind her ears. With her midcalf skirt billowing around her, she sat cross-legged on the baby blue matelassé spread on one of the two twin beds, surrounded by skirts and sweaters, stuffed animals, and an assortment of throw pillows that picked up the blue and mauve in the floral wallpaper. More clothes lay on Hadassah's bed. Aliza had shoved a pile aside so that I could sit.

"I'm going to the Valley for *Shabbos*," she said after apologizing for the mess of clothes. "A high school reunion. My parents said I have to go. I'm supposed to smile and pretend everything's fine, when Dassie could be. . . ." Her lips trembled. "I can't believe she ran away with a guy she met in a chat room. Why would she do something so *stupid?*"

"Hadassah never confided in you about being interested in anyone? Visiting chat rooms?"

"No. She probably figured I'd tell my parents. And to be honest, we aren't that close." Aliza shrugged. "She told her friend, though."

She tried to sound matter-of-fact, but I heard a touch of envy. Though my three sisters and I experienced the typical rivalries and spats, and we occasionally get on one another's nerves, we've always been close.

"Even though you're roommates?" I said.

"Last year I was in seminary. This year we don't see each other much. I get home from teaching after six, and I'm taking computer classes at night." She pushed a strand of hair behind her ear. "And dating." There was the ironic smile again.

"But you're the one Dassie phoned. How did she reach you, by the way?"

"On my cell. I guess she figured it was easier talking to me than to my mom or dad."

"What did she say?"

"That she was safe, and we shouldn't worry. She sounded nervous and hung up before I could ask her anything. I called her back, but she didn't answer."

"What about the second call?"

"Yesterday morning, you mean. She asked how our parents were doing. I said, 'How do you *think* they're doing?'" Aliza scowled. "She said to tell them she was sorry, that she hoped they'd forgive her. I *begged* her to come home. She said she couldn't. They probably had . . . relations, and she's ashamed to face my parents." The girl's face had turned pink.

I had a squirrelly feeling in my stomach. "Did you get the sense that she was being kept against her will? That she was afraid of this man?"

"I don't know. She sounded scared, like she was about to cry. I thought it was because she realized what she'd done. But she *said* she was safe. She wouldn't say that if she wasn't, right?"

Aliza's voice was imploring. Her eyes were anxious. I wanted to reassure her, but my unease was growing. I'm not sure why.

"Tell me about the morning Hadassah left, Aliza."

"There's not much to tell. I heard her do *negel vasser.*" The ritual morning rinsing of the hands. "And I heard her on the computer."

"Something for school?" I prompted when Aliza fell silent. "It may not be important, Aliza. Or it could be very important."

She traced a circle on the spread. "Dassie was on the Internet, instant-messaging someone. I heard a sound every time someone wrote back."

"What kind of sound?"

"Drums? Something like that." She hesitated. "I heard it before. A few weeks ago Dassie left and forgot to go off-line. Someone was IM'ing her, over and over. The sound was making me crazy, so I IM'ed the person and said Dassie wasn't home."

"Did you read the messages?"

"Just the last few lines. They were all the same. 'Where are you, sweetie?' That's how Dassie sometimes talks with her friends, so I thought it was a girlfriend."

With drums as a background noise? "Do you remember this person's screen name?"

"Something with 'For Jew' in it. But it was spelled J-U. Dassie found out. She yelled at me, said I was violating her privacy. It was probably this guy, right?" Aliza's eyes looked troubled.

That was my bet. "Maybe, maybe not," I said. "Do your parents know about this?"

"No." Aliza traced another circle on the spread. "I thought they'd be upset I didn't tell them right away. But it's not like I knew who it was." She looked up at me. "Can you tell them?"

On the wall facing the beds were two desks, one of which belonged to Hadassah. I switched on her computer and checked the documents she had recently worked on. A paper on the *Canterbury Tales*, another on the French Revolution. One file folder, COLLEGE APPS, included several versions of the essay Hadassah had written. I would have liked to view the websites she'd visited, but neither Aliza nor her parents knew Hadassah's password.

They couldn't tell whether any of her clothing was missing, either. Since she'd started driving, Hadassah usually shopped alone, and she often used her babysitting earnings for her purchases, so her parents weren't aware of what she bought.

Aliza wasn't familiar with her sister's wardrobe.

"We don't share clothes—well, except sweaters," she said. "Dassie and I have different figures. She's much taller, for one thing."

While Aliza sorted through the mounds of clothes on both beds, I rummaged through Hadassah's drawers and found clothing typical of the average Orthodox Jewish teenager, along with assorted memorabilia. Ticket stubs to Jewish concerts, letters from camp friends, an elementary school autograph book. Included among the letters was a photo of a brown-haired girl. I showed it to Aliza.

"That's Batya Weinberg," she said, her somber tone telegraphing bad news. "She was in Dassie's class. She died last May."

I looked at the thin young face and felt a twinge of sadness for someone I didn't even know. "What happened?"

"She had a heart attack. It happened very fast—like with that athlete who died on the field? They didn't know he had a heart condition. After Batya died, my dad had a psychologist talk to all the students. It wasn't just because of Batya. A boy in their class who had cancer died a few months before Batya. And the year before, another girl lost her sister in a car accident."

A heavy load of grief for one class. "Did Hadassah talk with this psychologist?"

"I guess. She was depressed about Batya and the other kids who died. Everybody was. But you'd have to ask my father."

I made a mental note to do that. "Aside from Sara Mellon, who else would your sister have confided in?"

Aliza looked sheepish. "Like I said, we're not close."

The backpack and overnight bag that Hadassah had taken to Sara's were in a corner of the room. The bag held her school uniform, underwear, opaque tights, and a pink vinyl zippered bag with toiletries. The school bag contained spiral notebooks, a notepad, pens, folders. I checked the folders and notebooks (in high school I'd written "Mrs. Zack Abrams" countless times), but I found no clue to the identity of Hadassah's Internet boyfriend.

In the closet I flipped through the clothes in the section Aliza indicated was Hadassah's. Most of the skirts and blouses (all long-sleeved, as Rabbi Bailor had said) were size two. A few were size 0, a size I'll never understand. And Abercrombie and Fitch, I heard, sells clothes in size 00.

"Dassie can eat a dozen doughnuts and not gain an ounce," Aliza said with envy when I remarked on the sizes. "I gained fifteen pounds in Israel and still haven't lost everything."

"Everybody gains weight in seminary." The wonderful fresh bread, the falafel, the chumous and tehina. "You look fine, Aliza."

"That's what my parents say, but tell it to the guys. They all want skinny, skinny, skinny." She sucked in her cheeks, then let out her breath with an uncertain laugh. "And tall. I'm short, so every ounce shows. But I'm on South Beach now, and I lost three pounds."

I've tried the South Beach diet. And The Zone, and a few others. So have my sisters and my mother, who is struggling with the pounds menopause has added. I mostly struggle with chocolate.

Aliza moved back to the bed and picked up a black sweater. "Dassie reads everything you write. She wants to be a lawyer, so I guess that's why." She folded a sleeve of the sweater, her eyes on me. "My father said you worked with the police to solve some cases."

"Not in an official capacity. But I *was* able to help them," I said, not wanting to sound immodest, yet hoping to give her assurance.

"Do you think you can find Dassie?"

"I don't know. I'm going to try."

She finished folding the sweater. "I don't care what people say if they find out. I just want Dassie home." Tears flooded her eyes. "I keep thinking, what if I'd told my parents about the IM. . . ."

"Don't." I took her hand. "If Dassie was determined to meet this man, she would have figured out a way, even if your parents had kept a watch on her."

"You really think so?"

I nodded.

Aliza left the room in search of luggage. I took advantage of her absence to poke through the trash can at the side of Hadassah's bed. Underneath crumpled papers, a handful of used unbent staples that poked my fingers, soiled cotton balls, and tissues stained with dark red lipstick, I discovered tags from Forever XXI, a trendy store. That was interesting. So was the stack of magazines under the bed: *In Style, Us, Teen Ink, Seventeen.* Maybe typical reading for a Torat Tzion girl, but it didn't fit with the girl who kept a basin and laver at her bedside so that she could perform the ritual morning hand-washing.

I pushed the magazines back under the bed, but kept the tags.

Chapter 8

Rabbi Bailor was in the dining room where I had left him, reading from a large text to the young boy on his lap.

"This is Yonatan," the rabbi told me. "Say hello to Mrs. Abrams, Yonatan. I was her teacher many years ago."

"Hello," the boy said shyly. He was blond and blue-eyed, like his mother.

"Yonatan is seven, but he gets to stay up late on Thursdays so that we can learn Torah. And tonight he asked a question I couldn't answer. Right, Yonatan?"

The boy grinned, producing dimples and revealing a gap where his two bottom front teeth should have been.

"I'm going to talk to Mrs. Abrams, Yonatan. Get ready for bed, and I'll come up and say *Sh'ma* with you."

Rabbi Bailor kissed the top of his son's

head and eased him off his lap. He watched him leave the room, then faced me.

"You talked to Aliza? She's a lovely girl, isn't she?"

"Very." I considered telling him his daughter was worried about her weight, but it wasn't my business. "She told me you had a psychologist talk to the students."

"Dr. McIntyre. He came to counsel students after the Weinberg girl died, and this year he's teaching a class for us. Batya's death was the third tragedy in that class. Aliza told you? It was a terrible time, terrible." The rabbi sighed deeply. "How do you explain the deaths of children to children? You talk about *Olam Habah*." The afterlife. "You tell them *Hashem* is a loving Father, that He has a plan we can't begin to fathom, that these souls have fulfilled their missions on this earth. But how can you expect them to understand when you don't?"

I have only recently begun to work through my feelings about God and Aggie's murder, so I had no answer for that.

"Did Hadassah talk to Dr. McIntyre?" I asked.

"Many times. She took Batya's death hard. Dassie's still seeing him. In fact, Dr. McIntyre is the first person I turned to when Dassie ran away. She's not answering our calls, but I thought maybe she would take his." The rabbi rubbed his palms against the edge of the table. "Dr. McIntyre said he can't initiate the communication. Dassie has his number. She would have to contact him."

"I'd like to talk to him. What about Hadassah's teachers? Maybe one of them can give us a lead."

Rabbi Bailor frowned. "I thought my brother-in-law explained, Molly. We don't want this getting out."

"I'm not planning to advertise your daughter's disappearance in the *Jewish Journal*." I blushed. "I'm sorry. That was *chutzpadik*."

"Yes, it was," he said quietly. "But you're right. You have to ask questions." The look he gave me was filled with sadness.

I would have preferred anger. "About her teachers?"

"Dassie likes most of them."

"Anyone in particular?" I prodded, curbing my impatience.

"She admired her history teacher, but he's not at Torat Tzion this year." Rabbi Bailor shut the text. "So did you learn anything from Aliza?"

I fingered the tags in my jacket pocket and told him about the instant message.

"At the time Aliza didn't realize it was important," I said. "Later, she was afraid you and your wife would be upset that she hadn't told you right away."

"Poor Aliza." He sighed. "She must feel terrible, carrying that around, worrying about what we would say."

"You should tell her that."

His dark eyes narrowed. "I don't need you to teach me how to be a parent, Molly."

My face burned. "I'm sorry. I didn't mean—"

He took a deep breath. "No, *I'm* sorry. Obviously, I haven't been doing a great job. Hadassah ran away. Aliza's afraid to talk to me. Gavriel—" He stopped. "I'll talk to Aliza. Thank you for telling me, Molly. I mean that."

"You can't blame yourself because Hadassah ran away, Rabbi Bailor."

"Who *should* I blame?"

He walked me to the door and took my jacket out of the hall closet.

"I read a recent commentary about Dinah," he said. "Before she was raped, the Torah refers to her as Leah's daughter. After the rape, she's *Jacob's* daughter. The change suggests that her father and brothers should have been aware that Dinah left her tent to see the daughters of the land perform. And the Rambam's son says her menfolk were negligent in guarding her. Not everyone agrees, but I can't stop thinking about that."

"You warned Dassie about chat rooms," I said. "You couldn't control her actions. Teenagers break rules. They take risks. It's almost an eleventh commandment."

"I was arrogant," he said, his voice humbled with anguish. "I thought that what happens to others would never happen to my family. I urge parents to use computer spyware, to Google their kids' names to see if any websites come up with their personal information. I didn't do that with Dassie. I thought she was safe."

His pain filled me with sorrow. I wished I had more to offer than words. "Dassie told Aliza she *is* safe, Rabbi Bailor. Until we know otherwise, I think you should take comfort in that."

Reaching into the closet, he removed a small manila bubble mailer from the inside pocket of his coat and handed it to me. "I received this at the office in today's mail."

There was no return address. Inside the mailer was a gold mesh bag with silver foil–wrapped chocolate coins, the kind kids get on Chanukah, along with a computer-printed message on a small sheet of paper that I was careful to hold by its corners:

> What DOES become of the broken-hearted?
> A penny for your thoughts, Rabbi. Or should I say a shekel? Or fifty?

There was no signature.

"That's a song reference. 'What Becomes of the Broken-Hearted?' " I looked up. "It's from him, right? Why didn't you show this to me earlier?"

"Because I'm not sure it *is* from him, and I don't want Nechama to know about it. I was hoping you'd say I was jumping to conclusions."

"Who else would send you an anonymous note?" I said, unable to check my irritation. I read the note again. "Do you have any idea why he chose this song?"

"Dassie must have told him I'm a fan of oldies. But why *this* song?" The rabbi shrugged. "Maybe he means he'll break Dassie's heart. Or maybe he's enjoying the fact that Nechama and I are broken-hearted. He's right about that."

"And the shekels?"

The rabbi hesitated. "It could be a biblical reference to the fine a rapist pays. Fifty silver shekels—a large amount in those days. That's aside from fines for pain, suffering, humiliation."

"How could you keep this from me?" I said again, angry now. "This changes everything. You have to go to the police."

He took the note from me, slid it back into the envelope, and dropped it in the mesh bag with the coins.

"If he raped her," I said, ignoring the pain that tightened the rabbi's face, "you have no choice. If the police can lift fingerprints from the note or the coins, and if he's in the system, they can identify him."

"You're friendly with the police, Molly. Can you ask them to check for fingerprints without telling them why? I touched the note, by the way, not the coins. I didn't think to be careful. I thought it was an early Chanukah gift."

I stared at him. "This man may have raped your daughter, Rabbi. Don't you think that's more important than her reputation?"

"If the police can't identify him, Molly, giving them Dassie's name is pointless."

I wanted to shake him. "Rabbi—"

"First, show them the note and the coins." He handed me the mailer. "Dassie told Aliza she's safe. Maybe he's just playing with me."

"And if he's not?" I said.

Chapter 9

==

"I hope this won't take long," Mrs. Mellon said after inviting me into her home. "It's almost nine, and Sara has a math exam tomorrow. I'm Faith, by the way." She frowned. "You said your name is Molly Blume? I thought Rabbi Bailor said *Abrams.*"

She was five ten or eleven, slender and practically hipless in a fitted midcalf black skirt. She had short auburn hair and hazel eyes that picked up the olive of her cashmere sweater and took my measure.

"Abrams is my married name. I use Blume for my 'Crime Sheet' column and articles. And I'm married only eight months. Old habits. . . ." I smiled.

She didn't. "I don't read police blotters. They make me nervous."

"They make *me* nervous, too."

She studied me to see if I was making fun, which I wasn't. "Molly Blume."

She tapped a finger against her lips. I was prepared for a comment about my name, which I share with James Joyce's lusty heroine. I'm often teased about that, and I blame my high-school-teacher mother, who should have known better.

Instead, Faith said, "Are you related to Steven Blume?"

"My father."

"He remodeled our kitchen. He did a fine job, but we're having problems with the dishwasher. That's not his fault, though." Her tone was grudging.

Thank God, I thought.

"And your mother's at Sharsheret, right? Celia Blume? Sara's older sister, Ronit, went there. Your mother taught her AP English. Ronit got a two on the exam, so she wasn't exempt from taking freshman English."

Unlike with the dishwasher, I sensed that blame was being assigned.

"You were divorced, right?" Faith said.

"Yes." The woman probably knew my bra size.

She nodded. "I know your ex–in-laws, the Hoffmans. They're nice people. Look, Molly, can I be direct?"

I wondered how she would characterize the conversation we'd had till now. Interrogation, really. "Absolutely."

"We love Dassie. We feel terrible for her parents. I can't begin to imagine what they're going through. But we don't want people finding out about Sara's involvement with Dassie's running away."

"I understand."

"Don't get me wrong. We don't approve of the fact that Sara covered for Dassie. Or that she lied to us." Faith Mellon's lovely mouth hardened. "But she's not to blame for what happened." The sharpness in her tone and eyes dared me to say otherwise.

"The Bailors don't blame your daughter." A half truth. "They're hoping I can help Sara remember something that may tell them where Hadassah is. Or who she's with."

Faith opened her mouth to say something, then clamped her lips together and turned on her heel. I followed her to a small den, where her daughter was sitting, rigid as stone, on a brown leather sofa. She jumped up when I entered, as though someone had poked her.

"This is Mrs. Abrams," Faith told her daughter. "She's here to talk to you about Dassie."

The teenager had her mother's willowy frame, though she wasn't as tall, and her eyes and long, straight hair were brown. She was wearing a long-sleeved blue oxford shirt, a pleated gray skirt that stopped inches above her ankle, and navy tights—the Bais Rifka school uniform my younger sister Liora had proudly worn for four years, similar to the Sharsheret uniform I'd been eager to chuck.

"It's nice to meet you, Sara. Call me Molly." I turned to the mother. "I'd like to talk to Sara privately, if that's all right."

I could tell it wasn't—not for mother or daughter. After aiming a look at me that could have split a diamond, Faith left the room and pulled the door shut with a click.

I sat on the sofa. After a moment Sara joined me. She chose the far end, and from the way she hugged her arms, I figured she wished there were more than several feet between us. A country, maybe.

"I can imagine how hard this must be for you, Sara. You and Dassie are best friends, right?"

"I don't know where she is. Honest." Her tone was defensive, but tears filled her eyes. She wiped them with her fingers.

"I believe you. How long have you known Dassie?" I was anxious to get answers, but knew I had to proceed slowly.

"Since kindergarten. We were in the same class until high school."

"You go to Bais Rifka, right? My sister Liora graduated from there two years ago. And my brother Judah teaches two classes there."

"Mr. Blume is your brother? I had him last year for Jewish History. He's cool. And Liora was choir head when I was a freshman." Sara lowered her arms. "My mom wanted me to go to Sharsheret. That's where my sister Ronit went? But most of my friends are at Bais Rifka."

"Except for Dassie." At the mention of her friend's name, Sara tensed. "I'm sure you want to help us find Dassie and bring her safely home. Tell me about Sunday, Sara. Dassie told her parents she was spending the night with you, right?"

The girl's face reddened. She studied her lap. "That was wrong. I know that."

"We all make mistakes," I said gently. "I've made plenty. What was Dassie wearing, by the way?"

"A black skirt and black sweater. She had the things in her overnight bag."

"Dressy clothes?"

"Uh-huh." Sara hesitated. "The skirt was shorter than she usually wears, and the sweater wasn't low-cut, but it was clingy. Her mom definitely wouldn't have been happy."

Clothes that probably belonged to the Forever XXI tags. "Did Dassie tell you where she was going that night?"

"To meet him. I don't know his name." A hint of sullenness suggested she'd been asked this question too many times. "Dassie wouldn't tell me."

"Not even a first name?"

She shook her head.

"Where were they planning to meet?"

"She wouldn't tell me that, either."

Sara sounded disappointed. I sensed that she'd experienced a vicarious thrill through her friend's illicit adventure.

"Had Dassie ever asked you to cover for her before?"

The girl's blush was an answer. "Twice. She told me she was going out with kids from school."

"Didn't your parents wonder where Dassie was going?"

"They go out a lot, and Dassie always made sure to be back before they came home." The blush deepened. "Sunday I knew she was lying. She kept checking her watch, and she had her makeup done. She said it was for fun, but I got her to tell me the truth, that she was seeing him that night and they'd met twice before. She was so *excited*. I think she wanted to tell *someone*."

Someone who would keep her secret. "If she met him before, Sara, why was she so excited Sunday night?"

"They were going someplace really romantic. I *tried* to talk her out of going. What if he was just pretending to be *frum*? What if he was a psycho? What if he tried to . . ." The girl's voice trailed off.

"Dassie said the other times, he didn't touch her. She trusted him completely."

That was part of the seduction. I thought again about the note, the reference to the shekels. The word "rape" flashed through my mind.

"Did he pick Dassie up Sunday night from your house?"

Sara shook her head. "She met him around the corner, on Alcott. He called her on her cell phone when he got there. I *tried* to talk her out of going," she said again.

"So how long have Dassie and this guy known each other, Sara?"

"A couple of months. I'm the only one Dassie told," Sara added with a touch of self-importance, forgetting for the moment that being the sole recipient of that confidence incurred responsibility, and guilt.

"Did Dassie tell you how old he is?"

"Twenty. She said he's really mature."

He could be twenty. He could be fifty. "Do you know what school he goes to, or what kind of work he does?"

"No. I *told* you, I don't know much about him. But no one believes me." The girl was on the verge of tears.

"I believe you, Sara." I patted her knee. "Tell me about the chat room."

"J Spot. J for Jewish? Dassie heard about it at school. You can meet people you wouldn't meet otherwise. And this one is safe, because everyone's *frum,* so you have a lot in common and a lot you can talk about, and—" Sara stopped. When she continued, she sounded flustered. "Anyway, that's what Dassie told me."

Sara had spoken with the authority of first-hand knowledge. I filed that away. "And then she got hooked. Why do you think that was?"

The girl hesitated. "It's tough when your dad is principal of your school. Dassie couldn't hang out with a lot of the kids, because her parents didn't approve of them. The school is Modern Orthodox, but some of the kids eat non-kosher food outside of school, and a few of them do other stuff."

"By 'stuff,' you mean sex and drugs?"

Sara nodded. "Dassie said some of the kids fooled around with marijuana. She *never* did," Sara added quickly.

I was saddened, but not shocked. The Orthodox community tries to shelter its children from the dangers of the secular world, but no community, I have learned, is invulnerable.

"What about her friends from Bais Rifka?"

"They kind of drifted apart. Different schedules . . ." Sara shrugged. "Dassie's still friends with some of them, but it's not the same when you don't see someone every day. And she doesn't like having to defend her school to them."

I could understand that. "Let's get back to Sunday night, Sara."

The girl picked up a needlepoint pillow. "Dassie said she'd be out till eleven. When she wasn't back by midnight, I was nervous, because my parents said they'd be home by one. So I tried her cell. Again and again and again." Sara's voice had taken on a breathless quality, as if she were reliving her anxiety. "Finally she answered. She said she'd be out late and would sleep at home and figure out something to tell her parents."

"How did she sound?"

"Excited. She was giggling half the time and—"

"And?" I prompted.

"She sounded drunk. I didn't tell her parents." Sara picked at a thread on the pillow. "Monday she phoned me after school. She said she was sorry she got me involved, and told me she was with him. I couldn't *believe* it. She said she was fine, everything would turn out okay. And she hung up. She didn't *sound* fine."

Almost the same thing Hadassah had told her sister. And like Aliza, Sara was looking at me for reassurance.

"Dassie's mom said she didn't blame me, but I know she did." The heightened color had returned to the teenager's face. "She wanted me to tell her everything I knew about this guy. But I don't *know* anything. She asked if Dassie was planning to run away with him. I said no way. Dassie would have told me, for sure."

My best friend, Aggie, I had learned years after she was killed, hadn't told me everything. If she had, she might be alive. Then again, maybe not . . . I brushed away the thought and the accompanying pain, wondered again if I would ever be free of it.

"Did Dassie tell you why she was attracted to him?"

"She said he was amazing. He was smart and kind. He made her laugh. He e-mailed her a photo, but she wouldn't show it to me. He made her promise, because what they had was private." Something flickered across the teenager's face.

Envy? Resentment at being shut out of her best friend's life? I could relate to both.

"Dassie said he really *listens* to her," Sara said. "And a couple of times he knew what she was thinking. Like one time, he said she'd make a great lawyer. That's *before* he knew she was planning to go to law school. And he guessed her favorite color, green. And her favorite music, and things like that. Dassie said that showed they had a bond. Like some married couples who finish each other's sentences? My mom and dad do that."

Mine, too. "So Dassie was serious about him?"

"I didn't think so when they started IM'ing. I thought it was just fun, you know? Talking to a guy, flirting, pretending he's your boyfriend? There's no harm in that, because he doesn't know your real name, or where you live or anything."

I had the feeling, again, that Sara was talking about herself. "What about teachers? Is Dassie close to any of them?"

"Not really. Well, her history teacher, but that was last year. I think she had a crush on him. She was hoping to have him for AP European History. He makes his students work like crazy, but almost all of them pass the AP test. She was upset when he left like that."

An odd choice of words, I thought. "Like that?"

"In the second week of September? Without telling anyone he was leaving? Dassie's father said the teacher had to quit because of a family emergency."

Something Rabbi Bailor hadn't mentioned. I wondered why. "You said Dassie's at your house all the time. Did she ever use your computer to visit J Spot?"

From the way Sara shifted her eyes I suspected that she had, and that she was struggling with what to tell me.

"A couple of times," she admitted.

"And you've been there yourself, right?" I said, stating my guess as fact.

She clutched the pillow to her chest as if it were a security blanket and slid down on the cushion. "Please don't tell my parents."

I promised I wouldn't and wondered how many more secrets I'd be asked to keep before the night was over. "Can you take me to the chat room?"

"Now?"

Sara's bedroom had pale yellow walls and a white daybed covered with a yellow lace coverlet. I stood a few feet from her desk while she logged onto the Internet.

"Okay," she said less than a minute later.

I moved closer and glanced at the screen.

Birch2 has entered the room.

I scanned the names in the chat room. Seven, including Sara's. "What's Dassie's screen name? You want to find her, right?" I said, toughening my tone when she didn't answer. "You want her safe, back home?"

"ST613."

ST. Estie. Esther is another name for Hadassah. 613 is the number of *mitzvot* in the Torah. "Is there a moderator in this chat room?"

Sara shook her head. "There's a *frum* website with a moderator, but it's not a live chat. You can talk about stuff that bothers you. J Spot is just for getting together with other Jewish kids."

"So how many times have you been to J Spot, Sara? The truth—I won't tell."

"Maybe six or seven."

I mentally multiplied that by ten. "So you could have been in the room with this guy."

"Maybe." The thought clearly troubled and intrigued her. "But I don't know his screen name. Honest."

"When were you in the chat room last?"

"Monday night. I just lurked. I don't even know why I went. It's not like Dassie or this guy would be there."

I pulled out my notepad and wrote down the URL for the chat room. "You said Dassie heard about this site from kids at Torat Tzion. Can you give me some names?"

She licked her lips. "Are you going to talk to them? Mrs. Bailor said no one's supposed to know about Dassie."

"I'm telling people that I'm writing an article about Jewish chat rooms, or the school. The names?" I prompted.

"Dassie mentioned two girls. Tara and Becky. I don't know their last names. She was friendly with another girl, but she died."

"Batya Weinberg."

"You heard about her?" Sara looked surprised. "Oh, the Bailors told you. Dassie was really upset about her."

I put my notepad back in my purse. "So I guess other kids from Bais Rifka visit this chat room, right?" I asked, aiming for casual.

"A few," she said, wary again. "I can't tell you who."

"I'm not asking. Sara, you *do* understand that chat rooms can be dangerous, don't you? Even *frum* ones?"

"I'm careful. I never give away any personal information. Neither do my friends."

"Dassie probably thought she was careful, too, Sara."

The look she gave me was filled with alarm and resentment. "You *promised* you wouldn't tell my parents."

"I'm going to honor that promise, Sara. I think *you* should tell them. They'll probably let you continue, with some guidelines."

"They won't." She slumped down on her chair.

"Think about it." I would be thinking about it, too. "Another question, Sara. Do you know Hadassah's password?"

"No. I wish I *did* know."

The good news was that I believed her. That was the bad news, too.

Chapter 10

I had learned enough to understand why Hadassah had been easy prey for someone she'd met in a chat room, but I still had no idea how to find her. Driving around the corner, I parked on Alcott and knocked on the doors of several houses on the chance that someone had seen the car that had picked her up Sunday night.

Of course, no one had.

I was on Pico, heading home, when I had a thought and drove back toward the Bailors' house. The street was filled with cars, and I had to park halfway up the block. My parents speak with nostalgia about the Los Angeles of their childhood, when you could leave your door unlocked and walk at night without fear, but I've read too much data about muggings in middle-class neighborhoods like this one, muggings that take place even in broad daylight.

So I hurried along the sidewalk, eager to escape the chill of the evening and the darkness that the street lamps did little to dispel, and
when I heard footsteps behind me as I turned onto the Bailors' walkway, I tensed and whirled around, my car keys in my hand, poised to
attack.

It was Reuben Jastrow. He was wearing a yarmulke and no glasses.

I dropped my hand. "Stalking me again?"

His face reddened. "I'm visiting my sister and brother-in-law."

Sometimes I speak without thinking. "That was a joke—obviously,
not a good one. Sorry."

"My wife often says I should lighten up. She's probably right." He
smiled tightly. "Did you learn anything from Hadassah's friend?"

I frowned. "How did you know I was there?"

"My sister told me you were planning to go there."

"Maybe *you* should be doing the detecting. That's *not* a joke."

"I'm sorry. My wife also tells me I can be pushy." Jastrow followed
me up the walkway. "I'm anxious to find Hadassah. We all are."

Jastrow rang the bell. A moment later Gavriel Bailor opened the
door and stepped aside to let us into the small entry off the living
room. He looked surprised to see me with his uncle.

"This is my nephew, Gavriel," Jastrow said. "Gavriel, this is Mrs.
Abrams."

"We met earlier today." I was struck again by how much the young
man resembled his father. The same nose, minus the bump; the same
soulful, dark brown eyes.

"I'll let my father know you're here," he told me. To his uncle, he
said, "*Ima*'s in the kitchen."

"I'll wait with Miss Blume."

Gavriel nodded and left us in the hall. I supposed Jastrow was being
polite, but I had nothing to say to him.

"He looks like a fine young man," I said to fill the silence.

Jastrow nodded. "Nechama gets phone calls almost daily from *shadchonim*. Gavriel is going out with an L.A. girl while he's home. She's
lovely, from a wonderful family."

I heard Rabbi Bailor's footsteps before I saw him hurrying toward us, his hand on top of his black yarmulke as if he were preventing it from flying off his head.

"Did you learn something?" he asked me eagerly after acknowledging his brother-in-law with a quick greeting.

Hearing the hope in his voice was painful. I shook my head and saw disappointment drag down the corners of his mouth. Jastrow's, too.

"Nechama's waiting for you," the rabbi told his brother-in-law. "Tell her I'll be right there."

Jastrow hesitated. After giving his brother-in-law a look, he wished me good night and passed through the dining room to the kitchen. Odd, I thought.

"So what *did* Sara tell you?" the rabbi said.

I gave him an edited summary, leaving out Sara's guess that Dassie had been drunk.

Rabbi Bailor sighed. "I had no idea Dassie felt so lonely at school. She was always smiling, always looking happy. Why didn't she come to us?"

"She probably didn't want to worry you, especially if she thought you couldn't solve her problems."

In high school and during several years that followed, I'd presented a happy demeanor to my parents, even though I'd been struggling with teachers and broken friendships and my growing doubts about Orthodox observance. Afterward my parents had asked the same questions: How is it that we didn't see, Molly? Why didn't you tell us?

"Sara mentioned that history teacher Hadassah liked," I continued. "She said Dassie was close to him. Maybe they're still in touch."

"I doubt it."

"It can't hurt to check. What's his name? Is he Jewish, by the way?"

"Greg Shankman." The rabbi said the name grudgingly. "Yes, he's Jewish. Why?"

His reluctance piqued my interest. "Just curious. I'll call you tomorrow for his contact information. Sara said Shankman left in September because of a family emergency. *You* said he wasn't at Torat Tzion this year."

"You're nit-picking, Molly."

" 'Examine the Torah's language carefully, and it will reveal fascinating meanings.' Isn't that what you taught us? Isn't that what the commentaries do?"

The rabbi forced a smile. "I'm delighted to know that you took my lessons to heart, Molly."

"There *was* no family emergency, was there?"

"Mr. Shankman's leaving has no bearing on Dassie." He glanced behind him. "My wife and brother-in-law are waiting for me. If you'll excuse me?"

"Was Greg Shankman fired?" The rabbi's stiffened posture gave me my answer. "He was, wasn't he?"

"I'm not at liberty to discuss Mr. Shankman."

His tone and diction spelled "lawsuit." "Shankman left in September, right?" I said, thinking aloud. "According to Sara, that's when Dassie met this man in the chat room."

"So?"

"So if Shankman was fired, maybe he *arranged* to meet Dassie in the chat room, to get back at you. That would explain the personal tone of the note."

"Ridiculous." The rabbi shook his head. "First of all," he said, taking on the traditional sing-song Talmudic cadence, "according to Sara, the man Dassie met is twenty. Mr. Shankman is closer to thirty."

"People don't always give correct personal data in chat rooms—or in personal ads, or online sites."

My last date via a Jewish site—"Tall, good-looking, spiritual, free spirit, affectionate"—had been a short, overweight, forty-year-old out-of-work computer programmer who thought buying me a drink entitled him to cop a feel.

And Kacie Woody's killer, I recalled, had pretended to be eighteen to gain her trust. And a thirty-four-year-old Phoenix police officer had pretended to be a teen when he sexually assaulted a thirteen-year-old boy less than two hours after he first met the boy in an AOL chat room.

"Anyway," Rabbi Bailor said, "Dassie saw his photo *before* she met him. She would have recognized Mr. Shankman."

"He probably e-mailed her someone else's photo. That's what they do."

"But Dassie met him twice before Sunday," the rabbi said. "If it was Mr. Shankman, she would have told Sara."

"Not if he convinced Dassie that she couldn't trust anyone with their secret. Actually, that would make the whole courtship more exciting. Forbidden love?"

"You have this all worked out," the rabbi said, impatient. "But I didn't hire Mr. Shankman. And he knew that it wasn't my decision to fire him."

"Why was he fired?"

"You haven't changed, Malka. Sorry—*Molly*. Always tenacious. Anything else?"

"You should call the police, Rabbi. The more I think about the note—"

"You're going to show it to your detective friend. Let's see what he finds out. I think this man is playing with me, Molly."

I frowned. "What makes you think so?"

"Just a feeling." Again, he glanced over his shoulder. "Is that it?"

He was either eager to get rid of me and my questions, or anxious to join his wife and brother-in-law. Maybe both.

"I'd like to ask Aliza another question. Is she home?"

"She's probably in her room. By the way, I talked to her about the IM thing. Thanks again for telling me."

"No problem."

At least I'd accomplished something.

Chapter 11

<hr>

Aliza was at her desk, applying pink-beige polish to her nails.

The mounds of clothes on the beds had disappeared.

"Nervous energy," she said, following my eyes. "We're all waiting for Dassie to show up, or at least *phone.*" Aliza capped the nail polish bottle and opened a bottle of topcoat. "I thought that was her phoning half an hour ago, because my parents were so stressed right after. But my dad said it was a parent. They're always calling him at home."

"It must be tough to be a principal. My mom teaches high school English, and she often gets calls from parents at home, too." "Emergencies" that are rarely that.

"My dad loves his job. Well, he'd love it more if he wasn't worried about losing it." She looked up at me, her teeth catching her upper lip. "I shouldn't have said that."

"I won't tell," I promised. "Why would your father's job be at risk, Aliza? He was a wonderful teacher. I'm sure he's a terrific principal."

To tell you the truth, I wasn't sure why I cared. Despite my sympathy for the rabbi during this crisis, I was still nursing a fourteen-year-old resentment. And though in my adolescent fantasies he'd never been the object of my revenge (I'd reserved that role for Rabbi Ingel, had pictured him being fired after confessing publicly that he'd maligned me), over the years I had often imagined Rabbi Bailor begging my forgiveness. But now I felt an inexplicable need to defend him against his detractors.

Aliza nodded. "My dad loves connecting with students, bringing them closer to Judaism. Most of them love him. And he's being honored in January at a Jewish educators' conference in New York."

"So what's the problem? If you can't tell me, that's cool."

"It's not a secret, really."

She busied herself applying topcoat. I sensed that she was deliberating, and didn't push.

"My dad and the secular principal don't get along," she finally said. "Dr. Mendes wants to get as many kids as possible into the Ivy Leagues. My dad encourages them to go to Israel, at least for a year. She thinks he tells them to focus on Jewish studies at the expense of secular subjects. Which isn't true." Aliza examined her nails and frowned. "My dad says you have to try to excel in *all* your studies. According to the Torah, wasting time is a sin."

That was the Rabbi Bailor I remembered. "You said *most* of the students love him?"

"A couple of months ago my dad wanted to expel a senior. Dr. Mendes didn't agree, because the student is planning to go to Harvard, and they didn't have proof. His dad and brother went to Harvard, too, so it's a big deal for him to go there."

"Proof of what?"

"I don't know. Anyway, my dad put this student on probation. So he missed the early decision deadline. Now his whole family's mad at my dad. Plus his father is on the school board. He gave a lot of money to build the school."

"Who's the student?"

"I have no idea." Aliza closed the topcoat bottle. "My dad never talks about students by name. The only reason I know all this is because I overheard him talking to my mom."

"So your parents are worried, huh?" I said.

"My dad says whatever happens is supposed to happen. My mom's worried, but she wouldn't mind if my dad got a job at a different school. One *shadchan* told my parents she might have a harder time setting me and my brother up because Torat Tzion is too modern. Can you believe it?" Aliza rolled her eyes. "My dad told the *shadchan* he's not interested in narrow-minded people."

"The *shadchan* or the families?" I smiled.

Aliza smiled, too. "Both."

"Actually, I have a dating question, Aliza." This was why I had come back. "Where would you go for the ultimate romantic setting?"

"Yamashiro Room," she answered without hesitation. "It's not kosher, so you can't eat anything, but you can have drinks if they don't card you. Plus you're going for the atmosphere and the view, which I heard is *amazing*. But it's not for a first date, or second."

I smiled. "The third date's okay?" In my sister Liora's circle, three dates means you're ready to pick out a ring, and china at the Mikasa outlet.

"Maybe the fourth." Aliza giggled. It was a lovely sound. "Yamashiro Room says you're serious. I've never been there, but one of my friends got engaged there a few weeks ago. Dassie said that's where—Oh." She gazed at me. "You think this guy took her there, right?"

I could hear the wistfulness in her voice. From the color that rushed to her face, I think she heard it, too.

"I know you've probably heard this before," I said, "but the right guy *is* out there for you. By the way, how *was* your date Saturday night?"

"Okay, but no magic. He'll call back," Aliza said. "The ones you don't want to, always do."

At least she was smiling.

Walking down the stairs, I said a silent thank-you to God for bringing Zack and me together, and a prayer for Aliza and for my sister Liora, who at twenty is starting to feel anxious about meeting her *bashert,* and for young women all over the country who were hoping to get to Yamashiro Room or its equivalent.

I was heading to the kitchen to say goodnight to the Bailors when I heard loud voices.

". . . don't have to tell her everything. She's not family."

Reuben Jastrow's voice. He sounded impatient, annoyed.

". . . ask her to help and leave her in the dark?"

Rabbi Bailor.

I should go, I thought. But curiosity is one of my vices, and since I assumed I was the "her" of this conversation, I had no trouble justifying my tiptoeing across the carpeted rooms and pressing my ear against the swinging door to the kitchen.

"She'll either find him or she won't," Jastrow said.

"*I'd* like to find him," Gavriel said.

"Gavriel," his father warned.

"She's my sister! She's your daughter! Don't you want to find this *menuval* and . . ."

"And what? Teach him a lesson? Beat him to a pulp so he won't prey on other young girls? Sure, I'd love to do that. And then this man will go to the police and file charges for assault, because it's not as though he kidnapped Dassie. She went with him of her own accord. And maybe he'll get your sister's name in the papers. That would *really* help her reputation, and the family's."

The rabbi's sigh was so loud I could hear it through the door.

"More important," he said in a gentler tone, "that's not the Torah way, Gavriel."

"I know."

"Do you?"

"Yes. I'm just so frustrated."

"Go learn, and hope that in the *z'chus* of your learning that Hashem will protect your sister. Go *daven* and ask Hashem to help us find her."

"And in the meantime?" Nechama said.

"We tell Molly."

"It won't help her find him," Jastrow said.

I pushed the door open and stepped into the kitchen.

"Tell me what?" I asked.

Chapter 12

They were sitting at an oak table at the end of the large room, underneath bright fluorescent light that caught the frozen expressions on their faces.

"He phoned," Rabbi Bailor said. "The guy Dassie's with."

"Chaim, you don't—" Jastrow began.

A look from his brother-in-law silenced him. "Gavriel, please excuse us."

"I'm not a kid, *Abba*."

"Gavriel."

There was a flicker of defiance in the young man's eyes. He stood. A few angry strides took him to the door. He shoved it hard and exited the room. The door swung back and forth several times.

"Tell her, Nechama," Rabbi Bailor said.

I didn't envy Nechama, caught between her brother and her husband.

"He phoned me on my cell not long after you left," she said. "I saw Dassie's number on the display, and I thought, thank God." Nechama shut her eyes briefly. "But it was him. He was using her phone."

Clever, I thought. And so cruel.

"I asked to talk to her. He said Dassie didn't want to talk. She'd asked him to talk for her. So I said, how do I know she's all right, that she's not. . . . ?" Nechama gripped the table edge so hard her knuckles turned white.

My heart pounded.

"So he called her. 'Dassie, come here, honey.' I *hated* that he called her 'honey.' I know he did it to upset me. But then I didn't care, because she was on the phone. '*Ima*, I'm okay.'" Nechama shut her eyes again for a second. "I was so happy to hear her voice, I started crying. 'Come home,' I said. She said she was fine. She felt terrible about causing us worry and pain. That was the only thing keeping her from being completely happy. 'Come home,' I told her. 'Please, come home.'"

Dassie hadn't been raped. Relief coursed through me. A second later I shot a reproachful look at Rabbi Bailor. He'd had knowledge—not "just a feeling"—and had let me worry.

"He took the phone again," Nechama said. "I heard him tell her he'd be right back, and I heard a door closing. 'Mrs. Bailor,' he said, 'I think you and the rabbi should know Dassie is in love with me. She's committed to me and wants to spend the rest of her life with me.'"

Not, "We're in love with each other, committed to each other. We want to spend our lives together." My relief was short-lived. I felt a chill snaking up my spine and avoided looking at the rabbi, who had stood and was pacing the length of the kitchen.

"I wanted to scream." Nechama moved her hands from the table and tightened them into fists. "I said wonderful, tell Dassie to come home, tell her we love her, we want her to be happy, and if you make her happy, that's what counts.' I almost choked on the words. He said Dassie needed to know that we were ready to accept him. I said, 'We're ready. Bring her home, you'll see.'

"He laughed. He said how could we be okay with our little girl running off with some man she met in a chat room? He said he didn't care what we thought, and soon Dassie wouldn't, either, because every day she was coming closer to needing only him. Not her parents, not her sisters or brothers, or her friends. 'We're like Romeo and Juliet,' he said. 'If I wanted to, I could tell her not to talk to you ever again, and she wouldn't, because she trusts me that much. And didn't the Torah say that when you marry, you should leave your parents and cleave to your spouse? Well, tell the rabbi that in God's eyes, his daughter and I are married.' " Nechama wiped the tears that had pooled in her eyes and spilled down her cheeks.

"In God's eyes?" I said.

"They had a ceremony. He gave her a ring." She looked down at her own gold wedding band.

"Is that binding?" I asked Rabbi Bailor.

He stood still. "It can be. If she wasn't coerced, if the ring belonged to him, if there were two valid witnesses."

I didn't know how to phrase the next question. "Did they . . ."

"They're waiting until she goes to the *mikvah,*" Nechama said. " 'Your husband should be proud of his daughter,' he told me. 'She wants everything to be kosher, although we're both eager. Monday seems so far away.' *Monster.*" Hate twisted her face.

The ritual bath and the laws of family purity are central to Orthodox Judaism, and many non-Orthodox women have also embraced this monthly rite that marks the end of a cycle in which life wasn't created, and prepares for the possibility of life in the coming month. You count seven days after the completion of your menses. Then, before you resume intimacy with your husband, you cleanse yourself and submerge yourself in the rainwaters of the ritual bath, just as Sarah did and Rebecca and Rachel and Leah.

Today was Thursday. Monday was in four days. "Did you recognize his voice?" I asked Nechama.

She shook her head.

"Could you tell how old he is?"

"No. He was whispering, I guess because he didn't want Dassie to hear him. He sounded intense, almost angry one minute, pleasant the next. I asked him what he wanted. Whatever it takes to bring Dassie home, I said, we'll do it. Just tell us what you *want.*"

"What did he say?"

"He said he wanted a hundred thousand dollars. Then he laughed again and said he was kidding, he didn't want money. He said Dassie was free to leave, that she didn't want to come home, which should tell us something. And even if she *did* come home, she was a married woman, forbidden to others. 'Ask your husband; he'll know.' Then he said, 'Isn't love grand?' And something like, 'It's a consummation Dassie and I both devoutly wish, so tell your husband I won't be paying the fifty shekels after all.' He said Chaim would know what that meant."

Nechama turned to her husband. "I asked you before, Chaim. What fifty shekels is he talking about?"

Jastrow was looking at his brother-in-law. If I could have backed out of the room, I would have, but Rabbi Bailor was standing in front of the kitchen door.

"He sent me a note." Rabbi Bailor told his wife about the coin and its reference, but said nothing about the song. "I didn't want to upset you, Nechama. And I'm glad I *didn't* tell you, because it was all talk."

She had been staring at her husband. When he finished speaking, she was still staring. I could hear the hum of the refrigerator in the dead silence.

"How could you keep that from me?" Her voice was quiet, hard as stone. "Who gave you the right?"

"I was protecting you, Nechama."

"Like you protected Dassie by letting her go to that school? Like you protected her by letting her have her own computer and keeping it in her room?"

Rabbi Bailor flinched. "You're right."

"What good does that do, Chaim? Will being right bring Dassie back? What else are you keeping from me?"

"Nothing. We'll find her, Nechama."

"And then what?"

Nechama buried her face in her hands. Rabbi Bailor moved toward her, but Jastrow had drawn his sister's head onto his shoulder.

Rabbi Bailor walked me to my car. I think he was anxious to get out of the house, away from a wife he couldn't console and a brother-in-law who could. His head was lowered, his shoulders hunched. I tried to think of something to say, but came up blank. Sometimes silence is best.

"I'm sorry I didn't tell you about the phone call right away," he said. "My brother-in-law was pressuring me, and Gavriel. . . ."

I didn't answer. We continued walking.

"The other day Dassie told me she'd heard about a boy and girl at a coed camp who had a mock wedding ceremony," he said when we reached the car. "She wanted to know if they were married if there was no rabbi. I told her the ceremony could be binding, and they might need a divorce. I thought she was just curious," he said. "What goes around, comes around."

I assumed he hadn't told his wife about that conversation. "You mentioned that for the marriage to be binding, you need a ring and valid witnesses. Where would he get witnesses?"

"I have no idea. To be honest, I'd be surprised if he *did* have two witnesses."

"So they're *not* married. Isn't that good news?"

"Not if Dassie doesn't know that. If she thinks she *is* married . . ."

"If," I have learned, is a huge word, filled with promise or foreboding. "Why didn't your brother-in-law want me to know about the call?"

"Reuben worried that you'd decide to bow out, that you'd insist on bringing in the police. Because the man joked about wanting money, and he sounds so . . ."

"Controlling, manipulative? Reuben was right, Rabbi Bailor. I think you *should* tell the police everything."

"You're going to give your detective friend the note and the coins, right? Maybe he'll find out something. Did anything strike you about the call, Molly?"

"The fact that this man mentioned Monday," I said. "It's as though he's giving you a deadline. Maybe he *wants* you to find him."

He nodded. "I noticed that, too. But I don't understand his game. Do you?"

I hesitated, then shook my head.

Several other things had struck me. Some that I wanted to think about, others that I didn't want to share with Rabbi Bailor because they were so worrisome.

Chapter 13

"Don't be disappointed if you don't learn any-thing," Zack said after he handed his car keys to the young valet.

"Liora said Yamashiro. Or the Grove, but that's in the middle of the Orthodox commu-nity, so Dassie wouldn't have risked being seen there. And Dassie mentioned Yamashiro to her sister, and to her best friend."

After leaving the Bailors, I had phoned Sara, then my sister Liora. Then Zack. He'd been happy to accompany me, but had insisted on driving. He claims I have a lead foot, and it's a steep uphill drive to Sycamore near Franklin and Yamashiro, which is 250 feet above Holly-wood Boulevard.

We walked toward the pagoda-style Moun-tain Palace (that's what "yamashiro" means) and climbed the steps to the entrance—ten or twelve steps; I wasn't counting. Definitely fewer than the original 300 that led up the hillside through magnificent Japanese gardens to the cedar and teak mansion, an exact replica of a palace near Kyoto, that the Bernheimer brothers completed in 1914 to house their Asian treasures. The treasures were auctioned off a decade later when one of the brothers died.

"It *is* beautiful, isn't it?" I said.

From where we were standing, we could look up and see the 600-year-old pagoda the brothers had imported from Japan. The oldest structure in California, I'd read.

"Disappointed that I didn't propose here?" Zack asked.

"Definitely not." Relieved, to be honest. That was where Ron had asked me to marry him. In the Sunset Room, to be specific. "And chocolate is always romantic."

Last Chanukah Zack had presented me with a huge *dreidel* filled with Godiva chocolates and a princess-cut diamond ring.

It was 9:50, too late to be seated in the dining room, we were informed with polite regret by the maître d' standing behind the tall, intricately carved hexagonal red desk in the lobby.

"I was hoping you could help me." I showed him Hadassah's photo. "My cousin was here Sunday night with a young man. Her parents haven't heard from her since, and they're beginning to become concerned, but they don't want to report her missing, because she's probably fine, and that would be embarrassing, if you know what I mean."

"Quite."

"The thing is, the young man probably knows where she is, but we don't know his name. My cousin may be with him right now, which is why we'd like to contact him. I really, really hope you can help us."

The maître d' frowned. "I'm not sure how."

"Could you show her photo to the staff? She was wearing a black skirt and long-sleeved black top, kind of clingy? Maybe someone can recall her, and the man she was with, maybe his first name? And then you could look through your receipts and find his last name."

The man sighed. "I don't have Sunday's receipts. Even if I did, it would take hours to go through all of them. And you're assuming that someone will remember this man's first name. That's highly unlikely, madam."

It was. Ridiculous, really. "Right. Sorry."

"Could you at least verify that my wife's cousin was here?" Zack said. "We'd appreciate your help."

The maître d' hesitated. Zack slipped him a twenty.

"I'll see what I can do." The maître d' palmed the bill. "You may want to wait in the lounge. The bar is open until one during the week, and the view is quite spectacular."

"I hope it won't take him till one to learn something," I whispered to Zack as we left the lobby.

Zack had never been here, so we walked to the heated, open-air garden court and strolled around, admiring the koi and silk tapestries and exotic plants.

"I wonder if those tapestries are the original ones," Zack said. "Yamashiro was restored, you know."

"Since when are you an expert on Yamashiro?"

"I read up on it. I always wanted to come here."

The lounge was crowded, but we nabbed a small table near the windows and ordered drinks that arrived almost immediately. A piña colada for me; a diet lemon Coke for Zack, who would be driving home—soon, he figured. He was certain the maître d' would strike out.

Gazing through the windows at the panoramic view of Hollywood and all of Los Angeles, I wondered which tiny dot of light signaled the room where Hadassah was. I sighed.

"Thinking about Hadassah?" Zack said.

"So much for romantic ambience. Sorry." I tasted my drink. The pineapple and rum mixture was sweetly tart, delicious. "I can understand why the Bailors are frantic. I would be, too, if my child ran away with a stranger. But it's sad that Hadassah's actions will taint her reputation forever, and her family's."

"That's the reality, Molly."

"Well, I don't have to like it." I sipped my drink.

"Not all the Yamashiro history is romantic, you know," Zack said. "Rumor has it that during the Depression, starving actresses hung out here hoping to be hired for the evening by men who could afford their company."

"Hooray for Hollywood," I said.

"After Pearl Harbor, a false rumor circulated that Yamashiro was a signal tower for the Japanese. The place was vandalized, and because of the anti-Japanese paranoia, the owners camouflaged the Asian architecture and used black paint to cover the carved woods."

"Is this supposed to cheer me up?"

"Rumors are powerful, Molly, even if they're not true. When the war ended, Yamashiro was converted into apartment units. A few years later, a new buyer planned to demolish the entire property and build a hotel and apartment building. But as the demolition was about to begin, he discovered all that beauty underneath the black paint."

"What's your point?"

"Sometimes we can't see behind the black paint, Molly. But the truth often emerges, eventually."

"I don't think that's a consolation for the Bailors." I stared into the darkness. "From what we know, this guy hasn't harmed Hadassah— yet. And he hasn't asked for money. Well, he joked about wanting a hundred grand, but then he said it wasn't about money. So what's in it for him?"

"Power, control. There are hundreds of predators like him lurking in chat rooms, pedophiles who prey on children, men who lure young girls and women to meet them."

And sometimes rape them, or kill them. I knew that's what Zack was thinking. The possibility made me shudder.

"A real estate agent from Anchorage had seventeen screen names," Zack said. "He'd pretend to be a girl and strike up a friendship with lonely girls. Then he'd try to set them up on a date with a teenage boy—himself. I'm sure Hadassah's guy made her feel safe, Molly. And he must have sensed her vulnerability. That's why he chose her."

I stirred my drink. "I don't think he *happened* to meet Hadassah in the chat room. I think he knew her."

Zack frowned. "What makes you think that?"

"Sara, the best friend, told me he knew things about Hadassah. That her favorite color was green, for example."

"Green is a favorite color for many people, Molly."

"He knew she was going to be a lawyer, Zack. He knew her favorite music. He's like a magician who sets up his cards, or a fortune teller who gets information on the client before the reading. The whole thing is rigged."

"What's this guy's motive?"

"Revenge? Rabbi Bailor wanted to expel a senior. He didn't, but there's still friction. Maybe this guy is trying to get back at the rabbi through Dassie."

"He's too young to fit with what Sara told you."

"Dassie could've given Sara misleading information. Or it could be someone else in the family. Like the brother."

"You're reaching, Molly."

"Maybe." I took another sip. "There's something personal about this. The note to Rabbi Bailor, the phone call. This guy has Dassie under his control. If he's not after money, why is he taunting them? And I'm bothered by what he said. About consummating the marriage?"

"From *Hamlet*." Zack nodded. " ' 'Tis a consummation devoutly to be wished.' "

"Hamlet's not talking about having sex with Ophelia. He's contemplating suicide. This guy also made a reference to Romeo and Juliet."

"Because Dassie ran away to be with him, because her parents wouldn't approve of him," Zack said, but he was frowning. "Did you mention this to the Bailors?"

"No. If I'm wrong, I didn't want to add to their worries."

The maître d' appeared. Behind him was a tall, leggy waitress, her platinum blond hair practically white against the black of her uniform shirt, on which "Yamashiro" was stitched in gold.

"This is Irene Jakaitis," he told us. "She remembers serving your cousin and the gentleman on Sunday night."

I jumped up so quickly that I rattled the table. Zack stood, too. The maître d' gave me a disapproving look as he handed me Hadassah's photo. Then he bowed and left.

"Irene, I *really* appreciate this," I said. "You're sure this is the young woman you saw?"

"Uh-huh. Her name was really different. Not Daisy, but close to it."

"Dassie?"

"That's it." Irene beamed. "She was a toothpick, even in this winter white outfit she was wearing. I mean, who can wear white, right?"

"I thought she was wearing a black outfit."

"She was when they arrived. She changed in the restroom. I kidded her date. 'Sweetie,' I said, 'you'd better feed your girlfriend or she's gonna disappear.' But your cousin said she keeps kosher and there wasn't anything she could order. So I'm thinking, wow, that must be hard, right?" She studied us, her eyes lingering on Zack's yarmulke. "You two keep kosher, too?"

I nodded. "Do you remember the man's name, Irene?"

The waitress shook her head. "Like I said, your cousin's name was unusual. But I hear so many names, I hardly remember any of them. Well, unless Brad Pitt walked in. His name I'd remember." She winked.

"What does this guy look like?" Zack asked.

She eyed Zack. "You're over six feet, right? He's a couple of inches shorter. Nice looking, but not drop-dead gorgeous. Brown hair, I think. He was wearing a beanie like yours. And they were into each other, you know? But without touching. Like, not even holding hands or anything." Irene placed a hand on her hip. "So kosher, huh. No bacon, right? What about wine? Does that have to be kosher, too?"

"Yes. How old do you think he is, Irene?" I asked.

"Midtwenties? Definitely older than your cousin." A frown clouded the waitress's amiable expression. "Are you cops or something? Is she under age?"

"We're not cops," Zack said. "We just want to find her, Irene. Honest."

"So how old *is* she? Twenty?"

"Almost," I lied, taking pity on Irene.

"I think it was all that makeup." The waitress sighed. "She definitely looked older."

"They had drinks?"

Irene nodded. "*He* did, a few. When she went to the restroom, he told me he was planning to pop the question, and he needed to get up the nerve to do the deed. Your cousin ordered a diet Coke, but she was getting mellow, if you know what I mean, so she probably had more than a sip or two of his. No wine, though. I brought over champagne after he proposed, on the house. Your cousin said no thanks. That's why I asked you about the wine."

"You heard him propose?" I asked.

Irene shook her head. "He did that outside. A lot of people get married at Yamashiro, because the view is so romantic. Anyway, when they came back in, your cousin had a ring. A plain silver band, but she didn't seem to care. And she had it on the index finger of her right hand. But then she moved it to her ring finger."

Eight months earlier, Zack had slipped a wedding band on the index finger of my right hand.

"They looked so happy," Irene said. "It was a perfect night. Well, it would've been, if not for his car. He came back in after they left and told the manager the valet dinged the driver door. I felt so bad for him. He was trying not to lose his cool, but he was really upset."

"So what happened?" I hoped a report had happened. A report would have a name and address, a phone number.

"The valet insisted the ding was there when he received the car. He'd written that on the parking ticket. My manager said your cousin's boyfriend could fill out a report, but he didn't want to. So they left."

So much for a report. I repressed a sigh.

"The truth is, it wasn't a big deal," Irene said. "You could hardly see the ding unless you were looking for it."

"You saw the car?" Excitement fluttered in my chest.

"A silver Altima. It looked brand-new. I felt like I was the maid of honor, you know? So I went to take a look, see if I could help."

"Did you happen to notice the license plate?"

"As a matter of fact, I did. It was one of those personalized plates, you know? R-C-K-Y-R-D. Rocky Road. That's my favorite ice cream, too."

Right now it was mine, too. I grinned so hard my cheeks ached. "I love you, Irene."

Irene laughed. "Hey, when you see your cousin, wish her *Mazal toff.* That's what you say when someone Jewish gets married, right?"

Chapter 14

Hadassah couldn't believe she was married. She didn't *feel* married, but the ring, a plain silver band, said she was.

She slipped it off and studied the indentation on her finger. There had been no rabbi, no witnesses, just the stars above them. She had asked her father about that a few weeks ago. "Why do you want to know, Dasseleh?" she had thought he would ask, had *wanted* him to ask. "Are you thinking of getting married?" Maybe he would have laughed.

But her father had asked nothing. He had frowned and told her, his voice uncharacteristically stern, that the ceremony could be binding, there could be serious ramifications. For a moment Hadassah had thought: *He knows.* But then he'd said, "This isn't a prank, Dassie. If any of your friends thinks . . ." Then he'd glanced at his watch.

She looked at the ring and wondered what would have happened if her father had asked.

She wasn't sure who had come up with the plan, when the plan had become real. "Your parents will never approve of me," he'd said the last time they talked, "especially your father." He had been so depressed that night. "Maybe we should stop seeing each other, Dassie. We have no future." The thought had paralyzed her. "No," she'd told him, "no."

"Then what?" he'd said. "We get married?"

Maybe, she'd told him, only half joking, because she couldn't bear the thought of not having him in her life. She was eighteen, an adult according to the law. She knew a lot of girls who were married at eighteen. If they were married, her parents would have to accept him. Maybe not right away, but eventually, because they loved her, and would come to love him and see how wonderful he was, how kind and caring, how much he loved her.

"He lied to you," her parents would say. "He tricked you, pretended to meet you when all along he knew who you were."

But that wasn't true. He hadn't known until she revealed her name, and that was when they started IM'ing, days after they'd met in the chat room. He'd been stunned, afraid to tell her the truth, afraid he would lose her. That's why he had e-mailed her someone else's photo.

She had thought there had been some mistake the first time they'd met, in the library. Her face had turned red with anger and confusion when she'd seen him. "What are you . . . ?" She had run out of the library, but he'd caught up with her, had explained why he'd kept the truth from her. "Your parents would have poisoned you against me," he'd told her.

And they had obviously been destined for each other. Forty days before a male child is conceived, he'd told her, a heavenly voice announces whose daughter he will marry, who will be his *bashert*.

"You are my *bashert*, Dassie, and I am yours. Soul mates. How else can you explain the way we met?"

She would tell that to her parents when their anger subsided. She had wanted to tell her mother tonight, but they'd had only a few seconds, and her mother had sounded so sad. *Come home, Dassie.* Her mother had cried. Hadassah had cried, too.

"That's why I don't want you to talk to your parents," he'd said when he came back into the room. "That's why it's best that I keep your phone. Not until they're ready to accept us. I don't want anyone to make you sad, Dassie."

And he was right, of course. He was right about so many things. He knew her so well. He had sensed even before they'd first talked that she'd been depressed. "You lost someone close to you, didn't you?" he'd said. It was almost as if he'd known about Batya.

Her parents were probably disappointed, not just angry. She knew all their arguments. What about seminary, Dassie? What about college and law school? "We thought you would marry someone more learned in Torah, someone with a *frum* background." She didn't need seminary, she would tell them. She could go to college in L.A., then law school, if that's what she still wanted. And maybe he wasn't as learned as her father or Gavriel, and he didn't have the perfect background, but he wanted to learn more, he loved Torah. Wasn't that the main thing? She would remind them that one of the greatest sages, Rabbi Akiva, hadn't started learning Torah until he was forty, that Rabbi Akiva's father-in-law, who hadn't approved of the man his daughter had wanted to marry, had come to love and admire his son-in-law.

They would tell her she was too young. "You have your whole life ahead of you, Dassie. You don't know what you're doing." Batya Weinberg had thought she had a long life ahead of her, she would answer. And Noah, who died of bone cancer, and Lisa, who was killed in a car crash.

She hadn't known it would happen Sunday. She had been surprised when he presented her with a silky white sweater and ankle-length white satin skirt, but she'd still had no idea. "Wear these for me," he'd said, so she had changed in the restroom. "Lovely," he'd said when he saw her. "Perfect," he'd said after he pinned a white orchid to her sweater. But she hadn't expected to stand with him under the night sky, the stars twinkling above, the lights of the city twinkling below them as he recited the blessing and slid the ring onto her finger. The truth was, she didn't really remember leaving the table or walking outside. She'd felt light-headed, wobbly. She rarely had alcohol—a little wine on *Shabbos*, four cups at the Pesach *Seders*. By the second cup, she was always dizzy. But he'd said, "This is a special occasion, Dassie," so she'd tried his drink and liked it.

And really, what was she waiting for? They could do this, cement their love and lives, or her parents would drive him away. He said that would happen, and he was right. Or she could die any day, like Batya or Noah or Lisa, who had counted on a hundred million tomorrows and were lying in their dark, cold graves.

"We may never get another chance," he'd told her. "Do you want to take that risk?"

She would never tell him, but she wished she could have had a real wedding, like the one her mother was planning for Aliza. She would have chosen a simple A-line satin dress, and a pearl headband attached to a cathedral veil. She would have liked to sit on a thronelike chair on a stage, where she would greet guests and accept careful kisses and wait for him to lower the top layer of her veil. She would have liked to hear her father's blessing, to feel his hands on her face, and his kiss. She would have liked to stand under a *chuppa* with a satin *tallit* roof, the family heirloom her parents had stood under and that Aliza and Gavriel and all her siblings would stand under one day.

She would have liked to capture on film the moment when he put the ring on her finger, when her mother raised her veil so that Hadassah could taste the sweet wine. She would have liked to clasp his hand while she waited for the bandleader to announce them for the first time, "Mr. and Mrs. . . . ," to race into the ballroom and duck under a procession of flower-adorned arches held by friends who would be squealing their delight.

She would have liked to dance with her mother and Aliza. She would have liked to be lifted high on a chair, nervous and excited, her hands gripping the sides of the chair—"Don't drop me!"—as her friends carried her to the men's side of the room and the raised chair on which he was sitting, waiting for her to come close enough so that he could stretch his hand and grab hers.

She would have liked all of that, but the main thing, she told herself again, was that they had each other.

Tonight she had waited anxiously in the other room while he talked to her parents. She'd been a little upset when he took the phone away, but of course, he had done it to protect her.

"Let them take their anger out on me," he'd said. He would take the blame for everything, and eventually they would come around.

"What did they say?" she asked when he returned. Not much, he told her, but she could tell from the way he avoided looking at her and the tension in his voice that he was lying. "Tell me," she insisted.

So he told her the truth, that her mother had said they'd never accept him or forgive Dassie, that Dassie had brought shame to the family, who would marry her now?

"My mother told me to come home," Hadassah said. "My mother cried."

Sure, she had cried, because she wanted Dassie under her control. "Go home, if that's what you want," he said. "You have to choose, Dassie."

She didn't want to choose, but he had sounded terribly sad, and she could hear that he was about to cry. She had never seen her father cry, or Gavriel, and she wasn't sure what to say, what to do. And yesterday he'd been in a dark mood. "Leave me alone, I have to think things through." She hadn't known how to handle that, either, but an hour later he was fine.

"I'm sorry," he'd told her. "I'm so worried about you, about us, I want to give you the world and take care of you. You know that, don't you?"

He'd been in a dark mood before, when he'd seen the damage to the car. A tiny dent. You could hardly see it. She'd been embarrassed by how angry he'd been with the valet. A little worried, because his face had turned so white, and then beet red. "I wanted the evening to be perfect," he'd said, "that's why I was so upset."

He was really upset tonight.

"Your parents offered me money to divorce you," he told her. "A hundred thousand dollars if I disappear forever and swear not to tell anyone. Is that what you want, Dassie? Because if that's what you want . . . Maybe you don't love me enough, the way I love you. I would die a million deaths for you."

She slipped the ring back on her finger.

Chapter 15

Friday, November 19, 7:43 a.m., 3100 block of Holly-ridge Drive. Unknown suspects broke into a residence and stole the victim's laptop, containing compromising pictures of famous actors and actresses. The suspects later fled the location.

"Well, golly, Miss Molly, you're up early." Andy Connors swung his long, boot-clad legs off his desk. "Or should I should say *Mrs.* Molly?"

"How are you, Andy?"

"No complaints. I'd be better if I didn't have so many cases, but that's the story of my life." He nodded at the stack of Blue Book binders on his desk. "Why do people decide to turn ugly right before the holidays?"

"I think you just complained," I said.

"I did, didn't I?" He chuckled. "So are you getting together for Thanksgiving with your whole *mishpacha?*" His flat Boston drawl gave the word a unique sound. "Did I say that right?"

"Perfect." Connors loves to use the Hebrew and Yiddish words he's started to pick up. "Zack and I will be with our combined families. What about you?"

"Dinner with friends. I'm doing the bird—a centuries-old Connors family recipe."

"Really?"

"No. I clipped it from the *Times.*" He gave me a lazy smile. "Sorry I missed you last week, Molly, and the week before. Lately I seem to be out whenever you stop by for your crime fix. So are you still enjoying married life?"

"Will you tease me again if I say it's wonderful?"

"Absolutely. It's indecent for anyone to be that happy. Probably a misdemeanor. Seriously, it's good to see you, Molly. You look beautiful, as always. Can I say that, or will your rabbi mind?"

I smiled. "I think Zack can handle it."

"I hope you're treating him right." Connors exaggerated a frown. "You're not dragging the poor guy into your investigations, are you?"

"Zack doesn't seem to mind. And I'm treating him *very* right." The piña colada and Irene Jakaitis's information had put me in a celebratory mood that had kept us both up past midnight. "Actually, I need a favor, Andy."

"And here I thought you were pining for my company."

"That, too."

"Liar." Connors stood and unfolded himself to his six-feet-two. "Grab a seat. I'll get us coffee. Medium or large?"

"Large, please. Regular, not decaf. With cream."

I'd had one cup this morning but still felt sluggish. Unlike Zack, who has to be at *shul* by six most mornings, I'm not an early riser. But I hadn't wanted to risk missing Connors, and I had to finish and e-mail my "Crime Sheet" column to my editor before noon.

"As for the favor," I said, "I'll let you decide how big it is."

He laughed and loped off to the end of the detectives' room. I pulled over a chair from the next table.

I'd met Connors when I took over the "Crime Sheet" for a class-mate from my UCLA journalism extension course, around the same time I began my first true crime book. That was over a year after Aggie was killed. Though I never articulated the thought at the time, I think I hoped that writing the column and examining true crimes would help me deal with the fog of grief, despair, and fear that shrouded my life after my best friend's murder. If anything, my column and books have reinforced my fears and my despair about the violence that in-creasingly confronts us. But I have taken heart that in some of the cases I've researched for my books, and in others that I found myself investigating, justice has been served.

And I did meet Connors. From the start he was more user-friendly than many of the LAPD detectives I've encountered (the nicer ones share photocopies of sanitized crime reports; the others force me to copy the crime data by hand), and despite those moments when my in-quisitiveness has pushed Connors to the wall and turned his bantering to caustic criticism, I know he's fond of me, just as I am of him. He's in his late thirties, has curly brown hair with a bald spot on his crown that doesn't strip him of one ounce of sexiness, and looks better in tight jeans than a person has a right to, although Zack comes in a close second. I don't know much about Connors's personal life, just that he left an ex-wife in Boston some years ago, and a few months ago he let slip that he'd met someone. I hope she's special.

"So what's the favor?" he asked when he returned, carrying two car-tons filled with steaming coffee.

"I'm hoping you can trace a California license plate for me."

He set the cartons on his desk, along with packets of sugar substi-tute and creamer that he dug out of his pockets. Then he sat down.

"Why?"

On the way to the Hollywood station I'd debated how much I could tell Connors without violating the Bailors' confidence. Not much, I'd decided. But there was no way I could find the information without his help. And I wasn't about to start lying to him, not even for Rabbi Bailor.

"This is delicate," I began, and realized I was using Jastrow's word. "I can't give you names, okay?"

"Not okay. I can't agree to do something before I know what's involved, Molly."

"All right." I tore open two packets of sweetener and stirred the contents into my coffee. "My friend's daughter ran off with a guy she met in a chat room. The family doesn't think she's in physical danger, but—"

"How do you know?"

"They heard from her several times. The last time was yesterday evening."

"Go on." Connors took a long swig of his coffee, which he drinks black.

"My friend is anxious to find his daughter and persuade her to come home."

"How old is the girl?"

"She turned eighteen a few weeks ago."

"So she's an adult," Connors said. "We're not talking statutory rape. What's so delicate?"

"This is an Orthodox family, Andy. A young woman running away with a guy may not be a big deal in the general world, but for an Orthodox family, this would be a huge stigma if people found out."

Connors nodded. "So where does the license plate come in?"

I told him what I'd learned.

Connors huffed. "Unbelievable luck. I've been trying to get a lead on a double homicide for three weeks. You go for drinks and hit the jackpot."

"Not *luck*," I said, annoyed. "An educated guess, deduction, and creative sleuthing."

"Whatever, Miss Marple. If you decide to give up your writing career, let me know and I'll put in a word with Bratton. Scratch that. He'd probably make you my superior."

"So will you help me, Andy?"

"I don't know." He swiveled in his chair. "What do you plan to do with the information?"

"Talk with this girl and try to convince her to come home. Apparently, she looks up to me. Plus the family thinks it'll be less confrontational if I talk to her. What?" I said when Connors frowned.

"Suppose this girl doesn't want to be found, Molly? Which is likely, considering that she's okay and hasn't come home. Maybe she doesn't want to live a religious life. Her choice."

"It *is* her choice, but that's not the case here. She *is* religious, Andy. She's strict about her observance."

Connors raised a brow. "So she ran away with a guy she met in a chat room?"

"From what I've learned, she's feeling neglected and isolated and doesn't have many friends. And she may be depressed. A classmate died last year of heart disease, and two other classmates died before that. Cancer and a car accident."

"Rough." Connors tsked. "So I'll ask you again, Molly. What if she doesn't want to come back?"

"I'm not going to tie her up and drag her home, if that's what you're worried about."

"Exactly. So what's your next move? Are you going to tell the dad, 'Sorry, your daughter's happy shacking up with her boyfriend'?"

Connors had me there. I took a long sip of coffee. "I don't know. I guess I didn't think it through."

"Would you give the dad the information?"

"I haven't thought about that."

"Well, think about it now. Suppose he tries to talk to his daughter. There's a struggle, someone's hurt."

I shook my head. "My friend would never hurt his daughter."

"In moments of extreme passion, people do the unexpected. You know that better than most people, Molly," Connors said in the gentle tone he uses when he's referring to Aggie. "And what if your friend decides to take out his anger or frustration on the guy his daughter's with?"

"He wouldn't do that."

"*You* may be sure. I'm not. Or what if the *boyfriend* gets physical with the dad? In either case, if anybody gets hurt, whose neck do you think will be on the LAPD chopping block, Molly? FYI, the answer isn't Tom Turkey."

"You're right," I said, glum. "Would you consider paying a visit to this guy, Andy?"

"To what end?"

"I don't know. Maybe you could scare him into letting her go."

"Has he raped her?"

"No."

"Has he assaulted her? Is he holding her against her will? Is she in any danger?"

"Define *danger.*"

Connors scowled. "Don't play games."

"He's brainwashing her. He intimated as much to the parents. And he's controlling her. He's threatened to cut her off from her family."

"He may not be Mr. Rogers, Molly, but from what you're telling me, he hasn't committed a crime and doesn't plan to. And the girl is an adult. Unfortunately, there's no law against stupidity."

"There's something else." I told Connors about the quote from *Hamlet* and the reference to *Romeo and Juliet*.

Connors gave a little snort. "So he's not an expert on Shakespeare, or he used the quote because the words fit his situation. Last I heard, Romeo and Juliet are still the epitome of young love."

"And the fact that he sent a note to the girl's father with a reference to 'What Becomes of the Broken-Hearted?' "

"Jimmy Ruffin. I love his stuff. So?"

I took the manila mailer from my purse and placed it on Connors's desk. "The note's inside, with some Chanukah chocolates. I was careful when I handled it, but my friend thought this was a little gift. He touched the note, but not the chocolates. He's hoping you can run the prints, if there are any, and identify this man."

Connors took a pair of latex gloves from a desk drawer and slipped them on. Then he removed the note from the mailer and read it.

"Your friend's a rabbi, huh?" he said, looking up. "What's a shekel?"

I explained.

Connors's expression hardened. "This guy raped her?"

"From last night's phone, apparently not. The thing is, Andy, this girl may be married."

"She is or she isn't, Molly. Unless she did a Britney Spears and changed her mind a couple of hours later."

"It's more complicated than that."

I told him that there had been a ceremony and that Dassie had a ring, that we didn't know if there had been witnesses, that the marriage hadn't been consummated. Then I explained about *mikvah.*

"I never heard of that," Connors said. "People really do that? Go without sex for two weeks every month? They don't even touch?"

From his awkward tone, I figured that "people" included me. "The idea is to elevate the physical into the spiritual, to make marriage more than just about sex."

"Sex isn't important?"

"It's *very* important. In fact, the marriage contract says the husband is obligated to give his wife pleasure. The two weeks when the couple abstains is supposed to make them feel like newlyweds, to heighten the anticipation and sustain the newness of the relationship."

"Abstinence makes the heart grow fonder?" Connors smiled.

"Something like that." I felt myself blushing. "I know virginity isn't a major concern for many teenagers, Andy, but in Orthodoxy it matters a great deal. Very observant Jews don't even touch each other outside of marriage. And suppose I *am* right, and this guy is contemplating a double suicide?"

"You're back to that? Shakespeare and Jimmy Ruffin."

"The song is morose, Andy." I'm an oldies fan, too, and had heard the song countless times, but I'd looked up the lyrics online last night before going to sleep. "Broken dreams, happiness being an illusion. It's about someone who can't find peace of mind, who believes he's lost everything and is doomed to an unhappy ending."

"Which probably fits half the guys in this station, but they're not about to kill themselves. And there's hope toward the end of the song," Connors said. "The guy is determined to search for someone to care for him."

"But it ends with the refrain, which is all about despair."

"That's your interpretation. It's a song, Molly. It's not a suicide note."

Zack had said that, too. "What if you're wrong?"

"What if I am? Suppose he *does* pull a Romeo. What makes you think she'd do a Juliet?"

"Nothing," I admitted. "But she may be depressed. She's under this guy's control, suggestible. . . . And what if he decides to kill her before he kills himself?"

Connors grunted. "A hell of a lot of *ifs*."

He put the note back inside the bag and removed his gloves. I drained the rest of my coffee.

"Did you tell the father about the car?" Connors asked.

I shook my head.

"What *did* you tell him?"

"That I might have a lead on Ha—on his daughter. I phoned him when I got back from Yamashiro. I didn't tell him where I'd been, or what I'd learned."

Connors gave me a knowing look. "Which means you were afraid of what he'd do with the knowledge."

In my mind I heard Rabbi Bailor telling his son what he'd like to do to the man who had lured his daughter, why he would never do it. *It's not the Torah way, Gavriel.*

"No. I wanted to check it out first, with you."

"Then why tell him anything?"

"Because he and the family are despondent, Andy. I wanted to give them hope."

Connors swiveled back and forth. "What's the car make and license plate?"

"A silver Altima. R-C-K-Y-R-D. Rocky Road?"

"Yum."

"*Thank* you."

"Don't thank me. I may check it out, see if the guy has a rap sheet, see if I can ID prints on the note, although my guess is the only prints we'll find will belong to your friend, the rabbi. Even if I identify this guy, I'm not promising I'll share the information with you."

My car was on Wilcox, in front of the station. I sat inside a few minutes, my hand on the ignition key, thinking about my conversation with Connors, about Hadassah Bailor.

'Tis a consummation devoutly to be wished. . . .

I took my hand off the ignition key and found my cell phone in my purse. After obtaining the number for my auto insurance broker, I phoned him and told him I'd been sideswiped in a hit-and-run but had managed to get the license plate of the car that had struck me.

"I'd like to know who owns that vehicle, Marty," I said.

"Sorry, but we don't have access to that information, Molly. We used to."

Damn. "What about the insurance company?"

"I'll check and call you back."

"It's important, Marty."

I gave him my cell number, turned on the radio, and listened to "Going to the Chapel." When my phone rang two minutes later, I flipped it open quickly.

"Did you get the name of the car owner, Marty?"

"This is Rabbi Bailor."

I should have looked at the LCD display. "Sorry, I thought you were my insurance company."

"You sounded anxious, Molly. Are you okay?"

"Annoyed, really. I had a little fender-bender, and the person who hit me just drove off. But I'm fine."

"Good. I hate to push, but did you learn anything about Dassie?"

"I don't have anything to tell you, Rabbi Bailor. I'll call as soon as I do." That was close enough to the truth.

"I have the phone numbers you wanted. Do you have pen and paper?"

My phone signaled that I had another call. I glanced at the display. The insurance broker. "I'm coming to the school today to talk to some of the students, so I'll get the information from you then. Thanks."

"About that. It seems—"

"I have another call, Rabbi Bailor. I'll see you later." I pressed the button to accept the new incoming call. "Marty?"

"I talked to the insurance company, Molly. You'd have to file a claim and fill out an insurance report, and then you still wouldn't get the information. And to be honest, unless the damage to your car is extensive, I'd advise you to pay for the repairs yourself. You had a claim a little over six months ago. If you file, your rates may go up."

"Even though I'm not at fault?" I asked, outraged by the unfairness of a rate hike resulting from my hypothetical damage.

"Two incidents in one year to one car is never good."

Neither is perjury. I've fibbed on more than one occasion to obtain information—I'd done so last night, with the maître d' and with Irene. I'm not happy about lying, but I do it when I think it's necessary, and when I'm not harming someone. That's a convenient rationalization, I know. But officially accusing someone of hit-and-run, even if I thought that person was despicable, or filling out an insurance report and signing the part where it says something to the effect that everything you've written is, to the best of your knowledge, true . . .

"Suppose I don't file," I said. "Suppose we just make inquiries? I just want to know who hit my car."

"It doesn't work like that. Sorry, Molly. You know what I say? Get the car fixed and be happy you weren't injured. Life's too short."

Chapter 16

Torat Tzion is a brick-faced, two-story building on Burton Way just east of Doheny. Burton Way, by the way, is one of those sneaky,
curvy L.A. streets that confuse tourists and
even some native Angelenos. It's a wide boulevard, separated by a median, that starts at San
Vicente and heads west. After passing Rexford
(and the Beverly Hills library and police
department), Burton Way morphs into Little
Santa Monica, narrows as it continues through
the retail mecca of Beverly Hills (think "Pretty
Woman" and Rodeo Drive) and Century City,
and finally merges with Santa Monica Boulevard. Along Burton Way are posh hotels, like
the Four Seasons and the unknown boutique
gem, L'Hermitage, where celebrities are known
to stay and where, more important, Zack and I
spent our wedding night. I imagined that the

rents in this upscale neighborhood were upscale, too, so the school probably had some angels.

I found a spot directly in front of the school, but by the time I entered the lobby, it was 12:40. I had hoped to be here earlier, but despite my best efforts, I hadn't finished my column until minutes before noon. Since *Shabbat* would start around 4:30, I assumed school would be out in less than an hour. Not much time to interview students.

The walls of the Feldman Family lobby, high-ceilinged and domed, were filled with a multitude of framed brass plaques. A host of angels, I thought. I read the names on a few of the plaques as I waited for the laconic guard to confirm that I had reason to be here before he checked my purse and had me pass through a metal detector. The presence of guards and other security measures in most Jewish schools and centers became a necessity five years ago, when Buford Furrow fired more than seventy bullets from an assault weapon into a Granada Hills Jewish community center and shattered our illusion of safety.

The bell clanged. Seconds later, doors to classrooms along a wide hall to my right and left were flung open, and teens came rushing out, like the bulls at Pamplona. The boys wore black slacks and white button-down shirts. The girls wore gray skirts with yellow sweaters or yellow blouses. Not the colors of my uniform, but for a surreal moment I was back in high school, washed in memories I didn't particularly like. The cliques, the blossoming doubts about religion, the boys (including Zack, who had dumped me without explanation) for whom I never felt pretty enough or sexy enough or thin enough or clever enough. Rabbi Ingel, who had accused me of something I didn't do. Rabbi Bailor, who had turned out to have feet of clay.

The rabbi, I learned, was in a meeting, but he'd left an envelope containing contact information for Cheryl Wexner and Greg Shankman with his assistant, Sue Horowitz, a buxom woman in her fifties with curly auburn hair, green eyes, and a warm smile. The lines around Sue's eyes and the deeper ones from her nose to her coral-lipsticked mouth suggested that she smiled often. Her southern drawl (she was born in Memphis, she told me) had me at "Hi, darlin'."

"Rabbi said to help any way I can," Sue told me. "Where would y'all like to start?"

She shut the door to her office, which she had made cozy with potted plants, one of which threatened to overtake her desk. Posters brightened the ecru walls, and a collection of vibrant-colored ceramic birds eyed me from the top of the black filing cabinet in the corner.

Sue offered me a seat, along with a cup of coffee I declined. I'd had two cups at home while working on my column and felt like the Energizer Bunny on speed.

"I'm writing an article about Torat Tzion," I began, but she stopped me.

"Rabbi told me about Dassie, Molly," she said in an undertone. "Can I call you Molly? I'd flay my skin before I breathed a word he told me in confidence," she continued before I could respond. "He's going through something awful, you know."

I told her I knew.

"So what do y'all need, Molly?"

"I'd like to talk to Dassie's friends. Tara and Becky. I don't know their last names."

"Tara Edelson and Becky Rothman."

"And since Rabbi Bailor doesn't want me to single them out, he said he'd arrange for me to talk to the girls in a group. I know it's late, but—"

"Didn't Rabbi reach you?" Sue asked. "He planned to tell the seniors first thing this morning that you'd be interviewing them, but Dr. Mendes—she's the secular studies principal. She said there was a problem."

So I had rushed here for nothing. My fault. While working on my column, I had shut off my cell phone and ignored a call on my home line from Rabbi Bailor. I'd assumed he wanted a progress report.

"What about Dr. McIntyre?" I asked. "Does he teach a class today?"

The door opened and a student poked his head in.

Sue scowled at him. "Don't y'all know how to knock, Brian?"

"Like this?" He rapped his knuckles on the door.

"You think you're cute, do you?"

"Kind of." He grinned. "Did Rabbi Bailor finish my letter of recommendation, Mrs. Horowitz?"

"When he does, you'll be the second to know. And if you don't learn some manners, I may just misplace it. That would be a shame."

The boy looked sheepish. "Sorry, Mrs. Horowitz." His head disappeared, and he pulled the door shut.

"Kids." Sue clucked. "Brian's okay, but some of them think because their parents pay tuition, they own the school."

"And the ones with parents on the board?"

"They *do* own the school." Sue laughed. "It doesn't make a difference to Rabbi Bailor. He's a principal with principle."

"What about Dr. Mendes? I understand that she and the rabbi don't see eye to eye, and he's worried about his job."

"Rabbi told you, huh?" Sue nodded. "Dr. Mendes is close to the board members, and to Robert Hornstein. He founded the school, and he hired Dr. Mendes."

"So Mr. Hornstein sides with Dr. Mendes?"

"On what day?" Sue sniffed. "Mr. Hornstein agrees with the last person he talked to. But Dr. Mendes has his ear. She's his golden child. Since she's been here, the number of kids being accepted into the Ivies has gone way up."

"Rabbi Bailor doesn't produce results?"

" 'Course he does. The kids love Rabbi, and he's changed lives. But the fact that kids are studying Torah in Israel and committing to keeping kosher and *Shabbat* isn't as sexy or exciting to the board as the fact that they're going to Harvard or Columbia or Penn."

"Do you think the rabbi may lose his job?"

"Not if the board members have half a brain among them. If Rabbi goes, I go." Sue pursed her lips. "But you were asking? Oh, right. Dr. McIntyre. He finished his class and said if anybody asked, he'd be in the teachers' lounge, photocopying an exam."

"Where's the lounge?"

"First floor. Take a right when you leave my office, then a left, and go down the hall. There's a plate on the door on your left. He's a good man, Dr. McIntyre, and a good teacher. The two don't always go together. I could tell you stories—but I won't." Smiling, she pulled an imaginary zipper across her mouth. "Rabbi would kill me." Then she turned serious. "He's been through a lot. Dr. McIntyre, I mean. He lost a child a few years back."

"I'm sorry to hear that."

"It can try your faith, losing a child." Sue pressed a hand against her bosom. "Rabbi says God put Dr. McIntyre here so he could connect with the kids when these tragedies happened. Rabbi said he told you about that, right?"

I nodded.

"And I do think being here, talking to these kids, is helping Dr. McIntyre. It gives him hope and a purpose."

"Speaking of teachers, Sue, do you know if Mr. Shankman is working in another school?"

"I don't. Back in October we had several calls about him. Nothing recently, so maybe he found another position. I hope so. Mr. Shankman is good people," Sue said. "Rabbi was sorry to see him go. I was, too."

I hadn't thought that Rabbi Bailor had lied to me, but confirmation is always gratifying. "Why was he let go?"

Sue pulled the imaginary zipper across her lips again. *"Shabbat shalom,* y'all."

Chapter 17

I found the lounge and knocked before entering. A copy machine was humming, spitting out pages. Hunched over a keyboard in front of one of several computers on a table that ran the length of the room was a middle-aged man with thick, unruly graying hair that matched the gray in his argyle vest. A slender, brown-haired woman in her forties was slipping folded yellow flyers into cubbies on the opposite wall. She was wearing a navy suit with a cream-colored blouse, plain blue pumps, and small pearl earrings. Administration, I decided.

"Dr. McIntyre? I'm Molly Blume. Rabbi Bailor may have mentioned that I'd like to talk to you?"

He looked at me, his fingers still on the keyboard, a blank expression in his brown eyes. Then he nodded. "Oh, right."

He swiveled and stood. He was taller than I'd realized, broader-shouldered. He turned to the woman. She was gazing at me, curious.

"Miss Blume is . . ."

"Doing a story on teenagers," I finished for him.

"You're the reporter," she said. "I'm Dr. Janet Mendes, secular studies principal. What paper do you write for, Miss Blume? Rabbi Bailor didn't say."

"Please call me Molly. I've written for the *L.A. Times* and other papers and magazines. I freelance."

The copy machine had stopped. McIntyre removed the page he'd been photocopying and placed another page on the window. The machine resumed its humming.

"I'm afraid I'm not familiar with your work," Dr. Mendes said. "Tell me more about this story."

Though my family thinks I'm a threat to Ann Rule, the queen of true crime, I'm constantly reminded of my anonymity. Right now anonymity was a plus.

"It's about teens and the Internet. I thought I'd interview students from private schools."

A cell phone rang.

"Sorry." McIntyre flipped open a phone he removed from a holder clipped to the waistband of his black slacks. He spoke quietly, then looked up. "I have to take this call. It may be a while."

I told him I'd wait. He left the room.

Dr. Mendes inserted the last flyer into its slot. "Rabbi Bailor said he was your teacher years ago, at Sharsheret. A small world. Is your mother Celia Blume?"

"She is."

"I'd never poach, but if she decides to leave Sharsheret, we'd love to have her teach here." Dr. Mendes smiled. "When you say 'teens and the Internet,' Molly, what exactly do you mean?"

"How they use it," I said. "What they enjoy most about it. Socializing in chat rooms, doing research, shopping, connecting with other teens. My pieces tend to evolve."

"And you've interviewed students at other schools?"

Ten to one, Dr. Mendes would check. "Torat Tzion is first on my list. I thought I'd start with the top."

I don't know why I said that—I was so obviously kissing up. But Dr. Mendes seemed pleased.

"We're proud of our students, and of our teachers who help them meet their goals. Your story sounds very current, Molly, but as I told Rabbi Bailor, I have concerns. For one thing, I wouldn't want classes disrupted, particularly since our students are preparing for midterms."

"I'd be happy to work around their schedule."

"More important, before we can allow you to interview any students, we would need parental permission."

Which ruled out talking to anyone today. "I wouldn't have to use names, Dr. Mendes. I'm trying to get an overall picture."

"Still, there may be liability issues. I could consult with the school attorney, but I'd prefer to take the safe route—and one that doesn't entail legal fees. And I'd like to see the questions you'll be asking."

While I wished she weren't so cautious, I could understand her concerns. "As I said, my piece is about how teens use the Internet. The frequency of use, patterns, the advantages and pitfalls."

Dr. Mendes frowned. "Pitfalls?"

"Or not," I said, backtracking as smoothly as a Michael Jackson moonwalk. "As I said, my story is elastic right now." Like my lies, I thought.

"All right. I'll send a letter to parents on Monday, with a release form. So perhaps you can do the interviews a few days after that." She frowned. "Although next week is Thanksgiving. Well, we'll see. In the meantime, please fax or e-mail me your questions. You can ask Sue Horowitz for my contact information."

"I'll do that."

"I'm sorry about the wasted trip, Molly. I hope you understand." Dr. Mendes walked to the door and had one hand on the knob when she turned toward me. "Can I show you around the school? We're proud of our facilities."

"Another time, thanks. The lobby is beautiful, by the way. I noticed that it's named for the Feldman Family. Is that the family with three Harvard men? Well, a father and one son so far. And a senior is headed for Cambridge next September, Rabbi Bailor said."

"Did he?" Janet Mendes looked surprised. "Rabbi Bailor meant the Prossers. They're one of the school's founders. Adam is one of our brightest stars. He hasn't made a decision yet, but we're assuming he'll follow in his brother Seth's footsteps and choose Harvard."

Adam Prosser, I repeated, committing the name to memory. "What are those, by the way?" I pointed to a stack of books I'd noticed on one of the tables that lined the walls. "Student yearbooks?"

"*Faculty* yearbooks, and pages for the senior yearbook. Mr. Hernandez, our history department chair, is the yearbook advisor, the lucky man." Dr. Mendes's tone was wry. "The seniors are planning to use one or more photos from each instructor's yearbook. They're aiming for nostalgia. Nostalgia can be quite embarrassing, I'm afraid, but the staff are all being good sports."

"What about you?"

"Oh, they won't find anything scandalous. I was always the good girl." She smiled and opened the door. "Would you like me to show you the way out? It's a large building, and you wouldn't be the first visitor to get lost."

"No, thanks."

"Oh, right. You're here to talk to Dr. McIntyre. So your trip won't be wasted after all." Again, there was a question in her eyes.

"Unless he needs parental permission."

She surprised me and laughed. "Touché. We live in litigious times, Molly. I don't like it, but it's a fact. Are you talking to Dr. McIntyre for your story?"

"Background information," I said. "The mystery of the teenager."

"When you solve it, I hope you'll share the secret. At school I pretend to know what I'm doing, but my two teenagers will tell you it's all a facade. It was nice meeting you, Molly Blume. I'm looking forward to getting your questions, and to seeing you next week."

Next week would be too late for Hadassah, who was counting the days before she went to the *mikvah* so that she could be intimate with a controlling man who joked about wanting a hundred thousand dollars and made allusions to suicide.

Maybe it wasn't a joke. Maybe I should have let Connors think blackmail was involved. That would have given him a legitimate reason to search for Hadassah.

Chapter 18

Dr. Mendes left. I'd been prepared to dislike the woman who was giving Rabbi Bailor a hard time, but she'd seemed friendly, approachable. Of course, she had no reason *not* to be friendly to me, especially since I was planning to write about the students in her school.

I crossed the room and looked through the stack of yearbooks. Rabbi Bailor's was among them. A yeshiva high school in Brooklyn. I flipped to the back and studied his senior photo. Charles Bailor. His dark hair reached almost to his shoulders, and he had a rakish air and a broad smile. I found other photos. One showed him on the basketball court, about to make a shot. In another photo he had his arms around a brown-haired cheerleader. I wondered when he'd changed his name to Chaim.

Next to the yearbooks was a box with a pile of clear plastic envelopes containing senior photos. I found the packet for Adam Prosser. He reminded me of Ron. It wasn't just his good looks—blond hair, blue eyes. It was the air of confidence and entitlement. Or maybe I was attributing qualities to Prosser that weren't there.

After glancing at the door, I pulled out the boy's senior photo and a family portrait and made copies of both. I removed the originals and my copies, along with copies Dr. McIntyre had left in the bin. I separated my pages from McIntyre's, returned his pages to the bin, and slipped my folded copies into my purse.

I was standing in front of the table with the yearbooks, the original photos in my hand, when I heard the door open. My back was to the door. I slid the photos inside the packet and turned around.

"Sorry, that took longer than I expected," Dr. McIntyre said. "Rabbi Bailor told me you wanted to ask me about Hadassah. I'm anxious to help you find her, but as you probably know, I'm bound by therapist–patient confidentiality."

"Actually, I'm not here to ask you about Hadassah. I wanted to talk to you about the man she's with."

McIntyre frowned. "I have no idea who he is. Unfortunately, even if I *did* know, I couldn't tell you."

"What if she's in danger?" I said.

"Even then, unless I could say with certainty that she was in immediate, *mortal* danger . . . Hadassah ran away with this man. She told her sister she was safe. Rabbi Bailor hasn't told me anything that would indicate otherwise."

"Can we sit down, Dr. McIntyre?"

I pulled out a chair from one of the tables, sat, and waited until the therapist reluctantly did the same.

"Did Rabbi Bailor tell you about the note he received from this man, and the phone call last night?"

"He did." Dr. McIntyre's nostrils flared. "I saw the note. Rabbi Bailor feels that this man is taunting him, and I have to agree. He's despicable. Scum."

"What about the phone call?"

"That's difficult to say." McIntyre sounded thoughtful. "I heard the conversation third hand. We've all played the telephone game, Miss Blume. Words often change when conversations are repeated. So do connotations."

"After I left the Bailors last night, I wrote down what Mrs. Bailor said." I took my spiral pad from my purse and read my notes aloud.

When I had finished, McIntyre nodded. "That's essentially what Rabbi Bailor told me."

"So what can you tell me about this man?"

McIntyre shook his head. "I'm not an armchair psychologist, Miss Blume."

"Just a guess," I said. "I won't hold you to it."

McIntyre removed his bifocals and rubbed them with a gray cloth that he took from his pants pocket. "This is purely speculation, you understand," he said, putting on his glasses. "As with the note, I sensed that this man enjoyed flaunting his control over Hadassah and, by extension, over the Bailors. He wants them to feel helpless. I'm sure you didn't need me to figure that out."

"Mrs. Bailor said he sounded angry and intense."

"That may be true. Or she may have *imagined* anger. It would be difficult for her to be objective about this man." McIntyre stroked his chin. "Also, he may have *feigned* anger to increase the Bailors' anxiety and helplessness. I didn't see his body language. I didn't even hear the conversation, so I can't comment on his tone."

"The thing that struck me, Dr. McIntyre, is that he told Mrs. Bailor that he and Hadassah were planning to consummate the marriage on Monday. Why tell her that?"

"Again, to show them that he's in control, that they can't stop the event. For deeply religious parents like the Bailors, it's like a ticking time bomb."

"I agree. But what if on some level this man wants to be found before the bomb goes off?" I told him about the quote from Hamlet and the reference to Romeo and Juliet, about the song.

Dr. McIntyre was frowning. "You're suggesting that he's contemplating suicide?"

"*Double* suicide." I let the doctor think about that. "It's possible, isn't it? You said yourself that this man has Hadassah under his control."

The therapist pressed his lips together. "This is exactly why I don't like speculating, Miss Blume."

"The fact that Hadassah ran away with this man and is still with him suggests that she *is* under his control, doesn't it?"

"That doesn't mean that she would allow herself to be convinced to take her own life."

"Maybe not by itself. But she was depressed about her friend's death, and the deaths of two other teenagers she knew. Rabbi Bailor told me she's been seeing you ever since Batya Weinberg died so suddenly."

"I thought I made it clear that I can't comment on anything Hadassah revealed during therapy. That includes anything related to Batya Weinberg's death." Points of red dotted the man's cheeks.

"Teenagers are at high risk for suicide, aren't they, Dr. McIntyre? I read about that all the time. It's the third highest cause of death among teens. Suppose this man wants to kill himself and encourages Hadassah to do the same. If she's in mortal danger . . ."

"You're presenting me with a theory based on literary allusions and song lyrics," McIntyre said. "Believe me, I would do *anything* to find Hadassah and stop this man from hurting her and other young girls."

"But do you think she's at risk?"

"Miss Blume, how many times can I say this? I can't comment on Hadassah Bailor. What you told me isn't enough for me to violate confidentiality. Even if I *am* worried about her, my hands are tied."

The troubled look in his eyes, the tremor in his voice—both told me he *was* worried. I had gone fishing and wasn't sure how I felt about what I'd caught. "So you *do* think Hadassah's at risk."

"I didn't say that." McIntyre's tone was guarded.

"But you could *say* it is. I spoke to a police detective this morning. If you tell him you think Hadassah is at risk, either from herself or from this man, he might take steps to find her."

"How? We don't know who this man is."

"I may have a lead."

Dr. McIntyre inhaled sharply. "What lead?"

"I can't tell you that. So will you talk to the detective?"

He didn't answer right away. "You're asking me to lie. I could lose my license."

"We don't know that it's a lie. And if it helps us find Hadassah?"

"I need to think about this." He drummed his fingers on the table. "If this man is contemplating killing himself, and having Hadassah do the same, why hasn't he done it yet? What is he waiting for?"

"The consummation," I said. "That's what he told Mrs. Bailor."

Having nothing to tell Rabbi Bailor, and something to conceal, I had hoped to leave without seeing him, but when I exited the lobby he was talking to several students. The conversation was animated. Rabbi Bailor was nodding and smiling. I wondered how he could function and act so normal, as if his world weren't upside down.

Leaning against a black BMW, one of several cars double-parked in front of the school, was a brown-haired young man in his midtwenties. He looked familiar. For a second or so I couldn't place him. Then I realized: He was number one son in the Prosser family photo.

I walked over to him. "I'm Molly Blume. I think I saw your photo in one of the old yearbooks. Your name is—?"

"Seth Prosser." He sounded bored.

"Nice to meet you, Seth. You have a brother here, right? Adam? You may have heard that Rabbi Bailor is being honored this January at an educators' conference. I'm talking to students and alumni to get background for a piece I'm writing about him."

"Sorry. Not interested." He checked his watch.

"It wouldn't take long. Maybe five minutes. It'll be painless, I promise."

"What I have to say you wouldn't print." He straightened up and raised a hand. "Yo, Adam!" he called.

I turned and saw a group of students exiting the school. Among them was Adam Prosser. He waved at his brother and held up two fingers.

"Well, if you change your mind, Seth, give me a call." I took a card from my wallet and handed it to him.

The rabbi was hurrying toward me, a principal turned father. I walked toward him.

"I'm sorry I couldn't see you, Molly. I was meeting with a parent. Any developments?"

"Not yet."

"Last night you said you had a lead." He sounded petulant. "Can you be more specific?"

"No, sorry." Telling him had been a mistake. "I *did* meet with Dr. Mendes. She said she'll send out release forms for the parents on Monday."

He grunted. "Monday is a year away. And who said Dassie's friends know anything?"

Adam Prosser and his friends were approaching.

"Have a good *Shabbos,* guys," Rabbi Bailor called to them over the honking of cars.

"You, too, Rabbi B," one of the boys said.

The others did the same. Prosser nodded stiffly, but looked straight ahead. A moment later he gave his friends high-fives and got into the BMW.

"I'd better be going," I told Rabbi Bailor. "Have a good *Shabbos.*"

He followed me to my car. "You'll phone me right away if you find out anything?"

"If I can tell you something, absolutely."

The rabbi frowned. "What do you mean, 'If you can tell me something'? Are you keeping something from me, Molly?"

I forced a smile. *"Now* who's nit-picking, Rabbi?"

The wind blew the bangs of my wig. I walked to the driver's side of my Acura and opened the door.

The rabbi walked around the car. "You can't even tell," he said.

I looked at him. "What?"

"You said you had a fender-bender? I don't see any damage."

A liar, my grandmother Bubbie G says, has to have a good memory. "Not *my* car," I said. "Zack's car."

The rabbi nodded. "As long as no one was hurt."

I ducked my head and got into the car before he could see my flushed cheeks.

Chapter 19

==

I had spoken to Connors and to McIntyre. I'd given the psychologist my card and Connors's phone number. Now all I could do was wait. I tried to put all that out of my mind while I stopped at Ralph's supermarket on La Cienega for nonfat milk, GOLEAN Crunch! cereal, a bag of Hershey's Kisses, and two pounds of fresh asparagus, which was on sale. The Molly Blume food pyramid.

I drove to Fairfax and Third and was pleased to find a parking spot in the usually overcrowded lot behind The Three Amigos discount produce store, where my family has been shopping for years. After navigating the narrow aisles and filling my cart, I chatted in my broken Spanish with the jet-haired, mustached clerk who rang up my purchases, including two bags of Clementine tangerines (Zack's favorite) and a box of blueberries—out of season and expensive, but I love them, and not just because they're high in antioxidants. When I opened my purse, I realized I'd left my checkbook on my desk before driving to Torat Tzion. The store doesn't accept credit cards. I had almost no cash. Sighing, I put the $3.99 four-ounce box of blueberries back on the shelf.

The things you do for love.

I arrived home at a quarter to four, with less than an hour until *Shabbat*. I took a shower and shampooed my hair, mercilessly flattened from two days of wig-wearing, then blow-dried it into the tousled curls Zack likes.

Zack had done most of the *Shabbos* preparations. He'd unscrewed the refrigerator lightbulb, heated water in the electric urn, set the timer that would shut off the lights throughout the house tonight and turn them on again tomorrow in the late afternoon. On the Sabbath we don't cook, or turn electricity or fire on or off. It sounds compli-cated and restrictive, I know. But except for a hiatus of several years after high school when I left Orthodox observance, I've been doing this all my life. And I look forward to being sealed off from the mundane activities of the world for twenty-five hours and reconnecting with my spirituality.

On the cloth-covered dining room table Zack had set a vase with yellow roses, and two silver candlesticks on a silver tray. I dropped a handful of coins into a silver-and-rosewood box—setting aside charity before the Sabbath is a helpful reminder to think of those less fortu-nate. Then I lit the candles, circled my hands above the flames three times to welcome the Sabbath and, hooding my eyes, recited the bless-ing and several additional prayers, including one for Hadassah Bailor.

The truth is, I didn't want to think about Hadassah—where she was, and with whom. I didn't want to worry about her, especially on the Sabbath, when there was nothing I could do. I told myself that Connors and Zack were probably right. I was investing too much in words, words Nechama Bailor may have misheard, words that never-theless filled me with apprehension and dread.

Finally, I prayed that Zack and I would be blessed with a child. I'd had mixed feelings when I didn't conceive the first few months of our marriage. A flutter of disappointment, a little relief, because we had just begun to learn our rhythms. A part of me had been loath to relinquish that special solitude. But I had turned thirty in April, and I wondered whether my failure to become pregnant when I was married to Ron—something I had viewed, in retrospect, as a blessing—had foreshadowed problems.

Zack was in the room. I hadn't heard him enter, but I could feel his presence. When I opened my eyes he was standing next to me.

"Good *Shabbos*," I said.

"Good *Shabbos*."

He placed his hands on my shoulders, and we kissed. A sweet kiss, not a sexy one. Unspoken between us was the hope that my being two days late meant I was pregnant.

"You look beautiful. New sweater?" He touched my sleeve. "Soft."

"Cashmere, on sale at Ann Taylor. Plus I had a coupon."

He smiled. "I didn't ask how much you spent."

"You never do. But I don't want you to worry. We can eat this week."

Zack's salary is generous, but L.A. is expensive. While we were lucky to find a fixer-upper in foreclosure (for the down payment, our parents supplemented our wedding gift checks and Zack's and my savings, and I suspect that my dad did the remodeling below his cost), our monthly mortgage payment can float a small country. I contribute my modest earnings from my "Crime Sheet" column, freelance articles, and true crime books, but Zack has refused to use the dividends from the investments I made with my divorce settlement. Maybe one day, for our kids, he says.

I was in the bedroom, putting on a necklace, when Zack appeared in the doorway.

"Ready to go?" he asked.

"I have to get a hat. Did you put away the groceries?"

"I did." He came up behind me. "Let me do that." He took the necklace and closed the clasp, then moved my hair aside and nuzzled my neck. "Thanks for the tangerines."

"You're welcome. Thanks for the roses." I turned and put my arms around his neck. "Please note that I gave up blueberries for you."

"I bought you three boxes."

"Three boxes is extravagant," I said, feeling a rush of love. It's the little things, I have learned, that often mean the most. "But so sweet."

I took a hatbox from a shelf in the closet.

Zack leaned against the dresser. "By the way, how did it go with Connors?"

I told him. I also told him about my conversation with McIntyre.

"Good thinking." Zack nodded. "You don't believe the suicide thing, though, do you? You said that to get McIntyre to talk to Connors, right?"

"To be honest, I have a bad feeling about all this, Zack. But I don't know if McIntyre will call Connors. And you may not think I'm so clever if Rabbi Bailor asks you about your car." I explained what had happened. "I'm sorry. He caught me off guard, and I didn't know what to say."

The phone rang. I couldn't answer it on *Shabbat,* but I could listen if the caller left a message.

Zack was frowning. "I don't want to lie to Rabbi Bailor, Molly."

Another ring. Maybe the caller was Connors.

"It's not as if you ever see him, Zack."

"And if I do?"

One more ring. Then the answering machine would pick up.

"I said I'm sorry, Zack. Rabbi Bailor took me by surprise." It wasn't our first spat, and it wouldn't be our last, but I hated the feeling. "Don't be angry."

"I'm not angry. I'm not happy, either." He glanced at the phone on his nightstand. "I know you want to find out who's calling."

"It may be Connors. But this is more important."

"I don't think there's much more to say, Molly. I have a problem with lying."

He left the room. I hurried to the answering machine in the den and heard Connors's voice.

". . . won't know till tomorrow, Molly. Call me after your Sabbath, and we'll talk."

Chapter 20

==

Zack was subdued and our conversation strained while we walked the five blocks from Citrus to Beverly and Detroit and B'nai Yeshurun, the synagogue where Zack has been serving as rabbi for a year and a half. I was contemplating apologizing again, but it was hard to find the right moment. Every few seconds, it seemed, we exchanged Sabbath greetings with men and boys of all ages who were making their way to one of a multitude of *shuls* in the area. And maybe, I told myself, it was better to leave things alone.

Since our wedding I've accompanied Zack to *shul* most Friday nights. Orthodox women generally don't attend Friday night services, but I don't mind being alone in the women's section. I enjoy the introspection the privacy affords, and the melodies sung with gusto and harmony by Zack and the other men standing on the other side of the wood-paneled *mechitza*.

I was in the middle of the last stanza of "L'cha Dodi" and had swiveled around to bow and greet the Sabbath Queen when I noticed a woman in the back row. We exchanged smiles. I turned back and sang the final refrain.

After the service I saw her in the lobby. She was putting on a black raincoat, and I caught a glimpse of a trim figure in a brown wool tweed skirt and camel turtleneck sweater. She was around five four, pretty in a quiet way. Fine lines around her mouth and hazel eyes put her in her late forties.

"Good *Shabbos*." I extended my hand. "I'm Molly Abrams. Welcome to the *shul*."

She shook my hand. "The rabbi is your husband?"

"Yes." She looked familiar. "Have we met?"

After eight months at playing rabbi's wife, I'm still an ingénue, and while I haven't committed any serious gaffes, a few weeks earlier I'd slighted a woman when I hadn't welcomed her back from a trip abroad. In a *shul* with a membership of over three hundred families, I was bound to slight other congregants. I hoped I hadn't offended the woman standing in front of me.

"I've attended services here once or twice," she said. "Someone pointed you out to me. The rabbi's charming new bride. Apparently, your husband was quite the catch." She smiled. "But to answer your question, no, we haven't met."

I relaxed. "Well, I don't know about the *charming*, but I'm glad we're meeting now. Are you new to the community?"

"I moved here almost a year ago from New York, but I haven't really met a lot of people. And I'm still *shul* hopping, trying to find my place."

From the brown hat on her chin-length highlighted blond hair, I had assumed she was married. The "I" suggested she wasn't. I glanced at her left hand. No ring. Divorced, I thought.

"There are plenty of choices, although I hope you'll like B'nai Yeshurun." I smiled. "Would you like to join us for dinner at my parents'? I know they'd love to have you."

My parents have raised us to follow the example set by Abraham, who is eponymous with hospitality. Zack and I often invite congregants for a *Shabbat* meal (the first few months we were universally turned down—the congregation wanted to give their rabbi and his bride time to get to know each other). And I'm always prepared in case Zack brings an unexpected guest. A tourist; someone who has just moved to L.A.; someone who, Zack suspects, can't afford a meal; someone who dreads spending *Shabbat* alone. Since marrying Zack I've become much more aware that people often hide loneliness behind a smile.

"I'd love to take a rain check," the woman said. "I'm having dinner with Rebecca and Henry Stone. I assume you know them?" When I nodded, she said, "I told Henry I'd meet him here. I guess it was *bashert.*"

"*Bashert?*"

"I'm Cheryl Wexner. I'm sorry, I thought I said. You left a message saying Rabbi Bailor suggested that you talk to me about Hadassah? I've become close to her, and I'm a little concerned about her. Is she all right?"

"Actually . . ."

I was debating how much to say when the double doors to the men's section swung open. Seconds later I exchanged "Good *Shabbos*" greetings with Henry Stone and introduced Cheryl to my father-in-law, Larry, who told me Zack was talking with a congregant.

"Have you seen Justin?" Cheryl asked Henry.

"He was talking with some of the other young people. I'll go check."

Henry left. I was accepting a kiss from my father-in-law—he looks exactly the way Zack will in twenty years—when my ex, Ron, strolled over. He's a Jewish Adonis, tall and blond and extremely good-looking. That, along with his zest for life, was one of the qualities that had attracted me. Apparently it attracted other women, too, which is why I divorced him eighteen months after our wedding.

"Me, too?" Ron offered his cheek.

When pigs fly, I thought, producing a smile. "I don't think so."

I've worked past my anger and hurt, but Ron still sets my teeth on edge. I was grateful to see Zack exiting the sanctuary and heading our way.

"Zack, this is Cheryl Wexner," I told him when he was at my side. "Cheryl, this is my husband, Zack."

"What am I, chopped liver?" Ron said. "I'm Ron Hoffman, Cheryl. I'm on the *shul* board."

"Nice to meet you, Ron."

"I'm the one Molly let get away. But she has good taste. She married my former best friend. My ex with my ex." He punched Zack lightly in his arm. "Two strikes."

Ron likes to make light of our divorce. I suspect he has two goals: deflecting criticism—or worse, pity—and making me and Zack uncomfortable. I couldn't tell whether Zack was annoyed. He hides his feelings better than I do. Cheryl Wexner definitely looked ill at ease.

"So what do you do, Cheryl?" Ron asked.

"I'm an educational consultant. I help students with their college and graduate school applications. Oh, Justin. Over here." She waved.

Walking toward us were Henry and a young man in his midtwenties. He had trendy narrow rimless glasses and wore a teeny red-and-black crocheted yarmulke on brown hair that was a little long and shaggy.

"I was wondering where you were," Cheryl said when he was at her side. She slipped her arm through his. "This is my son. Justin, this is Mrs. Abrams, the rabbi's wife. Justin is a screenwriter and the reason I moved here. He told me Los Angeles was paradise, and he was right."

Her eyes were animated, and I could hear the pride in her voice. "It's nice to meet you, Justin. What type of screenplays do you write?"

"I'm working on a futuristic thriller. Kind of noir, like *Gattaca?*"

"Molly's as noir as they come," Ron said. "She gets her jollies from looking at crime scene photos and hanging out with cops."

"Molly writes true crime books," Zack said.

"You've been published?" Justin asked me.

I mentioned my books and my pseudonym. I could tell from his politely blank expression, and his mother's, that they'd never heard of me.

"You study with Rabbi Bailor, right?" I said. "He was my teacher almost fifteen years ago, and Zack's."

"Mine, too," Ron said.

"It's nice that you're still in touch," Cheryl said.

Ron grinned. "Actually, Molly and the rabbi—"

"Have a special relationship." Zack put his hand on Ron's arm. "How do you like studying with him, Justin?"

"He knows his stuff," Justin said. "And he's cool. No pressure, you know?"

"Ready to go?" Henry Stone said.

Cheryl turned to me. "We can talk tomorrow night, Molly, or Sunday. Whatever is best for you."

"Talk about what?" Ron said.

"Sunday is fine," I told her, though if Connors came through, which I fervently hoped, there would be no need to talk to Cheryl. "I'll phone you."

"That would be lovely. I'm glad we met, Molly. *Shabbat shalom.*"

"*Shabbat shalom.*"

"Talk about what?" Ron said again after they left.

Chapter 21

My dad gave me a bear hug and a kiss and slapped Zack on the back. He's tall and broad-shouldered and has more gray than brown in his hair—no surprise, since he's fifty-eight, something I find hard to believe. My mom kissed me and Zack and disappeared into the kitchen, which was just as well, because she probably would have had heart palpitations if she'd seen Bubbie G jump off the den sofa as if she were a girl of eighteen, not a widow of eighty.

"Malkele," she said.

Macular degeneration has stolen most of the central vision from my grandmother's once bright blue eyes. I don't know what she saw as she held my face and kissed my cheeks, but I wanted the moment to last. I love the rose scent of her perfume, the velvet touch of her time-worn skin, which she smooths religiously with lotions she's accumulated over the years, lotions she would dot on my hands and cheeks when I was a little girl standing in the bathroom while she sat at her vanity table and applied makeup.

"You look beautiful, Bubbie," Zack said.

"Tenk you, Zack."

With her Polish-Yiddish accent, "Zack" came out as "Zeck." ("Zeck" is Yiddish for "sack," no correlation to his name, but I've given up trying to correct her.) Bubbie also pronounces most *th*s as *dees* or *tees,* and she often calls us by Yiddish endearments.

Sheyfeleh, shepseleh (they both mean "little sheep"), *mammeleh* (little mother), *zeeskeit* (sweetheart). We tease her about it, but she doesn't mind. In fact, she recently shared a joke about a mother whose son is leaving for his first day of school.

"Behave, my bubaleh," the mother tells the boy as they're waiting for the school bus. "Take good care of yourself, tateleh."

"I will."

"And eat your lunch, shain kindt."

"I will."

"Mommy loves you a lot, ketsaleh!"

When the boy returns from school, the mother asks, "So what did my oitzerel learn?"

"I learned my name is David."

Bubbie kissed Zack on both cheeks, too, and allowed him to escort her to the dining room and get her seated—no small matter, since she rejects most offers of help.

We were seven for dinner: Bubbie and my parents; Zack and me; Noah and Joey, two of my brothers. They both resemble my dad. Noah, twenty-five, is in his third year of law school. Joey, two years younger and two inches shorter, has a degree in computer programming but has joined my father's construction business and is enjoying working with him.

My youngest sister, Liora, I learned, was having dinner with my brother Judah and his wife, Gitty.

"What's the occasion?" I asked my mother in the kitchen after the men had recited *Kiddush* and we'd all enjoyed Bubbie's freshly baked *challa.*

My mother is fifty-seven, but can pass for her late forties. She has brown eyes, rich brown hair that she'd tucked into a black velvet crocheted snood, and a trim figure that she maintains with yoga and the Israeli dance class my sister Edie gives.

"No occasion," she said. "Gitty isn't feeling well. Liora offered to help with Yechiel so Judah could go to *shul,* and they invited her for dinner."

"Gitty's pregnant, isn't she?"

Yechiel was two, and my sister-in-law had commented that she and my brother Judah were looking forward to having another child. And at last Monday night's mah jongg game, she'd looked pale.

My mother looked flustered. "You'd have to ask Gitty."

"Sorry, I put you on the spot. Forget I asked." I resisted the urge to tell her I was a few days late. "Do you know Cheryl Wexner, Mom?"

She transferred the last slice of sweet-and-sour salmon from a Pyrex dish to a plate. "Where have I heard that name?"

"She helps students with college applications, and does educational consulting."

My mother nodded. "Some of the kids mentioned her. How do you know her?"

"I met her in *shul* tonight. I plan to invite her for a *Shabbos* meal, and I thought you might do the same. She's been living here almost a year and hasn't connected with the community. I think she's lonely."

"I'll give her a call this week. Is she married?"

"Divorced, is my guess. No ring, but she was wearing a hat. Her son was with her. Justin. He's in his midtwenties."

"That'll be nice for Joey and Noah."

"How's Noah doing? He looks so sad."

Two months ago, his fiancée had broken their engagement.

"He's having a hard time, but he'll be okay. I'd like him to start dating again, but he's not interested. It's much easier in romance books, isn't it? Well, not easier, but there are always happy endings."

My mother writes romance books under a pseudonym, Charlotte D'Anjou. My father's favorite pear. Recently, she was "outed," and she's nervous about reactions from her students and colleagues, and her principal.

"How's the book coming along, Mom?"

"I'm stuck on a scene. To kiss or not to kiss." She laughed. "Maybe I'll call you Sunday and you'll talk me through it." She handed me two plates. "For Zack and Dad. Serve Zack first," she instructed, as she always does.

"Not Dad?" I teased, knowing the answer.

"Your husband comes first." She smiled. "Speaking of husbands, is everything okay, Molly? You both seem preoccupied."

"Sorry. I *do* have something on my mind, but it has nothing to do with Zack." Half a truth, but there was no need to worry my mother.

"And Zack?"

What to say? "We had a little disagreement about the thing that's on my mind. But we're fine."

"Something you want to talk about?"

I shook my head. "It's confidential."

"But you and Zack are happy?"

"Very."

"Good." She patted my cheek.

When Ron and I were married, my parents took for granted that our marriage was sound until I told them otherwise. Sometimes I feel burdened with the need to reassure. No one's fault, just an aftershock of divorce.

My melancholy evaporated during dinner. I joined in the singing and conversation, which is always lively. And I listened attentively when Noah gave a *dvar* Torah about the week's portion that we would read in *shul* tomorrow.

Jacob leaving home after he has stolen the birthright. His dream of angels climbing and descending a ladder. His first meeting with Rachel.

"The commentaries explain why Jacob cried when he first saw Rachel," Noah said. "Jacob knew he wouldn't be buried with her. He was crying out of grief for their lost love." Noah folded the paper from which he'd been reading and placed it on the table. "Maybe that's one of the reasons we break a glass under the *chuppah* at a wedding, because even true love can't last forever. So we have to appreciate it while we have it."

"Well done, Noah." My father smiled.

"Ditto," Joey said.

Joey usually goes for quips. I'm sure that, like the rest of us, he realized this must have been a painful *dvar* Torah for Noah to give.

Under the table Zack took my hand and squeezed it hard. I squeezed back.

"Beautiful." Bubbie was sitting next to Noah. Her eyes had misted. "I wish for you what I had with your Zeidie, he should rest in peace." She pulled Noah toward her and kissed him. "You, too, Yossele."

"Noah first, Bubbie." Joey laughed.

"When love comes, you don't tell it to wait, *sheyfeleh*. You grab it and don't let go." She made a clutching motion with her hand. "I was seventeen when Zeidie and I were married. This was in '41, during the war. When the Germans came we were separated, and I didn't know where they took him. After the war I heard Zeidie was alive. In my heart I never gave up. Sometimes I think this is what kept me alive. Because I *knew.*" Bubbie G pressed a hand against her chest. "But to hear it?" She shook her head in wonder.

Bubbie rarely talks about her experiences in the Holocaust, which claimed most of her family. Parents, grandparents, four siblings, nieces, nephews, aunts, uncles, cousins. Many of the stories, my mother says, draw Bubbie back into a dark time too painful to revisit. But this was a wonderful story. Except for Zack, we had all heard it before, but I never tire of hearing it.

"A friend told a friend who told me," Bubbie continued. "Zeidie was in Sosnowice, she said. Our home town, in Poland. So I went with my friend Edja to the train station. We took with us a loaf of bread, because you couldn't buy food, you know. And you didn't need tickets. Everything was open. Nobody checked. Every day people were taking trains to look for someone. A father, a husband, a wife, a daughter. Most of the time, they were empty trips." Bubbie sighed and had a faraway look in her eyes.

"So we waited ten, twenty minutes until the train came into the station. Then we had to wait again before we could get on. Every minute to me was like an hour. Finally we were on the train, and the train started. A big noise, and we were moving." Bubbie mimed the motion.

"All of a sudden I hear people yelling, 'Genny, Genny! Yitzchok is here! Yitzchok is here!' Zeidie heard I was in Munich, and he came looking for me. He got off the train when it arrived in the station, you see, the same train I was going to take to look for him."

Bubbie's smile lit her face as though she were on that train, a twenty-one-year-old woman about to reunite with the man from whom she'd been separated for what had seemed like a lifetime. A man who, despite her hope, she must have feared she would never see again.

No matter how many times I hear the story, my eyes tear. I leaned close to Zack and whispered in his ear. "Ask her what she did."

"What did you do, Bubbie?" Zack asked.

"What did I do? I jumped off the train! I didn't want one more minute should go by before we would be together. At first I couldn't see him, because he was behind a bush, shaving. He wanted to look good when he saw me." Bubbie smiled. "But people were yelling, 'Genny is here, Yitzchok!' So then he moved away from the bush and I saw him. He shaved only half his face, and he looked so funny. And then we were laughing and crying and hugging and kissing."

"What happened to your friend?" Zack asked.

"Poor Edja." Bubbie G's smile was mischievous. "She was afraid to jump off, so she went all the way to the next town, and back, with the loaf of bread. Later, I teased Zeidie. If he was upset with me about something, I would tell him, 'For you, Yitzchok, I jumped off a train.' "

"You could have hurt yourself," Zack said.

"When you love someone, *tayereh kindt,* you don't think about danger." She dabbed at the corners of her eyes. "I would do it again."

Chapter 22

Hadassah had felt him watching her while she lit the *Shabbat* candles, tea lights that he'd set on a paper plate covered in tinfoil. He'd promised to buy her silver candlesticks, maybe for next *Shabbat*. She knew the blessings by heart and didn't need the white-leather–bound *siddur* he'd bought her, but she used it to show she appreciated his thoughtfulness. She had lit *Shabbat* candles alongside her mother for as long as she could remember, had mimed the hand waving and the blessing long before she could say the words or knew what they meant.

His presence had unnerved her. He had been brooding all day, his eyes on her wherever she went, she wasn't sure why. She'd been relieved when he left the apartment in the early afternoon, and though his absence had created a fertile ground for all her doubts to take root and blossom, she had tensed when she'd heard the key turning the lock.

But when he returned his mood was brighter, and his arms were filled with packages. Gifts for her—a pair of earrings, a cashmere shawl, a lipstick like the one she'd left in her overnight bag at Sara's, flowers that he put in a vase and set on the table.

He had bought food for Shabbat. Fish and chicken, salads, pasta, rice. "You shouldn't have to cook," he'd said. "You're a bride." She had teased him—"You just don't want me to mess up the stove." He hadn't laughed, and she was only half joking. He was fussy about the apartment and its contents. He insisted on washing the few dishes and glassware they used (mostly, he brought home pizza or deli sandwiches or Chinese). "You shouldn't have to lift a finger," he'd say, but she suspected he was afraid she'd chip something. The other day he'd pretended not to be upset when she'd left a glass on the coffee table. "It's no big deal," he'd said, rubbing mayonnaise into the teak, the ring from the glass so faint she couldn't see it. "It's as good as new." She had pretended not to see the look he gave her, almost like the one he'd given the valet. He'd had the car repaired the next day. "Good as new," he'd said that time, too.

He had dressed in the navy suit he'd worn to Yamashiro. He'd looked so handsome Thursday night that the sight of him had taken her breath away. It wasn't far to *shul*, he told her. There was a Chabad on Gayley, near UCLA, but the services didn't always start on time. It might be an hour and a half before he was back.

"If you don't want me to go," he said.

She walked him to the door, the way her mother walked her father every Friday night. She said, "Good *Shabbos*," and waited until he slid home the bolt with his key. "Just in case you fall asleep," he'd told her earlier, "because how would I get in? The *eruv* is up," he'd said when he saw her face. "Don't worry, I checked."

She hadn't been worried about the *eruv*, a man-made boundary that allowed him to carry on *Shabbat*. She'd been worried about being locked in. What if there was a fire, or an earthquake?

"There's a spare key in the kitchen," he'd told her, "in the green mug on the second shelf."

She decided to surprise him and put on the white sweater and skirt. Her wedding outfit. Sitting at the dining room table where the tea lights tried their best to illuminate the room, she opened the white-leather–bound *siddur*. It was a beautiful prayerbook, and she felt ungrateful longing for the one she'd left in the backpack at Sara's, some of its pages smudged where her fingers had rubbed the words, one page stained with the tears she'd shed when she found out Batya had died.

Her father probably had her *siddur*. She pictured him rushing to Sara's to pick up her backpack as soon as he heard, searching through it, hoping to find something that would explain why she had run off. "Come home," her mother had said. She had cried. That wasn't why Hadassah had run away, although maybe it was a teeny part of it. The "why," so clear to her Sunday morning, was no longer clear at all. Her certainty had crumbled, had been compressed into a hard ball of regret and anxiety that was lodged in her chest and sometimes made it difficult for her to breathe.

She wasn't sure who he was. He'd said all the right things, had known the words, the customs. "I'm no Rabbi Akiva, Dassie, but I learned enough . . ." But though he strapped on *teffilin* every morning, he did it awkwardly and barely kept the little boxes on his forehead and arm. She was almost sure he didn't say all the prayers, that he mouthed the words. And she hardly knew anything about his family. "You'll meet them," he'd said. "They'll love you."

This morning he had kissed her. She had never kissed a man before, aside from her father, and her eyes had widened in shock. She was intensely attracted to him and had wondered what it would be like to kiss him, but in her imagination, his lips were gentle in their passion. His kiss had been teasing one second, almost bruising the next. She had clamped her lips together.

"Don't," she'd said, "please don't." She had pushed him away.

"It's just a kiss, Dassie," he'd said, amused, then angry. "There's nothing wrong with a kiss. I'll bet your father kissed girls before he became a rabbi, and did other things he didn't tell you. Jacob kissed Rachel when he saw her. The Torah says so, in tomorrow's reading. And that was before they were married. You and I are married, Dassie.

In three more days we'll be as one. Nothing can separate us after that, except death."

She didn't like thinking about death. She had thought about it sometimes before Batya died, and after. She had wondered whether her life made a difference when no one seemed to see her anyway, when the loneliness felt like a black pit that was swallowing her up, when she was overwhelmed with pretending to be happy, making plans she had no hope of carrying out, like going to college and law school. She had said that to see her parents' reaction. Her mother hadn't been happy, but her father said, "If that's what you really want, Dassie." He had sounded so proud, and before she knew it, it was The Plan, and she was in a different school, her father's school, but she didn't see him more than she had before, and she felt lonelier than ever without her friends, so lonely that sometimes she sat in the bathroom stall and cried.

But she didn't want to die, not really. She had talked to Dr. McIntyre. "Think about how this makes you feel," he'd told her. "Are you hoping someone will see?" He had urged her to tell her parents, but she was eighteen, she had a right to privacy. "Write it down," he'd told her, "keep a log."

She had felt safe sleeping in the sleigh bed while he took the sofa bed. Until he kissed her. Now she wasn't sure she was safe, not just because of the kiss, he'd promised that wouldn't happen again until she was ready, but because of the way he was staring at her all the time. "I love looking at you," he said, when she told him he was making her nervous. "I would die a million deaths for you, Dassie." There was something sad in his glance, something that made her nervous.

The dark moods came more frequently. She had found him on the couch, his arms around his knees, rocking as if he were in a trance. She had read a story in English class about a boy who rocked on a toy horse so that he could discover the names of winning racehorses.

"I would die a million deaths for you, Dassie. Would you die for me?"

"The Rocking-Horse Winner." That was the name of the story. The boy had lost his mind.

She considered leaving right now while he was at *shul,* walking home even though it was probably four miles, maybe five, and she didn't know the way, and by now it was dark outside, the rose of sunset having long ago turned to gray, then black.

But he had locked the door.

"In case you're asleep when I come back," he'd said, "because then how will I get in?"

She was being ridiculous. She reminded herself of all the wonderful qualities she loved about him. His kindness, his laughter, his passion, his tenderness. The attentive way he listened to her, as if she were the only person in the world. And she had nothing to hide from him. She had bared her ugly secret, and he'd said, "Everything about you is beautiful, Dassie. I will kiss the hurts away."

She walked to the kitchen and found the green mug. There was the key, just as he'd promised.

She returned to the dining room and her prayers. "L'cha Dodi." *Come, my beloved.*

When she had finished her prayers, she set the table, handling the stoneware and goblets with care. Then she pulled a book from the wall unit and settled herself on the sofa. The room was chilly. She rose from the sofa and walked to the entry closet, where she had seen him store his bedding.

The closet was dark. From the reflected glow of the dimmed living room torchère, she could make out the light switch, but she couldn't turn on the light, not on *Shabbat*. She could also make out his green blanket and two pillows. The pillows were on top. She held them with one hand while she yanked at the blanket.

She hadn't seen the box underneath the blanket. It fell with a thump to the floor and landed on its side, spilling contents that clattered onto the hardwood floor.

She picked up a framed photo and felt a stab of anxiety when she saw that the protective glass was cracked. Slivers of glass were on the floor. She swept them with her hand and winced when she cut her palm on a shard. Stupid. She peered at her palm. It was bleeding. She touched it gingerly and felt a splinter on the fleshy part, below her thumb. She squeezed her palm to force the glass out, but the sliver was too small, embedded too deeply. The squeezing had increased the bleeding. She walked to the dining table and pressed a napkin to her palm until the bleeding stopped.

He would be a little upset about the photo, of course, but he'd understand. Or . . . she didn't know the neighborhood, but when he left the apartment on Sunday, she could look for a store that would replace the glass. She would tell him then.

"Good as new," she would say. They would laugh about it.

Her hand was throbbing. She found a broom and dustpan and swept up the glass fragments. Then she took the photo to the dining room table, removed a loose shard of glass, and looked at the photo. At first she was confused. Why did he . . . ?

She returned to the box. There were more framed photos, and letters, and other things that made no sense, until they did. She took everything to the table and stared at each item, one by one.

When she had finished, blood was pounding in her head.

She put everything back into the box, placed the lid on top, and shoved the box into the closet. She laid the blanket on top of the box, then the pillows.

She shut the closet door.

She was sure he would have an explanation for the things she had found, but she couldn't believe him anymore. Though he had left her alone for hours, she had never looked through his belongings. Now she did. She found vials of pills, drafts of a note that chilled her to the bone.

In the kitchen she took the spare key from the green mug and inserted it into the keyhole.

It didn't turn.

She removed the key, reinserted it, and tried to twist it in the lock.

She tried one more time, her fingers clammy now, shaking, her heart beating like a tom-tom.

Nothing.

He would have an explanation for the key, too. "It's defective," he would tell her. "I'll get you another one."

She started to cry, but crying wouldn't help her.

She didn't know where he'd put her cell phone. He had left his on a shelf in the wall unit. He had known she wouldn't use it on *Shabbat*.

But even on *Shabbat* she could use a phone in a life-or-death emergency. Her parents wouldn't answer, but the answering machine would pick up after four rings.

The answering machine was in her father's study at the front of the house. They might not even hear the ringing or the message, especially if they were singing or talking loud.

She could call someone else.

It was ten to six. Her father and the boys would be walking into the house right now, shaking off the cold. He would be taking off his black hat and placing it on the coffee table in the living room.

"Where are my girls?" he would say, the way he did when she was little, and she would race to him and jump into his arms, and he would spin her around and around and around.

She reached up, grasped the phone, and took it to the table. She had never used a phone on *Shabbat,* ever. Even holding it was a violation.

She thought again about the key that didn't work, about the pills, and the note. She flipped the phone open and turned it on. It seemed like hours, not seconds, before the display appeared on the small screen.

She had punched in the phone number when she heard the click of the key turning in the lock.

Her free hand found the shard of glass and closed around it.

Chapter 23

Saturday, November 20, 2:59 a.m., 1500 block of North Hobart Boulevard. A suspect broke into the home of a 54-year-old woman while she was sleeping. The suspect attempted to cover the victim with a blanket, and she woke up, screaming. The suspect then fled the location.

I dreamed about Aggie. Until eight months ago, when her murder had still been unsolved, I would dream about her all the time. In my dream she is wearing a long navy skirt and navy sweater, and the locket I gave her that wasn't on her body when the police found her. In my dream, as in life, she is beckoning to me to accompany her to a prayer vigil for a young woman stricken with cancer. *Come with me, Molly.* In my dream I follow her but never quite catch up. And that night, as I followed Aggie and turned the corner, hurrying after her, I saw Hadassah Bailor, wearing a satin white skirt and sweater, both splattered with blood.

I woke up with a start and a heavy feeling. Zack was snoring lightly in the full-sized bed next to mine. I didn't want to disturb him. So I slipped out of the bed and went to the bathroom and discovered that I wasn't pregnant after all. I didn't cry, but tears stung my eyelids, and I felt a sadness wash over me. Another month gone, and what if something was truly wrong?

In the morning Zack reached for me, but I shook my head and he nodded.

"It'll happen, Molly. I know it."

The day was uneventful. *Shul* in the morning, where I was Mrs. Molly Abrams, the rabbi's wife. I sat up front with my mother-in-law, Sandy, and although she may have sensed that I was quieter than usual, she didn't pry. After the services I made a point of greeting everyone I didn't know and people I did know, including my ex-mother-in-law, Valerie, who has taught me about grace in awkward situations but apparently didn't pass on that particular gene to Ron. He snubbed me in the refreshment hall—no doubt because I'd refused to tell him why I wanted to talk to Cheryl Wexner—and then told me I must be crushed by my lousy Amazon ranking for *Sins of the Fathers*.

Zack and I had lunch with his parents. They're attorneys—Sandy handles bankruptcies; Larry does litigation—and although they were disappointed when Zack deferred and then declined his acceptance to Harvard Law, they are immensely proud of "their son, the rabbi." And they have welcomed me into their family with warmth and affection and seem to have adjusted to not having Zack around 24/7.

"Larry and I are in intense therapy," Sandy teased me when I asked her if it had been hard to see her only child marry.

Zack's parents, like mine, are careful not to ask when we plan to have children, but most of their friends have become grandparents, and I'm sure they're eager to join that club. Maybe that unspoken (and probably invented) pressure contributed to my doldrums, along with my dream about Aggie and Hadassah. I made a good show of participating in the conversation, which was mostly a rehash of Bush's victory and Kerry's defeat. And I enjoyed the food. Marinated

London broil; a salad of asparagus, cherry tomato, and hearts of palm; angel hair pasta. I had two slices of the chocolate torte Sandy had baked.

But I was restless. I wanted to sulk, to feel sorry for myself. At home Zack and I studied the Torah portion together. He took a short nap. I read Hadassah's college essay and learned nothing. I went through a foot-high stack of back issues of the *New Yorker.* Then I read the current *People* and wondered if life as we know it could continue without Paris Hilton's face popping up everywhere. Zack left for *shul.* I played solitaire and watched the clock.

Hadassah was on my mind, and Connors's phone call. A minute after Shabbat ended I phoned him at home. His answering machine picked up. I left a message.

My laptop was on the desk in our den. I turned on the computer, connected to the Internet, and read my e-mails. Nothing significant, a large amount of SPAM. I deleted the SPAM, responded to e-mails, and checked my Amazon numbers for *Sins.* 84,000. Not exciting, not lousy. In my purse I found the website address for J Spot.

Seconds later I was on the site's home page. The background was a graphic of an open Torah scroll. I entered a screen name—ToraTora— and my usual password. After reading the conditions set by the site, I clicked I AGREE. A moment later I was in.

ToraTora has entered the room.

There were eight people in the chat room, including me and Birch2— Sara Mellon's screen name. They were discussing Thanksgiving plans.

Aleph36: I'm going to see *National Treasure* next Friday.
M&M: Me, too. I don't like turkey. It's fowl.
Sinai: Groan.
Lucky7: I have to work on my term paper.
Jewcy: Bummer.
M&M: You can buy one online.
DJ2440: That's cheating.

Lucky7: Duh.
M&M: Only if they catch you. ☺
Lucky7: Have you ever done it?
M&M: I don't have to. I'm naturally brilliant.
Jewcy: And modest. ☺
M&M: LOL
Lucky7: ROFL

LOL, I knew, was "laugh out loud." ROFL, "rolling on the floor laughing."

Sinai: Hey, ToraTora. First time?
ToraTora: Hi. Yeah, first time.
M&M: *Shavuah tov. Gut voch.* Have a good week.
Sinai: Welcome to our humble spite. ☺
M&M: LOL
DJ2440: LOL
Jewcy: Hi, ToraTora.
M&M: Jew or Jewess, ToraTora?

The sound of rolling thunder accompanied the appearance of an instant message in a box in the upper left-hand corner of my screen. Lucky7.

I accepted the message.

Never give your gender or any personal information.

I responded with "Okay, thanks!"

Lucky7 signed off from Instant Message.

I typed *"Shavuah tov* to you, too" and pressed SEND.

M&M: We're talking about buying term papers.
Sinai: Thou shalt not . . .
Jewcy: Spend too much. On one site they're charging twelve bucks a page. Twice that if you're in a rush. Not that I'd ever do it.

M&M: Yeah, sure.
Jewcy: No, really.
Sinai: Schools can find out now, M&M.
M&M: Shrek! And I don't mean the movie.
Jewcy: LOL
Lucky7: ROFL
Sinai: They use TurnItIn.
M&M: Turn it off!
Jewcy: RUK?
Sinai: My teacher was fired for cheating.
M&M: ?
Sinai: I heard he changed answers on AP exams.
Aleph36: OMG
Jewcy: POS
M&M: ABC

OMG, I assumed, was "oh my God." I was clueless about the others. RUK. POS. ABC. And I thought French was tough. I Googled INTERNET ACRONYMS AND TEENAGERS.

Lucky7: So how about those Mets?
M&M: I love all my classes, don't you?

I clicked on ACRONYMFINDER, typed in R-U-K. "Are you kidding." Obvious, once you knew it.

Sinai: LOL
M&M: Where do you live, ToraTora?

Another roll of thunder. Another warning from Lucky7.

I responded, "Got it, thanks," and returned to ACRONYMFINDER. P-O-S produced a list of possibilities, including "parent over shoulder." That one fit.

A-B-C, I learned, was "always be cool."

I was trying.

M&M: ToraTora, are you there?

Sinai: ToraTora went to Bora Bora.

Lucky7: LOL

ToraTora: LOL. I live on the west coast.

Sinai: Me, too. L.A.

Jewcy: Coast is clear. I'd love to go to L.A.

M&M: Be careful, Jewcy! L.A. is sin city.

Jewcy: Always am. ☺ L2M, Sinai, if I ever come to L.A. Just say where and when.

Sinai: You're all talk, Jewcy. You're going to yeshiva next year, not L.A.

I typed L2M. "Listening to music," or "love to meet."

Sinai: What brings you here, ToraTora?

ToraTora: A friend. She said J Spot rocks.

M&M: Which friend?

ToraTora: ST613.

M&M: ST hasn't been here in, like, days.

DJ2440: Maybe she's tired of you hitting on her.

Aleph36: She's really *frum*. She said her dad's a rabbi.

Jewcy: She's just not into you, M&M. ☺

Sinai: LOL

Lucky7: ROFL

M&M: w/e, man.

"Whatever."
Birch2, I saw, had left the room.

ToraTora: ST told me about a guy who chats here, too. For JU? Something like that.

Jewcy: For JU?

DJ2440: I only have eyes for ju. ☺

M&M: Justforju!

Aleph36: Right. He's been here.

M&M: I haven't seen him lately.

DJ2440: He's a lurker. I don't like his vibe.

Aleph36: Maybe they ran off together. ☺

M&M: Yeah, to Bora Bora. ☺ j/k

ToraTora: Do you guys know anything about him? My friend says he's kind of mysterious.

No response. I'd committed a breach of chat room ethics. The virtual silence was deafening.

M&M: So, ToraTora. What kind of yeshiva do you go to? Coed?

Another sound of rolling thunder.

Don't give out personal details! Be careful!

I typed "Thanks again for the warning!" but Lucky7 had signed off from Instant Message. I wondered whether he was an adult.

ToraTora: Yeah.

Sinai: Me, too. We get off two days for Chanukah.

Aleph36: It's early this year.

DJ2440: All the stores have Christmas decorations up.

M&M: Lord & Taylor is the best.

Jewcy: Macy's.

Sinai: Sometimes I feel a little left out.

Aleph36: It's easier when Chanukah and Christmas are around the same time.

Sinai: I don't think so.

The conversation segued into a discussion of the holidays.

ToraTora: Gotta go.

Sinai: Later, TT.

Lucky7: Later.

M&M: Come back soon. If Justforju shows, I'll tell him you're looking for him.

You do that, I thought, as I signed off.

An hour had passed since I'd phoned Andy. I tried him again. He wasn't home, but I didn't leave another message.

A few minutes later Zack returned from *shul.*

"Sorry it took me so long," he said. "Someone needed to talk to me." He took off his coat. "You look tense. Did you talk to Connors?"

"He wasn't in when I phoned. I left a message."

While Zack hung his coat in the closet, I gathered a silver cup and plate, a braided blue-and-white candle, and a silver box filled with cloves and allspice. I placed everything on the kitchen counter. Then Zack filled the cup with wine, lit the candle, and recited the *havdalah,* the blessing that officially separates the Sabbath from the rest of the week.

"*Shavuah tov,*" he said after he doused the flame in the wine that had spilled onto the plate beneath the cup.

"*Shavuah tov.*" I hoped it *would* be a good week.

"Do you want to go out, Molly, get something to eat?"

"I'd love to, but I'm waiting to hear from Connors."

"He may not call you back tonight, Molly."

"Or he'll call soon. But you're right," I said, seeing Zack's disappointment. "How about pizza?"

Zack changed into Dockers and a navy sweater that brought out the blue in his eyes. I put on a skirt and sweater and a baseball cap. We drove to a kosher pizza store on Fairfax crowded with teenagers who all seemed to be talking and laughing at a high pitch. I recognized a few of them—Torat Tzion kids. Adam Prosser wasn't among them.

"I feel ancient," Zack said.

"We *are* ancient."

We placed our order and chatted with people we knew while we waited twenty minutes for a table. Soon after we were finally sitting in a booth, the cashier called our name. I glanced at my watch.

"You want to phone him, go ahead," Zack said.

"Sorry." I laughed, embarrassed. "I'm that obvious, huh?"

"Let's just say spook work isn't your calling."

Zack left the booth and walked to the counter to pick up our order. I took my cell phone out of my purse and phoned Connors. I got his answering machine again.

"Andy, this is Molly. Give me a call when—"

"Hey, Mrs. Abrams. Nothing better to do on a Saturday night?"

"You're home."

"Apparently."

"Did you find the name of the car owner, Andy?"

"I left you a message yesterday. Didn't you get it?"

I could barely hear over the din. "Just the part where you said you wouldn't know until tomorrow. Meaning today. I didn't play the beginning."

Zack returned with our slices and set them on the table. "Connors?"

I nodded. "I'm in a pizza shop, Andy, and it's too noisy. Hold on."

After gesturing to Zack that I'd be right back, I slid out of the booth and worked through the crowd until I was outside. "Okay. You were saying?"

"I meant I wouldn't have *information* about this guy till today," Connors said. "I ran the license plate."

My heart thudded. "You have his name?"

"Can you hear me now?" Connors said, imitating the cell phone commercial. "Isn't that what I said? The guy's name is Greg Shankman."

Chapter 24

===

It took me a moment to respond. "Greg Shankman," I repeated, trying to keep all inflection from my voice.

"You don't sound surprised. Is that the name you were expecting?"

"I wasn't expecting *any* name. Thanks, Andy. I really appreciate this." It was chilly, and I had left my jacket inside. I hugged my free arm across my chest.

"Do you know the guy?"

Not a question I wanted to answer. "I've never met him, no."

"Not what I asked, Miss Molly."

I couldn't afford to lie to Connors. "He was the girl's teacher."

"A little extracurricular activity, huh? Kids and their teachers—seems to be the latest craze. Look at Mary Kay Letourneau. Can you believe they're getting married now that she's out of jail? Next thing you know, that'll be the next reality show: teachers and their teen lovers. At least Shankman and the girl waited until she was eighteen."

"I don't know about Mary Kay Letourneau, but based on what Shankman said to the girl's parents, he isn't in love with their daughter."

"Maybe not. Have you talked to him?"

"No. His name came up when I asked my friend about people his daughter might have confided in."

Connors snorted. "That's rich."

"Actually, my friend told me not to bother talking to Shankman. This will stun him."

"You can't tell him, Molly," Connors warned.

"I mean eventually, when he finds out."

Zack came out. He was holding my jacket and a cup of hot chocolate.

"So what are you planning to do with this information?" Connors asked.

Zack handed me the cup and draped the jacket over my shoulders. I smiled and mouthed a thank-you. He went back inside.

"What do you think I should do, Andy?"

"Nothing. *Nada.* Zip."

"Is that your final answer?"

"I'm not joking, Molly."

"Then why did you tell me?"

"To see if you knew anything about this guy. Which you do. I'm working on an angle, Molly."

"What angle?"

"Two months ago Shankman's girlfriend filed a restraining order against him. The order applies to their four-year-old daughter."

"So Shankman lost *two* loves that departed," I said, referring to the song. I took a sip of the chocolate.

"Whatever. I'm going to talk to the girlfriend. Maybe she'll give me a reason to have a conversation with Mr. Shankman."

"Tonight?" I felt a wave of relief.

"She's not home. I left a message on her voice mail. I'll call her again tomorrow."

"I think he's going to kill himself, and the girl," I said.

"Romeo and Juliet. We're talking life, not Shakespeare, Molly."

"He's separated. He can't see his girlfriend or daughter because the girlfriend filed a restraining order two months ago." I debated, then said, "That was either right before or right after he lost his job."

"He lost his job?" Connors's tone had sharpened.

"In September. He was fired—I don't know why."

"What does that have to do with your friend?"

Again, I deliberated before answering. "My friend is the principal at the school where Shankman taught."

"So Shankman is taking revenge?"

"He had nothing to do with firing Shankman. But Shankman isn't being logical. He's obviously lashing out at the easiest victim. The point is, Shankman may think he has nothing to live for."

Connors must have been pondering what I'd said, because he didn't answer right away. "We have till Monday night, right? That's when she'll go to this *mikvah?*"

"Unless Shankman decides not to wait."

There was silence on the phone. I listened to the cars driving by.

"Shankman's apartment is in West L.A.'s jurisdiction," Connors said. "I'd have to come up with a reason for my handling it."

"Can you talk to someone in West L.A.? Explain the urgency?"

"We don't know that it's urgent. For all we know, Shankman and your friend's daughter don't want to be disturbed."

"We can't wait till Monday, Andy."

"You promised not to tell her parents, Molly. If you tell them—"

"I won't." I could picture Connors's scowl.

"Because there's no telling what the father might do."

"I said I won't tell him, Andy."

"As long as we're clear. Don't make up a reason to ask your friend for Shankman's address."

The address was in an envelope in my purse. "I won't. Are you done?"

"And don't bother trying to look up Shankman's address," Connors said. "It's unlisted."

Shankman lived in Mar Vista, a mixed-income neighborhood southwest of Culver City within tantalizing proximity of Venice Beach. It was after nine when we pulled up in front of the house, a small one-story that was completely dark. There was no Altima in the driveway.

I rang the bell several times. Then, ignoring Zack's protest, I rang the bell on the house next door and told the woman who opened the door that I was Greg Shankman's cousin, visiting from Denver.

"Melissa left with Kaitlin this morning for Seattle," the neighbor said. "They're staying with her parents through Thanksgiving weekend. And Greg doesn't live here anymore. I guess you didn't hear, but he moved out a few months ago. Sad for the little girl," she added.

Connors had said that the girlfriend had filed a restraining order. I should have figured that the address Rabbi Bailor had given me was no longer valid.

"Do you happen to know where I can reach Greg?" I asked.

"He left his new address with me, and a phone number. Hold on, I'll get it for you."

When she returned she handed me a slip of paper with an address on South Manning.

"That's in West L.A. Greg didn't want to live far from Kaitlin. Tell him hello from Diane when you see him. I hope he's doing okay. He took the breakup real bad. But things seem better, and I'm hoping they can work things out."

The West L.A. address was a five-minute drive from Mar Vista. We found the building, located Shankman's name on the bank of mailboxes, and took the stairs to his second-floor apartment. There was no light coming from under his door, no sounds of occupancy.

I rang the bell. When no one answered, I rang again and pounded on the door.

"No one's home," Zack said. "Give it up."

"Then where is he? And where's Hadassah?"

"Maybe they went out."

"He wouldn't do that. I'm going to find the manager and ask him to check Shankman's apartment."

"Molly," Zack said, but I was already knocking on the door of the adjoining apartment.

Minutes later I was talking to Milt LaSalle, the overweight gray-haired building manager. He didn't seem overly concerned when I told him Shankman hadn't showed up two days ago for a family dinner.

"It's not like Greg not to call," I said. "We're really worried."

"He talked about going away for a few days," LaSalle said, but he took a huge ring of master keys and waddled up the stairs to Shankman's apartment.

Zack and I followed.

LaSalle rang the bell, then knocked. "Mr. Shankman?" he called. "Are you in there?"

He rang the bell again, called Shankman's name again. Knocked on the door. He found the key he wanted and inserted it into the lock.

"Door's not even locked," he said. He turned the knob and opened the door. "Mr. Shankman? Anybody home?"

LaSalle stepped inside and flipped up a switch on the wall that flooded the apartment with light.

It was empty. The living room, dining ell, kitchen, bathroom, bedroom. The dream had made me jittery. I don't know what I'd expected, but I was almost weak with relief.

"Looks okay," LaSalle said. "So maybe he forgot about your get-together."

"Where did he take her?" I said to Zack, my relief having quickly turned to alarm.

"Take who?" LaSalle frowned.

"Can I look around?" I asked. "Maybe he left a note to say where he went."

LaSalle looked dubious.

"Please," I said.

"Oh, all right. But don't break anything."

The place was immaculate. No trash in the kitchen or bathroom, no perishables in the refrigerator.

"I told you he was going away," LaSalle said with satisfaction.

I checked the bedroom. The sleigh bed showed no signs of recent use. Before LaSalle could protest, I opened the bedroom closet. There was no white satin woman's skirt, no white sweater. No black top that was a little too clingy. Only men's clothing. Suits, shirts, slacks, shoes.

On the shelves of the teak wall unit in the living room I saw photos of a man I assumed was Greg Shankman. He was tall, with curly light brown hair and brown eyes. Nice-looking but, as Irene Jakaitis had said, not drop-dead gorgeous. Young-looking, too—more like twenty-five than thirty. In some of the photos he was alone—on the beach, on a ski slope, in the park. In others he had his arm around a thin brunette. The girlfriend? There were also photos with the woman and a little girl with wispy blond curls, and other shots with Shankman and an older couple, probably his parents. One of the shots of Shankman and his girlfriend looked different. I peered at it and realized that the frame's protective glass was missing.

"Are you done here?" LaSalle asked, impatient.

"Just about. I really appreciate this."

LaSalle grunted.

There was a closet in the small entry. I opened it and switched on the light.

"You won't find him in there," LaSalle said. His chuckle turned into a wheeze.

Inside the closet were a jacket and a raincoat, an umbrella, a blanket and pillows. Under the blanket was a white cardboard box with reddish stains.

"Let's go," LaSalle said.

I could hear from his tone that I was out of time. I shut the light switch and stepped backward to close the closet door. My shoe crunched on something.

I bent down and picked up a sliver of glass.

"Come on," the manager said.

On the light maple floor I saw a sprinkling of reddish-brown dots. I touched them. They were sticky.

Zack bent down next to me. "Molly, we have to go."

I pointed to the spots.

"I lost my contact lens," I told LaSalle.

"Aw, jeez." He groaned. "Well, hurry up."

Crawling across the living room floor, I followed a trail of reddish-brown dots to the table in the dining area. I was careful not to touch them.

There was a small black-and-brown area rug in front of the sofa. I lifted a corner.

"How would your lens get under the rug?" LaSalle snickered.

"I'm shaking the rug to see if my lens is on it."

I looked under the rug.

"Find anything?" he asked.

"No."

The apartment building had an underground parking garage. La-Salle showed us Shankman's slot. The Altima wasn't there.

Chapter 25

The answering machine was blinking when we arrived home. The first call was from Dr. McIntyre. He was willing to talk to Connors and had left a message for the detective.

The second call was from Rabbi Bailor.

"Molly, call me as soon as you get in. It's—"

I paused the machine. My stomach muscles had tightened at the sound of the rabbi's voice. Right now I couldn't bear hearing his pain.

And I dreaded returning the call. What would I say? I know who your daughter is with, Rabbi Bailor, but I have no idea where he's taken her, what he's doing right now. I don't know whether she's alive or dead, and by the way, there's something on his apartment floor that could be blood.

The message light was blinking in admonishment.

I sighed and pressed PLAY.

". . . a miracle. Dassie's home! I can't believe it myself, but she's home."

My heart was pounding.

Zack had come into the room. "Who's home?"

"Hadassah Bailor."

I played the message again so that Zack could hear it. Then I phoned the Bailors. Gavriel answered. I paced while I waited for his father to come on the line.

"Molly? Can you believe it?" Rabbi Bailor was shouting his joy.

"I can't tell you how relieved I am for you." An image of the reddish-brown dots appeared in front of my eyes. I blinked them away. "When did Dassie come home?"

"Last night. Nechama answered the door. She almost fainted when she saw Dassie. I tried calling you after *Shabbos,* but your line was busy."

Probably when I was trying to reach Connors. "Did Dassie tell you what happened?"

"She doesn't want to talk," Rabbi Bailor said, subdued. "We phoned Dr. McIntyre. He said not to push her. He said she could be in shock."

"She just showed up at your front door? Where was she? How did she get home?"

"I don't know where she was, Molly. She walked home. That's the main thing, that she's home. The rest we'll deal with later. Dr. McIntyre is coming to see her. Maybe tonight. If not, definitely tomorrow."

"What about the man Dassie was with? Did she tell you his name or anything about him?"

"I told you, she's not talking. She's exhausted, poor thing. She slept all night and most of today."

"Did she tell you anything?"

"Just that she made a mistake, that he lied to her. I have to go, Molly. Nechama's calling me. I want to thank you for everything you tried to do. You gave us hope."

Rabbi Bailor hung up. I held the receiver a few seconds before I returned it to the cradle.

"What did Rabbi Bailor say?" Zack asked.

"Not much. Hadassah isn't talking. She may be in shock."

"Who could blame her?" Zack gazed at me. "You don't sound elated."

"I'm *thrilled* that she's home. I had a nightmare about her last night, and she was covered in blood. But I don't understand how she got away from Shankman, what made her decide to leave. And where *is* Shankman?"

"Rabbi Bailor didn't say how she got home?"

"He said it's a miracle."

"Sometimes a miracle is just that, Molly."

I listened to the third message. Dr. McIntyre, calling again to tell me the good news, Hadassah Bailor was home.

I phoned Connors. He wasn't in, so I left a message telling him that my friend's daughter had come home.

"Thanks anyway," I said.

I was fast asleep when the phone rang, and it took me a moment to realize that the sound wasn't part of a dream.

I fumbled for the receiver and brought it to my ear. "Hello?"

"It's Andy."

"She's home, Andy. My friend's daughter? I left you a message." I glanced at my clock radio. Three o'clock. "It's the middle of the night. Why are you—"

"He's dead."

I sat up too quickly. The room began to spin. "Who?"

"Greg Shankman. You told your friend, didn't you?"

I could hear the fury in Connors's voice. "No. I swear I didn't."

Zack stirred and opened his eyes. "Something wrong?"

"Shankman's dead," I told him.

Zack sat up and rubbed his eyes. He switched on his nightstand lamp.

"The apartment manager said a woman was there tonight," Connors said. "With a guy. That was you and Zack, right?"

My head throbbed. "Yes, but the apartment was empty."

"Who's your friend, Molly?"

"Tell me what happened."

"You first."

"No." I was clutching the receiver so hard my fingers ached. "Tell me what happened."

"You want to know what happened? This is me to my friend at West L.A. earlier today. 'Can you do me a favor, pretty please, run this guy's name, see if he has a rap sheet?' 'No problem, Andy.' And this evening, after you get me all nervous about the girl, I call again. 'Can we pay this guy a visit tonight?' 'Let me see.' So my friend calls back. 'What a coincidence, Andy. This guy's car went off the road and hit some big rocks, and guess what? He was in it.' *That's* what happened, Molly."

"Andy, I can't—"

"Don't bother," he said and hung up.

Chapter 26

Sunday, November 21, 11:03 a.m. Corner of Santa Monica Boulevard and Vine Street. A 21-year-old man refused to hand over his cell phone to the suspect and was punched in the face. The suspect grabbed the phone before fleeing westbound on Santa Monica Boulevard.

Connors's gray Cutlass was parked in front of our house when I returned from paying a *shiva* call to Mrs. Kroen. I'd phoned him early that morning, but he hadn't answered. I'd left a message telling him I would be home after eleven and would phone again. "I have to talk to you, Andy. Please."

At least he was willing to talk.

I walked up the driveway and entered the kitchen through the side door. Zack was brewing coffee—French roast vanilla. The smell was enticing and so was he. I'd been up for almost an hour after Connors's call until I fell asleep, and I hadn't heard Zack when he left for *shul.* He was wearing jeans and a sweatshirt and looked mighty fine. I wished I could kiss him. I wished Connors weren't there.

"How was the game?" I asked.

Zack plays basketball every Sunday. He needs the exercise, and it's his only break from the pressures of being a rabbi.

"We won. They got here a few minutes ago, Molly."

"They?"

"They" made it official. I hung my car keys on a hook, took off my jacket, and folded it over a kitchen chair.

"Connors and another detective. A woman. She didn't give her name. I told them I didn't know how long you'd be, but Connors said they would wait. I offered coffee, and they said yes."

"So we're entertaining them before they slap the cuffs on me?"

"Connors obviously thinks you told Rabbi Bailor about Shankman. You'll explain that you didn't, and everything will be okay."

"Right."

"I put them in the dining room—mainly because we have no living room furniture and I didn't think you'd want them to sit on the floor." He smiled. "Sorry, that was lame."

I smiled back. "Lame is welcome."

"I can cancel my meeting."

Not a good idea. He was meeting with the *shul* board. "I'll be okay. Go change into something more rabbinic."

I watched him as he headed out of the room and almost called him back. He must have sensed my indecision, because he turned around.

"You're sure?"

"I'm sure."

I filled two mugs with coffee and took them into the dining room. Connors was sitting at the table next to a strikingly pretty slender woman in her midthirties with shoulder-length dark wavy hair and green eyes that you'd have to be blind not to notice. She was wearing a camel sweater and had tied a multicolored wool scarf around her neck. She looked familiar, but I couldn't place her.

Connors took the mugs. "Thanks. These are for us, right? What about you?"

"Maybe later," I said.

He put one mug in front of the woman, kept the other, and sat down. "Molly, this is Detective Jessie Drake. Detective Drake, Molly Blume."

"Abrams," I said. I'm not sure why. All week I'd been explaining my different surnames to people. It was getting tiresome.

"Your husband is Zack Abrams?" Detective Drake said. She had a pleasantly husky voice, like Demi Moore's but not as raspy. "He didn't give his last name when we met. He teaches at Ohr Torah?"

"One class." Apparently, she'd checked out not only me but Zack. I found that interesting, and disturbing. I wondered if she was trying to intimidate me.

"Detective Drake is with West L.A., Homicide Division," Connors said, emphasizing the "homicide."

I sat down. "I know people at West L.A. I go there weekly to collect data for a column." That's probably where I'd seen her.

"The 'Crime Sheet,' " Jessie said. "Detective Connors told me. I'm surprised we haven't met. Who do you know at West L.A.?"

"Is this a coffee klatch?" Connors said.

I ignored him and named a number of detectives, including Phil Okum.

"My partner," she said. "We'd like to talk to you about Greg Shankman, Mrs. Abrams."

Down to business. "Call me Molly." I faced Connors. "I don't have more to tell you than I did last night." I almost said "Andy" but thought better of it.

"This is a courtesy, Molly," he said. "Detective Drake could have called you down to the station."

"Then you wouldn't be enjoying this freshly brewed coffee," I said.

Connors gave me a warning frown. I thought I saw a smile sneak across the other detective's face.

"Why don't we start over," she said. "I'll tell you what I know, and you can correct me if I get anything wrong. Okay?"

As if I had a choice. "Okay."

"You told Detective Connors you were concerned about a friend's daughter who ran away with a man she met in a chat room. You asked him to help you find this man, based on a license plate number you provided. Nicely done, by the way."

"Thanks."

If she wanted to play good cop, that was fine with me. It felt strange, though, to have Connors playing bad cop. I've had run-ins with other detectives, mostly those at Wilshire whom I had nagged for almost six years about Aggie's murder. I've never been on the outs with Connors. It made me angry, and sad.

"Last night Detective Connors told you the owner of the car was Greg Shankman," Jessie continued. "He instructed you not to give that information to your friend."

"I didn't."

"Then how do you explain the fact that Greg Shankman is dead, Molly?" Connors said.

"You said his car went off the road and crashed on some rocks. That would pretty much do it."

He glared at me. "You're hardly in a position to be a smart-ass. I trusted you."

"I trusted you, too." I glared back, then addressed Jessie. "I told Detective Connors that I feared Shankman would try to kill himself. Apparently, he did."

"There's a problem," Jessie said in a pleasant, unhurried voice. "The medical examiner believes that Mr. Shankman was dead before the car crashed."

I just sat there.

"Cat got your tongue?" Connors said.

I cleared my throat. "What was the cause of death?"

"That's not information we can share," Jessie said. "But you can see our problem, Molly. You had the name of the person who ran off with your friend's daughter. You left a message telling Detective Connors the daughter had returned home. When *did* she return home, by the way?"

"Friday night."

"Mr. Shankman died Friday night. So within a few hours of the time this girl suddenly returned home, the man she ran off with was killed." Jessie took a sip of coffee. "This is delicious. French roast?"

I nodded. In my mind I saw the reddish-brown spots on Shankman's hardwood floor.

"You were desperate to find her," Connors said. "I can understand that, Molly. Just tell me the truth, that you told the father."

I clenched my hands. "I didn't tell him."

"Then explain Shankman's death. Come on, Molly. You said you didn't know Shankman's name when we spoke Saturday night. Obviously, you *did* hear my message, and passed on Shankman's name to your friend."

"I *didn't* know his name. I heard you say you wouldn't know till the next day. I thought you meant the car owner's name. And you phoned on the Sabbath, Andy. You know I don't use the phone on the Sabbath. I'm Orthodox," I told Jessie.

"Very convenient," Connors said.

"But if you thought it was a life-and-death emergency, you *could* phone, right?" Jessie said. "And you feared Shankman would kill himself, and the girl. I've been studying Orthodox Judaism," she told Connors, who was staring at her, his mouth open. "I didn't know I was Jewish until a few years ago. Long story." She returned her attention to me.

"I didn't hear the message."

"Well, it's there," Connors said. "Why don't we play it so Detective Drake can hear it?"

"I erased it. I didn't see a reason to keep it."

He rolled his eyes.

"When have I ever lied to you, Andy? I can't believe that you think I went back on my word."

"You went to Shankman's apartment when I told you not to, didn't you?"

"You said not to get his address from my friend. I didn't. I already had it."

Connors grunted.

"If you didn't tell the girl's father, Molly, who *did* you tell?" Jessie asked.

"No one."

"You told Zack," Connors said with a "gotcha" tone. "He went with you to Shankman's apartment."

"Zack didn't phone anyone. We left for Shankman's apartment right after I talked to you."

"Let's assume you didn't tell anyone, Molly," Jessie said. "I see several possibilities. One, this girl's father, or someone else, picked up on something you said and used it to find Shankman. Two, the daughter, possibly in self-defense, killed him and staged the fatal car accident—with someone's help. I can't see her moving Shankman's body to the car on her own. Three, the daughter contacted someone who came to her rescue, killed Shankman—again, maybe in self-defense—and staged the car accident to avoid notoriety and protect the girl's name."

Those were all reasonable possibilities. I didn't like any of them. "Four," I said, "Shankman was killed by someone unrelated to my friend. Shankman's girlfriend filed a restraining order against him. I'd start with her."

Jessie nodded. "We intend to talk to her. But the timing is suggestive, wouldn't you agree? Why would the girlfriend choose this Friday night to kill him? And why would your friend's daughter leave that same night?"

I thought for a moment. "Suppose the girlfriend found my friend's daughter at the apartment and got into a heated altercation with Shankman. My friend's daughter was frightened," I said, thinking out loud. "She left. The altercation became violent. The girlfriend killed him and called someone to help her get rid of the body."

"Molly writes true crime books," Connors said. "You can tell she has a fertile imagination."

Jessie looked thoughtful. "Why would the girlfriend kill him?"

"In self-defense? She filed a restraining order. She must have had a reason."

"In that case your friend's daughter is a material witness, and we still need to talk to her. What did her father tell you about her return, by the way?"

"He said his daughter realized she'd made a mistake and came home. That was it." I wasn't about to tell them that Hadassah wasn't talking, that she might be in shock.

"You weren't curious?" Connors said. "That would be a first."

"I'm sure I'll hear the details at some point. They just got their daughter back, Andy. They're overwhelmed with relief and joy. I didn't want to intrude."

Jessie took another sip of coffee. "So what's the girl's name?"

"I can't tell you that."

"You may not have a choice," she said in that pleasant voice. "We can subpoena you, get a bench warrant for your arrest if you don't cooperate. I'd hate to go that route."

Connors said, "Even easier, we can ask the girlfriend what school Shankman was working at when he was fired in September. Then we'll have your friend's name."

"Then you don't need me to tell you." I didn't feel the need to volunteer that the girlfriend wouldn't be back until after Thanksgiving.

"We haven't reached her. We'd like to talk to the daughter as soon as possible. We're not saying she's involved with Shankman's death, Molly. And if Shankman was killed in self-defense . . ."

"I promised I wouldn't reveal her name, Andy. I told you that from the start. My friend is concerned about her reputation."

"A man is dead," Connors said. "I'd say that changes things."

"You were at Mr. Shankman's apartment last night, by your own admission," Jessie said.

I faced her. "Right."

"According to the manager, Mr. LaSalle, you were on your hands and knees, looking for a lost contact lens. Did you find the lens?"

"No, I didn't."

"What were you looking for, Molly?" she asked.

"Nothing."

"Not the lens?" She smiled.

"Aside from the lens." My palms were clammy.

"While you were looking for the lens, did you happen to notice bloodstains on the hardwood floor?"

"I can't say that I did."

"Careful wording. Oh, I forgot. You're a writer." Jessie smiled again. "When you left a message for Detective Connors last night, telling him the girl was safely home, you didn't tell him you saw blood spots on the floor."

"I didn't know there *were* blood spots."

"But that's what you suspected. You write true crime books and a crime column. So your instincts are sharper than the average person's, and if you saw reddish-brown spots on a floor, and you had reason to think something violent may have taken place in a room, you'd think blood. You violated a crime scene, Molly." Jessie sounded regretful, more than angry.

"I had no idea it was a crime scene."

"You were on your hands and knees, examining the floor. You picked up a rug and looked under it, too. Who knows what evidence you disturbed?"

"I was careful." I realized too late what I'd said. She had trapped me.

"Why would you be careful if you didn't know it was a crime scene, Molly?"

I just sat there, trying to meet those green eyes, wondering how much trouble I was in.

"Well, let me ask you this," she said. "If you had come home from Shankman's apartment, and you hadn't heard from your friend that his daughter was back home, would you have mentioned those spots to Detective Connors and assumed that something had happened in that apartment? That someone may have met with foul play?"

"Do I need a lawyer?" I managed to make that sound casual, but I was quaking.

"That depends," Jessie said. "What's your friend's name?"

I shook my head. "I have to think about this."

"Don't think too long," Connors said.

"There was more blood," Jessie said. "Especially near the closet, and under the rug. Someone cleaned up, but it's hard to get rid of blood. What else did you notice, Molly?"

"It was immaculate, everything neat and tidy. It looked like no one had been there for a while. And one of the photo frames was missing a protective glass."

"We noticed that, too. Did you touch anything, Molly? Doorknobs? Drawers? Knickknacks?"

"Doorknobs, and the bedroom closet door. I didn't touch any knickknacks or photos." In my mind I reviewed my walk through the apartment. "I touched the light switch in the entry hall closet."

"Did you touch the cardboard box in the closet?"

"No."

"Because there was blood on the box, too. That's interesting, isn't it?"

I pictured the reddish stains. "What was in it?"

Jessie smiled. "What about the knives in the kitchen?"

I blanched. "Is that what . . . No. I didn't touch any of the knives."

"Good. We'll have to get you printed, Molly," Jessie said. "For purposes of elimination. I'd like you to come down to the station tomorrow."

"I'll be there. Are we done?"

"What's your friend's name?" Jessie asked.

I didn't answer.

"Obstruction of justice, tampering with a crime scene. I can think of a number of other charges. One hour."

"What?"

"That's when we'll be back."

Chapter 27

My legs were so shaky I was surprised they held me up as I walked Connors and Jessie Drake to the front door. I watched them get into Connors's car and waited until the Cutlass turned the corner.

I phoned my sister Mindy. She's a real estate attorney, but I figured she remembered enough criminal law to advise me. I could hear her three children in the background as I gave her a summary of what had happened.

"Poor Rabbi Bailor," was the first thing Mindy said. "And his daughter. I can't imagine what they went through."

"What about the threats, Mindy? Detective Drake talked about obstruction of justice, contaminating a crime scene."

"She's trying to scare you, Molly. But she

can subpoena you, and she can get a bench warrant and have you arrested if you don't cooperate."

"Can I plead the fifth?"

"No, you can't. That protection applies only if what you tell the police will incriminate you."

"What do you think I should do, Mindy?"

"Cooperate. They'll find out Dassie's name from Shankman's girlfriend when they reach her, but they're right to want to talk to Dassie now. The colder the case, the colder the trail. Hours can make a difference."

I cleared my throat. "What if . . ."

"What if Dassie killed him?"

"Yes. The blood on the floor says *something* happened."

"Dassie may have killed him in self-defense. Or it was the girlfriend, like you suggested, or someone else we don't know about. But even if Dassie had nothing to do with his death, she may have vital information."

"You're right."

"Plus you have to consider your obligation to Connors, Molly. He's been a good friend all these years, and in running the license plate to get Shankman's name, and giving you that name, he bent a few rules. He could be in trouble with the department."

I hadn't even had time to consider that. "And my promise to Rabbi Bailor?"

"Talk to him, Molly. Explain the situation. He won't want you to put yourself in jeopardy."

There was every possibility that Connors or Jessie Drake had stationed someone in front of the house to follow me, but this wasn't something I could do over the phone.

Gavriel answered the door. He hadn't shaved in several days. The dark growth on his face enhanced his good looks and almost covered a cut on his chin.

I wondered if he would have a scar, like his father. "I heard the wonderful news about your sister," I said.

He nodded. "*Baruch Hashem.* We're all so grateful. I'll tell my father you're here. Do you want to wait in the dining room?"

I had just sat down when Rabbi Bailor entered the room. His smile could have lit a ballroom.

"I was going to call you again, to thank you, Molly. Like I said, you gave us hope. And I'll never forget your concern, your eagerness to help. Nechama will be sorry she missed you. She went for groceries, and then she's picking up the boys from school. Aliza went with her."

"Rabbi Bailor—"

"I'm sure you have a million questions, Molly. We do, too." The smile dimmed. "Dassie hasn't said much. Dr. McIntyre came last night. He said these things take time and cautioned us not to push her."

"Rabbi Bailor, two police detectives just left my house." I watched his face, hated the fact that I was doing it. "One of them, Detective Connors, knows that Dassie ran away. I went to him for help in finding this man."

"He's the one you gave the note and the coins to? Did you tell him Dassie's home?"

"Yes. Rabbi Bailor—"

"Please thank him for his efforts, Molly, and tell him I'm sorry I wasted his time. He can throw out the note and the coins. I certainly don't want them."

"Rabbi Bailor, I didn't tell Detective Connors Dassie's name, but now I have to."

The rabbi shook his head. "It's over. Dassie is home. She's safe. I don't want to know this man's name. I'm just grateful he's out of our lives. If Detective Connors wants to pursue the matter, that's up to him."

"The man Dassie ran away with is dead."

The rabbi turned ashen. "Dead?" He sat down heavily.

"He was in a car crash."

You're not to say anything about homicide, or about the blood in Shankman's apartment, Jessie Drake had warned before she left. *If you* do *say anything,* Connors had added, *we'll know.*

Rabbi Bailor frowned. "A man dies in a car accident. That's a terrible thing, but what does that have to do with Dassie? Why do they think she ran away with him?"

"The man is Greg Shankman."

The rabbi's eyes widened. "Shankman?"

I could swear his surprise was genuine, but if he *had* known, he'd had over a day to perfect his reaction. "Dassie didn't tell you who she was with?"

"I told you. She wouldn't talk." He dropped his head heavily against the back of his chair and stared up at the ceiling.

"The police want to talk to Dassie, to find out Shankman's frame of mind, since she was probably the last person to see him alive."

"He killed himself?" the rabbi asked, somber.

"They want to determine what happened, since they know that Dassie came home Friday night," I said, trying not to lie. "Detective Connors knows Shankman was fired. I told him on Friday, to convince him of the urgency of finding Shankman. Connors plans to talk to Shankman's girlfriend. Did you know Shankman had a four-year-old daughter?"

"No." The rabbi sighed deeply. "I didn't know much about his private life."

"The girlfriend will tell Connors that Shankman taught at Torat Tzion. So the police will learn Dassie's name, but they're pressuring me to tell them now. They can subpoena me and have me arrested if I don't cooperate."

"Of course you have to tell them, Molly. I'm sorry I got you involved." He picked up a pencil and rolled it between his fingers. "When you said maybe it was Greg Shankman, I thought you were crazy, remember? He called a few weeks ago to tell me to expect a call from a principal. I told him I'd give him a strong recommendation. And all this time he was trying to ruin my daughter? Why?"

I heard anger in the rabbi's voice, and deep pain. I don't know if there's anything worse than betrayal.

"Why was he fired, Rabbi Bailor? He's dead, so I doubt that there would be any legal ramifications if you told me."

"Still, it's *loshen horeh*." Gossip. He put down the pencil. "You can give the detectives Dassie's name, Molly. But she's in a fragile state. I don't know if she'll talk to them. By the way, what did you tell them about her?"

"What you told me. That Dassie came home Friday night, that she'd realized she made a mistake."

"And the police think Greg was despondent, so he killed himself." The rabbi formed a steeple with his fingers. "If you had told me two days ago that the man who did this to Dassie committed suicide, I wouldn't have rejoiced, but I wouldn't have been heartbroken. But now Dassie is home, and that man is dead. He's someone I knew, someone I liked, someone who left behind a young daughter. And he can never do *teshuvah* for what he's done."

Rabbi Bailor sat lost in thought. I'm not sure what triggered his realization that there was another, more grim explanation for Shankman's death, but I could see his expression turn from sad contemplation to alarm.

He dropped his hands to his desk. "The police think it's suicide, or something else? I'm not a fool," he said sharply when I didn't respond. "What did they ask you about Dassie?"

Connors's warning was in my head. I chose my words. "They wanted to know how Dassie got away from Shankman, and why she left Friday night."

"So they think it's too coincidental—that she came home, that Greg is dead. But if he didn't kill himself, then—"

The look the rabbi gave me was filled with horror. "They think *Dassie killed* him?"

I didn't answer.

"So the car accident—someone made that happen?" His face was gray. "Where did it happen? When?"

"I don't know. Dassie didn't tell you anything when she came home, Rabbi Bailor?"

"I told you she didn't." He centered his yarmulke. "Now you're a detective, Molly?"

"The police will ask you the same thing."

"Dassie said he lied. Over and over. He lied, he lied, he lied. That's all she said."

"She never said his name?"

"*Never.*" The word had the force of a *shofar* blast. "If you saw her Friday night, Molly, you would understand. She walked almost four miles. Her hair was wild, she was crying, out of breath. She collapsed in Nechama's arms."

"It's probably more like seven miles from Mar Vista to here," I said, my head pounding.

"Mar Vista?" The rabbi looked puzzled. "That's Greg's old address. When he called the last time, he told me he'd moved. I keep forgetting to ask Mrs. Horowitz to change the information in our files."

It was a reasonable explanation. I hoped it was true. "Can I talk to Hadassah, Rabbi Bailor?"

"She's not talking. Not to me, not to Nechama, or Aliza. Not even to her uncle, even though they're very close. Or to Dr. McIntyre. She doesn't say a word."

"Can I see her?"

Hadassah was lying so still I thought she was sleeping, but when I neared the bed I saw that her blue eyes were wide open. Her strawberry-blond curls were splayed against the Wedgwood blue pillow. Her face was pale, her lips almost invisible. She was wearing long-sleeved flannel pajamas with a yellow lollipop design.

"Dassie, Molly Blume is here to see you," her father said. "She was your counselor in B'nos years ago, remember? You read all her books and articles?"

There was no response. The eyes could have been colored glass for all the expression they showed.

Rabbi Bailor straightened up and gave me a look. See? He walked to the door.

I knelt at her side. "Dassie, I'm so happy you're home. Everyone is. We were all worried about you. I know you're tired, but if you ever want to talk, I'm ready to listen."

Her arms lay on top of the white lace-bordered sheet. I reached over and took her slender hand. She jerked her hand up, bending her elbow, as if she were swatting at a fly. The wide sleeve of her pajama rode up, and I found myself staring at the red cuts that began at her wrist.

I followed Rabbi Bailor downstairs.

"I don't know what I'm going to tell Nechama," he said. "For the first time in almost a week, we woke up happy."

My grandmother says, what's the use of a beautiful dream if the dawn is chilly?

Chapter 28

Hadassah was afraid to dream.

Friday night, after her mother had hugged her and gripped her face so tightly with both hands as she kissed her that Hadassah winced; after her mother undressed her and cried, "What happened to you, my poor baby!"; after she helped her into her pajamas and into bed— after that Hadassah had fallen into a deep, restless sleep.

When she woke up it was the middle of the night and the house was still. She needed to use the bathroom. She flipped back her comforter and swung her legs off the bed, and that was when she saw the blood that trickled down her arms and legs and dripped onto the pale hardwood floor as she hurried past the kitchen and the dining ell to the closet where she had hidden when she heard the key in the lock, the shard of glass in her sweaty hand—

Don't drop it, Dassie! When she heard his footsteps, she had held her breath so tightly that she could feel her ribs. If he looked for her in the bedroom—Dassie, honey, where are you? Why is the light out? Are you okay?—if he did that, she could unlock the front door and run down the stairs and pound on someone's door, Help me! Please help me! But the footsteps came up to the closet. She could hear his breathing, could hear the squeak of the knob as he twisted it, could see a tiny, dim sliver of reflected candlelight when the door opened. What the hell? he yelled. He grabbed her arm, and she lunged at him, the pointy end of the shard aimed for his throat.

It had taken her a few seconds to realize that she'd been dreaming. She lay drenched in sweat, her heart beating too fast, pumping the blood too quickly all through her body. A dream, she told herself. She was in the bed that had been hers since she was three. She was safe. The bleeding had stopped. But she didn't want to have that dream again, because the next time she didn't know if she could make it out of the closet. Her father had told her people never died in their own dreams, but she had read that wasn't so. And if she died in her dream, she knew she would really die, forever. That was why she had taken the shard and shoved it between the mattress and box spring, just in case.

Shabbos morning, after her father and the boys left for *shul,* and her mother had checked on her before going downstairs to say her prayers—"How are you doing, sweetie? Can I get you anything?"— Hadassah had slipped out of bed and found two boxes of the No-Doz tablets she kept hidden in an old shoe box filled with tapes. Her friend Tara had given her some Ritalin pills that she'd filched from her brother, who had ADD. A lot of the kids used Ritalin, especially before finals and AP exams, but Hadassah had been too nervous to try it, and No-Doz did the trick.

And last night, she hadn't dreamed. That was good.

Everyone was so concerned. Her mother, her father, her uncle, Dr. McIntyre. Even Gavriel had come into the room, shuffling awkwardly from foot to foot. "I'm glad you're okay, Dassie." Sara kept calling and wanted to see her. "I told her you're resting, honey," her mother said. And Aliza had come home from her weekend reunion late this morning. Hadassah could tell that Aliza was uncomfortable, tiptoeing around the room, talking in a whisper on the phone, coming over to the bed every once in a while. "Do you want to talk, Dass? I was so scared for you, I cried every night."

Most of the time Hadassah hadn't answered. Sometimes she had shaken her head, or nodded. After a while she realized that if she lay still and stared straight ahead, people would leave her alone. She didn't know how long she could do that. A few days. Longer, if she had to. But then what? And even with the No-Doz she would have to sleep eventually. And then the dream would return.

Molly Blume had been here. She had touched Hadassah's hand, and Hadassah had instinctively jerked her arm. That had been a mistake. Hadassah hadn't seen Molly's face, but Molly must have noticed the marks. There was nothing Hadassah could do about that now. She was relieved that Molly had seen her left hand, not her right. Hadassah hadn't realized at first that the shard had lacerated her right palm. Her mother had gasped when she'd seen the cuts.

"You must have fallen on something terribly sharp," she said. She had applied antibiotic ointment and wrapped her hand in a gauze bandage. "If it's not better by tomorrow, Dassie, if it looks infected, we'll go to the emergency room." Later that night her mother had unwrapped the bandage to show Hadassah's father the cuts. "Do you think we should go to the emergency, Chaim? Or maybe we should take Dassie to Dr. Miller. He's only three blocks away." But her father had said no. And an hour ago he'd reapplied the ointment and replaced the bulky gauze with several small bandages that weren't noticeable.

"The police will be here soon, Dassie," he had told her, smoothing the last bandage onto her palm. "They want to talk to you about Greg Shankman. Greg is dead, Dassie," her father said, still holding her hand. "He was in his car when it crashed. Molly wouldn't say, but I think the police believe he was killed."

Hadassah's eyes filled with tears. She stared at the wallpaper and imagined tiny cells of fear attaching themselves to the oxygen cells her heart was pumping through her body.

Her father blotted her tears. "They'll want to know how you got away, Dassie, how you got home, all the details. But you don't have to tell them anything you don't want to, Dassie. We love you, Dassie."

The police came an hour later. Two of them, a man and a woman. "My daughter may be sleeping," she heard her father say, so she arranged her hands, palms flat against the comforter. After the man made Hadassah's parents leave the room, the woman took a chair from Hadassah's desk and put it next to her bed.

"I'm Detective Jessie Drake," she told Hadassah. "You can call me Jessie. I know you've gone through a terrible ordeal, Hadassah, but we have to ask you a few questions.

"Do you remember what happened Friday night, Hadassah?

"What time did you get home?

"Did you walk home all the way, or did you get a ride?

"Did you call anyone to help you, Hadassah?

"Was Mr. Shankman there when you left the apartment?

"Did he try to hurt you, Hadassah?

"We want to help you, Hadassah.

"Is there anything you want to tell me, Hadassah?"

Chapter 29

Monday, November 22, 9:38 a.m., 5500 block of Carlton Way. A married couple got into an argument, and the woman attempted to stab her 49-year-old husband in the chest with a knife. The woman failed to cause any serious injury to her husband and fled the scene.

Shankman's death made the morning news.

I was chugging along on the treadmill in our spare room, working up a sweat while watching a local station to make the time pass and reach my goal of two miles more quickly. So far the news had been unremarkable. The original Scott Peterson jury would sit for the penalty phase; Dan Rather would probably be stepping down, and maybe Tom Brokaw (I'd much rather lose Rather); Arnold "The Governator" Schwarzenegger was urging a California football team to play only in-state games;

Eisner was still battling Disney. Traffic was next, then the weather, reported by a pretty, voluptuous young woman who was pointing to a map of the San Bernardino Mountains and talking about a cold front. I found her Dolly Parton twin peaks distracting and imagined that the temperatures of male viewers were rising. No cold front here—more like hot and bothered.

I was about to switch the channel when I heard the gray-haired male anchor say, ". . . breaking news about the death of a popular local high school teacher."

I brought the treadmill to an abrupt stop, my heart pounding from exertion and anxiety. A second later Shankman's photo filled the screen. It was a formal shot—he was in a dark suit and tie, his light brown hair carefully combed. I wondered where the station had obtained it.

"Lydia Martin is coming to us live from Mulholland Drive about a mile west of Coldwater Canyon, where twenty-nine-year-old Greg Shankman met his death," the anchor continued. "Lydia."

Now the screen showed a thirty-something woman. The wind was blowing her long dark hair as she stood at the side of the two-lane road.

"Kevin, I'm only feet away from the spot where, some time Friday night, Greg Shankman's car plunged onto the rocks below," the field reporter said, pointing to her left. "Shankman left his apartment in West Los Angeles. But where was he headed? And what happened? Police have few clues and no witnesses, and ask anyone with information to contact the West L.A. station."

"Do they think it was suicide, Lydia?"

"It's possible, Kevin. Neighbors told us Greg Shankman was depressed. In September he suddenly left the Orthodox Jewish high school in the heart of Beverly Hills where he had been teaching for several years. And his girlfriend of five years, Melissa Frank, had ended their long-term relationship and obtained a restraining order."

"Thanksgiving is in three days, and psychologists talk about holiday pressure," the anchor said. "Do we know why Shankman left the school?"

"School officials won't comment. The sad irony is that reconciliation was in the air. Melissa and their four-year-old daughter, Kaitlin, returned last night from Seattle, where they had hoped Shankman would join them for the Thanksgiving weekend. Melissa and Greg were talking about getting married. But this Thanksgiving will be sad for Melissa and Kaitlin. And there will be no wedding bells, and no holiday celebration for Greg Shankman. Back to you, Kevin."

I wasn't surprised that the media had picked up the story. The estranged girlfriend, the restraining order, the violent car crash, the fact that Shankman had taught at an Orthodox Jewish school—all that made for interesting material. Janet Mendes was no doubt grateful that the reporter hadn't named the school. I didn't know whether other media would mention it. And if other reporters followed the story, they would soon learn that there was only one Orthodox Jewish high school "in the heart of Beverly Hills."

At least the media didn't know that the police suspected foul play, I thought as I took off my sweats and sneakers and prepared to shower. I wondered again whether I should have refused to give the police Rabbi Bailor's name. Melissa Frank had returned last night. They would have obtained the name of the school from her.

"You did the right thing," Zack had told me when he returned from his board meeting.

That's what Connors had said, too, his tone somewhat conciliatory.

I still felt miserable—about giving the police Rabbi Bailor's name, about my rift with Connors and what was possibly the end of our friendship, about the concerns I was having about Hadassah Bailor and the marks on her arms.

Thinking about the police reminded me that I'd told Jessie Drake I would stop by today to have my fingerprints taken—"for purposes of elimination," she had said. I generally collect data for my column on Mondays and Tuesdays. I would start at West L.A.

I had finished reciting my daily prayers and was putting on makeup when the phone rang. I hurried to my nightstand and picked up the cordless receiver.

It was Cheryl Wexner.

I'd forgotten that I'd told her I'd call her about Hadassah. So much had happened since Friday. I felt as though a week had gone by. I apologized and told her things had come up—a lame equivocation, but the best I could do.

"I understand completely," Cheryl said. "When I didn't hear from you, I was going to phone *you*, but I got caught up in work, too. November and December are my busiest months, because of college deadlines. I *do* want to talk to you about Hadassah, Molly, but that's not why I'm calling you. I heard on the news that Greg Shankman died in a horrible car accident. I thought you might know Greg? He taught at Torat Tzion, and you're close to Rabbi Bailor."

"I never met Greg, but I know he was Hadassah's teacher last year." I wondered what Cheryl would say if she knew that until last week I hadn't spoken with Rabbi Bailor in almost fourteen years. "I did hear about his death. It's a tragedy."

Whatever Shankman had done, it *was* a tragedy—for his parents and any siblings he might have, for his little girl, for his girlfriend, whether or not she had been planning to reconcile with him.

"I saw him less than two weeks ago," Cheryl said. "I can't believe he's dead."

"How did you know him?"

"Dr. Mendes, the secular studies principal at Torat Tzion, introduced us. I met with her soon after I moved here and told her I'd appreciate referrals from the school. I have a B.A. in history, and Greg teaches history. We got to talking, and we became friends. The reason I'm calling, Molly—the TV reporter said people who have information about Greg should call the police. Friday night your ex-husband said you deal with the police, and you write true crime books. So I was hoping you could advise me. Justin, really. He's the one with the information."

I was glad she couldn't see my face. "What kind of information?"

"He'd rather explain in person. I know you're busy, but he's home now, and if you could meet with him as soon as possible?"

Chapter 30

Cheryl lived on the corner of Ogden and Oakwood in Beverly-Fairfax, only blocks from Bubbie G, on the ground floor of the two-story building with multiple turrets that my sisters and I had called "the castle" when we were kids. My parents lived in the area before they bought their house on South Gardner. So did many Orthodox Jews before they moved half a dozen blocks east toward La Brea.

The neighborhood is a mix of old and new. The "new" includes the Bicentennial Post Office, a natural foods store, and the huge mustard-colored Broadcast apartment building above it. The "old" is Television City and the CBS building, where my mom and her friends used to spend their summers watching quiz shows being filmed. Some of the "old" is now a memory, like the Pan Pacific Theater, where my parents went on their first date, and the Art Deco Pan Pacific Auditorium, where in the 1960s you could see the annual Home Show or GM's Motorama, or a boxing or wrestling match, or Elvis, live. My optometrist had a huge black-and-white panoramic aerial photo of Beverly-Fairfax and the Pan Pacific Auditorium. I loved looking at it, trying to locate my parents' home and Bubbie G's apartment. A few years ago he remodeled his Wilshire office, and the photo came down.

The neighborhood is also populated more and more by hip singles who park their sporty cars fender to bumper on the narrow streets that were never meant to accommodate so many vehicles, parked or moving. Which is why I had to circle Cheryl's block twice before I gave up and parked a block away.

Cheryl opened the door as soon as I rang the bell, and I had the feeling she'd been watching for my arrival. There was no entry hall. I stepped into a large barrel-ceilinged living room painted pale gray and furnished with a navy chenille sofa, a chrome-framed glass coffee table, and two tall chrome-framed cabinets, one on either side of a small plaster-faced fireplace, that held books and curios. Several plants added color to the room, along with framed museum prints on three of the walls.

"I'm afraid you may have come for nothing," Cheryl said, her voice awkward with apology. "It was Justin's idea to phone you, but now he's having second thoughts. He doesn't want to get anyone in trouble."

She was wearing a black turtleneck sweater and jeans that made her look more hippy than she had in her skirt Friday night. I could tell she'd been crying.

"Why don't you tell me what you know, and we'll go from there." I handed her a bag. "A little something from The Coffee Bean & Tea Leaf and me to welcome you to Los Angeles. They're all kosher, by the way."

"This is so sweet, Molly." She opened the bag and inhaled. "Smells heavenly. You'll have to share some of this with me."

"I got an assortment of Danish, including the crumble cheese, which is my favorite. The coffee is Jamaican Blue Mountain regular and Mocha Java Blend decaf. I've never tasted either one, but they sounded good."

I followed her through the dining room ("My office," she said, pointing to a stack of folders, a thick college directory, and individual college catalogs piled on the table) to a breakfast nook off a galley kitchen with a pink ceramic tile counter and outdated wallpaper with pink and gray bubbles. While Cheryl put up a pot of the Jamaican, I sat at a round white Formica table and arranged the pastries on a platter she took down from a cabinet.

"I told you Greg and I are good friends?" she said when she joined me at the table. "Justin is close to him, too. That's why he's taking this so hard."

"Do you have other children?"

"No. Justin has a half sister. I divorced his father when Justin was three. I should never have married Simon. He was head over heels in love with me, and well-to-do. He wanted to give me the world. I thought I loved him, too, but I was on the rebound. There's nothing like a first love, is there?" She sounded terribly sad.

Zack had been my first love. We had dated in high school, and I'd had visions of happily-ever-after, but a carton of cottage cheese has a longer shelf life than our relationship did. I had pined for him long after we'd broken up. As for Ron, part of his attraction, I later admitted to myself, was the fact that he'd been Zack's best friend. Easy loves, heavy damages.

"It can color your whole life," Cheryl said. "It took me years to get over him, even after I divorced Simon. Sometimes I wish I'd never met him. He moved on, of course. Wife, kids. No picket fence." She laughed uneasily. "God, listen to me. I'm not usually this maudlin. I think it's because of Greg. One minute he was alive, the next . . . I was telling you about Justin. Where was I?"

"You said his father remarried." I took a crumble cheese Danish from the platter and broke off a piece.

Cheryl nodded. "Stacy's a nice woman. I'm glad they found each other. She and Simon had Tina soon after they married. From the time they brought her home from the hospital, Justin felt he came second. I'm not sure he did, but that's how he felt. It's not an unusual story, but when it's *your* story, it's the only one that counts. And Justin is creative, and creative people tend to be more sensitive, I think. Don't you?"

I nodded. "Justin lived with your ex?"

"Sometimes. Sometimes he lived with me. He couldn't find his place. And it didn't help that Simon and I aren't on the same page about religion. I'm Modern Orthodox. Simon and Stacy are stricter. And Justin—well, until about a few months ago, he was ready to chuck the whole religion. Sometimes I think he was trying to get back at Simon and at me. But then Greg told him about Rabbi Bailor and convinced him to meet with the rabbi. They hit it off. But I'm not sure if Justin wants to continue learning with him."

I could hear footsteps above us. Someone jumping. "When did Justin move to L.A.?"

"A year ago. After college he decided he wanted to write screenplays. He was always a writer, always making up wonderful stories." Her smile lit up her face. "He moved here to pursue his career and kept telling me how wonderful L.A. is, so I came to visit and ended up staying." She bit a piece of the croissant she'd taken. "This is amazing. How's yours?"

"Too good," I said, impatient to get to the reason I'd come.

"Anyway, I was ready to leave New York. I was never happy there. Business-wise, it's worked out. I do much of my consulting and application guidance online, and I'm getting more and more referrals from local schools. And being with Justin is wonderful. He's a part-time waiter—the typical Hollywood story—so it made sense for him to move in with me. I've learned not to ask where he's going or what time he'll be back, but it's hard to accept that your little boy is all grown up when he still comes to you for money. And of course, you're not allowed to ask what it's for." There was a hint of annoyance behind the smile. "I know Justin hates asking, and I don't mind helping him. It's only until he sells his first screenplay. I just *know* that'll happen soon. He has the talent. It's just a matter of time, and connections."

"So Justin became close to Greg," I said, hoping to get back on track.

"Sorry. You didn't come to hear my life story." She laughed ruefully.

"To be honest, I haven't made close friends yet, and you're easy to talk to. People probably tell you that all the time. I didn't mean to go on and on."

"You didn't," I said. "I'm interested in hearing about your background."

"You're being kind, but thanks. Anyway, Greg was like an older brother. If Justin was having girl trouble, he'd turn to Greg. And Greg would read his material and make insightful comments. Greg is—" she stopped. "Greg was very bright and knowledgeable, and not just about history."

"You said Justin has information about Greg that the police may find useful?"

"It's about what happened in school, at Torat Tzion. Greg was accused of inappropriate behavior with one of the senior girls."

"It was all lies," Justin said.

He was standing in the doorway, his hands in the pockets of his jeans. His hair was tousled, and he looked as though he'd just woken up from a troubled sleep.

"Feeling better, honey?" Cheryl asked.

He shrugged.

"Come sit down." She pulled out the chair next to hers. "Mrs. Abrams brought treats."

"Molly, please," I said. "When people call me Mrs. Abrams, I think they're talking about my mother-in-law."

Justin walked over, but he remained standing, shifting from leg to leg. "I don't know what my mom told you."

"Just what you heard." Cheryl patted the seat of the chair. "Why don't you tell Molly what happened, Justin."

"I'm not sure *anything* happened. That's the point. I don't want to tell the police something and get someone in trouble if it has nothing to do with Greg's accident."

"You said this girl lied about Greg," I said. "When was this?"

"In September, the first week of school." Justin took his hands out of his pockets. "She told the principal that Greg said he'd give her an A if she put out. It was all a lie, everything."

"Why would this girl accuse Greg falsely?"

"To discredit him." Justin sat down. "She's tight with a guy in her class that Greg had accused of cheating."

"How could Greg be sure?" Having been falsely accused of cheating, I'm sensitive about the subject.

"Greg watched him for two years. The kid cheated on tests, plagiarized papers. All the teachers knew it, but no one could figure out how he did it, so they couldn't prove it. And his family helped build the school."

"Adam Prosser?"

Justin narrowed his eyes. "You know?"

"I guessed. I heard rumors about him."

"Well, it was driving Greg crazy," Justin said. "Over the summer he spent hours in the UCLA library stacks and online, and he finally had the goods on Prosser. The kid had copied some papers almost verbatim. He bought others online. Greg found a website that helped him trace that."

TurnItIn? That was the site one of the kids in the chat room had mentioned.

Cynthia put a pastry on a plate and set it in front of her son. "You haven't eaten all day, Justin."

"And Greg confronted the boy?" I asked.

Justin nodded. "Prosser denied it, of course. Greg wanted to give him a chance to come clean before he told the principal. But the next day the principal called Greg into her office and told him a senior was accusing him of sexual harassment. Amy Brookman."

A name I hadn't heard. "Didn't Greg explain why Amy was lying? That he'd found proof Prosser had been cheating?"

"Sure. But Greg didn't have the proof with him that day. He said Amy gave a convincing performance. She cried. She said she was so depressed she had to go on Prozac. And she gave dates when she met with Greg alone and he came on to her." Justin grunted. "Greg stayed after hours to *help* her. That's the thanks she gave him."

Justin tore off the top of the Danish, then dropped it and pushed the plate away.

"When did this alleged harassment take place?"

"Amy said Greg was coming on to her and threatening her all last year. She's hoping to go to Columbia or Penn, and a B average won't cut it. So she didn't tell."

The coffeemaker was gurgling. I could smell the nutty flavor wafting toward me. Above us there was more jumping.

"But all of a sudden, in September, Amy's no longer afraid of Greg?" I said.

"She was still afraid, but she felt she had to speak up. She claimed Greg was picking on Prosser because he's the one who encouraged Amy to come forward. She couldn't let Greg get away with his lies." Justin rolled his eyes. "She also claimed she wasn't the only one Greg hit on."

"Who else?" I asked.

"Another girl in her class."

"Did this other girl accuse Greg, too?"

"She died last year. They said she had a heart attack."

"Batya Weinberg?"

He looked at me, curious. "You heard about her too, huh? Amy said she killed herself because of Greg. How sick is that, to make up garbage like that? What was Greg supposed to do? Ask the Weinbergs to sign an affidavit saying their daughter didn't kill herself?" Justin tilted his chair back.

I nodded, but wondered with some unease whether Batya *had* killed herself. Dr. McIntyre, I recalled, had seemed edgy when I'd brought up her name.

"Plus Amy said if anyone was guilty of cheating, it was Greg," Justin said.

"In college?"

"At Torat Tzion," he said, impatiently. He brought his chair to an upright position. "They said Greg changed kids' answers on the APs."

"Why would Greg do that?"

"He *didn't* do it." Justin scowled.

Cheryl put her hand on her son's. "Molly knows that, honey." The coffeemaker had shut off. She stood and took the few steps into the kitchen. "They said he did it for the status. Greg was proud that almost all of his students passed the AP. They passed because he prepared them so well." Cheryl took three mugs from a cabinet.

Sara, I recalled, had said that Dassie had hoped to have Shankman for an AP history class. That Shankman worked students hard, that almost everyone in his class passed the AP exam. And someone in the chat room had mentioned a teacher who changed answers on an AP exam. Was that chat room visitor someone from Torat Tzion?

"I can still see Greg the night he told us what had happened," Cheryl said, holding one of the mugs. "He was devastated. Shocked, hurt. He didn't know how he would support himself. He'd moved into a new apartment. He'd just bought a new car. More than that, he loved teaching. Working with kids, helping them reach their potential. He couldn't see himself doing anything else."

My mother loves teaching for the same reason. So does my brother Judah, who won't give up his two classes even though his Judaica store is thriving. I found it hard to reconcile Greg Shankman, model teacher, with the man who had lured Hadassah from her home and threatened to rape her. My mother says the truth can have many faces. Maybe Greg had been both people.

Something was nagging at me. I reviewed in my mind what Justin had told me. "You said other teachers suspected Prosser of cheating, Justin. Wouldn't that have rung bells and shown him to be a liar?"

Justin looked at his mother.

"Tell Molly," she said. "She'll understand."

But he drummed his fingers on the table and waited until Cheryl had brought the mugs to the table and was sitting again.

"Justin," she said.

He sighed. "Prosser found out that Greg had a thing with a senior at the high school where he taught before he came to Torat Tzion." He was looking at me, daring me to say something.

All I could come up with was, "Oh."

"He made a mistake," Justin said, his tone just short of belligerent. "People make mistakes. That didn't mean Amy was telling the truth about the harassment."

I wondered how certain Justin would be of Shankman's innocence if he knew about Hadassah. "How did Prosser know this?"

"He found a letter from the student in Greg's briefcase. She said their affair was partly her fault, but mostly it was Greg's. He took advantage of her. She was his student. She was too young to know what she was doing. Now she had to deal with the repercussions. Her therapist said she had to work though her anger so she could make decisions about her life. She didn't want to hurt him, but she had to consider what was best."

"She was going to go to the authorities?" I took a tentative sip of the coffee.

Justin shook his head. "She was planning to make their breakup permanent and was thinking of moving to Seattle."

For a moment I didn't put it together. "Melissa Frank," I said. And the repercussion was their daughter?

"Greg showed me the letter when he got it," Cheryl said. "He and Melissa had been having problems, and he'd moved out. He looked like the world was coming to an end. It wasn't just losing Melissa. It was losing Kaitlin, their daughter. Recently, though, he was hopeful. He said he and Melissa were talking about getting back together. I thought maybe he was in denial, but the news said something about reconciliation, too."

"What about the letter?" I asked.

"Prosser made a photocopy," Justin said. "He got hold of a list of Melissa's classmates. He located a dozen or so and found one who was willing to talk."

"And he showed the letter to the principal?"

"His father did. He's on the board of the school. And the kid told Greg if he showed his proof to the principal, Amy would phone Melissa and tell her what Greg had done to her, and to the Weinberg girl. Greg couldn't take that chance. He was hoping he and Melissa could work things out. But if Amy talked to her . . . So he never showed anyone the proof, and the school fired him."

The cheese Danish that had looked so tempting minutes earlier held no interest for me. "Justin, I'm going to ask you something that will upset you, but please understand that I'm just trying to get a clear picture. Okay?"

He stiffened.

"How do you know Amy isn't telling the truth?"

"Because I know Greg." He clenched his jaw. "He would never do something like that. And I talked to Amy's best friend. She told me Amy is crazy about Prosser and would do anything for him."

"How did you meet the friend?"

"I found out where the Torat Tzion kids hang out. I hooked up with this girl and got her to confide in me." A sly smile flashed across Justin's face. "They ruined Greg's life. I wanted to do something, to help." There was no smile now, only anger.

"And this girl told you Amy lied about Greg?"

"Not in so many words," he admitted. "I think she got scared."

"Do a lot of the kids know about all this?"

"As far as I know, just Prosser and Amy. And maybe Amy's best friend. They had to be careful. If word got out, it would all backfire, and they'd be in serious trouble."

It was too much to absorb. I had spent several days and countless hours worrying about Hadassah and trying to find her. In the process, I'd felt increasing outrage toward the man who had taken advantage of her. Nothing that I had heard now diffused that outrage, but my feelings had become complicated.

"Justin, your mother told me you didn't know if you should go to the police. What does all of this have to do with Greg's death?"

"At first Greg was planning to go to the local Jewish newspaper with the story, and maybe the Jewish bureau of education. He even talked about going to the *Times*. He was so angry and depressed. He felt so helpless."

"Wasn't there anyone he could talk to? Someone who would help?"

"He tried talking to Rabbi Bailor. He told the rabbi Amy was lying to protect Prosser. He didn't tell him about his girlfriend and daughter. He didn't know how the rabbi would take that. But Rabbi Bailor told Greg he didn't have a say about hiring or firing outside of Judaic studies. Plus he and the other principal were butting heads. Greg told the rabbi he understood, but he felt let down. Rabbi Bailor talks the talk, but he sure doesn't walk the walk." The young man's lips curled in derision.

Cheryl squeezed her son's hand. "There probably wasn't anything he *could* do, Justin. He did write Greg a letter of recommendation."

"Whatever. The thing is, Greg decided he couldn't talk to anyone.

Because if he did, the whole thing would come out about Melissa. He couldn't do that to her, or his daughter. The last time I talked to him he sounded terrible, like he had nothing to live for. And then today my mom and I heard he was killed in a car accident. And the first thing I thought was, that wasn't an accident. He killed himself. But they made him do it. And they should pay, shouldn't they? Somebody should."

Justin wrapped his hands around his mug. "But if I tell the police, everybody will know Greg killed himself. Melissa, too. They'll have to tell her. And what if Kaitlin finds out? People talk. You know how that is. What kind of legacy is that to leave your daughter? What I'm asking is, do you think I should tell the police or leave it alone? It's not like telling them is going to make a difference, is it? Nothing I say or do will bring him back."

Chapter 31

Bubbie G's hands were floury when she opened the door. "Such a surprise." She wiped her hands on her red-checkered apron and stood on tiptoe to kiss me.

"I was in the neighborhood and decided to stop by, Bubbie. Something smells good."

"Mandelbrot." The Jewish equivalent of almond-flavored biscotti. "Bella came a few minutes ago. I'm popular today." She winked.

Bella Grubner was sitting on Bubbie's olive green velvet couch. She's one of Bubbie's many friends, most of who are Polish-born Holocaust survivors, many of them widows. Bella is big-hearted, but when it comes to gossip, she could teach Liz Smith a few moves. Hence Bubbie's wink.

Bella has a big frame, too. The hug she gave me was practically a Heimlich maneuver.

"You look beautiful, Molly," she said. "If I

didn't know you were wearing a *sheitel,* I would think this is your own hair. Custom, yes? How much did you pay?"

"It was a gift," Bubbie said. "From her parents."

"How's your husband, Molly? Such a good-looking man."

"He's great, thanks."

"You're married eight months already, no?" She eyed my stomach. "I see you put on a little weight. Good news?" She smiled.

"Chocolate," I said.

Bella looked confused, then smiled. "It'll happen, Molly." She patted my arm. "With some people it takes longer. My niece was married three years, and now she has twins. *Kenehoreh,*" she added quickly, to ward off the evil eye.

"Molly has to talk to me about something," Bubbie said. "Private."

"Oh?"

"Police business," I said, assuming a solemn expression. "I need Bubbie's advice."

"Oh." Bella looked at Bubbie with envy.

According to my mom, Bubbie G *qvells* in telling her friends that her granddaughter is chummy with LAPD detectives and is in the know about crime around the city. My former seventy-eight-year-old thrice-widowed landlord, Isaac, took similar pleasure in bragging to his poker buddies about his "well-connected" tenant. Now that reading even large-print material has become frustrating for Bubbie (she found the magnifying machine my parents rented from an eye institute too cumbersome), she has my mother read my column to her every Tuesday and phones to tell me her favorite entries. She's an ardent fan of true crime books and crime fiction—she passed on that love to me—and she rushes to the library to get the latest audio books on tape.

After Bella left, I followed Bubbie into the kitchen, where eight two-inch-high loaves were cooling on racks on the white-tiled counter.

She placed one of the loaves onto a cutting board. "Don't let Bella upset you, Molly. She means well."

"I know. But it *has* been eight months, and I didn't get pregnant with Ron, either."

"Bella can say foolish things, but she's right." Bubbie picked up a knife. "It's in *Hashem*'s hands. And eight months isn't so long, *sheyfeleh*. Sara, Rivka, Rachel—they all waited longer."

I watched, nervous, as she sliced each loaf on the diagonal into one-inch slices, but though Bubbie has only limited peripheral vision, her fingers were sure.

When the slices were in the oven, lying on their sides on a greased cookie sheet, Bubbie brought tea and sugar cookies to the breakfast room table.

"Something is bothering you, Molly," she said. A statement, not a question. "You have a heavy heart. Friday night, too. It's about having a baby, or something else?"

I'm always amazed by how much my sightless grandmother can see. "A man was killed," I said. "Not a nice man, but still."

She nodded. "And?"

"I'm afraid the killer may be someone I know, somebody in the community. And I'm having mixed feelings about the man who was killed."

I told her everything, beginning with Reuben Jastrow's appearance in the lobby of my San Diego hotel. She listened without interrupting, nodding once in a while as she sipped her raspberry tea.

"If I had never gone to Detective Connors," I said when I had finished, "he would never have found out about Hadassah Bailor. He wouldn't have known that the Bailors had a motive."

"The rabbi and his brother-in-law asked you to help, Molly, to use your police connections. This is why they came to you. And the rabbi knew you were going to show the detective the note." Bubbie leaned across the table and took my hand in both of hers. "You went with good intentions. How could you know this would happen? And if, *chas v'shalom*, the rabbi or his family is involved, the truth will come out, Molly, with or without you. This is what was meant to be."

"And what do I tell Justin, Bubbie? Should I encourage him to go to the police?" I had told Cheryl and her son that I needed to think before I advised him what to do.

Bubbie sipped her tea. "This Justin thinks Shankman killed himself, yes? He says Shankman decided not to tell his story to the newspaper. But you're thinking, maybe Shankman changed his mind, yes? And if he did, and this boy who cheated found out, or his father did . . ."

I nodded. "And the boy or his father, or both, went to Shankman's apartment to persuade him not to go public, and they ended up fighting. But where was Dassie when this happened?"

The oven timer pinged. I beat Bubbie to the counter, slipped the mitts on my hands, and moved the cookie sheet to the cooling rack. The mandelbrot were golden brown, flecked with green and red from the chopped pistachios and cranberries Bubbie had added to the dough.

When they were cool enough to touch, Bubbie put a handful in a brown paper bag. Then she handed me a small plastic bag inside of which were a sugar cube and a clove of garlic.

"Put this in your *chulent*," she said, referring to a traditional meat, beans, and potato stew cooked all night in a Crock-Pot and served for *Shabbat* lunch. "I got it yesterday morning at Gusta's grandson's bris. It's a *segulah* for having children."

I had heard about the tradition. "You really think it works, Bubbie?"

"It can't hurt. And you'll have a delicious *chulent*." She smiled.

At the door she kissed me again.

"Should I suggest that to Connors, Bubbie? That this boy who cheated, or his father, might have been worried that Shankman was going to talk to the *Times* and other papers?"

She shook her head. "*Besser gornisht tsu machen aider tsu machen gornisht.* Better to do nothing than to make something into nothing. I know you're worried about the Bailors, Molly, and maybe you want the police to look elsewhere. First find out if there's something."

I probably should have waited a day or so before visiting Melissa Frank, but Justin's story was in my head. And maybe there *was* "something." So instead of going to West L.A., I drove to Mar Vista and parked in front of Melissa's house.

The neighbor I had met Saturday night answered the door. I tried to remember her name. Diane.

"You were here the other night," she said. "Greg's cousin. This must be a terrible time for you."

My lie had come back to bite me. I nodded, feeling lower than dirt, and asked if I could speak to Melissa.

"I'll check. She's trying to get some rest, poor thing. The next few days will be crazy. She's been on the phone since she got back last night from Seattle. She had to tell Greg's parents, and she's been talking to police, and to reporters. I don't know how they found out, but they did." Diane scowled. "I don't think it's sunk in yet, though. And Melissa hasn't figured out a way to tell Kaitlin. But I know she'll want to see you."

"I'm not Greg's cousin," I said.

She stared at me. Her face turned red.

Mine was hot with shame. "I needed to find Greg. I said that to find out where he lived. I'm sorry."

"I think you should leave." Diane started to shut the door.

"Melissa may want to talk to me."

"I doubt that."

"Please tell her this is regarding one of Greg's students at Torat Tzion. If she doesn't want to talk to me, I'll understand."

"Wait here."

Diane looked at me as though I were a snake about to slither through the opening of the door. A minute or so passed before she reappeared.

"Melissa wants to know your name and your connection to Greg."

"My name is Molly Blume. I—"

"That's what you said last time."

"That *is* my name. I never met Greg, but someone asked me to talk to him about a delicate matter. That's what I was trying to do Saturday night."

"Greg was dead Saturday night. The police said his car went over the road Friday night."

"I didn't know that when I came here."

"I'll tell Melissa."

I waited again. The afternoon sun was bright, but the day was chilly. I hugged my arms.

Diane returned. "Melissa doesn't want to talk to you."

"Will you give her my card? In case she changes her mind." I hurried to get a card from my wallet before she shut the door. "Please tell her she can phone me night or day."

Diane glanced at the card and grunted. "You're a reporter. I should have known."

"If you could just give Melissa the card," I said.

"I don't think so." She slammed the door.

I dropped the card in the mailbox and left.

Chapter 32

I had been to the West L.A. station many times, but never to have my fingerprints taken. I parked on Butler, passed through the Pizza Hut orange tile entry and, feeling like Hester Prynne walking around with that A on her chest, took the stairs to the second floor detectives' room.

Jessie Drake wasn't at her desk, but she had left word that I would stop by. Another detective rolled my prints.

"Detective Drake needs this for purposes of elimination," I told him, though he hadn't asked.

"Uh-huh. Did you want to leave a message for Detective Drake?"

I debated writing a note saying I had information and a possible lead regarding Shankman's murder. Bubbie G's cautionary words flashed in front of me.

"No, thanks. Please tell her I was here."

I spent an hour copying crime data at the station, then drove to the Wilshire station, where I did the same and exchanged a warm greeting with Detective Hernandez, and a lukewarm one with Detective Porter, who liked me better before I helped solve Aggie's murder, but now seemed to be thawing.

I arrived home after four and checked my voice mail. Zack had phoned to say he had to visit a congregant in the hospital, so I should eat without him. My sister Edie reminded me that mah jongg would be at her house tonight, instead of Gitty's. "Be on time," she added. And my friend Penny wanted to know if I'd disappeared.

There was no message from Melissa Frank. I hadn't really expected to hear from her.

I returned Penny's call. I hadn't seen her since my wedding, and I missed her. We spoke for over half an hour, covering much of what had happened to both of us in the past seven months. Between Zack, my family, and my writing projects, I often find myself too busy to stay connected with many of my friends, so I enjoyed catching up.

We made a date to see a movie the Saturday night after Thanksgiving—Penny and her husband Bob, Zack and me. I wrote the information in my planner and checked my e-mail. My Amazon numbers had improved—*Sins* was now 22,800—but someone had posted a nasty review. Probably Ron.

I had stopped at the Fairfax Fishery on the way home. I sprinkled garlic salt, paprika, and teriyaki sauce on two trout fillets, covered one in plastic wrap, and put it in the fridge. I broiled the other, ate it with a salad and couscous, and slapped a Post-it on the fridge with cooking instructions for Zack. I added a heart.

I phoned the Bailors and spoke to Nechama. She told me Dassie was resting more comfortably, but wasn't talking much.

"I don't know if you heard the news, Molly. A man who was Dassie's teacher last year died in a car accident. We don't know if we should tell Dassie."

I didn't know whether Nechama Bailor was a great actress, or whether her husband was keeping another secret from her. I didn't want to think about the possibility that the rabbi was keeping other, darker secrets.

"Mom's playing instead of Gitty," Edie told me as I was hanging my coat in the entry closet. "I think she's pregnant."

"Mom?" I like teasing Edie because she's so easy.

"Very funny. Did Gitty say anything to you?"

I shook my head. Even if my sister-in-law *had* told me, I wouldn't have admitted that to Edie. She takes her seniority seriously, and she would have been hurt.

My mother and Mindy were in the breakfast room, setting up the tiles. Aside from having inherited our mother's brown eyes and brown hair, my sisters and I don't look alike, although people see a familial resemblance. Edie, five feet two, is the shortest, with chin-length highlighted hair (she and I are both assisted blondes). Mindy, next in line, is five-ten. I'm five-six; Liora is five-four.

My mother, who taught all us Blume girls mah jongg, has been playing every Monday for over thirty years, but her group has extra players, which is why she could sub for Gitty. Liora plays, too, but she's not as passionate about the game as we are, and most of her nights are occupied with dating. Like Aliza Bailor, I thought.

I took out my four dollars and placed my tiles on my rack. Mah jongg has elements of fourteen-card gin and Rummy Q. It involves luck and strategy and a familiarity with the numbered Chinese characters painted onto the ivory-like tiles (Cracks, Bams, Dots, Flowers, Soaps). No matter how tired or preoccupied I am when I arrive, I know I'll find relaxation and comfort in the form of nosh and conversation, which is rarely serious.

Tonight was no different until the second game, when Edie brought up Shankman's fatal crash.

"They didn't identify the school," Edie said, naming a tile and tossing it onto the table, "but it's obviously Torat Tzion. I hope there's no scandal involved. Have you heard details from the cops, Molly?"

"Not that I can say." I scooped a handful of warm popcorn from the bowl.

She looked at me shrewdly. "So there *is* something."

I tossed a tile. "Three Bam."

"If Shankman was planning to reconcile with his girlfriend, why would he kill himself?" Edie asked.

"Maybe it was just a terrible accident," my mother said. "Why read into it? Let him be." Her tone was sharp. For my mother, that's unusual.

"You sound as if you knew him, Mom," I said.

"He gave a session on teaching AP classes at an all-day educators' conference sponsored by the Bureau. He impressed me as being knowledgeable and passionate about his students. And he was so young. Not even thirty."

We finished the game without much talking. Mindy won. We turned the tiles facedown, mixed them, and set up for another round.

I passed Edie three tiles. "Speaking of APs, I hear that kids cheat on them." Not my smoothest segue. "Is that going on at Sharsheret, Mom?"

"There's definitely cheating, although I don't know about on the APs," she said. "We talk about it at every faculty meeting. We're vigilant, but students are creative. And cheating is epidemic."

"And endemic," Mindy said. "If there's a test, someone will cheat. How are they doing it now?"

"The usual. They write information in teeny letters on their palms or on the inside of their fingers, or on a stretched rubber band. Two weeks ago my colleague caught a student who peeled off a water-bottle label, printed math theorems on the back, and glued the label back on."

"Clever," Edie said.

"And cheating has gone hi-tech," my mother said. "Kids text-message answers with their cell phones. At one school, they used a device to get their teacher's password and steal his exams and his answers. And they buy term papers online. It's big business. Go to Google, type in 'term paper.' You'll get thousands of sites. 'Plagiarism-free papers, guaranteed. Custom research. Best prices.' It's sickening."

"It's commerce," Mindy said.

"How do I cheat—let me count the ways." I poured myself a glass of diet peach Snapple.

"Why is that legal?" Edie asked Mindy. "Why don't they stop the people who are selling the papers?"

"They claim they're providing a service. They're not in control of whether the student neglects to credit his sources." Mindy shrugged. "A Wal-Mart heiress allegedly paid her roommate twenty thousand dollars over three and a half years to write papers and other assignments."

"I heard that." Edie nodded. "They named a university sports arena after her." She frowned. "What was her name?"

"Paige."

"How much per page per Paige?" I said, and we all laughed. "But that can't work for the APs, Mom. Students don't know the questions or essay topics until they're in the room taking the exam."

"No, but someone who takes the exam in New York or Ohio phones the answers to a friend in an earlier time zone." My mother looked at her tiles. "And with camera phones, they can take a picture of the questions or material and e-mail the page or pages."

"So why don't schools ban cell phones during exams?" Mindy asked.

"That's Sharsheret's new policy. I'm sure other schools have done the same. But parents complain. They want to be able to be in touch with their children, in case of an emergency. Anyway, as soon as we figure out how to stop one form of cheating, they come up with another method."

"Like car thieves," Edie said. Her Suburban had been stolen and stripped two months earlier. "I knew kids who cheated in high school and in college. They thought it was cool, no big deal."

"It's more complicated," my mother said. "There's incredible pressure for students to excel, to get into the Ivy Leagues. And the competition can turn ugly. A friend at another school told me that a top-ranked senior lowered her rival's grades on her transcripts to improve her own chances of getting into the top schools. Eventually, the truth came out, but still."

"What happened to the girl who changed the grades?" I asked.

"All her college acceptances were withdrawn, and she didn't graduate with her class. I don't know what she's doing now."

"Writing term papers for sale," Mindy said. "Or running a political campaign."

"Obviously, that's an extreme example," my mother said. "But kids in college prep tracks have insane schedules. Sixty or seventy pages to read a night, labs, term papers, exams they have to ace every semester—double all that if they're in a yeshiva. Plus all the extracurricular programs they *have* to take, because every other student is taking them to show admission boards that they're well-rounded, exceptional students and leaders of tomorrow."

"That's quite a speech." Mindy smiled.

"It was, wasn't it?" My mother's laugh was self-conscious. "I wish I had answers. In the meantime, kids come to class like zombies because they drink coffee or take caffeine tablets so they can pull all-nighters. If it's not caffeine, it's Ritalin."

"Like the mom on *Desperate Housewives,*" Edie said. "Desperate Schoolchildren."

"It's not funny." My mother gave her a warning look.

"Or Desperate Teachers," Mindy said. "I heard that's going on, too."

Edie looked appalled. "Teachers cheating?"

"It's the pressure," Mindy said. "With the No Child Left Behind law, if kids don't do well, the school could lose federal funding. So teachers 'help' students along."

"How?" I asked.

"They drop hints during an exam, or write the correct answers on the board. They change answers on score sheets, give out the real exam as the sample test. Sometimes they give extra time to take a standardized exam, or they don't include a poor student's results."

"But what about on an AP test?" I asked my mother.

"I don't see how a teacher could tamper with the essay. But with the multiple-choice sections, the teacher could change the blackened ovals. Or the proctor could do it."

"Why would a teacher do that?" Edie asked.

"Status," Mindy said. "Bragging rights."

"So this is what my kids have to look forward to?" Edie said. "Wonderful."

"Next on *Oprah,* 'Teachers who cheat and the cheaters who teach them,' " I said.

Zack was studying Talmud on the phone with a friend when I came home after eleven. I blew him a kiss and went into the bedroom, where I changed into flannel pajamas. I save the sexy stuff for the right time of the month.

I was brushing my teeth when I heard the second phone line ring. I rinsed my mouth and hurried to my nightstand. Maybe Melissa Frank had changed her mind and was willing to talk to me.

I picked up the receiver. "Hello?"

"Molly? This is Irene."

"Irene, this is *such* a coincidence. I was going to phone you tomorrow at the office."

"At the office?" She sounded confused.

I realized the voice didn't sound right. "You *did* say your name is Irene?"

"This is Irene Jakaitis. From Yamashiro? We met Thursday night?"

"Oh, of course. Sorry. I thought you were a different Irene."

Irene Gurstner: my friend, and the therapist who helped me work through Aggie's murder and other traumas.

"You said I should call if I remembered anything else," the waitress said. "Well, I didn't, but I thought you'd want to know that someone phoned about your cousin and the guy she was with. He said he was her father."

I sat down on my bed. "When was this?"

"Friday afternoon, after four? The maître d' said this man told him you were here Thursday night, asking about his daughter, Dassie, and the guy she was with. The maître d' told him, yes, your cousin was here. The man wanted to know who you talked to, because he wanted to thank her. Meaning me. So the maître d' called me to the phone, and the man thanked me and wanted to know what I told you, because he said you didn't give him details. Did you?"

"Not so many, no," I said, my heart sinking.

"Anyway, I told him about the wedding ceremony and about the damage to the car, how it almost ruined the evening. So he said, right, you told him about that. But I thought something was funny."

"What do you mean?"

"He said he couldn't remember the license plate number of the car. I mean, how can you forget Rocky Road, right?"

"Right." Perspiration beaded my lip. "So you told him what it was?"

"Uh-huh. I didn't see why not to. If he's not your cousin's dad, why would he be calling? But the more I got to thinking about it, the whole conversation was strange, you know? So that's why I'm calling you. I thought you'd want to know. By the way, did you ever talk to the guy who was with your cousin?"

Irene had obviously not seen the news about Shankman. "I'm sorry to say he was in a fatal car accident, Irene. It was on the news today."

"Oh, my God! What about your cousin?"

"She wasn't in the car."

"Thank God. That's why I don't like watching the news or listening to it. It's always so depressing." Irene sighed. "They were such a sweet couple, you know?"

Chapter 33

Hadassah wondered when the detectives would be back.

They had searched the house yesterday evening, when they came a second time. Hadassah had heard them walking up the stairs. Her father had just returned from *shul*. She heard him say, "My daughter's resting, she's not up to talking," speaking louder than he usually did, so she knew he was trying to warn her, like last time. When they entered the room, her arms were under the comforter, and the shard was where she had put it, between the mattress and box spring. She kept her eyes sealed while the detectives opened her dresser drawers and the closet door.

The male detective said, "Rabbi Bailor, we have a witness who saw a young woman Friday night a few blocks from Mr. Shankman's apartment building. The woman fits your daughter's description. She was wearing a white blouse and skirt. She was running and she looked upset. Where are the clothes your daughter was wearing when she came home Friday night?"

Her father said, "I don't know. I'll ask my wife."

Hadassah didn't know what her mother had done with the clothes. She hadn't asked Hadassah about the white silk sweater and satin skirt she'd never seen before, or about the stains splattered across both—stains she must have suspected were blood. She had bundled the skirt and sweater and taken them away after she'd helped Hadassah into pajamas and bandaged her palm. Or maybe before. Hadassah couldn't remember, and some things weren't clear. Her mother must have shown the clothes to Hadassah's father. "Chaim, what should we do with these?"

Her father hadn't mentioned the clothes to Hadassah. Maybe he had thrown them away in a stranger's trash bin. Hadassah hoped so. She never wanted to see them again.

The detectives left the room. Hadassah wasn't sure whether they were gone for good, so she didn't move. When the woman returned twenty minutes later, her partner, Phil, wasn't with her. Neither was Hadassah's father. Jessie shut the door and pulled over a chair, the way she had the first time. Even when Hadassah's eyes were open, she looked straight ahead, so she didn't really know what Jessie looked like, just that she had long dark hair. But her voice was low and soothing, and she spoke as if she had all the time in the world. She had the kind of voice that made you feel safe, like Dr. McIntyre's.

"How are you, Hadassah?" she asked. "I'm sure you're frightened. I would be, if I were you. You went through a terrible ordeal, and we're all glad that you're okay.

"We know that you were at the apartment with Greg Shankman, Hadassah. We found his blood in the apartment. We found someone else's blood, too. Was it yours, Hadassah? If he tried to hurt you and you fought him, you have nothing to worry about, but you need to tell us.

"Maybe you were scared and phoned someone to help you. I can understand that. I would have been scared, too. Did you phone someone, Hadassah? Did Greg try to hurt the person you phoned? That would be self-defense, too, Hadassah. We just want to know what happened.

"We have the clothes you were wearing Friday night, a white skirt and blouse. Your mother washed them, even though they say 'dry clean only.' I guess she wanted to get the blood out. Greg's blood. The thing is, Hadassah, even if you wash clothes, it's hard to get all the blood out, especially in the seams. I think there *is* blood in the seams. The lab guys will find it, even the tiniest amount. And lab tests will tell us if it's Greg's blood. But it would be so much easier if you told us now. Then we won't have to bother you again.

"I think Greg tried to hurt you, Hadassah," Jessie said. "I think you fought him off, and I'm so glad you did. I think that's how you got his blood on your white blouse and skirt. It *is* his blood, isn't it?

"And then you phoned someone you could trust. You needed help. I would have phoned for help, too. And that person said, 'Get out, Hadassah. I'll take care of everything.' And he *did* take care of everything, because there's nothing of you in that apartment, Hadassah. Not your clothes, or makeup, or cell phone. But we know you were there, Hadassah."

Hadassah decided her father was with the other detective, Phil. That's why he wasn't here with her.

"We talked to your friend Sara," Jessie Drake said. "Sara told us that when you left her house you were wearing a black skirt and sweater, and you had a black purse. And inside your purse were your wallet and your cell phone and makeup and house keys. But we didn't find any of those things in Greg's apartment, Hadassah. Not the clothes or purse or wallet or cell phone or keys. And we didn't find any of those things here, in your house.

"Do you know where your clothes are, Hadassah? Or your cell phone or wallet? Or your purse? Or your keys?

"What do you remember, Hadassah?

"Is that Greg's blood on the clothes you wore Friday night, Hadassah? If you tell us, you'll feel much better, I promise. I know you don't want to get anyone in trouble, Hadassah, especially people you love.

But you know the truth is going to come out, don't you? If you called someone to help you, and if that person protected himself against Greg, well, we understand that. It's self-defense.

"Was it your father, Hadassah?

"Was it your brother?

"Don't be afraid, Hadassah. Just tell me the truth."

Hadassah wasn't sure how long Jessie Drake stayed, although she seemed to be talking and talking forever in that slow, quiet voice that made Hadassah want to open her eyes and tell her everything. She couldn't tell Jessie, ever, but she longed to tell someone. If she did, maybe the sounds and smells and images would go away and she wouldn't be afraid to sleep. The click of the key turning in the lock. The scent of her own fear as she cowered, shivering, in the total darkness of the closet. The impossibly rapid beating of her heart when she heard the doorknob being twisted open. The shock in his eyes when she jammed the glass shard into his throat, his howl, the blood that came spurting out when she yanked the shard out, prepared to strike again.

He had pressed his hand against his throat and staggered backward. She had shoved him, hard. So hard that he lost his footing. Even before his head slammed onto the hardwood floor with a loud thunk, she ran to the door. Sliding the deadbolt, she pulled the door open. She found the stairwell and, her footsteps echoing like artillery fire, raced down the stairs to the ground floor.

She caught a glimpse of herself in the mirror in the lobby. Blood was on her hand, her face, stark against the white of her clothes. The blood was warm, sticky, metallic. She wiped her face with her hands. Hugging her arms to camouflage the stains on her chest, she fled the building.

Right or left? She didn't know. And she couldn't ask anyone. She couldn't risk drawing attention to herself.

She turned right and ran blocks before she realized she was going in the wrong direction. A man walking by stared at her. She waited until he passed. Then she turned and jogged up dark streets until she saw the bright lights she hoped were Olympic Boulevard. Her breath was ragged. She had miles to go. The shard was in her hand. She had become aware of the stinging pain coming from her palm. She stopped and saw the blood that oozed from the cuts. She continued moving, but slowed her pace.

She remembered with sudden panic that she had called for help. She didn't know if he'd received her message. If he had, he would be arriving any second to save her. She wanted to warn him, but the phone was on the closet floor. She had needed to keep one hand free, and in the other she had been gripping the shard. She'd been terrified that the phone's ringing would betray her, so she had switched it to vibrate mode and flipped it shut after whispering into it the address she'd found on an envelope in the box.

It's Dassie. Help me, please.

She heard footsteps now, coming up the stairs. Maybe it was the police. But it was her mother, wanting to know if Hadassah needed anything before she went to sleep. Hadassah shook her head. "Sweet dreams, baby," her mother said.

Hadassah wondered at what point, if ever, Dinah had allowed herself to sleep without worrying that Schechem would plague her dreams. She had been thinking about Dinah since Friday night. She had many questions she would have liked to ask her father, though she didn't know if he had answers.

Had Dinah tried to escape after Schechem kidnapped and raped her and held her captive? Had she waited, certain that her father or brothers would save her? How had she felt, knowing that two of her brothers had killed to avenge her? And how had those brothers felt about the blood they had shed? And what about the rest of the family? After the fact, did they ever talk about what had happened?

Hadassah's father had told her that, according to the *Midrash*, Dinah had been taken in by one of the brothers who had rescued her. She had given birth to Schechem's daughter, Osnath, who was adopted by a wealthy Egyptian, Potiphar, and eventually married her uncle, Joseph. He recognized her through the amulet her grandfather, Jacob, had given her.

But that was in the *Midrash*, not in the Torah. The Torah never mentioned Dinah again. It was as though she had ceased to exist. Because Dinah's story was concluded, her father explained.

Sometimes Hadassah thought it would be easier if she ceased to exist. Other times she wished she had a protective amulet, like Osnath's. She wedged her hand between the mattress and box spring and touched the shard. She wondered when her own story and that of her family would be concluded, and how.

Chapter 34

Tuesday, November 23, 9:18 a.m. Along Kingsley Drive and Sunset Boulevard, a 54-year-old suspect assaulted a 19-year-old female until she lost consciousness. The suspect later fled the scene.

I'd been sorely tempted to phone Connors as soon as I hung up with Irene Jakaitis, but my vindication came with a stiff price tag. Zack had commiserated with me about my dilemma. Sleep on it, he'd advised.

Morning didn't bring wisdom or resolution. I was anxious to redeem my good name with Connors and repair our bruised friendship. Irene would verify that someone had dogged my steps and learned the license plate number of the car that belonged to the man who had lured Hadassah away from her home, a man who now lay in a morgue, a victim of foul play. In all likelihood that someone was Rabbi Bailor.

Before falling asleep, I'd reconstructed what I thought was a logical sequence of events, based on two facts and on numerous assumptions—never a wise idea.

The facts: Late Thursday night I'd told the rabbi I had a possible lead, but I'd refused to elaborate. Friday afternoon, someone spoke to Irene Jakaitis and elicited the license plate number of Dassie's date's vehicle.

My assumptions: Rabbi Bailor had questioned my story about the fender-bender. His suspicions raised, he'd queried his daughter Aliza about my second visit Thursday night and learned that I'd wanted to know where someone would go on a romantic date, that the place was Yamashiro, and that I suspected Dassie had gone there Sunday night.

My deduction: Rabbi Bailor had spoken to Irene.

Another assumption: The rabbi had recognized the license plate and had known on Friday afternoon that the man he was seeking was Greg Shankman.

And then what?

That was the question that had given me a restless night, the reason I was loath to report my conversation with Irene Jakaitis to Connors.

And I could be wrong. I had no proof that Rabbi Bailor had made the call, no reason to think he'd recognized the license plate aside from the fact that Shankman was dead. Even if the rabbi *had* identified Shankman, I had no proof that he'd acted on that knowledge. He could have shared what he'd learned with someone else. His son, his brother-in-law, Dr. McIntyre.

I needed to know the truth. I needed to know whether Rabbi Bailor had manipulated me, just as Connors had been convinced that I'd manipulated him. So I drove to Torat Tzion, and I fervently hoped that my assumptions, like Connors's, were wrong and I would learn that, as Bubbie G would say, "something" was in fact "nothing."

Two local television news vans were stationed in front of "the Orthodox Jewish school in the heart of Beverly Hills." I parked around the corner and walked to Burton Way. When I neared the school, I looked straight ahead, avoiding eye contact with three reporters who were leaning against the vans, lying in wait. I have several contacts at the *L.A. Times* but almost none in television or radio, so I wasn't worried about being recognized.

I did recognize Lydia Martin, the field reporter who had covered Shankman's death. She was tiny in person, almost skeletal in a black wool pants suit. She caught up with me as I headed to the lobby.

"Do you teach at Torat Tzion?" Lydia asked, mangling the school's name.

"No." I tried opening the lobby door. It was locked.

"Did you know Greg Shankman, the history teacher who died Friday night?" she asked.

Answering her had been a mistake. I rapped on the glass.

"What about Hadassah Bailor, the principal's daughter? We've learned that the police have talked to her about Mr. Shankman's death."

Someone, either at Hollywood or at West L.A., had obviously leaked the connection. I did my best to keep a blank expression. It's no secret that the media rely on "unnamed sources" at police stations around the city. I wondered if the unnamed source was Connors, or Jessie Drake. Maybe they'd wanted to shake things up.

"Can you tell me anything about Mr. Shankman's relationship with Hadassah Bailor?"

The guard approached. He'd been casually efficient on Friday. Now he stood with his feet spread apart and his muscular arms folded across his puffed out chest. Mr. Clean, or Popeye after ingesting a can of spinach.

"No media," he said.

"I was here Friday." My business card says I'm a columnist and freelance reporter. I took out my driver's license and held it against the glass door.

He scanned the license. "What's the nature of your business?"

"I'm here to see Sue Horowitz."

The guard walked to his desk and picked up the phone.

"Who is Sue Horowitz?" Lydia asked. "Is she connected with Hadassah Bailor?"

Lydia was like a puppy yipping at my heels. I continued to ignore her, and after half a minute she gave up and walked back to the van.

Part of me was annoyed with her persistence. The other part sympathized. I am often that yipping puppy.

The guard put down the phone and nodded at me. A moment later he unlocked the lobby doors.

"Not you," he told Lydia, who had returned faster than a stain on a newly shampooed carpet.

"Are you an attorney?" the reporter called as I slipped into the lobby.

But she was talking to glass. After relocking the doors, the guard checked the contents of my purse. I passed through the metal detector and was headed to Sue's office when I saw Dr. Mendes exiting an office. Same suit, different blouse.

She turned and headed in the opposite direction.

"Dr. Mendes," I called, hurrying to catch up. "Molly Blume?" I added, when she didn't acknowledge me.

She stopped and turned around. The principal looked harried and had shadows under her eyes.

"I can't talk to you now, Molly. I assume you heard about Mr. Shankman? The students are upset, of course. Many of them knew him. And I'm sure you saw the media camped outside?"

I nodded. "I can imagine this is a tense time for everyone."

"Yes, and I don't think it's going to get better any time soon." She smoothed her hair behind her ear. "So I'm afraid we'll have to indefinitely postpone your interviewing students. I'm sorry."

"I understand. I *would* like to discuss something with you, when you have a moment. There's been talk about cheating going on at Torat Tzion."

"Cheating is a fact of life at every school, Molly." Her words were measured, her patience strained. "I'm sure your mother will tell you the same thing." She glanced at her watch.

"I don't mean students. Apparently, there was a problem with Mr. Shankman and the APs he proctored."

Dr. Mendes stiffened. "Where did you hear that?" she asked, her voice razor sharp.

"I'm afraid I can't reveal my source. Is that why Mr. Shankman was fired, Dr. Mendes?"

"I can't comment about Mr. Shankman, Molly. As far as I know, there was no irregularity with any of the APs he gave or proctored. Mr. Shankman was a dedicated teacher, always professional. I would be surprised and saddened to find out that he tampered with exams." She sighed. "Although from what the media is saying, there's a side to Mr. Shankman none of us knew."

"So you're saying he *may* have tampered with exams?"

She frowned. "I'm not saying anything of the sort. That would be irresponsible and slanderous and unfair. Mr. Shankman can't defend himself. And rumors about what he may have done wouldn't be fair to his students, or to the school. Promise me that if you learn anything else from your source, you'll come to me before you print anything?"

I promised that I would.

Sue was on the phone when I entered. She held up two fingers and motioned for me to sit. I gazed at the ceramic birds on the filing cabinet.

"You picked a bad day, darlin'," she said when she hung up. "The phone hasn't stopped ringing since I got here, and I've got more than twenty calls to return. Y'all heard what happened to Greg Shankman, right?" She sighed. "It's too much to take in. First they said he's dead. Now they're saying he was killed."

"The media?" I hadn't listened to the news this morning. Obviously, a mistake.

"Them, too." Sue puckered her lips. "Two detectives came yesterday. A pretty woman and a mountain of a man. They searched Rabbi's office and his closet, and Dassie's locker. I can't imagine what they thought they'd find."

The woman, I guessed, was Jessie Drake. The man didn't sound like Connors. Probably Phil Okum, Jessie's partner. "Did they take anything?"

"Nothing from Rabbi's office or closet. I don't know about Dassie's locker. They asked me about Mr. Shankman. Why he was fired, did he have run-ins with kids, and if yes, which ones. I told them they'd have to talk to Dr. Mendes. She has Mr. Shankman's file."

I was gratified to learn that the police were pursuing other avenues. "Is Rabbi Bailor in today, Sue?"

"He is, but he's not taking calls or seeing anyone. Dr. Mendes is

dealing with the press and the parents. I don't know which is worse."
After a quick glance at the door to the rabbi's adjoining office, Sue
leaned across the desk. "Now they're saying Mr. Shankman is the one
Dassie ran away with," she said, her voice just above a whisper. "The
media, I mean. I still can't believe it, but I guess it's true. They said he
had a little girl, that he was depressed because his girlfriend broke up
with him. But why would he do that to Dassie? And why would she
run away with him? Did Rabbi tell you anything?"

I shook my head.

"I don't have the heart to ask him," she said. "He's been going
around in a daze since Monday."

The phone rang. Sue picked up the receiver and told whoever was
on the line that she'd be happy to take a message for Rabbi Bailor.

"Is there something y'all wanted to ask me, Molly?" she said when
she hung up. "To be honest, I was surprised when the guard told
me you were here, now that Dassie's safe at home. Thank God," she
added. "That's a miracle and a half, isn't it? That she got away, I mean.
She could've been in that car with Mr. Shankman."

I nodded. "I wanted to talk to someone who knew Mr. Shankman,
to try to get a handle on why he would do that to Rabbi Bailor's family. You said the rabbi liked him."

"He did. I think that's why Rabbi is taking this so hard, Molly."

"Maybe Mr. Shankman just lost it, you know? Being fired, losing his
girlfriend, losing his daughter. I heard he bought a new car right before
he was fired. I guess he thought he'd lose that, too, if he couldn't make
the payments. Did you ever see it?"

Sue shook her head. "It's not like we have a parking lot for faculty
or staff. Just two spots—one for Rabbi, the other for Dr. Mendes. The
rest of us have to find street parking. I've had my share of parking tickets, thank you very much." She sniffed.

A dead end, I thought.

"I know Greg was excited when he bought the car," Sue said. "It
was his first new one."

"Maybe Rabbi Bailor would know," I said. "Men are into cars."

"Darlin', Rabbi wouldn't know a Moped from a Lexus. Ask him

anything about the Torah, and he'll cite chapter and verse. But cars?" Sue smiled.

"I think they said on the news that Greg Shankman had one of those specialty license plates."

"Did he? Oh, right. I remember he talked about getting one." The phone rang again. Sue picked up the receiver. "Torat Tzion. I can check, but it'll take a few minutes." She placed her hand on the receiver. "It was nice seeing y'all. You take care now."

Chapter 35

==

Lydia Martin and company were still on the sidewalk when I exited the lobby. Pretty soon they would take root and sprout leaves, I thought as I headed for the corner. Lydia took a few steps toward me but stopped and turned her attention to a man who was approaching the school from the other direction. Lucky me. Poor him.

Fifteen minutes later I was home. After putting a load of laundry into the washing machine and talking to Zack, I sat at my desk and began entering the data I'd collected yesterday from Wilshire and West L.A. It's not an exciting activity, and the column doesn't pay much, but I'd hoped that a byline would give me a toehold in the media world. Five years later I haven't won a Pulitzer, but I've developed contacts at several papers for whom I freelance regularly. And once in a while I come across a crime I find puzzling or intriguing, enough to make me investigate. One investigation turned into the true crime book I'd recently finished, *The Lady From Twentynine Palms.*

Today I didn't find anything intriguing—mostly car thefts, residential burglaries, a number of street muggings. While my fingers typed, my mind returned to my conversation with Sue. Not a total waste. I'd learned that Jessie Drake was investigating possible run-ins between Shankman and one or more of his students. I wondered whether the detective was merely being thorough or whether she was following a lead. And if so, what lead.

I had also learned that Rabbi Bailor was oblivious to cars. If so, he probably wouldn't have recognized Shankman's license plate number. And if he'd tried to identify the car owner, he would have reached a dead end, as I had.

So maybe Rabbi Bailor *hadn't* known on Friday that Hadassah was with Greg Shankman . . .

Then why had Hadassah left that night? I pictured the wounds on her arm, the blood on the floor, on the box. There had been more blood, Jessie Drake had said.

Hadassah's blood? Shankman's?

I wrote both names on a sheet of paper, circled them, and connected the circles with a line.

Shankman must have assaulted Hadassah. Somehow she escaped. Had she killed him in self-defense?

Someone had tried to remove the blood. The same person who moved Shankman from his apartment to his car and drove the car off the road? Hadassah wouldn't have been up to the task. Someone had also removed any signs that Hadassah had been in the apartment. From the little I knew about the teenager, I didn't think she would have had the presence of mind to eliminate evidence.

Unless someone had directed her.

Jessie had suggested that Hadassah had phoned for help, and I had to admit that made sense. But whom had Hadassah phoned?

And what if Shankman was alive when Hadassah phoned? Shimon and Levi, Dinah's brothers, had murdered Schechem and his townspeople to rescue their sister and avenge her honor.

With an objective mind and a heavy heart, I wrote Rabbi Bailor's name and Gavriel's, drew circles around them, and connected them to Hadassah. I debated, and added a circle for Reuben Jastrow.

Maybe Hadassah hadn't phoned anyone. Maybe she ran home and told her family what had happened. And Rabbi Bailor, alone or with Gavriel, went to Shankman's apartment and removed Hadassah's belongings. And transferred Shankman's body to his car, and drove the car off the road?

Saturday night, after *Shabbat*, not Friday night. Rabbi Bailor wouldn't have violated the Sabbath to protect his daughter. Or would he?

The ringing of the phone startled me. It was Cheryl Wexner.

"I'm afraid to turn on the news and learn the next awful development," she told me. "They're saying Greg was killed, that he had a relationship with Hadassah Bailor."

"I know." I told Cheryl about the reporters I'd seen in front of the school.

"Honestly, I don't know what to think. My first reaction was that they're making this up. But they're careful about what they put on the air, aren't they? They could be sued. And if what they're saying is true . . ."

"I know," I said again, trying to decide what to tell her.

"But I don't—Oh." Cheryl was quiet a moment. "When you phoned Friday, Molly, you said you needed to talk about Hadassah. It was about Greg, wasn't it?"

"I didn't know when I phoned you that Greg was involved," I said, glancing at the circles I'd drawn. "Hadassah ran away with someone she met in a chat room. The Bailors asked me to help find her."

"Because you have police connections," Cheryl said.

"Something like that. Rabbi Bailor thought Hadassah might have confided in you and mentioned something that would help us identify who she was with."

"She never said a word about Greg, probably because she knew I would have talked her out of getting involved with him." Cheryl sounded pensive. "But didn't you say Hadassah met someone in a chat room?"

"I think Greg pretended to meet her there. By the time they met face-to-face, Hadassah was hooked. And her friend told me Hadassah had a crush on him. I'm sure Hadassah didn't know about his girlfriend or daughter. Rabbi Bailor didn't."

"But why would Greg do something like that? And why would he pick Hadassah?"

"Maybe he resented Rabbi Bailor for not going to bat for him, and took out his resentment on his daughter."

"That's not the Greg I knew."

"Obviously, he had a psychological problem, Cheryl. He dated his high school student. He fathered a child with her." On my paper I wrote "Melissa," circled her name, and connected the circle to Shank-man.

"One mistake doesn't mean he was a predator," Cheryl said, but her voice lacked conviction.

"Maybe he *was* harassing Amy." And Batya Weinberg, I thought. "Greg may have been wonderful to Justin, and not so wonderful with young girls."

Cheryl was silent. I added Batya's name and a question mark.

"I can't tell Justin," Cheryl said. "This would break his heart. He's been upset for months about Greg. When he heard Greg had died, he broke down and cried. He was much calmer after he talked to you, by the way. Thank you for coming."

"I didn't do anything."

"You listened. You cared."

"Has Justin decided to talk to the police?"

"Do you think he should?"

"I don't know. If Greg wasn't planning to go public with this whole thing, then I don't see how Justin's information would help the police in their investigation."

"Into Greg's murder, you mean. I can't absorb that. Who would want to kill him?"

I decided to let Cheryl work that out for herself. "By the way, Cheryl. When we met, you mentioned you were concerned about Hadassah, too. Why?"

"I thought she was depressed. After you phoned me on Friday, I contacted Rabbi Bailor to make sure it was all right to talk to you. He told me you were a friend of the family and were trying to help Hadassah. I could tell that he couldn't talk, that someone was in the office."

"Could be."

"The thing is, I feel guilty, Molly. I met with Hadassah several times. She was under tremendous stress. I don't think she wanted to go to an Ivy League college, or law school. She was doing that for her father. And she talked about Batya Weinberg a great deal. The girl Justin mentioned, the one who had a heart attack? Hadassah hinted one time that Batya might have killed herself. So I was worried, because Hadassah and Batya were close, and I had recently read about cluster suicides."

"I read about that, too." A teen commits suicide. Soon after, one or more close friends do the same. A frightening thought . . .

"Anyway, I didn't know if I should tell Hadassah's parents. I didn't want to alarm them unnecessarily. And I knew that Hadassah was seeing Dr. McIntyre, so I assumed she talked to him about Batya. And I told him what Hadassah was doing, just in case she *didn't* tell him, and her parents didn't know."

"Doing?"

"Cutting herself. A lot of teens do it. I saw her arm. She made up some story about being scratched by a neighbor's cat, but I didn't buy it."

Chapter 36

===

Melissa answered the door. I recognized her from the photo in Greg Shankman's apartment, but the photo hadn't shown the freckles. She was wearing jeans and a black cable-knit V-neck sweater over a white T-shirt. With her brown hair in a ponytail, she looked more like a teenage babysitter than a mother of a four-year-old.

"I thought you were my friend Judy," she said. "Do I know you?" Her voice was friendly, open.

"I'm Molly Blume. I stopped by the other day?"

It took a second or so before accusation replaced the friendliness. She narrowed her eyes. "You said you were Greg's cousin."

"I'd like to explain," I said. "I don't blame you for being upset."

Behind her, a voice called, "Mommy? Can I go on the swing now?"

"In a sec', hon." Melissa faced me. "You're a reporter, right. That's what your card said."

At least she hadn't slammed the door shut. "I freelance, and I write books and a weekly column."

"I talked to reporters Sunday night, but I didn't tell them much more than they knew. They were here when I got back from Seattle. How did they find out so fast?" She shook her head.

"I know this is a terrible time for you, Ms. Frank, but if I could have a few minutes of your time?"

She studied me. "You told my neighbor you wanted to talk to me about one of Greg's students. What about him?"

"Greg suspected him of cheating. I think Greg found proof. I'm wondering if you could tell me more about that."

"Why?"

"I'm wondering if that had anything to do with his death."

She thought that over, then opened the door wide. Stepping inside, I was assaulted by the overpowering scent of days-old floral arrangements that filled the living room. Stacks of toys and the boxes they had come in covered the floor.

"People have been bringing stuff since we came home," Melissa said. "I won't have to cook till next year. Kaitlin, say hi to Mommy's friend Molly."

The little girl was feeding a doll with a miniature bottle. She was wearing a sweater with Disney characters over black leggings, sitting the way only children can—bent legs wide apart, her weight on her shins, her red-and-white sneakers touching her hips, her little butt an inch off the carpet.

"Hi, Kaitlin." I smiled.

"Can we go outside now, Mommy?" She had a sweet, round face, blond curls, and a hint of her mother's freckles.

And no father, I thought. Hearing that Greg Shankman had a daughter was one thing. Seeing her in the flesh was more painful.

"Sure, baby." Melissa smiled at her daughter. "She's been cooped up indoors, poor thing," she told me.

Kaitlin put down the bottle, held on to the doll, and jumped to her feet. Swinging the doll by an arm, she raced down a narrow hall to a door that led to the backyard and waited for us to catch up.

A red metal swing set took up most of the small yard, which was enclosed with a cinder-block wall and brightened with pockets of pansies and straggly impatiens. In the corner were a pink tricycle and a yellow scooter.

Melissa strapped her daughter into a swing and set it in motion. The swing creaked as it moved back and forth. The girl squealed. From where I stood, it looked as though her red shoes were touching the gray-blue sky.

"I haven't told Kaitlin," Melissa told me in a sad, low voice. "I haven't found the right time, or the words to tell her she's never going to see her daddy again. First they said maybe Greg killed himself. Now they're saying he was killed. I don't know what to believe."

"Do you know anyone who would want to kill Greg?"

She shook her head. "Greg got along well with people. His students loved him. Well, except for this one kid you were asking about, a big-time cheater."

"Greg didn't tell you his name?"

"Higher, Mommy! Higher!"

"He may have. I don't remember." Melissa pushed the swing harder. "He spent the summer getting the goods on this kid. I'd asked him to move out, so maybe he needed something to focus on. Anyway, the first week in September Greg had proof. He showed it to the principal, but she told him it wasn't enough. So he quit. He didn't want to teach in a school where they took the word of a cheater over his."

Not the same version I'd heard. I wasn't surprised that Shankman hadn't told Melissa that he'd been fired and accused of sexual harassment.

"Greg was intense, you know?" Melissa said. "And impulsive. And he got into moods where he thought the whole world was against him. That's one of the reasons we split up."

"Is that why you got a restraining order against him?"

"I'm sorry that got out. I didn't want his parents to know." Melissa sighed. "Greg had crying jags when I asked him to move out. And he kept coming to the house, begging me to take him back. He said his life was over, he didn't want to live without us, stuff like that. He scared me, and Kaitlin." She looked at her daughter. "I had no choice."

"But things obviously improved if Greg was going to join you for Thanksgiving."

"He was calmer." Melissa nodded. "He'd pulled himself together. Two weeks ago Sunday we spent the day together, the three of us. We went to the park, had a picnic lunch. It was a nice day." The swing slowed. "I did it for Kaitlin. Maybe I gave Greg false hope. That was the last time I saw him," she said, with sadness I hadn't heard before.

"More, Mommy!" the girl called.

"So you weren't about to reconcile?" I asked.

Melissa pushed the swing again. "The TV reporter said we were setting a wedding date. That's not true. We had major problems. I didn't know if we could get over them. I told Greg, that Sunday. But he was a good dad, and I wanted Kaitlin to have him in her life."

"Did you talk to him after that Sunday?"

"He phoned every day, mostly to talk to Kaitlin. He said he was in Sedona—that's in Arizona? He was trying to make decisions about what he was going to do. Obviously, he lied. He didn't go anywhere."

I felt a stirring of interest. "What kind of decisions?"

"For one thing, the principal called him a couple of times. She wanted him to come back. And the kid that cheated? The brother went to see Greg at his apartment, to talk things out. Greg said it was too little, too late. But he didn't have anything else, so I told him to consider the principal's offer."

The swing came to a stop.

"Again," Kaitlin said.

"Maybe you should get off now, honey," Melissa said. "I don't want you getting sick."

"I won't."

"One more time, and that's it. But tell me if you feel funny, promise?" Melissa gave the swing a shove. "She gets a little nauseous sometimes," she told me.

"That happens to one of my nieces," I said. "Did you talk to Greg Friday night?"

"Friday afternoon. He sounded tense. I asked him what was wrong, but he wouldn't tell me. I asked if he was planning to come to Seattle for Thanksgiving. He said he'd let me know."

"Did you go to his apartment to see if he was okay?"

"The police asked me that, too. As far as I knew, Greg wasn't *at* his apartment. And if he was having one of his moods, I didn't want to be around him. The next thing I heard, he died in a car accident, in L.A. They said he killed himself. And now they're saying someone killed him."

We had come full circle. I had learned a few details about Shankman's life, but nothing surprising or revealing.

"And today they said he was involved with a girl." Melissa huffed. "A high school senior, the daughter of the Jewish studies principal of the school where Greg was teaching. I don't know what Greg was thinking. Well, obviously he *wasn't* thinking. I guess all his talk about wanting to reconcile was just that—talk. Or maybe he took up with this girl because he figured we were over."

She grabbed the back of the swing and brought it to a stop. "Okay, Kaitlin. That's it for now."

She undid the straps, removed her daughter from the swing, and set her down. The girl's face was a little pale.

"Can I go on the scooter, Mommy?"

"In five minutes. Rest your tummy."

"My tummy's fine," she said, beginning to whine.

"Your baby's, then. I think she needs a nap, honey. Don't you think so, Molly?"

"I do," I said.

" 'Kay."

Holding the doll so that its legs grazed the ground, Kaitlin walked a few feet, plopped onto the grass, and rocked her doll in her arms.

"She can spend hours with that doll," Melissa said, watching her.

"Did Greg ever talk about Rabbi Bailor, Melissa?"

Melissa nodded, her eyes still on her daughter. "Greg said the rabbi was a good man. But when Greg needed help with this cheating thing, the rabbi wouldn't get involved. Greg was steamed about that. I thought he was over the whole thing, but he told me he was going to go public about the cheating at the school."

My stomach muscles tightened. "When was this?"

"One of the days he was supposedly in Sedona. He said he was going to talk to the newspapers, and write an article about cheating in schools."

"About this boy, you mean?"

"And cheating on the AP exam. Greg said he knew who was doing it."

"Who?" I said, with greater intensity than I'd intended, but Melissa didn't seem to notice.

"He wouldn't say. Greg was going to give this boy one last chance to come clean. If the kid refused, Greg was going to go public. He didn't care about the consequences. He hoped I wouldn't, either."

"What consequences?" I asked, though I knew.

"A girl at the school—not the rabbi's daughter—accused Greg of coming on to her. If Greg showed the school his proof, the girl was going to call me. Greg swore it wasn't true, but . . ."

"I don't mean to offend you, Melissa, but I understand he was your teacher when you first started dating."

Her face turned a deep shade of pink. "I guess that'll be tomorrow's headline. I was seventeen. I trusted him. He said he'd never done anything like that before." She looked at her daughter. "I'd better take Kaitlin inside. It's chilly."

Back in the living room, I picked up my purse from the side of the sofa, where I had left it.

"Do you know what Greg did with this proof, Melissa?"

"He said something about keeping it in a safe place. A safe deposit box, probably. This morning one of Greg's students called. He was sorry to hear about Greg and hated to bother me, but Greg had some papers the student had written a while back. He said if I found anything, when I got around to it, no rush, to please let him know. I told him Greg took everything when he moved out, but the boy gave me his number in case I came across anything."

"What was his name?"

"Adam Prosser. That's the boy who cheated, isn't it?" Melissa said.

Last night my mother had mentioned a senior who'd tried to sabotage a rival's academic career by tampering with her transcript. Tampering with grades is one thing, I thought on my drive home from Mar Vista. Murder is another. Adam Prosser was a cheater, and he might have had his heart set on Harvard, but I couldn't see him killing Greg Shankman to get there.

I *could* see him going to Greg's apartment Friday night to reason with him. Or maybe Prosser's father had made the visit. Or the brother? And if the argument had turned violent? And if somebody grabbed a knife . . .

Had Hadassah witnessed the confrontation and run out? If Cheryl was right, and the cuts on Hadassah's arms were self-inflicted, they weren't evidence of a struggle. I remembered the tissues I'd seen in Hadassah's wastebasket. I had thought the dark stains were red lipstick. Maybe they were blood. And I recalled Rabbi Bailor's comment: *Dassie's sleeves are so long you can barely see her wrists.*

But if Hadassah had left during the confrontation between Prosser and Shankman, why was she refusing to talk? Rabbi Bailor had told me his daughter might be in shock. That was possible. That was also a convenient excuse.

And who had removed her belongings?

Back in my house, I folded the laundry and came up with no answers. I returned to my desk, added a circle with Adam Prosser's name, and linked it to Shankman's. Melissa had told the police about Greg's decision to go public. Now that she knew Adam's name, she was planning to phone Jessie Drake with the new information.

I was tempted to phone Jessie, too, in case Melissa didn't make Prosser her priority. She had a child to worry about, and maybe funeral arrangements, too, once Shankman's body was released, though his parents would probably make most of the decisions. It must be awkward and painful, dealing with your child's grandparents when you've obtained a restraining order against their son. Maybe the Shankmans had taken comfort from the media reports about a reconciliation.

Even though, according to Melissa, there *was* no reconciliation.

The media had probably wanted to romanticize the story, give it more pathos. Maybe they'd heard talk of reconciliation from the neighbor. She had seemed hopeful, I recalled. So had Cheryl.

I wrote RECONCILIATION?? on the bottom of my page of circles.

Maybe Melissa had changed her story after she'd talked to reporters. . . . After she heard about Hadassah?

I ran the angles through my mind. If I were Melissa, and I had learned that while my ex-boyfriend and I were talking about getting back together, he was having a fling with a high school senior, I would be furious and humiliated. The police might consider that a motive. So if I wanted to divert suspicion from myself, I would downplay my interest in reconciling. And maybe that explained why Melissa had been willing to talk to Molly Blume, a reporter, to get that point across.

I considered phoning Jessie about Melissa, but I had nothing concrete, and I knew she'd see it for what it was: an attempt to divert suspicion from the Bailors. And my heart wasn't in it. Having met Kaitlin, I didn't want Melissa to be involved in her ex-boyfriend's murder.

So I phoned Rabbi Bailor's office. I wanted to know how Dassie was doing, whether she'd shed light on what had happened.

"Rabbi left a few minutes ago," Sue said. "His wife phoned, and he went right home. But I'll tell him y'all called."

"Thanks, Sue."

"By the way, you were asking about a specialty license plate? I remember all about it now. It was R-C-K-Y-R-D. Rocky Road? The ice cream flavor? Mr. Shankman told me about it when he picked up some papers a few weeks after he was let go. He said it cheered him up when it came in the mail. Rabbi was in my office when Mr. Shankman stopped by. He told Rabbi about the plate, and Rabbi laughed and said, 'Too bad it isn't kosher.' Rabbi's cute, isn't he?"

Chapter 37

This time Jessie Drake didn't pull over a chair.

She came into Hadassah's room with her partner, Phil, in the middle of the day, when Hadassah's father wasn't home, or her brother. Hadassah had heard the doorbell. She had shut down the computer only seconds before she heard footsteps on the stairs and hurried to her bed. If Jessie had touched the still-warm screen, she would have known.

Hadassah's mother walked in behind the detectives. "My husband's on the way home," she said. "I called him. If you can wait until he gets here?"

But Jessie said they had to talk to Hadassah. *Now.*

The "now" was serious, filled with threat. So Hadassah knew today would be different, even before Detective Drake started speaking, her voice not unpleasant but tougher.

Hadassah knew that her mother heard the threat, too. "What's going on?" she asked. Hadassah could hear the tremor behind the bluster in her voice.

Jessie said, "We matched hair from your brush to hair we found in Greg Shankman's bedroom, Hadassah. We're pretty sure we can match the DNA from your hair to the DNA of the blood we found on the floor. So we know you were there, Hadassah."

"I want you to wait until my husband comes home," Hadassah's mother said.

"We showed your photo to a witness who saw a young woman a few blocks from the apartment on Friday," Jessie continued. "The witness identified you, Hadassah. So you were there Friday night, and something made you run from the apartment. If it was self-defense, you have nothing to worry about. But you have to tell us who helped you. No more games. I am out of patience, and so is the district attorney. He is ready to file charges."

"My daughter needs a lawyer," Hadassah's mother said. "I don't want you asking her any more questions until she has a lawyer."

Hadassah was surprised by how calm her mother sounded, how strong. It was as though another person had suddenly inhabited her body.

Phil said, "Mrs. Bailor, your daughter is eighteen. She's an adult. If she wants an attorney, she can ask for one. That's her right, but you can't do it for her."

"She's not well," my mother said. "You can see that. She can't make decisions. She needs a lawyer."

Jessie said, "Phil, can I talk to you?"

Hadassah thought Jessie sounded worried.

"Don't say a word, Hadassah," her mother warned. "Your father will be home any minute. He'll call a lawyer."

Hadassah's fingers bunched the top sheet. She could tell Jessie Drake about hiding in the closet, the air warm and close and filled with the scent of mothballs. She could try to explain about the photo and the other items in the box, about the pills and the note, about all the lies, everything he'd told her was lies. She could tell Jessie Drake about the way he was staring at her, about the kiss and the worry of what he'd do next, about the green mug and the key that wouldn't open the door lock. About feeling trapped. She could tell Jessie how terrified she'd been when she'd heard the click of the lock that told her he was back, that he had been talking of death and dying. *I would die a million deaths for you, Dassie. Would you die for me?* She could tell Jessie Drake that she hadn't wanted to die.

So when she lunged at him with the shard, was that self-defense? Hadassah had thought so at the time. She hadn't meant to kill him. She had heard the click of the lock and picked up the shard to defend herself. She had wanted to escape to the safety of the family she should never have left. He had grabbed her free arm, and her hand had driven the glassy point into his throat, and she couldn't take that back, ever. Not even in her dreams.

Maybe he wasn't dead when she left him lying on the floor and ran out. She couldn't tell that to Jessie. Jessie and the district attorney might agree that Hadassah had acted in what she believed to be self-defense.

But if he was alive when Hadassah left?

Hadassah didn't want to think about that, but she had been thinking about little else since Sunday morning, when her father told her. "Greg Shankman is dead," her father had said, holding her hand while he bandaged her palm, careful not to ask questions about the deep cuts. "You don't have to tell the police anything, Dassie. We love you, Dassie."

If Hadassah explained, Jessie might believe her. But she would ask the same questions she'd asked before:

What happened after you left the apartment, Hadassah? Who moved Mr. Shankman's body to his car? Who removed all your things? Your clothes, your cell phone, your wallet, your keys.

Hadassah didn't know. That's what kept her awake at night, more than the No-Doz.

Jessie would ask about Hadassah's father. But Hadassah didn't know what to tell her about her father, or her brother. Her mother had opened the door Friday night. She had cried out when she saw Hadassah as though she'd seen a ghost, "Thank God! Thank God!" Hadassah had collapsed in her arms, sobbing, and her mother had sobbed, too.

"Thank God! Thank God!" She had held Hadassah to her chest and rocked her the way she had when Hadassah was a little girl.

"Oh, how I wish *Abba* knew you were home!" her mother had exclaimed, brushing the tangled curls away from Hadassah's face, which was streaked with tears and flecks of blood Hadassah hadn't wiped off. "He went with Gavriel to a *sholom zochor* for Tova Gordon's new baby boy."

Hadassah wasn't sure what time her father and brother had come home. Late, because her mother had started to worry. "Where can they be? I hope they're all right: You hear terrible things, people being mugged while they're walking on Friday nights."

When her father returned, he had come into her room. She had been waiting for him, watching the doorway, and had seen his large shadowy form in the meager light of the hall. He had knelt at the side of her bed and wrapped her in his arms, had stroked her hair and face. "He lied, *Abba,*" Hadassah said. "He lied about everything."

"It's going to be okay, Dassie," her father told her. "Everything is going to be okay."

Unspoken between them was the understanding that there would be no questions. No one asked her anything or looked her in the eye. Not her father, not her brother or uncle, or her mother or sister.

Dr. McIntyre had wanted to prescribe a sedative. "You've been through a terrible experience, Hadassah. If you want to talk . . ."

Hadassah wondered if Dinah had talked to her brothers about the people they had killed. Schechem, and the others. She wondered if Dinah had avoided looking in people's eyes, too.

"Okay, Hadassah," Jessie Drake said. "If you want a lawyer, that's your right. I know that we're going to find Greg Shankman's blood on your clothes. We'll arrest you. The district attorney will get a court hearing to determine competency. You and I both know you're competent. You're afraid to tell the truth."

Hadassah heard her father as he bounded up the stairs.

"If you're protecting someone, Hadassah, tell us," Jessie said. "This is your last chance. You can talk to us, or—"

"I want you to stop badgering my daughter, Detective," Hadassah's father said, running into the room. "She hasn't done anything wrong. She doesn't have to talk to you. That's her right."

"Why doesn't she tell us that?" Phil said.

"Obviously, she can't. *I'm* telling you. You have no proof that she was involved with Mr. Shankman's death. If you did, you would arrest her."

Hadassah could hear her father's panting.

"We'll be back, Hadassah," Jessie said.

After the detectives left, Hadassah's father took her hand. "I won't let them hurt you, Hadassah. I promise."

Chapter 38

==

Nechama Bailor looked more haggard than the last time I had seen her. She told me her husband was unavailable, but the way I was feeling, a Sherman tank wouldn't have stopped me.

"I have to talk to him, Mrs. Bailor."

"He's tied up, Molly." She smiled apologetically. "Call a little later."

"I'm sorry, I can't do that."

I couldn't decide whether she looked more startled or offended as I stepped around her and headed to the rabbi's study. The door was closed. I didn't bother knocking.

Rabbi Bailor was pacing and talking on the phone when I entered. I caught him in midstride. He frowned. "Please hold on," he said to the person on the other end and covered the receiver with his hand.

"This isn't a good time, Molly."

"It isn't a good time for me, either, Rabbi Bailor." I sat on the chair facing the desk.

"The police are this close to arresting Dassie, Molly. I'm trying to get hold of an attorney." He spoke with barely contained exasperation.

"By all means, finish your call. I'll wait."

He removed his hand from the receiver. "Can I call you back?" he said into the phone. "Ten minutes? Thank you." He put the receiver down and folded his arms. "What's so important?"

"You knew on Friday that Dassie was with Shankman, Rabbi Bailor." My voice was calm, but my nails dug into the arms of the chair. "You phoned Yamashiro Room. You spoke to the waitress I questioned Thursday night. You learned Dassie had been there Thursday night with a man who thought his car was damaged by the valet. You recognized the license plate number of the car. R-C-K-Y-R-D. Shankman's Altima."

The rabbi dropped his hands to his side. "I didn't phone Yamashiro Room, Molly. I didn't speak with anyone there. You can believe me or not."

"Then who *did* call? On Friday Detective Connors left me a message, telling me it was Shankman. He ordered me not to tell you. With Shankman dead, he thinks I *did* tell you."

"I can't help what Detective Connors thinks, Molly."

"You jeopardized my credibility with him, Rabbi Bailor. You've probably ruined our friendship. That may not matter to you, but it matters a great deal to me."

Rabbi Bailor looked at his watch.

"When I came here Sunday, you pretended to be shocked when I told you Shankman was dead, and that he was the man Dassie met in the chat room. But you *knew* it was Shankman."

"I *was* shocked that Shankman was dead. Again, you don't have to believe me, Molly, but that's the truth."

"But you knew on Friday that Dassie was with Shankman, didn't you?" I demanded.

He looked me in the eyes. "Yes."

"And Sunday you pretended you didn't know."

He sat at his desk. "I'm sorry I misled you, Molly. It's a difficult situation. I didn't want to involve you more than you were already involved."

"That's a long definition for lying," I said.

He flinched. I felt no satisfaction, only sadness. I had harbored resentment toward the rabbi, but had never doubted his honesty.

"You've said your piece, Molly. I apologize. I can't do more."

"You can phone Detective Connors and tell him how you tracked down Shankman's identity."

"I didn't track him down."

I thought about what Rabbi Bailor *had* answered, and what he hadn't. I considered who else would have traced my steps and talked to Irene Jakaitis.

"Your brother-in-law called Yamashiro, didn't he?" I said. "He spoke to the waitress and got the license plate number."

The rabbi made no denial. That and a twitch in his cheek confirmed my guess. I should have realized it was Jastrow. He was determined to help his sister. He had come to three book signings to vet me. He had driven two hours to meet with me in San Diego and pretended to be Rabbi Bailor to accomplish what he wanted. The other day I had teased him about being a detective.

"Reuben told you what he'd learned," I said. "So you went to Shankman's apartment."

"I didn't know his address, Molly."

"You said Dassie walked four miles from his apartment. So you knew where he lived." Another lie, I thought.

"I knew he had moved to West L.A. His street address was in my Rolodex at school. I didn't know it by heart. I don't know the addresses of *any* of the Torat Tzion staff by heart," he said with a surge of impatience. "Why would I?"

"So you drove to the school Friday and—"

"Ten minutes before *Shabbos*? That's when I learned it was Shankman. And then I drove to his apartment? On *Shabbos*?"

"If you thought it was a life-and-death emergency," I said, using the same argument Jessie had used on Sunday.

"From what Shankman told Nechama, nothing was going to happen until Monday. How could I risk being *mechallel Shabbos* if Dassie was safe?" Rabbi Bailor picked up a staple remover and clicked it several times. "I considered getting his address and walking there," he admitted. "I decided to wait until Saturday night, when *Shabbos* was over."

I stared at him, incredulous. "So you went to *shul*, came home, made *Kiddush*, ate a meal with your family, and sang *zemirot*. You did all that knowing where Dassie was? That she was with a man who had taunted you and told you he raped her?"

"But he *didn't* rape her." The rabbi put down the staple remover. "He was trying to brainwash her, yes. But twenty-four hours wouldn't make a difference. I didn't think she was in physical danger, Molly. His deadline was Monday."

I reminded myself that I'd never communicated my fears about the double suicide to Rabbi Bailor. Maybe that had been a mistake.

"It was a test from *Hashem*," the rabbi said. "Not an easy one. Maybe I learned that it was Shankman right before *Shabbos* so I wouldn't be able to act on that knowledge. If I had gone there, if I had witnessed Shankman hurting her, who knows what I would have done?"

"Did Dassie tell you he assaulted her?" I could tell that he regretted his words.

"She didn't tell me anything. She said he lied. She was emotionally spent."

"Shankman is dead, Rabbi Bailor. Somebody killed him. Why won't Dassie tell the police what happened? Because she's in shock?" I said, with sarcasm.

He scowled. "Is that so hard to believe? She was with this man for almost a week. He had her under his control. Even if he didn't assault her, Dr. McIntyre said Dassie could be suffering from posttraumatic stress."

"What time did she come home?"

The rabbi sighed. "Is that important?"

"It is, to me. You owe me answers, Rabbi Bailor. What time?" I asked again.

"Around eight o'clock? Maybe a little later."

"You're not sure?" I reviewed the little the rabbi had told me about

Dassie's return. "You said Dassie collapsed in your wife's arms. You weren't home, were you?"

"I was at a *sholom zochor,* with Gavriel," he said, his voice steady.

"I see."

His face was flushed. "That's the truth, Molly."

I let that hang in the air. "So what time did you return from the *sholom zochor?*"

"Around ten. As soon as I arrived home, my *Hatzolah* radio went off. The call was for an address on Beverwil. I drove there, but two other members had already responded. So I drove home."

Hatzolah, which means "rescue," is a community emergency response organization. My dad is a trained member. So is Zack. When you hear the call, you respond with your member number and wait until you're authorized to drive to the location.

"So you weren't authorized to respond?" I asked.

"I just went. I was thinking about Dassie, where she was."

Having caught the rabbi in one lie, I didn't know whether I could believe anything he told me. He might have responded without authorization to the call. Or he might have used the call as an excuse to drive on the Sabbath without arousing his neighbor's curiosity—but not to Beverwil.

"And Gavriel?" I asked.

"I'm not sure when Gavriel came home. He was planning to visit friends after the *sholom zochor.*"

"Did you tell Gavriel about Shankman?"

"I'm tired of this, Molly. This isn't a courtroom."

"How did Dassie get away from Shankman?"

He glared at me. "I don't know." Each word was a separate sentence.

"When I was at his apartment Saturday night, none of her belongings were there. She must have had clothes, toiletries, a purse. And her cell phone," I said. "Shankman used it to phone your wife. Did Dassie bring those things home with her?"

"No. I have no idea who took them."

"Your brother-in-law?"

"I didn't ask him." The rabbi placed his palms on the desk and leaned toward me. "You tried to find Dassie, Molly. For that, I'll always be grateful. But I don't owe you any more answers. I have to protect myself and my family."

"If you didn't do anything wrong—"

He snorted. "You think it's so simple? Don't be naïve." He pushed his chair back and stood. "I'm finished talking about this. If you have more questions, go to your good friend Detective Connors."

Heat rushed to my face. "Are you saying it's my fault the police know Dassie was with Shankman?"

"You told Connors the father of the girl you were looking for was a rabbi. You told him the man she was with was fired from the school where the rabbi was a principal."

"I was trying to find her. I didn't know Shankman would be killed."

"You're right." The rabbi sighed. "It doesn't matter. What's done is done. This was meant to be."

"Did you ever wonder why Greg Shankman *chose* Dassie, Rabbi Bailor?" I had his attention now. I should have stopped. "He was angry with you, because you let him down. He was angry, because you did nothing when Amy Brookman accused Greg of sexually harassing her, even though she was lying to protect her pal Adam Prosser, who everybody in the school knows is a pathological cheater. He was angry because when he was about to lose his job, you said, 'Sorry, Greg, you're a nice guy, but gee, this is out of my hands.' Why does that sound so familiar?"

Rabbi Bailor's face was mottled with color.

I picked up my purse and stood. My legs were shaking, and I felt physically ill.

"You know what, Rabbi Bailor? I tried to help. I put my heart into finding your daughter. I may have said more than I should have, but I did it because I was anxious to find her. And at least I *tried*. When have *you* tried?"

Chapter 39

I don't remember what Nechama said when I saw her. She was standing outside the study when I opened the door. I mumbled good-bye and managed to wait until I was in my car before bursting into tears. Ten minutes later I was still sitting. The key was in the ignition. My hands were on the wheel. I was too distraught to drive.

My head was pounding. I swallowed two Advil tablets and downed them with a long swig from a water bottle I always take with me. But analgesics wouldn't erase the memory of my spiteful, childish outburst.

"You hurt me, I'll hurt you back, harder."

And nothing I could say would erase the pain I'd seen in Rabbi Bailor's eyes. I hoped Nechama hadn't overheard. It was one thing to wound the rabbi, another to wound their marriage, which, from what I had seen, was already strained by their daughter's disappearance.

The truth about an awful truth is that it isn't always necessary to share it. And as Bubbie G says, a word is like an arrow—both are in a hurry to strike. Though fourteen years had passed, that day, I realized, I had been in a hurry to strike.

The West L.A. detectives' room was almost empty when I arrived, close to four-thirty. Jessie was at her table. She looked up when I approached.

"I'm about to head home," she said. "If you're here for information, Molly, I don't have any."

"Do you have a few minutes?"

"That's about all I *do* have. How can I help you?"

I pulled up a chair and sat. "I had an interesting conversation with Melissa Frank today. She told me Greg was planning to go public with proof about the cheating that was taking place at Torat Tzion."

"Adam Prosser." Jessie nodded. "Ms. Frank phoned this afternoon and gave me his name."

"Prosser is the reason Greg was fired," I said.

Jessie raised a brow. "Ms. Frank didn't tell me that."

"Melissa didn't know." I summarized what I'd learned from Justin. "Melissa told me the secular studies principal, Dr. Mendes, was talking to Shankman about his returning to Torat Tzion. Prosser's father is on the school board. Suppose the father goes to Shankman's apartment to cut a deal. Prosser says he'll agree to let Dr. Mendes reinstate Shankman if Shankman drops the cheating charge. Shankman refuses. Things take a violent turn. Shankman is killed."

Jessie had been listening with interest. She tapped her fingers together. "And where is Hadassah Bailor during all this, Molly?"

"Not in the apartment. Shankman either frightened her or assaulted her. She escaped before Prosser arrived."

"We have the clothes Hadassah was wearing when she came home Friday night, Molly. A white skirt and sweater. Mrs. Bailor laundered the clothes, but the lab found bloodstains in the seams."

I swallowed hard. "How do they know it's blood?"

"They used antihuman hemoglobin. It's an antiserum that reacts specifically and only with primate blood. So unless Hadassah came in contact with a bleeding monkey, the blood is human." Jessie wasn't smiling. "My guess is the lab tests will show it's Shankman's blood. So while your theory is interesting, it doesn't account for the blood on Hadassah's clothes."

"But you won't know for sure that it's Shankman's blood until you have the lab results, right? When will that be?"

"Ordinarily, the lab would spray Luminol on the suspect area and examine it in a dark room, or in a container. Any blood would show up with a bluish color. But Mrs. Bailor used bleach. On silk and satin—interesting, don't you think?" Jessie paused. "Anyway, some bleaches react with Luminol and give a false positive. So the lab is doing DNA analysis. That takes at least two days, probably longer."

"It might not be Shankman's blood," I said. "I talked to someone today who suspects that Hadassah was cutting herself. Self-mutilation?"

Jessie nodded. "Who told you that?"

"Cynthia Wexner. She worked with Hadassah on her college applications. They became close."

I told Jessie what Cynthia had noticed. I also told her about the marks I had seen on Hadassah's arm, about the stained tissues. About her father's comment, that she always wore long sleeves.

"Suppose you're right," Jessie said. "Hadassah leaves before Prosser arrives, and the blood on her clothes is hers. Who cleaned up Shankman's blood? Prosser?"

"Yes. And he moved Shankman to the car and staged the crash to cover up the murder."

"But what about Hadassah's belongings? She was in that apartment from Monday through Friday, Molly. We found hair fiber and other trace evidence on the bed and on the sofa. We matched it to fibers on clothes we found in her closet. Why would Prosser remove Hadassah Bailor's things? Leaving them for us to find would be smarter. It would point us in her direction."

Jessie was right. I considered, then said, "Maybe Rabbi Bailor removed them Saturday night."

"We searched his home and his office, and Hadassah's locker at school. We didn't find anything. Not her cell phone, or the purse the friend said Hadassah was using, or her house keys."

I wondered if Rabbi Bailor had stashed Hadassah's belongings at his brother-in-law's house. "Speaking of phones, can you find out if Hadassah called anyone Friday night?"

"We subpoenaed her cell phone company's records. We should have that information tomorrow."

"What about Shankman's land line?"

"His phone has an LCD display and a record of the most recent outgoing and incoming calls. No calls Friday. In fact, no calls since the previous Saturday. A lot of people use their cell phones as their main phone."

"And Shankman's cell phone?"

"He made several calls to Ms. Frank and to his home number. He also phoned Torat Tzion, the *L.A. Times,* and the Bureau of Jewish Education." Jessie hesitated. "And the law offices of Mulligan, Raslin, and Prosser."

"Interesting."

"That doesn't mean Prosser went to Shankman's apartment, Molly."

"I know. Did you find any fingerprints, aside from Shankman's?"

"Hadassah's. We lifted her prints from items in her house and matched them to prints we found in the apartment. We found Ms. Frank's prints, and her daughter's. Ms. Frank told us she visited Shankman several times."

I pictured Kaitlin on the swing, saw her curls flying. "That's it?"

"We have unidentified prints that match prints we found on the Altima. Shankman's prints, by the way, were on the steering wheel, but not on the handle or driver's door."

"Maybe the prints belong to one of the Prossers."

"Or to Rabbi Bailor, or his son. I know you're trying to help prove that the Bailors aren't involved with Shankman's death, Molly. Unfortunately, Hadassah *is* involved. Her father may be, too. Or her brother."

"Did Rabbi Bailor tell you where he was Friday night?"

"He said he was at a party for a newborn boy, and then he responded to an emergency call."

So the rabbi was being consistent either in his lie, or in his truth. "Detective Drake, we know Shankman was killed Friday night. Rabbi Bailor wouldn't have driven Shankman's car on the Sabbath, even to protect his daughter. The brother wouldn't have done it, either."

Jessie shrugged.

"Can you tell me what killed Shankman?"

She swiveled in her chair.

"Detective Connors believes I betrayed his confidence," I said. "I didn't identify Shankman to Rabbi Bailor or anyone in his family."

She studied me a moment before answering. "I can't give you all the details, Molly. I can tell you the victim's shirt was soaked with blood, and there was some blood on both front headrests in the vehicle, but comparatively little blood on the seat or seat backs, or in the back of the vehicle. If he was alive when he sustained the injuries from the crash, and those injuries caused massive bleeding, there would have been blood spatters all around him. The fact that we found so little blood suggests he was dead when he was placed in the car. People don't bleed postmortem."

I nodded. "What about the murder weapon? You asked me if I had touched any of the knives."

"The medical examiner hasn't done the autopsy yet. Until he does he can't determine the cause of death. But from his preliminary findings, which he based on the size and nature of the wounds, Shankman sustained several types of injuries." Jessie neatened a stack of papers. "I really have to go. I have a date, and I don't want to be late. You may know him. Ezra Nathanson? He teaches at Ohr Torah. Your husband subbed for him a few times." She cocked her head. "Did I say something funny?"

"On Sunday, when you said Zack was a rabbi, I thought you'd checked us out. You made me nervous."

"I intended to," she said, seriously.

"I do know Ezra. I didn't know he was seeing anyone."

"We're taking it slow. As I mentioned, I'm studying Judaism, but I'm not ready to commit to Orthodoxy."

"You said you found out recently that you're Jewish?"

Jessie nodded. "My mother was a hidden child during the Holocaust. She was the only one of her family who survived. She married my dad—he's Episcopalian—and never told him or anyone else that she was Jewish. I found out by accident when I came across some photos of her family."

I tried to imagine what Jessie must have felt. Shock? Confusion? Hurt? "What about your mother? Has she found her way back to Judaism?"

"Hardly." Jessie smiled wryly. "And she's not thrilled that I have. It's a challenge. But life is definitely not boring."

"So how did you meet Ezra?"

"That's a long story." She moved her chair back and stood. "Maybe we can talk more another time. I *really* have to go. I'll walk out with you."

"One more question?" I rose and returned my chair to the adjoining table. "What was in the box in the closet?"

"Nothing. Interesting, because we found blood on the inside and outside of the box." Jessie picked up her purse and slung it over her shoulder. "If you want to help the Bailors, Molly, convince Hadassah to talk to us. If she doesn't, as soon as we get the lab results about the blood, I'll have to arrest her. I really don't want to do that."

"Even if she killed Shankman in self-defense?"

"If that's what happened, why doesn't she tell us?"

Chapter 40

Over an early dinner I told Zack what I'd said to Rabbi Bailor, and felt like crying again during the telling.

"I don't blame you for being upset, Molly," Zack said. "It was unfair of Rabbi Bailor to blame you for what happened. You were anxious to find Hadassah."

"I told him it was his fault Shankman chose Dassie. That was a horrible thing to say, even if it's true." I poked at the roast chicken on my plate. "And it may *not* be true. How do I know what was going on in Shankman's head?"

"Give it a day or so, Molly. Then, only if you want to, you can call Rabbi Bailor."

"I can't face him, Zack. His daughter could have been killed, a man is dead, and I'm focused on my own petty hurts over something that happened fourteen years ago."

"You admired him. You felt he let you

down. It's hard to get over something like that. I'm sure Rabbi Bailor feels terrible about what he said, too, Molly."

My eyes teared again. I wiped them with a napkin.

"Did you ever consider confronting Rabbi Ingel?" Zack said a few minutes later. "He's the one you're really angry at, Molly."

"Oh, please." I put down my fork. "The man is in total denial. He'd never admit he was wrong. I saw him at a wedding after my divorce. I could tell what he was thinking from the way he looked at me: 'You see, Malka, I was right about you,' " I said, mimicking the rabbi's high-pitched tone. " 'You're a failure.' "

Zack laughed. "You sound exactly like him. But isn't it possible that you were being sensitive, Molly?"

"It's possible," I admitted. "I felt like a failure. And I'm not exactly objective about the rabbi. Mindy says I give him too much power over me. Every time I see him, all those emotions come flooding back."

"He doesn't represent Orthodoxy, Molly. For every Rabbi Ingel, there are tens of open-minded, sensitive, compassionate rabbis who don't use fire and brimstone to force their students into a cookie-cutter mold."

"I know. I married one of the good ones." I smiled. "But it took me a while to figure that out."

I had told Zack about the doubts I'd had in my late teens about Orthodox Judaism, about the questions I'd been afraid to ask. I'd drifted away. Then one evening, two years later, Mindy had dragged me to a lecture where I'd heard a dynamic, fascinating rabbi, very much like the Rabbi Bailor I had first known and admired. I had signed up for his class out of curiosity and had gradually found my way back to Orthodox observance.

Zack said, "Rabbi Ingel's still at Sharsheret, so your mom sees him all the time, right? Isn't that awkward?"

"She's not a fan. Basically, she and my dad feel sorry for him. They think he's sincere in his zealousness, but narrow-minded and clueless. And tactless." I sighed. "I need a hug, Zack."

"I'd love to give you a hug. I'm sorry."

"You don't make the rules." I ate an asparagus spear.

"So what did Detective Drake tell you?" Zack said.

"Trying to change the subject, huh?" I repeated what I'd learned. "So maybe that *is* Hadassah's blood on her clothes, not Shankman's." I looked at Zack's face. "You don't think so, huh?"

He shrugged. "It'll be interesting to see who Hadassah phoned Friday night, if anybody."

"Detective Drake hopes to know tomorrow. By the way, she's dating Ezra Nathanson."

Zack raised a brow. "Ezra and a cop? Huh. She's Jewish?"

I told him about her background. "She seems very nice. More important, she's investigating the Prosser angle."

Zack left to teach a Talmud class. I cleared the dishes while I talked to Edie and to Mindy, who told me Liora had flown to New York the night before. A *shidduch* date, my mother confirmed when I phoned her.

"On paper, he sounds great," my mother said.

"On paper they all sound great. Speaking of paper, how's your book?"

"I'm still blocked."

"Tell me what has you stumped."

Fiction was infinitely more appealing than reality. We talked plot for half an hour. My mother hung up to take her nightly walk with my dad. I watched *Scrubs,* then phoned my friend Irene.

"I miss seeing you every *Shabbos,*" she told me after we'd caught up. "Why did you have to get married and switch to your husband's *shul?*"

Irene always makes me smile. "It kind of goes with the territory. Irene, what can you tell me about cluster suicides?"

"For one thing, they account for only five percent of suicides. Why?"

I told her about Hadassah and Batya Weinberg, and Greg Shankman.

"I heard about that on the news," Irene said. "What a tragedy. So you think Shankman planned to kill himself and get Hadassah to do the same?"

"Either that, or murder-suicide. I know it sounds crazy."

"It's not crazy at all, Molly. Suicide among young people has been on the rise. They're under greater stress than they ever were—stress from school, peers, family. And there's a romantic image—Romeo and Juliet. They don't think about the messiness of death. They do it to make a point, or to make someone feel sorry. Do you know for a fact that the Weinberg girl killed herself?"

"No."

"She died last year, you said? Cluster suicides are defined as three or more suicides that take place in a short period of time in the same area—like within a school, or a town. But there are copycat suicides. That's when someone kills himself because a friend has done it, or a celebrity. Often, the attraction is the notoriety or glamour. What makes you think Hadassah was contemplating suicide?"

"I don't know that she was. But from what I've learned, she's been depressed, overwhelmed with school, lonely. She was very upset about Batya Weinberg's death and the deaths of the other kids she knew. Also, someone close to her thinks Hadassah is cutting herself."

"Oh."

I didn't like the "Oh." "Is there a correlation between cutting and suicide, Irene?"

"Some people—mostly cutters—say the release of tension provided by cutting *prevents* suicide, but most therapists believe there's an increased risk. Not every person who self-mutilates is suicidal, Molly, but cutting the wrist is a step closer to slitting a wrist."

I pictured Hadassah's scarred arm and winced.

"Several of my patients self-mutilate, Molly. Most of them are teenage girls, although one woman is in her forties. Some tear their hair. Some burn themselves. Most of them cut themselves—with razors, staples, safety pins, knives. Whatever's available."

"I found a few unbent staples in Hadassah's trash can," I told Irene. "But why do they do it?"

"Did you see *Thirteen?* That was in theaters last year. It's about a teen who self-mutilates."

"Holly Hunter played the mom, right? I didn't see it. It sounded too depressing."

"It's definitely not a feel-good film. To tell you the truth, I worry that susceptible teens may see films about self-injury and get ideas. There's a whole culture of cutters. They have websites. They have a cut-of-the-month club, where they get together and show off their latest cut."

"Nice," I said.

"They do it for the glamour and the attention. But underlying all that is a serious emotional problem. Basically, a teen who cuts into her skin is lonely or suffers from family neglect. She has feelings of worthlessness and self-loathing. She may be depressed. She may be overwhelmed with school. She may be grieving over someone she's lost. A lot of cutters have other psychological problems. They may be bipolar, or have eating disorders."

So much of what Irene had described fit Hadassah. I thought about Hadassah's clothing. Size 0. "I get the psychology, Irene. But how does cutting make this person feel better?"

"She's in emotional pain, right? By cutting herself, she's localizing the pain and bringing it to the surface. And she's relieving the tension."

"And when the tension builds?"

"She cuts again. Sometimes the cuts get infected. Or she cuts too deeply, or too close to a vein. I had one patient who shared a razor with a male friend. The friend was HIV positive. Lucky for my patient, she tested negative."

"Very lucky," I said.

"Cutters self-mutilate with increasing frequency and intensity. It's like with any addiction. After a while, two glasses of Scotch doesn't give you the high they did. So you drink more. Cutting is a tough addiction to break, but with therapy, there's a good chance. There's a hospital-based program in Naperville, Illinois, that treats only patients who injure themselves. It's called S.A.F.E. ALTERNATIVES. The clinical director, Wendy Lader, says skin is a bulletin board. By cutting themselves, teens are saying, 'Can you see how much pain I'm in?' "

"Now you see me." I felt overwhelmed with sorrow for Irene's unnamed clients, for Hadassah Bailor, for anyone who felt the pain of invisibility.

"You said Hadassah's home," Irene said. "How is she?"

"She's not talking to anyone." I explained what I had witnessed. "Her father says she may be suffering from post-traumatic stress."

"That could very well be. Is she under a doctor's care?"

"Yes. Dr. McIntyre. He's a psychologist, or psychiatrist—I'm not sure. He teaches a class at Torat Tzion."

"Well, as long as she's under his care."

"So from what I've described, Irene, do you think she's at risk of killing herself?"

"How can I answer that, Molly? I've never met her. I've never talked to her. But the trauma of whatever she went through—being controlled, being manipulated, possibly assaulted—none of that bodes well. And from what you told me, she still hasn't dealt with whatever pushed her to cut herself in the first place. And suppose she killed this man, even in self-defense. She may still feel responsible for his death, and for bringing all this trouble to her parents' doorstep. I assume her family knows she's cutting herself?"

"I don't know."

"Well, if they don't know, they should."

I had intended to tell Rabbi Bailor before our conversation took its emotional turn. The way things were now, I didn't feel comfortable calling him. Maybe I would raise the subject with Dr. McIntyre.

Irene and I talked a while longer. After I hung up, I logged onto the Internet and responded to several e-mails, among them two letters from fans. I checked my Amazon ranking. Still in the 20,000 range. Then, on a whim, I visited J Spot.

I recognized most of the names in the chat room, including Birch2. I made a mental note to talk to Sara again about her online activities.

DJ2440: So the odds of getting into medical school aren't great unless you're a music major.

Lucky7: Musicology, not biology.

M&M: Lame-o-rama.

Jewcy: Say something, Birch.

Birch2: Not much to say. I have to do homework. 'Night.

M&M: Don't go up a tree, Birch.

Lucky7: LOL

Birch2 has left the room.

Aleph36: Dude, you're putting me to sleep. You guys are booooooring!!! Kerry was better than this.

M&M: My parents split their vote.

DJ2440: I'm Bushed.

M&M: Ambushed?

Lucky7: Hey, ToraTora. Where've you been?

ToraTora: Bora Bora.

Lucky7: LOL

ST613 has entered the room.

M&M: Hey, ST. Shalom.

I stared at the screen. ST613 was Dassie. Just hours ago Rabbi Bailor told me his daughter was emotionally spent. Now she was well enough to get out of bed?

Maybe he didn't know.

Lucky7: What's up, ST?

ST613: Not much.

Jewcy: Still down in the dumps, huh?

DJ2440: Like last night? Tell us why.

ST613: Nothing special.

M&M: ST is blue. Boo-hoo.

Jewcy: Cool it, M&M.

So Dassie had been in the chat room last night, too.

Lucky7: So why are you sad, ST?

ST613: I'm okay.

M&M: A horse walks into a bar. The bartender says, why the long face?

Sinai: LOL

DJ2440: ROFL

ToraTora: ROFL

M&M: My mom was sad yesterday, 'cause JFK was killed November 22.

DJ2440: My mom and dad talk about where they were when they heard.

Lucky7: Where were you when they dropped the charges against Kobe Bryant?

Sinai: My teacher was killed.

M&M: No way!

Lucky7: When?

Sinai: Friday night. It's been on the news.

DJ2440: So what happened?

ST613 has left the room.

M&M: Give, Sinai.

Sinai: Remember I said a teacher cheated on the AP exam? He's the one.

DJ2440: Dude!

Lucky7: Killed, how?

Sinai: His car went over a cliff and landed on rocks.

M&M: Yuk! Splat!

Lucky7: Gross, M&M.

Sinai: They're saying someone killed him and put him in the car to make it look like an accident.

DJ2440: OMG

Sinai: He was a nice guy. . . .

Chapter 41

Hadassah was on the computer when her father came into her room. She thought he would be angry. "What are you doing out of bed?" he asked. "Are you feeling better?"

She heard surprise in his voice, and hope. So she told him yes, she was better, and maybe tomorrow she would go outside to get fresh air. She wasn't ready to go to school, not yet. She wasn't ready to face everybody, her classmates and teachers. Or even Sue, who was warm and loving and would hug her and tell her, "Thank God, you're okay, that's the most important thing, Hadassah. Thank God it's over."

Hadassah knew that it wasn't over.

Something must have happened today. Her father sat on the side of her bed and held her hand, not the bandaged one. He was careful about that. "Dassie," he said, his voice so serious, so heavy, so filled with sadness, just like seven years ago, when his mother died, so Hadassah knew that he was going to prepare her, that the police were coming to arrest her. But he said, "Dassie, I have to ask you a question." And she thought, *Molly told him.* "Look at Dassie's arms, Rabbi Bailor, don't you see the scars?"

It was right after Batya died. Hadassah was confused when she heard, how could somebody be there one day, sitting next to you in class? And the next day she was dead? Hadassah's father told her it was a heart attack, but Hadassah knew that wasn't true. Batya wasn't sick, she looked like everybody else, like Hadassah. That was a frightening thought, that you could go to sleep at night and not wake up the next morning. Although that was what Hadassah said every morning after she rinsed her hands and her eyes. *Thank you,* Hashem, *for returning my soul, for returning souls to dead bodies.*

Like Batya's. Everybody was crying, "Oh my God! It's so awful." Hadassah thought it was awful, and frightening, but she didn't cry. For a long time, even before Batya died, Hadassah felt as if she were watching the other Hadassah on a television show. Sometimes she thought people didn't really see her, so maybe she wasn't real.

Blood was real. Blood was life.

The first time Hadassah cut herself, after Batya's funeral, she used a soda can tab and ran it along the inside of her wrist. Just a small cut, just a few beads of blood. The pain was sharp for a few seconds, and then it was gone. But pain was good. So was blood. Pain meant Hadassah was alive, real, not like Batya, and Noah and Lisa, who felt no pain.

Hadassah didn't think Batya cut herself. But she knew Tara did. Hadassah saw her arm once when they were changing for gym. "My cat scratched me," she told Hadassah. Mrs. Morton, who taught them Jewish laws and was their senior advisor, was so pleased when Tara starting wearing long sleeves, even in the late spring and early fall, when it was so warm. "I think you're having a positive effect on her," she'd told Dassie. There were probably other cutters in the school. There was one in Bais Rifka, Sara had told her. And maybe there were more. Hadassah was careful when she was around Sara. They used to get undressed in front of each other, but now when Hadassah slept over, she made sure to change into pajamas in the bathroom. "You're getting so *frum*, Dassie," Sara teased. A few weeks ago Aliza had come into their bedroom unexpectedly, right after Hadassah had showered. "You're bleeding!" Aliza had said. "Look at your legs and your arms!" Hadassah had told her she'd started itching like crazy all over. Maybe it was something she ate, or something in the detergent. So she'd started scratching and scratching and all of a sudden she was bleeding. Aliza said, "Maybe you should tell Mom." So Hadassah said, "I told her. She said I should take Benadryl." And her sister said, "You better take a lot, Dassie. You look gross."

Hadassah had shown him the cuts. She had worried that he would be disgusted, but he'd said, "Everything about you is beautiful, Dassie. I will kiss the hurts away." And he had showed her *his* scar, on his right wrist. "In the end I couldn't do it," he told Hadassah. "I was waiting for you."

She knew what her father would say. "Why didn't you tell us, Dassie? You know it's against the Torah, Dassie. You're not allowed to do anything to hurt yourself. You're not allowed to mutilate your skin, not even for a tattoo." Hadassah had thought about that when she cut herself. Each time, she told herself, This is the last. On Yom Kippur when she stood next to her mother and Aliza, and beat her breast with her fist, "For the sin that I have committed before You," she had made a silent promise to stop. But she couldn't stop.

That's why she had told Dr. McIntyre. Dr. McIntyre had wanted to tell her parents, but she was eighteen, an adult. He couldn't tell them without her permission. He had advised her to keep a log. "Write down every time you cut yourself, Hadassah. Write down what you're feeling before you do it, and when you do it, and how you feel right after." So she wrote everything down in a small notebook. The notebook was in her purse, along with her car keys. Someone had taken her purse and all her other belongings from his apartment.

Her palm throbbed.

She hadn't cut herself since coming home Friday night. There had been too much blood. On her palm, on her clothes, on the floor of his apartment. And he was dead. Her father had told her.

The shard was there, between the mattress and the box spring. She had checked to make sure before getting up to sit at the computer. She thought about using it. Just a scratch. She would be careful, it was so sharp. *What the hell!* he'd yelled.

Now her father stroked her hand. "Dassie, did he ever tell you why? Why he tricked you, why he did this to you? Did he say he was angry with me? Is that why?"

So her father didn't know.

Hadassah lied, because what was the point of telling him? "Your father," he had told her, "breaks people's hearts and pretends he doesn't see them. He's being honored at an educators' conference, but what he's really teaching is that you care about yourself and don't think what you've done to other people. Your father doesn't want to see that—oh, no, not Rabbi Bailor."

Anyway, it didn't matter. Because that wasn't why. It was Hadassah's fault that a man was dead, that a little girl would never see her father, would never feel his arms holding her, kissing her scrapes, telling her everything would be okay. Hadassah had seen her in the photos. She had seen the picture books and puzzles in the box in the closet. And when the police came back, as Hadassah knew they would, her father would say, "I did it, Detective Drake." He had told Hadassah he would protect her. She had heard in his voice when he had burst into the room that he was ready to do it right then. But even if he had done something, which Hadassah didn't really believe, not her father (and not Gavriel, though Dinah's brothers had killed the entire male population of a city for her), even if he *had,* that was Hadassah's fault, too.

And it wasn't over.

Chapter 42

Wednesday, November 24, 8:24 a.m. Along Sunset Boulevard and Vista Street. The suspect approached a 39-year-old man in his car and asked for the time. The suspect then held a knife against the victim's chest, demanding money and his cell phone. The suspect later fled the scene in an unknown vehicle.

I had promised to make squash quiche for Thanksgiving dinner, which my parents were hosting. Almost twenty adults and seven kids, so I picked up three butternut squashes and two quarts of soy milk at the market.

While the rinsed and pierced squashes baked in the oven, I did an hour's worth of crime data entry and talked to Edie, who phoned during a break in the Israeli dance class she teaches, to find out whether I'd learned anything new about Hadassah and Greg Shankman. I told her I hadn't. When the squashes were soft, I scooped out and mashed the flesh. I whisked in flour, sugar, softened margarine, soy milk, and three eggs, and poured the mixture into three quiche pans we'd received as wedding gifts. It's a simple recipe, but my mind had been on Shankman, which is why fifteen minutes after the quiches were in the oven, I remembered the cinnamon I hadn't sprinkled on top of each quiche. I took out the pans, sprinkled the quiches with cinnamon, and set them back in the oven.

The quiches needed another hour of baking. I checked my e-mail, deleted forty-three offers to meet "cheating housewives," and visited J Spot. Some of the regulars were there, and several new names. I lurked for a few minutes and logged off.

Since talking with Melissa, I had thought again and again about Adam Prosser and his father, and the phone call Greg Shankman had placed to the father's law offices. I wondered what the father looked like. Then I remembered the copies I'd made on Friday of the Prosser family photo and Adam's photo.

The copies, in my purse, were folded in half. I took them out, unfolded them, and moved aside the top page, with Adam Prosser's smiling face. Mr. Prosser was standing in the center of the family photo, his arm around the waist of a woman I assumed was Mrs. Prosser. On either side of the parents was a son. Adam and his brother. Mr. Prosser was a large man. Large enough to lift a body and haul it out of an apartment into an elevator that would take him to a car in the garage?

I picked up the photocopy to take a closer look at Prosser and realized I was holding two sheets of paper. Maybe I'd accidentally made two copies of the family photo.

But the second page, I saw, wasn't a copy of the photo. It was a copy of an article. For a second I was puzzled. Then I remembered that Dr. McIntyre's photocopied material had been underneath the copies I'd made of the Prosser photos. While separating our photocopies, I'd obviously kept one of his.

The article was from a website and was titled "SMART CHAT." I skimmed a few paragraphs of text that discussed the appeal of chat rooms. The rest of the page contained safety tips for parents to pass on to their children:

Never give a real name or location.

Never meet anyone you talk to in a chat.

Remind your child that people you meet in chat can give false information, including age and gender.

Never use a sexually suggestive screen name.

Don't give out your e-mail address in a public chat.

There were more tips for children, followed by advice for parents: to monitor their children's chats, to communicate regularly with their children about who they talk to online, to move computers from their children's rooms to a public area.

I assumed that McIntyre had been planning to share these tips with his students at Torat Tzion. A good idea, even if it had been too late to protect Hadassah. I put the sheet aside and pulled over my page with circles. I added a circle for PROSSER—Seth or father?—and connected it to Shankman's.

Thinking about McIntyre reminded me that I'd intended to ask him whether the Bailors knew that Hadassah was cutting herself. I found his card in my purse, phoned his office, and listened to his recorded voice informing me that he would be out of town until after Thanksgiving. "In case of emergency, please call Dr. Hobart at. . . ."

I hung up. Hadassah's self-mutilation was troubling, but I didn't know whether it was an emergency. And McIntyre had probably informed the Bailors. I recalled how agitated he'd been about the possible danger Hadassah faced. He had seemed genuinely anxious to help. Anxious enough to talk to Connors, even though doing so would have put the therapist in legal and professional jeopardy. Sue Horowitz had mentioned that McIntyre had lost a child a few years earlier, that teaching at the school gave him hope and a purpose. Maybe that loss had convinced him to contact Connors.

I imagined McIntyre's reaction when Rabbi Bailor told him Hadassah had run away. I wondered whether Hadassah had confided anything about Shankman to her therapist. *Even if I knew who he is,* McIntyre had said, *I couldn't tell you.* Rabbi Bailor had mentioned that he'd asked the therapist to try contacting Hadassah, that McIntyre had explained that he couldn't make the call, that Hadassah would have to call him.

Dassie has his number.

It occurred to me with a jolt that if Hadassah had phoned someone for help Friday night, maybe that someone was McIntyre. She was under his care. She trusted him. He didn't have to worry about violating the Sabbath. . . .

I played the scene in my head. Shankman assaults Hadassah. She defends herself. If Jessie Drake was right, and the blood on Hadassah's clothes was Shankman's, Hadassah injures him. With what?

Jessie Drake had asked me if I'd touched the knives in Shankman's apartment. I pictured Hadassah running to the kitchen, grabbing a knife . . .

Or maybe it wasn't a knife. Saturday night, I'd found a sliver of glass on the floor near the closet in the living room. And one of the photos in the wall unit had been missing its protective glass.

Hadassah and Shankman fight. The frame is knocked down. The glass shatters. Hadassah picks up a shard and defends herself. She stabs Shankman. He falls down.

She's terrified. She phones McIntyre.

McIntyre asks whether Shankman is alive. But if Shankman is alive, wouldn't McIntyre instruct Hadassah to phone 911? Or would he tell her to leave the apartment, and contact 911 himself?

But from what I knew, there had been no phone call to 911. Which meant Shankman was dead when Hadassah phoned McIntyre.

So Hadassah leaves—either on her own, or because McIntyre tells her to. McIntyre arrives and finds Shankman dead. He removes Hadassah's belongings, transfers Shankman's body to Shankman's car, and drives the car off the road.

I shook my head. It was a stretch to believe that the therapist would tamper with a crime scene by removing Hadassah's belongings, even if he wanted to protect her. I couldn't see McIntyre moving Shankman's body and staging the car accident.

I rewound the scene and started again. Hadassah is worried by something Shankman says or does. She phones McIntyre. *Help me.* She struggles with Shankman and wounds him with the knife, or the shard. McIntyre arrives and finds Shankman assaulting Hadassah. She's covered with blood. McIntyre steps in. Struggles with Shankman. Shankman is killed. Hadassah feels guilty about having involved McIntyre, so she refuses to tell the police what happened.

But if Shankman was killed in self-defense, why *wouldn't* she tell the police?

Unless . . . Hadassah wounds Shankman and flees the apartment. She assumes McIntyre has responded to her call for help. She doesn't know whether Shankman was alive or dead when she left. When she learns Shankman is dead, she wonders. . . . She's afraid to ask the therapist, and he doesn't say anything to her because he believes that she killed Shankman. So neither one says anything to the police.

Shankman removes Hadassah's belongings.

And then?

I shook my head again. I was up against the same wall.

"I'm going to have to charge y'all tuition if you keep coming here, Molly," Sue said when I entered her office a little before noon. She smiled. "If you came to see Rabbi, you're out of luck. He's teaching a class and won't be finished till twelve-ten."

That suited me fine. "I was hoping to talk to Dr. McIntyre. I'm thinking of doing that article about teenagers and the Internet. I thought I'd get his views."

"Oh, honey, he won't be back till after Thanksgiving. He took ill Monday and canceled his classes, and he told me he wouldn't be in his office today, so don't bother trying him there. And if y'all are thinking about interviewing students, I don't think that's going to happen, not with all the media attention the school's been getting. Dr. Mendes is in a *mood.*" Sue clucked. "I can't say I blame her."

"I did try phoning Dr. McIntyre this morning. A recording told me the line was disconnected," I lied. "Do you have another number where I can reach him?"

"Just his office number." Sue flipped through her Rolodex and read off a number. "Is that the number you tried?"

"That's it." McIntyre's office number had a 310 area code. That could be Pico-Robertson, Beverly Hills, Century City, Santa Monica, Long Beach, Carson. "What about a home number, Sue?"

She frowned. "That would be in his file. But I couldn't give you that information, Molly."

"I understand. Well, maybe I dialed wrong. I'll try his office number again. By the way, I know that the Prossers are unhappy with Rabbi Bailor, because he put Adam on probation."

"Rabbi told you?" Sue nodded. "Rabbi did what was right. Like I said, it doesn't matter to Rabbi how much money a family gives the school."

"I met Seth Prosser the other day. Adam's brother? He definitely didn't seem happy with the rabbi."

Sue grimaced. "Seth has a temper. He barged in here one day when all this was going on, demanded to see Rabbi. He was yelling. 'He won't get away with this. He'll be sorry.' Stuff like that. I told him to come back when he learned some manners. That boy was always high strung."

"Is he an attorney, like his father?"

"He was going to law school, but I heard he took a year off."

The phone rang. Sue answered. "Torat Tzion. No, Ariella didn't mention a dental appointment, Mrs. Linzer." Sue listened. "Right now? All right, I'll get her. Do you know which class she's in right now?" Sue sighed. "Okay, I'll find out. But please make sure she brings a note tomorrow. You're welcome."

Sue hung up. "You'd think I had nothing better to do. It was nice seeing y'all again. Good luck with your article."

"As long as I'm here, Sue, I can ask you a few questions for my article, too. You can give me your perspective."

"Well, I don't know what I can tell y'all about teens and the Internet, except that, judging from my kids, they spend way too much time on it."

"I'd love to hear some details."

She smiled. "All right, then. Let me find out what class this girl is in and tell her that her mom's waiting outside."

Typing on her keyboard, Sue accessed a document and found the information she wanted.

When she left, the door was open. I shut the door and walked to the filing cabinet. The multicolored birds squatting on top of the cabinet glared at me. With a silent apology to Sue, I opened the top drawer and thumbed through the folder tabs. No MCINTYRE.

His folder wasn't in the second drawer. Or the third. I found a folder for PROSSER. I wrote down the Beverly Hills address.

I didn't know where Sue had gone, but it couldn't have been far. She would be back any minute. Any second, for that matter.

I tabbed through the folders of the fourth drawer. Nothing.

The ringing of the phone startled me.

I turned and looked at Sue's desk. There was a shallow top drawer on the left. Below that was a deep drawer. A filing cabinet?

The phone was still ringing. I wished the answering machine would pick up. I hurried to the desk, pulled open the bottom drawer, and there it was: McIntyre's file. The drawer was crammed with files, and I had to jiggle the manila folder to get it out.

The phone stopped ringing.

Inside the folder was a single sheet of paper. McIntyre's photo, passport size, was stapled to the upper right corner. On the sheet were his home address in North Hollywood, and his home phone number, with an 818 prefix. Another address and phone number, also in North Hollywood, for the person to notify in case of an emergency. Nancy McIntyre. I wrote that down, too.

I heard footsteps.

My heart thumped. I closed McIntyre's folder and jammed it back into the drawer.

I was shutting the drawer as the door opened.

I sprinted to the black filing cabinet and was holding a parrot when Sue entered. Thank God this one couldn't talk.

"These are cute," I said. "You collect them?"

She nodded. "They are, aren't they? Some people do salt shakers or ashtrays. I like birds."

I put the parrot back on the filing cabinet. "By the way, Sue. My mom teaches at Sharsheret. She says the AP course instructors proctor their own AP exams. Is that how it works here?"

"Sometimes. But if a teacher isn't available, someone else will do it. Usually, Dr. Mendes."

Interesting. "I'm surprised Dr. Mendes would have the time."

"Well, she's very much a hands-on principal. I have to say I admire that about her. She's a stickler for detail, too. She wants to make sure everything is right."

"And I guess she makes sure all the information the students have filled out is correct, huh?"

"Oh, yes. She collects all the AP exams and mails them back to the testing center. And she goes over every teacher recommendation before it's mailed out. All right then, Molly Blume. What would y'all like to know?"

"Actually, Sue, I had a call while you were out, and I'll have to take a rain check. Maybe we can talk next week?"

"Whenever." She smiled. "You're a breath of fresh air, Molly. I can see why Rabbi likes you."

That made me feel worse.

Chapter 43

I took Coldwater Canyon, one of the serpentine roads that connects L.A. to the San Fernando Valley. The road climbs until it reaches Mulholland. Then it descends. When I reached Mulholland I thought about the spot where Greg Shankman's car had careened off the road onto the rocks below, but I had no interest in viewing the scene of the crime.

McIntyre lived on Whitsett, north of Ventura Boulevard. Like many of the homes in the Valley, his was ranch style. There was a car in the driveway, but no one answered the door after I rang the bell several times. To the side of the door were editions of the *L.A. Times*, from Sunday through Wednesday. I wondered if he'd gone on vacation.

Nancy McIntyre lived less than half a mile away. I wasn't sure what she could tell me, if anything, but as long as I was here I decided to pay her a visit. I didn't know whether she was Dr. McIntyre's mother or sister, or another family member.

As it turned out, she was his ex-wife. She was in her early fifties, I guessed, petite and trim, with short dark brown hair and hazel eyes. She was wearing a hot pink sweater and black slacks.

I introduced myself, told her I wanted to talk to her ex-husband in regard to an article I was writing about teens and the Internet, that I'd learned he wasn't in his office today, but hadn't found him at home, either.

"How did you get my home address, Molly?" she asked.

"I looked it up online," I said.

"Try again." She folded her arms. "My address isn't listed. Neither is John's. You have ten seconds to tell me how you found me and what you're doing here. At that point I will definitely shut the door, and I may call the police."

I didn't need ten seconds. "I got hold of your husband's file at the school where he works," I said.

She frowned. "Why? And please don't insult my intelligence by repeating that lie about your article."

"One of his students, Hadassah Bailor, is also his patient. She ran away with—"

"John told me about her," Nancy interrupted. "He was terribly distressed. And then yesterday I heard on the news that the girl had a relationship with a teacher whose car crashed off of Mulholland Friday night, correct?" The woman narrowed her eyes. "What's your connection?"

"I was asked by the family to find her."

"I see. And what's John's connection? Aside from being this girl's teacher and therapist?"

"I think Hadassah phoned him that night for help."

Nancy stood for several seconds, her arms folded, not really looking at me. "I think I liked your story better," she said. She opened the door. "Come in."

We sat in a small den on a hunter green chenille love seat that showed signs of wear. Against one wall was a cherry desk with one of those vintage phones with the round dial. On another wall was a book-case filled with books and photos.

"Please sit down," she said. It was more like an order than an invitation.

I sat. She remained standing and rested a hip against the desk.

"John hasn't been himself the past few days," Nancy said. "I knew something was wrong."

"When did you last talk to him?"

"This morning. I talk to him every day. Sunday we were supposed to have dinner, the way we do most Sundays. John said he was coming down with a cold, but I knew better. I know what you're thinking: How nice that we've managed to stay amicable. We're not amicable, Molly. John loves me. I love him. We are best friends. We just can't live together."

"I see."

The look she gave me was fierce. "No, you *don't* see, so why do you feel compelled to say you do? I find it tiresome and condescending. What do you know about John?"

"I've only talked to him once. Rabbi Bailor speaks highly of him. The rabbi's assistant, Mrs. Horowitz, told me Dr. McIntyre is a good teacher and a good man."

"He is. Did she tell you we lost our daughter?"

I nodded.

"Did she tell you how?"

"No." I had the feeling I didn't want to hear.

Nancy took a photo from the bookcase and handed it to me. "That's Victoria."

I looked at the young face in the photo. Dark brown hair, blue eyes, a sweet smile.

"She killed herself when she was fifteen," Nancy said. "She met someone online ten months before that. They started instant messaging. He told her he was sixteen. He was fifty-three. He taught high school math in Dallas. He came to the house one day when he knew John and I were at work, and he molested her."

Her recital had been unemotional, flat. I supposed that was the only way she could bear telling it.

"I'm so sorry." Tears welled in my eyes.

"Everyone is sorry, when they hear." Nancy took the photo and held it to her chest. "Vicky didn't tell us right away. She was ashamed. She was afraid we'd be angry, that we'd blame her for giving this man information that allowed him to find her. We knew something was wrong. She wasn't eating. She had difficulty sleeping. Her grades were falling. She was obviously depressed. I did something I'd never done before. I read her journal. She'd written everything down."

Nancy studied the photo before returning it to the shelf. "She was angry at first, because I'd violated her privacy. But I think she was relieved that her terrible secret was out. John didn't want to treat Vicky himself, so he took her to a therapist, who put her on an antidepressant. Vicky seemed better. We all felt safer. Three months later she hanged herself. A few months ago we learned that the antidepressant she was taking can cause suicidal tendencies in some teenagers. Apparently, it had been banned in Britain last December."

I had read articles about the FDA report and its findings. Prozac, I recalled, had been cleared. But a list of other antidepressants hadn't. And families were urged to take a depressed teen not to a pediatrician, but to a psychiatrist, who would provide therapy and carefully monitor the dosage and effects of the antidepressant.

"Vicky died five years ago," Nancy said. "John has been punishing himself ever since. He spent his life helping people deal with emotional and psychological problems so that they could lead healthy, fulfilling lives. But he couldn't save his own child. He couldn't understand why Vicky hadn't come to him earlier, why he hadn't seen that something was terribly wrong when she was on the antidepressant. It ate at him." Nancy paused. "People say they understand. They can't possibly. I hope they never can."

I nodded.

"You know they say losing a child can either bring a couple together or destroy their marriage? After a year and a half, I realized we couldn't continue living each day as a memorial to Vicky. Every day we were dying a little more. So I called friends I hadn't talked to in over a year. I took an interest in my appearance. I went back to work. I'm an occupational therapist. But John?" Nancy sighed. "John couldn't do it. And he resented that I could. He accused me of betraying Vicky's memory. And I was afraid he was going to pull me into Vicky's grave with him. So we divorced."

Nancy put her hands on the desk. "Do you want to know what John does almost every night, Molly? He eats dinner—usually by himself, unless I join him. He's lost touch with most of his friends. Then he goes out. To a singles bar, to a club. He watches young girls, and if he sees them talking to men, he goes over and warns them to be careful. And when he comes home, Molly, he goes online and visits teen chat rooms and warns kids not to reveal personal information."

"Lucky7," I said.

Nancy looked startled. "How did you know?" she demanded.

I told her about my visits to J Spot.

"That was Vicky's screen name," Nancy said, her voice gentled. "John took it over. I think it makes him feel she's still alive."

"When did he start visiting J Spot?" I asked.

"After Hadassah Bailor ran away. He hadn't thought to monitor J Spot. He's blaming himself for that." She stood straight. "Tell me why you think Hadassah contacted John on Friday night."

"It's just a theory," I said, and explained my reasoning.

"John is obsessed with protecting young women," Nancy said when I had finished. "A few months ago he followed a man and a young woman from a bar to the man's apartment. The man spotted him lurking and called the police. They arrested John. He called me. I talked to the police and explained." Nancy sighed. "At the school where he was teaching before Torat Tzion, parents complained that he was asking his female students questions about their boyfriends and their Internet habits. Things like that. Needless to say, John wasn't rehired."

"Nancy, would Dr. McIntyre have moved Greg Shankman's body and staged the car accident?"

"The John McIntyre I married?" Nancy shook her head. "The John McIntyre trying to atone for his daughter's death?" She left the question unanswered. "Aren't you going to ask me if John would have killed to protect Hadassah?"

I couldn't tell what she wanted. "Would he?"

"I don't know, Molly. That's sad, isn't it? I've urged him to see someone, to get help. Maybe now he'll listen."

If it wasn't too late. "When I stopped at his house, before I came here, I saw Dr. McIntyre's car in the driveway, but he didn't answer the door. And Mrs. Horowitz told me he called in sick on Monday."

Chapter 44

The car was still there.

I parked on the street behind Nancy and followed her to the front door. She picked up the newspapers, rang the bell several times, then unlocked the door with a spare key. Like Saturday night all over again, I thought, as I followed her inside. I hoped the ending was different.

"John?" she called. "It's Nancy."

There were no house sounds—no music, no TV, no dishwasher running, no drone of a vacuum that would explain why he didn't respond.

"John?"

A shrill whistle broke the silence. I jumped at the sound. So did Nancy. We passed through the living room and dining room to the kitchen, where a kettle was boiling. She turned off the flame. The sink and counters were filled with dishes.

He was in his office. Nancy entered the room. I stayed in the hall, but from where I was standing, I could see Dr. McIntyre sitting at his desk. His hands were on the keyboard of one of the two computers that faced him.

Nancy stood behind him and placed a hand on his shoulder. "John, didn't you hear the doorbell? Or the kettle?"

"Just a second," he said, not turning around.

"John, honey, I was worried about you."

"I told you I was fine," he said, irritated. "I think I had a touch of the flu."

"You canceled all your classes this week, John."

"Stupid!" he exclaimed. "You see that post, Nancy?" He pointed to the screen. "The poster said she takes gymnastics. She named the sports center, and the city! Anyone can find her." His fingers flew on the keyboard.

Nancy massaged his shoulder.

"I can't be everywhere, Nancy."

"I know, honey. That girl you told me about, Hadassah Bailor? I know you were terribly worried when she ran away with that man."

"Hadassah's safe now."

"That's wonderful. I think you helped her, John. Did you?"

I held my breath.

He moved the computer mouse and clicked. "Do you have any idea how many chat rooms there are, Nancy?"

"Did you help Hadassah Bailor, John?"

He inched the chair to the right and rested his hands on the keyboard of the second computer. "She called my emergency number. Friday night. She left a message."

"So you went to Mr. Shankman's apartment? John, this is important." She removed his hands from the keyboard and moved the mouse away. "John, tell me what happened."

He dropped his hands to his lap. "She was whispering, but I could hear how terrified she was. 'Help me, please.' That's what she said. She gave the address and the apartment number. I had to help her, Nancy."

"Of course you did, John." She squeezed his shoulder. "So what happened?"

"I didn't get the message right away. There was a problem with my service. When I got to the apartment, the door was unlocked, but Hadassah wasn't there. He was on the floor, lying on his side."

"Mr. Shankman?"

McIntyre nodded. "I checked for a pulse. He was dead, Nancy. His shirt was covered with blood. There was a gash in his throat. And his head. . . ." McIntyre made a retching sound.

"Why didn't you call the police, John?"

"I was afraid they would arrest Hadassah."

"But she called you for help, John." Nancy stroked his arm. "On your emergency number. If he assaulted her, and she killed him in self-defense, the police wouldn't have arrested her."

"The back of his head, Nancy. It was . . . horrible. Somebody . . . There was a marble statue on the floor. An owl. It was covered in blood. I was afraid the police would say it wasn't self-defense. Because why didn't she run after she stabbed him? Why did she smash in the back of his head? If I had gotten there in time, Nancy. . . ."

"You did your best. John, did you take Hadassah's belongings from the apartment?"

"She must have panicked, Nancy. She was terrified. But she shouldn't go to jail. Shankman was a monster. He deserved to die."

"Did you move Shankman's body to his car, John?"

"No."

"Someone moved his body to his car and crashed the car, John. I heard that on the news. I'm sure you did, too."

"I didn't move his body. Why would I do that?"

"To protect Hadassah."

"I didn't move his body, Nancy."

"Are her things here in the house, John?"

He didn't answer.

"John, the police know Hadassah Bailor was at Shankman's apartment. We have to call them. You understand that, don't you? Where are her things, John?"

"I took the marble statue. I wiped off the blood, and the fingerprints."

"John—"

"They're going to think I killed him, Nancy. They're going to find out about Vicky, and the other incidents."

"I'll stay with you, John. I'll explain everything, and they'll believe me. Where are Hadassah's things, John?"

"In my bedroom closet."

He returned his hands to the keyboard and typed. Nancy turned to me and nodded. She put her arms around him and kissed his head.

I phoned Jessie Drake.

Chapter 45

===

They found Hadassah's black purse, inside of which were her cell phone, house keys, and a small journal. They also found a plastic bag with makeup and toiletries and clothing. A cashmere shawl, earrings, a skirt and a clingy black sweater, an ivory lace nightgown with a tag still attached. Wrapped in a towel was a black marble owl.

I stood in the hall, watching. I checked my watch and was surprised to see that it was almost four. Two hours had passed since Nancy and I had arrived.

A short while later Jessie came out of the room.

"What now?" I asked her.

"We have to take Dr. McIntyre for questioning."

"I think he's telling the truth, Detective Drake."

"Call me Jessie. I think you've earned it." She smiled. "McIntyre may be telling the truth, Molly. But he does have what will probably turn out to be the murder weapon."

"He mentioned a gash in Shankman's throat."

"As I said, the autopsy hasn't been done yet. But the injury to his head was significant."

I tried not to, but I pictured a hand slamming the black marble owl against the back of Shankman's head. I felt queasy. "Did Dr. McIntyre tell you what time he arrived at Shankman's apartment?"

"He says it was around six-forty. He says his service delayed giving him Hadassah's message, which she placed at five-fifty-three. We'll check with the service to verify that he's telling the truth."

"You think he's lying?"

"We can't rule out the possibility that he killed Shankman. You said his daughter killed herself because she'd been molested by a teacher. Friday night he finds himself in a room with a teacher who tried to seduce a student, and maybe assaulted her, and perhaps intended to kill her? Could be he was reliving the past, but this time he was determined to render justice."

It was so sad, I thought. Carrying around that pain, that guilt. "What about the Prossers? Are you forgetting about them?"

"Not at all. I spoke to the father, Gerald. His wife was out of town for the weekend, visiting her parents. Gerald and the boys were home. They alibi each other."

"Naturally."

"But," Jessie said, "a neighbor saw the car pulling out of the driveway Friday night, just before six."

"Interesting," I said.

"And the older brother, Seth, left law school at the end of last semester. Apparently, he has a drug problem. He was in rehab through the end of the summer, and he's taking the year off before he goes back."

I drove home and phoned Zack to tell him what had happened. I debated phoning the Bailors but decided not to. If McIntyre was telling the truth, either Hadassah had killed Shankman, or someone else had.

My quiches had been sitting on my kitchen counter for hours. I put them in the refrigerator and phoned Jessie.

"Did you check Hadassah's cell phone calls?" I asked.

"A few minutes ago. She placed a call to McIntyre at five-fifty-three. So McIntyre is telling the truth about that. She also placed a call to her home."

"Thursday night, you mean. Shankman phoned Hadassah's mother."

"No, Friday night, at five-fifty-two. There are a few other calls, including one to 911, also at five-fifty-two. My guess is she hung up before she talked to a dispatcher. We'll check out all the calls."

"You're sure about the Friday night call to the Bailors?"

"I'm sure. I'm sorry, Molly."

"She could have placed the call to her parents but decided against leaving a message. The same as with the 911 call."

"She could have. Absolutely."

I could hear that Jessie was humoring me. I was sick at heart. Rabbi Bailor had said he was home Friday night, having *Shabbat* dinner with his family before he and Gavriel left for the *sholom zochor*. But was that true?

I was restless. It was four-thirty. Zack wouldn't be home for more than an hour. I read a few chapters of a book, but I couldn't concentrate. My sister-in-law, Gitty, phoned. I pretended to be surprised when she told me she was pregnant, and was commiserating with her about her morning sickness when a beep on the line told me I had another call. My caller ID showed that the call was from Yamashiro. I said good-bye to Gitty and pressed FLASH.

It was Irene Jakaitis. I wondered what she could possibly tell me now.

"Your cousin must be so relieved," she said.

"Relieved?"

"You know, about her boyfriend? I finally saw the news, about the car crash. It was awful."

"We're all glad she's safe."

"No, I mean that *he's* okay. Your cousin's boyfriend."

"Irene, he was in a fatal car crash. The man my cousin was with is dead."

"Well, I guess we're talking about some other guy, Molly. Because the man they showed on the news? Greg Shankman, I think they said? The one whose car went off the road? That's not the man your cousin was with Thursday night at Yamashiro."

I was speechless. I leaned against the kitchen counter.

"Molly? Are you there?"

"Irene, are you sure about this?"

"Positive. Like I told you, I'm bad with names. But I'm good with faces. What I can't figure out, though, is what your cousin's boyfriend was doing in this guy's Altima. I guess he borrowed it, huh? That explains why he was so freaked by the damage to the car."

Chapter 46

Bubbie G says speed is good only for catching flies. I thought about that and decided to wait before phoning Jessie Drake.

I drove to the Bailors. Parked in front was Jastrow's dark blue Volvo, so I wasn't surprised that he answered the door. He didn't look thrilled to see me.

"I need to talk to Hadassah," I said. "It's urgent."

Jastrow sighed. "Miss Blume, we appreciate all your efforts, and I hope you won't take this the wrong way, but my brother-in-law retained an attorney for Dassie, and the attorney instructed us not to talk to anyone."

"Where's Rabbi Bailor?"

"In his office. My sister is out. As I said—"

"Tell him Greg Shankman wasn't at Yamashiro with Dassie."

Jastrow grunted. "Of course, he was."

"I spoke with the waitress fifteen minutes ago. You know, Irene Jakaitis? The one you phoned Friday afternoon?" Jastrow had the grace to blush. "She just saw the news coverage for the first time, along with a photo of Shankman. She's positive he's not the man who was with Dassie Thursday night."

Jastrow froze. "But the license plate . . ."

"Obviously, someone else was driving Shankman's car."

"Who?"

"That's what I want to ask Dassie. She knows. Maybe that's the person she's protecting, although I can't imagine why."

"Dassie's not here. She's feeling a little better, thank God. She walked over to visit her friend, Sara. It's just a few blocks, and she needed the fresh air."

"Call Dassie and tell her to come home."

Jastrow hesitated, then stepped aside to let me in. He left me in the hall and walked to his brother-in-law's office.

While I waited, I reviewed what I'd worked out on the drive here. Shankman had told Milt LaSalle, the apartment manager, that he was going away for a few days on vacation. With Melissa he'd been more specific: He'd told her he was going to Sedona to think things over and make some decisions. Like Melissa, I'd assumed that Shankman had lied about going away. Just as I'd assumed that he'd assaulted Hadassah.

But if Irene Jakaitis was right, and I had no reason to think otherwise, someone else had "met" Dassie through J Spot and lured her away. Someone, I still believed, who had known enough about her to impress her with his "insight." Someone who, while Shankman was away, had appropriated Shankman's car and apartment.

Dr. Mendes had probably known that Shankman was going away. According to Melissa, the principal had talked with Shankman several times over the past few weeks. Had she mentioned his travel plans to Gerald Prosser? Had Prosser calmed his son: *Don't worry, Adam, as soon as Shankman's back from vacation, we'll resolve this issue?*

Had Seth known?

Seth was high-strung, Sue had said. And according to Jessie, he'd been in rehab for a drug problem. So he'd been in town in September, when Dassie first met her anonymous boyfriend. And Sue Horowitz had said that the law school dropout had threatened Rabbi Bailor. *He'll be sorry.*

Maybe it had started as a prank: Humiliate the daughter. Embarrass the rabbi. Maybe he'd wanted to blackmail Rabbi Bailor to remove the probation—and then it turned into something more sinister. What a double coup, and what malevolent irony, to complete the seduction by using the car and apartment that belonged to Shankman, the man who was the cause of Seth's brother's problems.

But how had Seth gained access to Shankman's apartment and car? Melissa, I recalled, had said something about Seth going to talk to Shankman at his apartment. . . .

I heard footsteps and saw Rabbi Bailor and his brother-in-law walking toward me. They both looked grim.

"Listen," I said, prepared to forestall an argument.

"She's not there," Rabbi Bailor said. It was more a wail, really. "Dassie's not at Sara's. She never showed up."

My chest was so tight I couldn't breathe. "When did she leave here?"

"After five. A half hour ago? Reuben said it wasn't Shankman. But that's not possible! He's dead! Dassie—" He stopped himself.

"I want to see her room," I said.

I didn't wait for permission. I raced up the stairs to the bedroom and heard footsteps following me. The bed had been neatened. The computer was off. The room was filled with flowers. On the nightstand between the two beds was a stack of get-well cards and the envelopes they had come in.

"All her friends have been sending cards and flowers," Rabbi Bailor said. "And calling. That's why she wanted to go to Sara's. For a little normalcy."

An envelope in the stack caught my eye. The return address said ADAM PROSSER. I pulled it out and showed it to Rabbi Bailor.

"Where's the note?" I asked.

"I don't know."

"Don't you find it odd that Dassie is friendly with a boy who hates you?"

"I've never discussed any Torat Tzion student with Dassie. She has no idea that the Prosser boy and I have our difficulties."

I checked the trash can. I looked under Dassie's bed. The magazines were gone. A section of the bedskirt was stuck between the mattress and box spring. I lifted the mattress, bent my head, and looked underneath.

Something was there. I slipped my hand into the space and pulled out a blue card.

> I saw your father leaving the apartment
> Friday night when I came back from shul.
> Greg Shankman was dead. Killed.
> I could tell the police, but I won't, ever.
> I would die a million deaths for you, Dassie.
> JUSTFORJU

I showed Rabbi Bailor the note.

"That's a lie." His face was red with outrage. "Do you have any idea who wrote this?"

I took the card from his shaking hand. "Possibly."

"Who—"

"I could be wrong. I was wrong about Greg Shankman." I didn't want to think about my role in his death. "As soon as I learn anything conclusive, I'll let you know. In the meantime, call Detective Drake and tell her Dassie has disappeared."

"You think Dassie went with this man voluntarily?"

"She may have. She may love him. She may feel obligated. Rabbi Bailor, are you aware that Dassie has been cutting herself?"

He looked as if I'd slapped him. "Cutting herself?"

"Self-mutilating. Cheryl Wexner suspected it and told Dr. McIntyre."

"Dr. McIntyre never said a word." The rabbi sank onto Aliza's bed. "When Dassie was a baby, I used to put a mirror in front of her nose to make sure she was breathing. I worried about every sniffle. She had croup, so I stayed up nights with her, worrying. And then she grew up, and I thought, now I don't have to worry so much. So now you're telling me she's cutting herself? Why?"

"I spoke with a psychologist, Rabbi Bailor. She said cutting is sometimes a prelude to suicide. That's why I was so worried last week, because I thought this man might convince Dassie to kill herself. A double suicide," I said.

I explained the references to Hamlet and Romeo and Juliet. "Whatever Dassie's involvement with Shankman's death, she may feel guilty."

"I can't believe Dassie would kill herself." Rabbi Bailor frowned. "And if he can't convince her? What then?"

I could see from the terror in his eyes that he'd answered his own question.

Chapter 47

The maître d' remembered me. He didn't look pleased, but he agreed to get Irene. I tapped my foot impatiently until he returned after what seemed like an hour but was only a few minutes.

"Irene is extremely busy," he told me, basking in disapproval. "But she said she'll be out as soon as she can."

"Thank you."

More waiting—not my strong suit. I phoned Zack to tell him where I was and what had happened. Then I phoned Rabbi Bailor.

"I talked to Detective Drake," the rabbi told me. "She's putting out an all-points bulletin. Reuben and I drove around the neighborhood, but there's no sign of Dassie."

I saw Irene approaching. She waved as if we were old friends.

"Can you tell me what you're thinking?" he asked. "Please."

"When I'm sure. I have to go, Rabbi." I hung up before he could say anything else.

"That's something about the car, isn't it?" Irene said when she was at my side. "Did you figure out who borrowed it?"

"I have an idea."

On the way to Yamashiro I had stopped at home for the photocopy I'd made of the Prosser family. I took the photocopy from my purse and showed it to her.

"Do you recognize anyone in this photo, Irene?" I held my breath.

She peered at the photocopy for a long moment, then shook her head. "Nope."

Not the answer I'd expected.

"Are you sure?" I pointed to Seth. "What about him? This was taken a few years ago, but he looks pretty much the same."

She took another look. "No, sorry. Not even close."

I had been so certain. Thank God I hadn't said anything about Seth to Rabbi Bailor.

"You think your cousin's boyfriend stole the car, don't you?" Irene said. "I'd hate to believe that. He seemed so sweet."

"To be honest, I'm not sure of anything anymore. Well, thanks anyway, Irene. If you remember anything—"

"I *did* remember something. Your cousin's boyfriend was writing a screenplay. That probably doesn't narrow it down, 'cause half the people in Hollywood are writing screenplays, right?"

"Right."

"Or trying to get into acting. I am, too. Shocker, huh?" Irene smiled. "I don't plan to be waiting tables long. But I'm patient. If it's meant to happen, it'll happen, right? Anyway, I guess that's why he gave me such a nice tip. One waiter to the other, you know?"

My heart was drumming in my chest. "He was a waiter?"

Irene nodded. "You don't look good. Are you okay, Molly?"

"Irene, did he mention what kind of screenplay he was writing?"

She thought a moment. "He said it was like a movie I saw,

with Ethan Hawke and Uma Thurman. I don't remember the name."

"*Gattaca?*"

"That sounds right. It's kind of sad, isn't it? About Ethan Hawke and Uma, I mean. I thought that one would last, didn't you? I guess it's hard to find true love."

Chapter 48

Hadassah's head ached. She tried raising her hand to massage her temple and realized he'd tied her hands. Not so tightly that they hurt, and he'd been careful to avoid the scars above her wrists, but the knots were tight enough so that she couldn't undo them even if she could reach them with her thumbs.

She was lying on a bed in a small room that glowed with the light of candles. Some of them had a fruity scent. Others were musky. There was another smell, too, and the combination was making her nauseated. From outside the room she heard music. The sound track from *Romeo and Juliet*. His favorite.

He was sitting on a folding chair, watching her. When she opened her eyes, he hurried to her side and put his hand over her mouth.

"Please don't scream," he said. "I would never hurt you, Dassie. Don't be afraid."

She nodded. He removed his hand.

"I had to tie your hands, Dassie. You were thrashing. I was afraid you'd hurt yourself."

She knew he was lying. She had been walking to Sara's, thrilled to inhale the crisp evening air after being indoors for so long. Suddenly he was standing in front of her. "I've been waiting for you, Dassie," he said. A cloth covered her face. She smelled something sickly sweet. Then everything was black.

"I could watch you sleep for hours," he said now. "I did that in the other apartment. You didn't even know."

He ran his fingers through her curls. She cringed at his touch, but lay still.

"This isn't how I wanted it to be," he said. "Greg is dead. Because of you, Dassie." His voice was soft with reproach. "But I still love you."

Her lips were dry. She licked them. "Water," she said.

He left the room and returned with a glass. Sitting on the side of the bed, he raised her head and brought the glass to her lips. The water was cold, with a hint of chlorine.

"Why did you ruin everything, Dassie? Why did you run away?"

"I was scared. You lied to me. It was his apartment. I was scared," she said again. She didn't want to tell him that his talk of death and dying had frightened her. She didn't want to say the word *death*.

"We wanted to be alone. Where should we have gone? I would have explained."

"You took away my phone. You locked the door. The key didn't work. I felt trapped."

"You gave me your phone to protect what we had," he chided. "Remember? I had no idea the key didn't work. I would never hold you against your will, Dassie. How could you think that?" He stroked her cheek. "I waited so long for someone like you, pure and true. Someone just like me. We're the same, Dassie."

She recognized the lyrics from the song. "Their" song.

"I brought you a new nightgown." He walked to the chair and held up a creamy white satin gown edged with lace, just like the first one he'd bought her.

"It's beautiful," she said.

He frowned. She thought he knew she was lying, but he said, "Why aren't you wearing the ring?"

Friday night, after coming home, she had realized that the ring was on her finger. She had taken it off and put it in a dresser drawer, in case he wanted it back.

"I was afraid my parents would take it away, so I put it somewhere safe," she told him.

She had no idea what he planned to do, but she knew enough to be afraid. She'd thought she would never be as terrified as she had been on Friday night, but Friday night she'd had a phone, she had called for help. Friday night, she thought, biting her lips to stop their trembling, she had stabbed a man who had done nothing to deserve it. Now he was dead. So maybe she deserved to die, too.

"Where are we?" she asked.

"An apartment. It's empty, except for the mattress and box spring. I brought the sheets, because I wanted everything to be pretty. I brought the candles, and the wine I bought for *Shabbat*." He leaned close. "I would die a million deaths for you, Dassie. Would you die for me?"

"Yes," she lied.

Wine would make her drowsy, but it might make him drowsy, too. Hadassah had learned about Yael, who saved the Jewish people by inviting the enemy general, Sisera, into her tent. Yael plied Sisera with cheese to make him drowsy. And when he was asleep, she took a peg and a hammer and drove the peg into his forehead.

Hadassah didn't have a peg. She had taken the shard with her, she wasn't sure why. It was in the pocket of her sweater.

She didn't know where he had put her sweater.

And her hands were tied with rope.

Chapter 49

I found a spot in front of my favorite house with the multiple turrets. I still hadn't figured out what to say, but I locked the car, walked the few steps to the apartment door, and rang the bell.

Cheryl opened the door. "Molly, what a lovely surprise. No treats from The Coffee Bean this time?" She smiled.

I forced a smile in return. "Sorry."

"I'm just joking." She furrowed her brow. "Are you okay? You look upset."

"It's been a long day. Is Justin here?"

"You came to see how he's doing?" She squeezed my hand. "You are so sweet. He left an hour or so ago and took my car. He said he'd be out late and not to wait up. I'll tell him you stopped by. Can I fix you a cup of coffee?"

"No, thanks. Maybe another time." I wasn't sure whether there would ever be another time. Even if there were, nothing would be the same. "Do you know where to reach him? I wanted to ask him something about Adam Prosser."

"I don't, sorry. He lost his cell phone and hasn't had a chance to buy a new one. He called me earlier and said he was using a friend's cell, but he didn't leave me the number, and I don't have caller ID. I'm making a salad. Do you mind if we talk in the kitchen? I don't want the lettuce to wilt."

We walked to the kitchen. Cheryl stood in front of the sink and rinsed some vegetables. I sat at the table, just as I had two days ago.

"I saw the get-well card Justin sent Dassie the other day," I said. "That was thoughtful of him."

From Yamashiro, I'd returned to the Bailors' and to Dassie's room, where I found the blue envelope that matched the blue card. The return address said CHERYL WEXNER. I hadn't said anything to Rabbi Bailor or to Mrs. Bailor, who looked as though she'd died. As soon as I'd left their house, I phoned West L.A. and left a message for Jessie to call me.

Cheryl looked at me, surprised. "He sent her a card? That *is* thoughtful."

I could see in her eyes the beginnings of something that wasn't quite alarm. "I didn't realize Justin knew Hadassah," I said.

"She came here half a dozen times to work on her application. She and Justin met once or twice. To tell you the truth, if she wasn't so young, and so religious, he might have been interested in her. I'm not sure he'll ever be Orthodox. Although people do change," she said. "Rabbi Bailor wasn't always rabbi material."

"Neither was my husband."

It would have been easy for Justin to get hold of the contents of Dassie's file when his mother was away. I had read the essay—there had been nothing revealing. Had there been a questionnaire? *Write down your favorite color, your favorite foods, what music you like, your hobbies, your talents. What significant events have shaped your life?*

Cheryl peeled a cucumber. "Anyway, Rabbi and Mrs. Bailor would never have allowed Hadassah to go out with someone they didn't hand-pick. And not with a screenwriter. I'm sure they want her to marry someone who learns Torah every day. I don't blame them."

An edge of anger in her voice said otherwise. Had Justin been angry, too? Was that why he'd done what he had—because he hadn't felt good enough for the rabbi?

"Anyway," Cheryl said. "I'm so relieved Hadassah's safe at home. I meant to ask you, did you tell the Bailors about the cutting?"

"I did. They're upset, but now they know to keep an eye on her. And of course, she's going to continue therapy. It's sad how many at-risk teens there are. You're lucky that Justin wasn't scarred by the divorce. I know you said he had a rough time, but he seems to be doing well."

"He's a sensitive young man. I think I told you that? And so creative." She put down the peeler and turned toward me. "Between us, Molly?"

I nodded.

"Justin tried to kill himself two years ago. He slit his wrist. Thank God I got him to the hospital in time. He had therapy, and he's been on medication since. He hates being on meds, but I tell him thank God they're available. His father tells him, too." Cheryl set the cucumber on a wood cutting board and sliced it. "Don't tell Justin, but that's why I moved to Los Angeles. He was three thousand miles away, and I worried that he wouldn't remember to take his meds. And I *do* like it here."

"I'm glad. By the way, how was dinner with the Stones?"

"Lovely." Cheryl flashed a smile. "They invited me for Thanksgiving dinner. And I'm planning to have them for lunch the following *Shabbat.*"

"Did Justin enjoy it, too?" I hoped my tone was nonchalant.

Everything indicated that Dassie had been with Justin. The get-well card, Irene's comments. But if he had been with his mother and the Stones on Friday night, how had he seen Rabbi Bailor leaving the apartment?

"Oh, Justin didn't go for dinner," Cheryl said. "He joined me for services at *shul,* but he had other plans. Young people are so secretive, aren't they? But I'm glad he has friends, especially lately. He was doing so well until Greg was fired. He took it so personally."

So Justin had been at the apartment. Had he seen Rabbi Bailor leaving? Or was that a lie?

Cheryl rinsed a tomato and set it on the cutting board. "Would you like to stay for dinner? I can defrost another steak. I'd love the company."

"I wish I could, but Zack is expecting me home. You mentioned the other day that Justin wasn't going to continue studying with Rabbi Bailor. That's too bad."

I wondered where Justin was right now. With Hadassah? Had she lied about going to Sara's? Had he talked her into running away with him a second time?

"Yes, well, he was terribly disillusioned when Rabbi Bailor didn't support Greg," Cheryl said. "And some of his anger toward the rabbi is my fault, I'm afraid."

"I don't understand."

Maybe Justin had communicated with Dassie. I had seen her in the chat room last night. Maybe he'd IM'ed her: *Come with me, or I tell the police about your father.*

Cheryl laughed, nervous. "I don't know why I'm telling you all this. You're not going to think well of me."

"Try me," I said, hating the fact that I was eliciting information under the promise of friendship.

"God, I haven't talked about this in years." She cut the tomato and tossed the chunks into a glass bowl, along with the cucumbers. "Justin and I have always been close—probably too close. I was a single mom with an only son, and Justin is so empathetic. I talked to him about personal things as if he were an adult. I treated him like a friend. That was wrong. I regret it."

I nodded, my mind on Justin. What if he'd followed Dassie while she was walking to Sara's? What if he'd snatched her?

"You remember I told you about my first love?" Cheryl said. "Justin came across some love letters I'd kept, and some mementos. So I told him about it. It was a mistake. I must have sounded bitter—I *was* bitter. For a long time, really. And after the first time, it became easier to talk about it with Justin. And poor Justin." Cheryl sighed. "He took on my hurt, and he decided this man had ruined my life. Justin believes that I never gave Simon a chance, that he and Simon and I could have been a happy family. And you know, he may be right."

I had learned the other day that Cheryl liked to talk. I wanted to yell at her. *Hurry up! Get to the point!* I pictured Dassie walking to Sara's, unsuspecting. I pictured Justin grabbing her and forcing her into his car. I couldn't begin to imagine her terror.

Cheryl took a handful of lettuce leaves, sealed the bag, and put it in the refrigerator. "But it's too late, isn't it? You can't redo your life. I've tried to explain that to Justin, but he won't listen to me. So I was surprised and a little nervous when he began studying with Rabbi Bailor. But Justin really liked him." She tore a leaf and tossed the parts into the bowl.

I was confused, not really focused. "Because . . . ?"

She stopped what she was doing and looked at me. "Oh, I thought you understood, Molly. Charlie Bailor was my first love. *Chaim,* now. We dated our senior year of high school."

I hoped my face didn't reveal my shock. That was why Cheryl had looked familiar. I'd seen her photo in Rabbi Bailor's yearbook. Her hair had been brown then, and she'd been decades younger.

"We came from similar backgrounds," Cheryl said. "Orthodox, but not heavy-duty. Charlie never said so, but I was sure we'd get married—maybe in our junior year of college. And on a school-sponsored weekend at the end of that May, we *did* get married, kind of." She sounded wistful.

"You had a ceremony," I said. "With a ring."

She nodded. "All the rabbis and teachers were finally asleep. A group of us drank beer. And then we were outside, Charlie and me and the others. We were a little drunk, and someone put a lace kerchief on my head and a bouquet of flowers in my hands. And Charlie put a ring on my finger and said the blessing. And he kissed me, right there under the stars. It was silly and beautiful." Her eyes glistened.

I sensed that in her mind she was at that weekend gathering, standing under the stars.

"We didn't think we were married, of course. It was just a joke. But I kept the ring. I still have it, as a matter of fact. I don't know why."

"I'd love to see it," I said.

"It's nothing special."

She wiped her hands on a dish towel and left the room. While I waited, I pulled out my cell phone, called West L.A., and left another, urgent message for Jessie.

Cheryl returned. She had an odd expression on her face—a mix of annoyance and bewilderment, maybe a little concern. I had probably worn the same expression when I saw the credit card charge for flowers that Ron had bought and I had never received.

"I can't find it," she told me. "I saw it a few weeks ago. I can't imagine where it is. I don't think the housekeeper would have taken it. It's not worth much."

"You were telling me about you and Rabbi Bailor?"

She picked up the peeler and another cucumber. "Someone talked Charlie into going to Israel for the year, instead of straight to college. At first he wrote me all the time. He called me, too, but not as much. Phone calls from Israel were very expensive then. But after a few months the letters didn't come as often, and the calls stopped. And then he wrote me a letter. He said he really liked me, but his life was taking a different direction, and he hoped I'd understand. And I heard from someone who was in touch with Charlie that Charlie went to a different yeshiva, a stricter one. And that he changed his name to Chaim."

I wondered if Cheryl was aware that bitterness had crept into her voice.

"I phoned him. I told him whatever direction he was taking, I would take with him. But he said that wouldn't work, that he wasn't the same person, that he knew I would find someone who would make me happy. I wasn't going to beg, you know? The next letter came a year later. He was getting married and wanted to talk about the ceremony we'd had. The rabbi who was going to perform the wedding told Charlie that if we had two valid witnesses, we'd need a divorce. Charlie didn't want to take any chances, so he wanted to give me a *get*, a divorce. A divorce!"

Her voice shook. She slammed the peeler on the board. "I was so hurt. I didn't answer his letter. Or his phone calls. But my parents said Charlie was right. What if I met someone? Without a divorce, I couldn't get married. So I phoned Charlie, and he sent me a *get,* from Israel. And someone hand-delivered it. And that was it. And it *hurt,* Molly." She wiped her eyes. "God, I thought I was over this, but it just doesn't go away, does it?"

Better love me a little, Bubbie G says, but love me long. "Did Rabbi Bailor know that Justin was your son?"

"No." Cheryl came to the table and sat down. "Wexner is Simon's last name. Charlie—Chaim—doesn't know who I am. I never heard from him after I received the *get,* but I kept tabs on him. I was kind of obsessed with him." She blushed. "It was stupid, and unhealthy. I knew he'd moved to L.A. I knew he was a principal at Torat Tzion. I saw him when I first moved here, the day I went to meet with the secular stud- ies principal, Dr. Mendes. I think I told you? Charlie passed me in the hall. He didn't even recognize me. I recognized him, even with the beard. I was going to say something, but then I didn't."

"But Justin knew."

She nodded. "That's why I was surprised that he agreed to study with him. Greg convinced him. He told Justin that Chaim was a great guy. I think Justin was curious, you know? And then Greg was fired— and well, here we are."

I didn't know where to begin. "Cheryl, I have to tell you some- thing."

She frowned. "Something's wrong? Is it Hadassah? Did she . . . ?"

I took her hands. "Cheryl, you know what they're saying on the news, that Dassie ran away with Greg? It's not true."

Her eyes widened. "But Greg is dead. Someone killed him."

"Cheryl, Thursday night Dassie was at Yamashiro with the man she met in the chat room. She was with Justin."

She yanked her hands free. "That's crazy!" She got to her feet. "Why would you say something so awful?"

I took the blue get-well card from my purse and handed it to her. "Justin sent this to Hadassah."

She looked at the envelope as if it were tainted. Then she took it, pulled out the card, opened it, read it.

Her face had turned the color of putty. She dropped the card on the floor and moaned. She started to sway. I stood to help her, but she sank back onto the chair and buried her head in her hands.

"My God," she whispered.

"Cheryl, did Justin know that Greg was going away?"

She looked up. "Greg asked him to water the plants and take in the paper. Justin was disappointed that Greg didn't want him to use the car, but it's new. My God," she said again. "But Justin would never hurt Greg. He *loved* Greg."

"I know he did. Cheryl, Dassie is missing."

She stared at me.

"She left her house to walk over to a friend's, but she never showed up. Do you have any idea where Justin is right now?"

"You don't know that Hadassah is with Justin."

"You're right." I nodded. "But we don't know that she isn't. I'm very concerned about what they might do. I'm concerned about both of them, Cheryl."

"He takes medication, Molly. I make sure he does."

"Where is he, Cheryl?"

"He wouldn't hurt Dassie." She bit her lip. "Are you going to call the police?"

"I have to. You know that."

"Justin will panic. The last time, after he was in the hospital? They sent him somewhere for a few months. He told me then he would never let anyone do that to him again."

"Where is he, Cheryl?"

"I don't want him hurt. I can't believe he did anything to Greg. You heard him, Molly. You heard how upset he was about what happened to Greg, about what those kids were doing."

I didn't answer. I could see her torment.

"He's been making extra money painting apartments," she said. "He finished a job yesterday, but he said he had to do some touch-ups."

"Do you know the address?"

"I can find out. The apartment building belongs to one of my clients. That's how Justin got the job."

Chapter 50

Paint, Hadassah realized. That's what she smelled.

She told him it made her feel ill. "Can we go somewhere else?" she said.

Outside, she could run. She could scream. She could draw attention to herself.

"There's nowhere else," he said. "But we won't be disturbed." He scowled. "It wasn't supposed to be like this. Greg said he would be gone until Wednesday, and then he was going to Seattle, to be with Kaitlin. If he hadn't come home earlier, everything would be different."

Kaitlin, Hadassah said silently. Now she had a name for the blond-haired little girl. Tears stung her eyes.

"Why did you stab him, Dassie?" he said, mournful. "If you hadn't stabbed him . . . Why would you try to kill him?"

She was amazed he hadn't figured it out.

How was that possible? She realized with a wave of relief that he didn't know that she'd been hiding from him, that in the dark she had thought she was stabbing the person who had imprisoned her for a week.

"I was frightened," she said. "It was dark. I thought he was a burglar." Lying wasn't so difficult, she found, and she was telling him what he wanted to hear.

"There was so much blood," he said. "All over his shirt. There was a gash in his throat, Dassie. Here."

He traced a line across her throat, pressed his thumb into the hollow of her neck, against her windpipe. She found it hard to breathe, but forced herself to relax.

He moved his thumb. "What did you stab him with, Dassie?"

She almost said a knife, but he would know she was lying. She decided he was testing her.

"A piece of glass. It was cold, and I wanted a blanket," she told him. "The box fell, and a frame broke."

He nodded. "You saw the photo. Why didn't you trust me, Dassie? Why didn't you wait and let me explain?"

"I was scared. I heard the key in the lock. I knew it was too soon for you to be back. I picked up a piece of glass from the floor, from the photo. He came into the apartment. He grabbed my hand. I was *terrified.*" She didn't have to pretend about that.

"So you stabbed him." He was watching her, nodding. "And you called your father for help, with my phone. Does your father have it?"

"I don't know."

She had phoned home, but had hung up without leaving a message. She had hung up on 911, too, because all she had was seconds, and what if they didn't believe her? So she had phoned Dr. McIntyre. She knew his number by heart. But she didn't know whether Dr. McIntyre had contacted her father. That had tormented her. And she didn't know whether her father had been in the apartment.

"He fell," she said. "I thought I'd killed him. There was so much blood, and his scream . . ." In the dark, before she fell asleep, she could still hear it.

"Greg said it was my fault. You were the one who stabbed him, Dassie, but he blamed me." His voice trembled with indignation.

The significance of what he had said struck her. She almost wept.

"He didn't recognize you in the dark, Dassie. He found your purse. He saw the *Shabbat* candles. 'What's going on, Justin?' "

He was rubbing his fingers together, starting to rock.

She had left him alive. Her heart was pounding. "It was my fault," she said. "I should have stayed."

"He saw your clothes in his closet. He yelled at me. 'What have you done, Justin? Where are the phones, Justin? Are you crazy, Justin?' "

Two cordless phones and their stations had been in the box, along with the toys and the puzzles, and the letters from a woman named Melissa, the woman in the photos with the little girl. Kaitlin.

"I'm not crazy, Dassie."

"No, of course not," she said.

"His cell phone was in his hand. He was going to call my mother, or the police. I begged him not to, but he said I needed help, I was sick. He turned away from me. He wouldn't *look* at me. So I took that stupid owl and hit him." Tears were streaming down his cheeks. "I didn't mean to hurt him, Dassie. I wanted him to *put down the phone*. If you hadn't stabbed him, if you hadn't run away . . ."

"It's my fault," she said when he paused, because it was her cue to sing the refrain to this sad, sad song. She wasn't really listening. Her hands were bound, but she felt freer than she had in days.

"And my father?" She held her breath.

"I heard the door open and hid on the balcony. I didn't see him, but I heard him walking through the apartment. He took all your things. He wanted the police to blame me for everything, Dassie." His voice shook. "Even though it was your fault, and Greg's. Greg was supposed to come back Wednesday, not Friday. So I had to move his body to the car. I had to crash the car. What else could I do?"

"I should have waited for you," she said.

His rocking slowed.

"I shouldn't have let you take the blame."

"The important thing is that we're together, that we love each other." He stopped. "You were scared, so you tried to protect yourself. Is that how you cut your palm? With the glass?"

"Yes."

"Poor Dassie." He spread her hands apart and kissed her lacerated palm. He frowned. "What did you do with it? With the piece of glass? I didn't find it."

His elbow was pressing against her thigh. "I threw it away."

"Good." He wrapped a curl of her hair around his finger. "My mother said it wouldn't work. 'She's not for you, Justin.' Your father didn't think my mother was good enough for him, either. Did you know that?"

"No." She didn't know whether this was one of his lies.

"He gave her a ring, the ring I gave you. You didn't throw it away, did you?" he demanded, pulling the curl.

She winced at the pain. "It's in my drawer."

"He said the blessing, 'Behold you are sanctified to me according to the laws of Moses and Israel.' It was a promise in front of witnesses, Dassie. He broke his promise. He broke my mother's heart. Do you know what becomes of the broken-hearted? Do you think that was right, Dassie?"

She shook her head.

"He broke Greg's heart, too. He could have helped him, but he didn't. So maybe, when I first e-mailed you, I was angry at your father. I tricked you, Dassie. I read your file. I knew all about you before we met. But I fell in love with you. Do you believe me?"

"Yes."

"You understand why I did it? You're not angry?"

"I understand. I'm not angry."

"Tell me you love me, Dassie."

"I love you," she said, choking on the words.

"And we'll be together forever?" he said. "Because I'm not like your father. I won't break my promise. I gave you my mother's ring."

She nodded.

"Say it. Say we'll be together forever."

"We'll be together forever."

"You're lying."

She froze.

He traced her lips with his finger. "You know we can't be together, Dassie. The police will find out we killed Greg. They won't let us be together."

Her heart hammered in her chest. She was surprised he couldn't hear it.

"True love doesn't end, Dassie. Romeo and Juliet. Othello and Desdemona. Tristan and Isolde. They die, but their love stays pure."

She stifled a sob.

"I would never let you feel pain, Dassie."

He stood abruptly, shaking the bed, and walked to a corner of the room. His back was to her, but she could see him reaching into his pants pocket.

"I went to the *mikvah*," she said.

He crouched, then stood and turned around. He was holding a goblet.

"Last night, after I read the card you sent," she said, "I knew you would come for me."

He returned to her side.

"You bought a nightgown," she said. "Don't you want me to wear it, for you?"

"When it's time."

He raised her to a sitting position and brought the goblet to her lips. "Drink," he said.

She took a sip of the wine. It was ruby red, dry. It tasted bitter, but dry wines *were* bitter. Or maybe he had put something in it, something he'd taken from his pocket. She thought about the vial of pills she had found among his things.

"More," he said.

She drank. Wine dribbled down her chin. He caught the drops with his finger and licked them. Then he drank from the goblet.

"I want to be with you, one time," she said. "Don't you want that, too?"

She raised her bound hands.

Chapter 51

We lost precious minutes while Cheryl looked for the phone number of the client who had hired Justin to paint the apartment. Another five minutes passed before she reached the client on his cell phone.

"Everything is fine," Cheryl said, her voice amazingly calm. "I'm sure Justin did a beautiful job. I want to take him something to eat."

"Ask him for directions," I whispered to Cheryl.

"How do I get there?" she asked. She scribbled on the margin of a newspaper that lay on the table. "Okay. Thanks." She hung up.

I tore off the segment of newspaper. The address was in Hollywood. Connors's jurisdiction. "What's the apartment number?"

"201." Cheryl put a hand on my arm. "Let me talk to Justin first, Molly. He'll listen to me. I know he will."

I picked up my purse and ran out of the apartment, with Cheryl at my heels. I didn't want to talk in front of her. I unlocked the car, told her to get in, and phoned Connors at home. His line was busy. I tried West L.A. and left an urgent message for Jessie.

From Cheryl's, it was a fifteen-minute drive without traffic to the Hollywood apartment, double that in the rush hour we were in. I drove to Melrose, turned right, and headed east.

We didn't talk, although every few minutes Cheryl said, "Justin will listen to me."

She had a right to hope, but the repetition was making me antsy. "Read me the instructions again, Cheryl."

"Take Highland to Sunset, Sunset past Vermont . . ."

I reached Highland in less than ten minutes, but it was a parking lot. When I neared Santa Monica, I made a sharp right. Cars were moving well at first, but blocks later, we slowed to fifteen miles an hour.

I made a left onto Cahuenga and took that to Sunset. More traffic. I turned right on Sunset. I tried not to think about Hadassah.

"Justin won't hurt Hadassah," Cheryl said, as if she were reading my mind.

I tried Connors again. This time he answered.

"What?" he said when he picked up. Connors has caller ID, so he knew it was me.

Not a warm reception. "Shankman wasn't with the girl," I said.

"Come on, Molly."

"Just *listen.*" In a low voice, I told him what I'd learned.

"Where's the mother?" he asked. "With you?"

"Yes. She says he'll listen to her."

"Let's hope she's right," Connors said. "Her son has her car, right? What's the make and license plate number?"

I asked Cheryl, and relayed the information to Connors.

"Can I talk to him?" Cheryl said. "What's his name?"

"Detective Connors." I passed her my phone.

"Detective Connors? This is Cheryl Wexner, Justin's mother. Let me talk to him. I know what to say, to calm him." She listened. "He would never hurt anyone, but if he's frightened . . . He's just a little confused. What?" She furrowed her brow. "All right. Yes. Thank you."

Cheryl handed me the phone and leaned against the headrest. She shut her eyes. I couldn't imagine what she was thinking.

"You're sure about this guy, Molly?" Connors asked.

"Yes." I gave him the address and apartment number. "His mother's not sure he's there. Can you tell Detective Drake? And give her my cell number, please?"

Minutes later my phone rang. I flipped it open.

"Two units are on the way," Connors said. "Where are you?"

"Ten blocks away."

"I should be there in two minutes. Detective Drake is on her way."

I made a right on Sunset.

"We're in radio contact with the units," Connors said. "When they get there, if they think Hadassah is in immediate danger, they're going in."

"Got it."

"Don't tell the mother."

"Right."

"The cell phone they found at Dr. McIntyre's isn't Hadassah's, by the way. It's Justin Wexner's."

"Yes."

"Detective Drake's guess is that Wexner has Hadassah's phone. You think he killed Shankman?"

"Yes."

"And you think he plans to kill himself and the girl?"

"Right."

"See you there."

Connors hung up. I shut the phone and put it on my lap.

"What was he asking you?" Cheryl was wringing her hands.

"He wants to make sure I have the right directions."

It seemed like an hour, but it was only minutes before we arrived. I parked the car down the block, near two black-and-whites.

"Wait in the car," I told Cheryl, but she undid her seat belt and was standing on the sidewalk before I was.

"He'll listen to me, Molly," she said. "If they go in, they'll frighten him."

Connors walked toward us. I introduced him to Cheryl.

"My son will listen to me," she told him.

"Someone's in there," Connors said. "We can hear music, but nothing else."

I didn't want to think about the possibilities. "Maybe Mrs. Wexner can phone her son," I said.

"Justin lost his cell phone," Cheryl said. "I told you that. I don't know the number of the phone in the apartment, or if there is one."

"Detective Drake has your son's phone," Connors said. "We think he has Hadassah Bailor's, but we don't know if it's charged."

"He used it Thursday night, when he phoned her parents," I said. "Hadassah had it with her the Sunday she left home. So he must have charged it."

"I don't have her number," Cheryl said.

"It's programmed on his phone. I got the number from Detective Drake." Connors handed Cheryl a slip of paper with the number.

"I don't want to scare him," Cheryl said. "What should I say?"

A minute ago she had been so confident, I thought.

"Tell him you're concerned about him," Connors said. "Keep him talking."

Cheryl took her cell phone out of her purse and made the call.

Chapter 52

"Make a wish, Dassie."

He blew out all the candles except one and switched on the light. She blinked at the sudden brightness and forced herself not to flinch when he sat on the side of the bed.

"You won't try to run away?" he said.

"I would have gone with you, Justin, if you'd asked. I was shocked to see you."

"I IM'ed you, Dassie. Over and over. I told you we had to talk. I tried you a hundred times, I saw you were online. But you didn't answer."

"I was afraid my parents would see." She held her bound wrists toward him. "I understand why you did what you did, Justin. It was my fault, all my fault. I want to make it right."

She didn't know where the words came from. They weren't her words, or Dinah's. Dinah's brothers had come to save her, but no one was coming to save Hadassah.

He stared at her. An eternity passed before he leaned closer and fingered the rope, another as he undid the knots.

She massaged her wrists.

Her head pulsed when she sat up. She was dizzy. Maybe it was the wine, or what he'd put in it. Or the reaction to whatever had been on the cloth he'd held over her nose and mouth. She inched to the edge of the bed and slowly pushed herself to a standing position. She didn't know where he had put her shoes. Her legs were wobbly.

I am Yael, she told herself.

She picked up the nightgown, which he had laid on the end of the bed. She ran her hand across the silky fabric. "It's beautiful, Justin. I'll change in the bathroom. I won't be long."

"I broke the lock. I didn't know if I could trust you, Dassie . . ."

"I don't blame you," she said, hiding her dismay. "Where's my sweater, Justin? It's warm in here, from all the candles. It's probably chilly in the bathroom." She saw his frown. He didn't believe her. "This is my first time, Justin," she said shyly.

She cast her eyes downward. She wondered how Yael had convinced Sisera that it was safe to enter her tent.

"I'll wait outside the door," he said after what seemed like an eternity. "You can change in here."

Her heart sank. He picked up the goblet and blew out the last candle on his way out of the room.

He shut the door. She tiptoed across the carpeted floor to the window and looked out at security bars. Straight ahead, only a few feet away, was the neighboring building. The blinds on all the windows were shut.

She felt a wave of tiredness as she moved to the closet. Maybe she would find a hanger, a belt, something she could use. She heard the creak as she opened the closet door.

She knew he had heard it, too.

"What are you doing, Dassie?" He sounded playful.

"Looking for something to hang up my clothes."

"Just leave them on the side of the bed."

The closet was empty.

"Are you ready?" he called.

"Almost."

Her hands shook as she unbuttoned her blouse. She undressed quickly, leaving her clothes at the end of the bed, and slipped the nightgown over her head. The room was warm, but she shivered. A blanket of goose bumps covered her arms.

She lay down on the bed. Her eyelids were starting to feel heavy, and she fought the urge to shut her eyes.

"Dassie?"

He opened the door and approached the bed. He sat on the edge and stroked her face.

"You're so tense," he said.

"I'm a little nervous."

"Don't be."

He brought his face to her lips and kissed her softly. She tasted the wine.

"I've waited so long for someone like you, Dassie. Do you really love me?"

"With all my heart."

"Forever?"

"Forever."

He moved away. "Is this why you wanted your sweater, Dassie?"

In his right hand was the shard. The glass gleamed in the light.

She stared at it.

He grabbed her hands and pinned her arms above her head. "You lied, Dassie. You broke your promise."

Her heart lurched wildly in her chest.

With his free hand he placed the tip of the shard in the hollow of her throat. "This is what Greg felt, Dassie. You were going to kill me with it, too, weren't you?" He sounded sad.

His breath was warm on her face.

"It was for me, not for you," she said. "I didn't know you were coming for me, did I?" She saw indecision in his eyes. "I cut myself with it this morning. I can show you."

He hesitated.

"I was ashamed to tell you," she said. "It's so ugly. I promised myself I wouldn't do it again, but I couldn't stop. Help me stop, Justin."

He lowered her hands and released them. She turned her right palm up to show him the angry, bright red line.

"Poor Dassie." He stared at her arm. "I told you I would kiss your hurts away." He bent his head.

Her scream startled him. It was her scream and Dinah's. It was the howl of the man she had stabbed and left for dead, an eldritch screech filled with terror and fury. Using both hands, she shoved his shoulders, hard.

The shard flew out of his hand as he toppled backward to the floor and hit his head against the chair.

She jumped from the bed and lunged for the sliver of glass. It was invisible against the beige carpet. She pawed the carpet, swept her hand across it in wide arcs.

And then she saw the sliver of glass. She grabbed the shard, wincing as the sharp edge opened her wounds.

She scrambled to her feet while he braced himself on the chair and stood.

He took a step toward her.

"Dassie, I would never—"

She raised her hand and pointed the shard at him. "Don't."

Chapter 53

Wednesday, December 8, 9:30 p.m. Along the 900 block of Northwestern Avenue. A suspect took out a screwdriver from his waistband and pointed it at the victim, saying, "I'm going to kill you."

We heard the scream when we were steps away from the apartment door. Cheryl had called Hadassah's cell phone several times. Justin never answered. By then Jessie had arrived, and Cheryl's conviction had returned.

"Let me tell him I'm here," she'd begged. "Justin will talk to me. I *know* he will."

Connors and Jessie drew their weapons. He broke down the door. I grabbed Cheryl's arm to stop her from following Connors and Jessie into the apartment, but she wrenched her arm free and ran inside. I went in after her.

They were in the bedroom. Justin was all in black. Hadassah was wearing an ivory nightgown, edged in lace and streaked with blood. My nightmare come true, and hers. Her right arm was raised in a fist. At first I didn't see the long sliver of glass she was aiming at Justin. He was standing a few feet away.

He looked dazed when Connors told him to put his hands on his head. Cheryl, her face a sickly gray, said, "Please, honey, do what they say."

So Justin put his arms on his head, but he didn't take his eyes off Dassie.

"Dassie, tell them I didn't want to hurt you," he said as Connors pulled his arms behind him and cuffed his wrists. "Tell them it's what you wanted, too."

Hadassah was shaking. Jessie put an arm around her shoulders, gently unbent her fingers, like the petals of a rose, and removed the shard. Even from where I was standing, I could see that Hadassah's palm was bleeding.

"*Tell* them, Dassie." Justin turned to his mother. "*Mom?*"

The "*Mom?*" has stayed with me, and Hadassah's scream.

I phoned the Bailors. I didn't name Justin. I told them Hadassah was safe and put her on so they could hear for themselves.

Connors found an empty vial of sleeping pills in Justin's pocket, and Hadassah thought Justin had put something in the wine he'd made her drink. Jessie drove her to the Cedars-Sinai emergency room, where doctors treated her lacerated palm and pumped her stomach while other doctors tended to Justin.

Zack met me at Cedars. We sat with Cheryl for hours, in the same waiting room where Nechama Bailor was reading psalms and Chaim Bailor was pacing in long, anxious strides.

It was a strange non-reunion, surreal in its irony. Rabbi Bailor looked with mild curiosity at the woman whose arm I was holding when I arrived. A second later I could see that he'd realized she must be the mother of the man who had brought all of us here. He told me later he hadn't recognized Cheryl, hadn't seen in her the young girl he had married one May evening under a canopy of stars. He had wondered who she was, but had kept his distance. What do you say to someone whose son intended to kill your child?

I had worried how Cheryl would react when she saw Rabbi Bailor, but she avoided looking at him. She picked at the skin around her thumb and talked to Zack and me about Justin, her hopes for him, her fears. Every few minutes she got up and walked to the desk to ask an emergency room volunteer when she could see him. She must have been overwhelmed with anguish over what her son had planned to do, profoundly relieved that he hadn't been successful. She was probably troubled by the thought that sharing with a sensitive son decades of resentment toward the man who had broken her heart had contributed to the avalanche of events that had brought two families to this sad, sad crossroads.

Later that night I drove Cheryl to her apartment and tucked her into bed when she was too tired to talk. In the morning I accompanied her to the Hollywood station and waited with her while Justin was booked. He's on a suicide watch now, in county jail. Jessie told me the district attorney is going for second-degree murder. Justin's father flew out to see him and has retained a top-notch attorney to defend his son.

After Thanksgiving dinner at my parents', Zack and I visited Cheryl and made sure she ate the food my mother sent. Since then I've stopped by several times. Cheryl seems pleased to see me, but I know I'll always be a reminder of the night that changed her life. She told me that people in the community have been dropping off meals, and she's received more phone calls and invitations in the past few weeks than she has in the year since she moved here. It's sad that it takes a tragedy for people to notice you.

Melissa is moving to Seattle. She was shocked and saddened to hear about Justin. Greg had talked about him fondly, and often, and Justin had bought Kaitlin the yellow scooter I'd seen in the yard. Greg's parents found papers in their son's safe-deposit box, including a folder with proof of Adam Prosser's cheating. They left the folder with Melissa. She gave it to me.

I sent a copy of the contents of the folder to Janet Mendes. I sent another copy to Robert Hornstein, the founder of Torat Tzion. That probably explains why Dr. Mendes was anxious to meet with me.

"I wish we'd had this in September," she told me in her office.

I said, "Uh-huh," in a tone that told her I wasn't buying what she was selling. Then I repeated what I'd learned about Amy Brookman's accusation, and told Dr. Mendes I couldn't reveal my source. For what it's worth, Dr. Mendes appeared shaken, but I've learned that people and their reactions aren't always what they seem.

"Of course, we're going to make sure appropriate measures are taken," she told me. "I hope you don't feel it necessary to make this public, Molly."

Greg had wanted to go public, but I didn't see any good in dragging Torat Tzion through the media mud, especially since "appropriate measures" included expelling Adam Prosser and Amy Brookman, and removing Gerald Prosser from the board.

As for Dr. Mendes, my mother heard a rumor that the secular studies principal will be leaving Torat Tzion at the end of the year. I can't prove she doctored the AP exams, and maybe she didn't. I'm curious whether AP scores at Torat Tzion will be as uniformly high this May as they have been in the past few years.

The storm blows over, the driftwood remains.

Connors and I are okay, I think. He believed my explanation about the license plate, but I still feel an occasional twinge of hurt that he doubted me. And I've made a new friend in Jessie. We met the other day for coffee, and Zack and I plan to go out with her and Ezra.

Dr. McIntyre has taken a leave of absence from Torat Tzion and his practice. He's undergoing therapy. Nancy is hopeful. And the district attorney won't be filing charges.

Hadassah is back at school and is seeing a therapist. She plans to go to seminary in Israel, though not necessarily this coming September. She needs to heal first, in body and in spirit. She told me she's dreading her court appearance in the event Justin's case goes to trial, but she's strong. Jessie told her the injury she inflicted on Greg was superficial, despite the profuse bleeding. But Hadassah still feels guilty. She has nightmares about him and wonders when they'll stop. I didn't tell her that seven years later, I still dream about Aggie, and I wasn't even there when she died.

I don't think we'll ever know what Justin was thinking when he attacked the man he'd loved like a brother. He told Hadassah he was desperate to stop Greg from phoning Cheryl or the police. My friend

Irene thinks it's more complicated. She thinks Justin had built up resentment toward his real father, who, in his mind, had abandoned him for a new family; that he transferred that resentment first to Rabbi Bailor, who had betrayed his mother, and then to Greg, who was about to betray him.

Irene is probably right. She usually is.

Rabbi Bailor was stunned when I told him that Cheryl Wexner was his high school sweetheart, that Justin was her son. "I don't think I ever saw her," he told me. That was probably true, in more ways than one.

The rabbi insisted that he had championed Greg Shankman's case, though unsuccessfully. I'd like to think that's true. It's possible that Greg's disappointment with the rabbi's efforts was unreasonable.

Rabbi Bailor also told me he'd defended me fourteen years ago. It seems Rabbi Ingel had insinuated to others that Rabbi Bailor was a little too fond of me, that maybe fondness was clouding his judgment.

"I was a coward, Molly," he said. "I failed you. I failed myself."

There are things Rabbi Bailor could have done fourteen years ago, but I am ready to move on. There are things Charlie Bailor should have done when he became Chaim, though I'm not sure any of them would have kept him from breaking Cheryl's heart. Cheryl told me that she and the rabbi talked the other day.

"I should have done that years ago," she said.

A small vengeance, Bubbie G says, poisons the heart.

Maybe that's why I phoned Rabbi Ingel last week. I planned to tell him how I'd felt all these years, to get closure, to rid myself of the poison. He stopped me before I could say anything and told me he was glad I'd called.

"Maybe I was a little hard on you, Malka, but I did it for your own good. And I was right, wasn't I? My words made you turn your life around."

There is nothing you can do if someone doesn't want to see.

I've been checking out J Spot from time to time. Birch2 is a frequent visitor. I thought long and hard, then phoned Sara and told her that if she didn't tell her parents about her online activities, I would. But I'm not Lucky7, and as Dr. McIntyre said, you can't be everywhere.

In case you were wondering, Liora's date turned out to be a dud, but on the plus side she's racking up frequent flier miles. I put her in touch with Aliza. They seem to be hitting it off—and not, Liora said with a laugh, just because they're both eager to find their true loves.

The last time I saw Dassie, she asked me whether I thought Justin loved her. Or had it been all about vengeance? she wanted to know. I told her he probably loved her.

"Like Shechem?" she said. "He came to love Dinah."

"Like Schechem," I agreed.

It occurred to me that Cheryl's love had fostered vengeance, that her son's vengeance had turned into a distorted love. That Greg Shankman had loved inappropriately, and then not well.

Last Friday I added the garlic clove and sugar cube Bubbie gave me into my Shabbos *chulent*. Bubbie was right about the *chulent*. It was delicious. As for bringing a baby, time will tell. In the meantime, I count my blessings that I am with someone I love.

Tonight as Zack lit the first candle of Chanukah in our menorah at home. It was also the first anniversary of our engagement. Zack gave me a beautiful necklace and four boxes of blueberries. And Godiva chocolates, of course. I gave him a leather desk set he'd been eyeing. No Clementines—they won't be available until next year.

After dinner with our families, we had drinks at Yamashiro and invited Irene to join us on her break. The Bailors had sent her flowers, and she had an audition tomorrow that looked promising. Life was good, she said.

Zack and I strolled through the gardens and watched the koi. Then we walked outside and looked at the starry night.

Molly's Butternut Squash Quiche
(compliments of my daughter Sabina)

1 butternut squash, or one package precooked
squash
½ cup flour
½ cup sugar or Splenda sugar substitute
½ stick margarine, softened
2 cups soy milk or pareve (nondairy) creamer
3 eggs
cinnamon

Buy a box of precooked squash. Or . . . wash
and pierce a squash and bake at 350° F. for an
hour and a half, or until soft. Scoop out the
flesh, and mash it in a bowl.

Add flour, sugar (or Splenda sugar substitute),
softened margarine, soy milk (it's nondairy) or
nondairy creamer, and eggs. Whisk, or use an
electric mixer for a smoother consistency.

Pour into quiche pan or round aluminum pan. Sprinkle top with cinnamon.

Bake at 350° F for an hour and fifteen minutes or until golden brown.

Serve hot or at room temperature. Cold isn't bad, either.

Serves eight to twelve people, depending on how generously you slice it.

One slice is never enough. ☺

Glossary of Hebrew and Yiddish Words

abba (noun, ab´-ba). Father.

Baruch Hashem (Ba-ruch´ Ha-shem´). Thank God. Literally, Blessed be God.

bashert (noun or adjective, ba-shert´). Destiny, or destined.

bas Yisroel (noun, bas Yis-ro´-el). Daughter of Israel. A complimentary description.

Besser gornisht tsu machen aider tsu machen gornisht. Better to do nothing than to make something into nothing.

bris (noun). Literally, a covenant. The ritual circumcision performed on a male when he is eight days old.

bubaleh (noun, bub´-ba-leh). Little doll; little grandmother. (Affectionate term.)

challa (noun, chal´-la or chal-la´). Braided loaf of bread. Plural: *challot* (chal-lot´) or *challas* (chal´-las). See my book, *Dream House,* for recipe.

Chanukah (noun, Cha´-nu-kah). Eight-day Festival of Lights in the Jewish month of Kislev, which usually falls in December or in late November.

Chas v´shalom (chas ve-sha´-lom, or chas ve-sha-lom´). God forbid.

chulent (noun, chu´-lent). Sabbath stew made of meat, potatoes, barley, and several kinds of beans.

chuppa (noun, chup´-pa). Wedding canopy.

chutzpadik (adjective, chutz´-pa-dik). Audacious; galling.

chutzpah (noun, chutz´-pah). Audacity; gall.

daven (verb, da´-ven). To pray.

drash (noun). Sermon.

dreidel (noun, drā´-del). A four-sided top used to play games on Chanukah.

d´var Torah (noun, d-var´ to´-rah). Sermonette, explication on the Torah.

eruv (noun, e´-ruv; also, e-ruv´). An artificial or natural boundary within which one may carry items on the Sabbath.

frum (adjective). Used to describe someone who observes Orthodox Judaism.

get (noun). Jewish bill of divorce.

Gut voch. A good week. A phrase uttered after the Sabbath ends to wish someone a good week, and the title of a song. In Hebrew, *Shavuah tov.*

Hashem (noun, Ha-shem´). God.

hatzolah (noun, ha-tzo´-lah). Rescue. Also, *hatzalah* (ha-tza-lah´).

havdalah (noun, hav-dal´-lah or hav-da-lah´). Literally, separation. The blessing that marks the end of the Sabbath and separates it from the rest of the week.

ima (noun, ee´-ma). Mother.

kenehoreh (ke-ne-hor´-eh). Also, ke´naynehoreh (ke-nain´-e-hor´-eh). A frequently used phrase that is an elision of *keyn ayin horeh* (kān a´-yin hor´-eh). Let there be no evil eye.

ketsaleh (noun, ket´-sa-leh). Kitten (endearment).

Kiddush (noun, kid´-dush or kid-dush´). A prayer recited over wine at the beginning of a Sabbath or holiday meal. Also refers to refreshments served after synagogue services on the Sabbath or other Jewish holidays.

kindt (noun). Child.

Kleine kinder, kleine freiden; groisseh kinder, groisseh laiden (phrase, klein´-e kin´-der, klein´-e freid´-en; grois´-seh kind´-der, grois´-seh lai´-den). Small children, small joys; bigger children, bigger sorrows.

Kol ha´kavod (phrase, kol ha-ka-vod´). Kudos.

kosher (adjective, ko´-sher). Ritually correct. Most often used in reference to dietary laws.

lashon harah (noun, la-shon´ ha-rah´; also, *loshen horeh* (lo´-shen ho´reh). Slander, gossip.

L´cha Dodi (l´-cha´ do-di´). Sabbath song, part of Friday night prayer service. Literally, "Come, My Beloved."

mammeleh (noun, mam´-me-leh). Little mother (endearment).

mandelbrot (noun, man´-del-brot). Almond-flavored biscotti. Literally, almond bread. Also, *mandelbroyt*.

Mazel tov (ma´-zel tov). Literally, Good luck; figuratively, Congratulations. Also, *Mazal toff.*

mechallel Shabbos (verb or noun, me-chal´-lel shab´-bos). One who violates the Sabbath, or to violate the Sabbath. Also, *mechallel Shabbat* (me-chal-lel´ shab-bat´).

mechitza (noun, me-chi´-tza). Partition in a synagogue or hall to separate men and women.

menuval (noun, me-nuv´-el). A loathsome person. Also, adjective, (me-nu-val´), loathsome.

mikvah (noun, mik´-vah). Ritual bath. Also, *mikveh*.

mishpacha (noun, mish-pa´-cha or mish-pa-cha´). Family.

mitzvot (noun, plural, mitz-vot´). Positive commandments. Also, *mitzvos* (mitz´-vos).

negel vasser (noun, ne´-gel vas´-ser). A ritual daily rinsing of hands performed upon rising.

oitzerel (noun, oi´-tze-rel). Little treasure (endearment).

Olam Habah (noun, o´-lam ha´bah; also: o-lam´ ha-bah´). The afterlife, the world to come.

Pesach (noun, pe´-sach). Passover.

qvell (verb). To take joyous pride in.

Rambam (noun, Ram´-bam or Ram-bam´). Rabbi Moshe ben Maimon, also known as Maimonides. A renowned twelfth-century scholar, he served as physician to the sultan of Egypt and authored the *Mishna Torah,* a systemic codification of Jewish law, and *The Guide to the Perplexed.*

Seder (noun, se´-der). Feast held on the eve of the first day of Passover, commemorating the Exodus from Egypt. Plural, *sedorim,* or, colloquially, *Seders.* Jews living outside of Israel observe a second Seder on the eve of the second day.

segulah (noun, se-gu´-lah; se-gu-lah´). An object or prayer connecting the recipient with a special beneficial quality; treasured possession.

Shabbat (noun, Shab-bat′). Sabbath. Also, *Shabbos* (shab′-bes).

Shabbat shalom (Shab-bat′ sha-lom′). May you have a good Sabbath.

shadchan (noun, shad′-chan). Matchmaker.

shadchonim (noun, plural, shad-chon′-im). Matchmakers.

shain kindt (phrase, shine kindt). Beautiful child (endearment).

Shavuah tov (Sha-vu′-ah tov). A good week. See *Gut voch,* above.

sheitel (noun, shei′-tel). Wig.

shekel (noun, shek′-el). A monetary unit, a coin. Plural, shekalim (she-ka-lim′) or colloquially, shekels.

shepseleh (noun, shep′-se-leh). Little lamb (endearment).

sheyfeleh (noun, diminutive, shā′-fe-le). Little lamb (endearment).

Sh′ma (noun and verb, she-ma′). Literally, hear. The first word of a prayer recited three times daily. Parents recite this prayer with their young children at bedtime.

shidduch (noun, shid′-duch). Arranged match between a man and a woman.

shiva (noun, shiv′-a or shiv-a′). Literally, seven; the seven days of mourning for a deceased relative.

shofar (noun, sho′-far). Trumpet, or ram's horn used on Rosh Hashanah and Yom Kippur.

sholom zochor (noun, sho′-lem zo′-cher). A party for a newborn male, held on the Friday night after his birth. Also, *shalom zachor* (sha-lom′ za-chor′).

shrek (noun). A fright. Colloquially, Yikes! Or, what a *shrek!*

shul (noun). Synagogue. Plural, *shuls.*

siddur (noun, sid-dur′ or sid′-dur). Prayerbook.

Sukkot (noun, suk-kot´). Eight-day harvest festival that begins five days after Yom Kippur. Also, Succos (Suc´-ces).

tallis (noun, tal´-lis). Prayer shawl. Also, *tallit* (tal-lit´).

Talmud (noun, tal´-mud). Body of work composed of the Mishna—the oral law—and Gemara, its commentaries.

tateleh (noun, ta´-te-leh). Little father.

tayereh kindt (phrase, ta´-ye-reh kindt). Dear child (endearment).

teffilin (noun, te-fil´-lin; te-fil-lin´). Phylacteries: black boxes containing verses from the Scriptures that males use in daily prayer.

teshuvah (noun, te-shu´-veh or te-shu-vah´). Repentance.

Torah (noun, To´-rah or To-rah´). The Bible; also, the parchment scroll itself.

tznius (noun, tzni´-us). Modesty. Also, *tzniut* (tzni-ut´).

yarmulke (noun, yar´-mul-ke). Skullcap. The Hebrew is kippah (kee´-pah or kee-pah´).

yeshiva (noun, ye-shi´va or ye-shi-va´). School of Jewish study.

z´chus (noun, zeh-chus´). Merit. Also, *zechut* (ze-chut´).

zeck (noun). Sack.

zeeskeit (noun, zees´-keit). Sweetheart. Also, ziskeit.

zeidie (noun, zā´-die). Grandfather. Also, *zeidi, zeide, zeideh, zaydie.*

zemirot (noun, ze-mi-rot´; plural of ze´-mer). Songs usually sung during the Sabbath or holiday meals.

Please turn the page for a
Reading Group Guide to
Now You See Me . . .

A Reading Group Guide for Now You See Me . . .

Two years ago a teacher at an Orthodox Jewish high school told me she suspected that a few of her female students were cutting themselves.

"How do you know?" I asked.

I recall being disturbed and saddened, but not shocked. The Orthodox community attempts to shelter its own from the dangers of the secular world, but no community is invulnerable.

"Five months ago these girls were pushing the envelope, coming this close to violating the school's dress policy," the teacher said. "Now their sleeves cover their wrists—even when the temperature's in the eighties. So I know."

I had been contemplating writing a novel about teens at risk. I had a folder thick with articles I'd clipped from newspapers and magazines: Teens and the Internet. Teens and chat room predators. Teens who self-mutilate. Teens who cheat. Teens with eating disorders. The risk of suicide for teens taking antidepressants.

Now You See Me explores the challenges faced by young people on the verge of adulthood, young people who are eager to establish their own identities, but are frightened and confused. Young people who may feel disenfranchised, isolated, burdened with their parents' expectations and their own feelings of inadequacy, pressured by their peers, and desperate to fit in.

Young people, and those no longer young, who feel that no one really sees them.

Rochelle Krich

Questions for Discussion

1. Molly initially resists agreeing to search for Hadassah Bailor. She feels inadequate to the task and has unresolved issues with Hadassah's father. Did you sympathize with her reluctance, or did you find it petty? What made Molly overcome that reluctance?

2. Rumor and innuendo can permanently damage a person's reputation, and by extension, that of a family, especially within a close-knit, traditional community like Hadassah's. Can you understand why the Bailors didn't want to involve an outsider in their search for Hadassah? Would you have handled the situation differently?

3. What was your impression of Rabbi Bailor? Of his wife, Nechama? Of their son Gavriel? Of Aliza, Hadassah's sister? Of Reuben Jastrow? Did your impression of these characters change throughout the course of the novel?

4. How would you describe the dynamics of the Bailor family? Do you think the Bailors are representative of the average American family? In what way, if any, did they contribute to Hadassah's feel-

ings of isolation? Do you think they ignored signs that Hadassah was unhappy, or was Hadassah effective in hiding her feelings?

5. How did you feel about Sarah, Hadassah's best friend? Do you fault her for keeping Hadassah's secret about her online boyfriend?

6. Aside from the opening chapter, I intended to tell the story entirely from Molly's point of view. But Hadassah insisted on having her own voice. How did her voice affect the story?

7. At what point did you become worried about Hadassah's safety? What factors intensified your concern? Did you fear that, like Shakespeare's Juliet, she would kill herself?

8. Do you think teens are at greater risk today than they were a decade ago? If so, why? Does the media exaggerate and possibly contribute to the problem? How can we reduce the risks teenagers face? How can we protect them? Empower them?

9. Do you think that parents are naïve about the dangers of the Internet and lax in monitoring their children's online activities? Aside from the tips mentioned in the novel, do you have other suggestions?

10. Do you see a difference between cheating on an exam and buying term papers or other material online? In what ways do schools and parents contribute to the problem? Why don't teenagers view plagiarism as cheating?

11. Was Molly justifiably angered by Rabbi Bailor's equivocations and lies? Did he "owe" her the truth, even if that truth jeopardized him and his family? Molly herself equivocates—with Connors, with Rabbi Bailor and others. Is she being hypocritical?

12. What was your impression of Cheryl Wexner? Do you think she was inappropriate in making her son her confidant? At what point

did she first suspect that Justin was somehow involved with Greg Shankman's death? Was she in denial?

13. Were you shocked to learn that Justin killed Greg? Do you believe that Justin felt remorse? Do you view Justin as evil or damaged goods?

14. The death of a child can create tremendous stress on a marriage. Discuss the relationship between the McIntyres. Do you see a possibility of their remarrying?

15. I had originally intended to have Molly rescue Hadassah from Justin, but Hadassah ultimately saves herself, transforming herself from "Dinah" to "Yael." Was this transformation believable?

16. Do you believe that Rabbi Bailor attempted to defend Molly when he was her teacher fourteen years ago?

17. At the end of the novel, Hadassah asks Molly if she thinks Justin loved her. Do you believe he did?

18. Discuss the title, *Now You See Me,* as it applies to the characters in the novel.

About the Author

ROCHELLE KRICH is the author of many ac-
claimed novels of suspense, including *Blues
in the Night* (which introduced Molly Blume),
*Dream House, Shadows of Sin, Dead Air, Blood
Money,* and *Fertile Ground.* An Anthony Award
winner for her debut novel, *Where's Mommy
Now?* (which was adapted as the TV movie *Perfect Alibi*), Krich lives in Los Angeles with her
husband and their children.

Visit Rochelle Krich's website at
www.rochellekrich.com.

About the Type

This book was set in Monotype Dante, a typeface designed by Giovanni Mardersteig (1892–1977). Conceived as a private type for the Officina Bodoni in Verona, Italy, Dante was originally cut only for hand composition by Charles Malin, the famous Parisian punch cutter, between 1946 and 1952. Its first use was in an edition of Boccaccio's *Trattatello in laude di Dante* that appeared in 1954. The Monotype Corporation's version of Dante followed in 1957. Though modeled on the Aldine type used for Pietro Cardinal Bembo's treatise *De Aetna* in 1495, Dante is a thoroughly modern interpretation of that venerable face.